Praise fo

'A propulsive, sinister, gripping tale about the dark
side of human nature that is hard to put down.'
Alex Michaelides

'Original, creepy and devastatingly clever. I raced through
The People Watcher yet didn't want it to end.
Utterly addictive. I loved it!'
Andrea Mara

'Deftly plotted and deliciously twisty, this
character-led thriller is a step outside the rest.'
HEAT

'Absorbing and richly detailed, *The People Watcher*
is a novel with real heart.'
Lisa Ballantyne

'A taut and immersive story about a troubled,
complex but ultimately enchanting character. Twisty
and dark as the night itself, it is beautifully written,
compulsive and impossible to put down. A triumph.'
Neil Lancaster

'Another corker from the author of *The Memory Wood*.'
SAGA magazine

Also by Sam Lloyd

The Memory Wood
The Rising Tide

THE PEOPLE WATCHER

Sam Lloyd

PENGUIN BOOKS

TRANSWORLD PUBLISHERS
Penguin Random House, One Embassy Gardens,
8 Viaduct Gardens, London SW11 7BW
www.penguin.co.uk

Transworld is part of the Penguin Random House group of companies
whose addresses can be found at global.penguinrandomhouse.com

First published in Great Britain in 2023 by Bantam
an imprint of Transworld Publishers
Penguin paperback edition published 2022

Extract on p. 154 from *The Collected Poems* by Robert Frost © 1969 Holt Rinehart
and Winston, Inc., published by Vintage Books. Extract reproduced
by permission of The Random House Group Ltd.

Every effort has been made to obtain the necessary permissions with
reference to copyright material, both illustrative and quoted. We apologize
for any omissions in this respect and will be pleased to make the
appropriate acknowledgements in any future edition.

A CIP catalogue record for this book
is available from the British Library.

ISBN
9781529177428

Text design by Couper Street Type Co.
Typeset in 11.5/14.5pt Dante MT by Jouve (UK), Milton Keynes
Printed and bound in Great Britain by Clays Ltd, Elcograf S.p.A.

The authorized representative in the EEA is Penguin Random House Ireland,
Morrison Chambers, 32 Nassau Street, Dublin D02 YH68.

Penguin Random House is committed to a sustainable future
for our business, our readers and our planet. This book is made
from Forest Stewardship Council® certified paper.

Dedicated to
Vrinder Singh Randhawa

Here's to Mexican Hat
(and many other adventures)

When I spot torchlight cutting through the pines towards our caravan, I know it's over. I remain at the window regardless, watching the December dark.

Outside, the grass is hairy with frost. Across the clearing, close to the forest's edge, stands another caravan just like this one. They'll search it first. When they don't find us there, they'll look here. They'll see the forced-open door. And that will be the end.

Shrugging off my blanket, I touch the back of my skull, seeking out its unnatural depression. A doctor – one of the many who've treated me over the years – once told me that female skulls are thicker than male ones. Only by a little, but maybe just enough to have saved me.

You were lucky, she said.

I guess she hadn't read my file.

Sound explodes from the forest. I hear snapping branches, a ripping of undergrowth. Then a black mass crashes into the clearing.

The stag is enormous, maybe two hundred kilos. It halts in a pool of moonlight, breath blasting in white gouts. Grabbing my Celestron binoculars, I dial in the focus wheel. Even now – knowing what's coming – I can't resist a closer look. Once a snoop, always a snoop; I think that's what they say.

As I watch, the animal swings its rack of antlers towards those dancing blue-white beams. For a moment it remains motionless, flanks quivering. Then it bolts into the night.

Drawing the curtains, I unfurl my makeshift blackout sheet. Once I'm satisfied no light can leak out, I turn on my torch. It reveals the utter squalor in which we've been living these past few days: overflowing rubbish bags; crushed water bottles; discarded sippy cups; a battered copy of *The Gruffalo*; empty cans of Peppa Pig spaghetti; a vast sack of used nappies.

The entire caravan should stink. And yet, when I breathe, my head fills with ghost scents: lemon, fried butter, bubble gum.

Neurologists call this phantosmia, not uncommon in folk whose brains have pogoed around their skulls as hard as mine. My olfactory hallucinations can happen at any time, but mainly when life's getting too much. That's true for my vertigo, too.

I stand, clench my teeth, wait for my surroundings to settle. Then, one hand braced against the cabinets, I edge through the galley kitchen to the bedroom.

There he is.

Two years old and perfect.

He lies beneath two heavy blankets. Right now, only his head is visible. I see soft skin. Hair like pale silk. We might have been living in squalor, but at least I kept him clean.

He frowns in sleep, flinches away from my light. Then he blinks his eyes open and squints up at me. 'Mummy?'

My breath goes. My throat aches. 'Sorry, kiddo.'

Three days and three nights – that's all we managed. Seventy-two hours of cold misery.

My plan failed. Thinking back, it was hardly a plan at all: a taxi ride, a train ride, another taxi; then a midnight hike through forest to this holiday park closed for winter.

He sits up, rubs his eyes. I wonder if he senses it, too: our time together running down, running out.

'Are you warm enough?' I ask.

'Cold.'

It's yet more evidence of my failure. Back when I was planning this, I assumed that these caravans, even in winter, would still have mains power. They don't – and their gas cannisters have disappeared, too.

I slump down beside him and rub his back. Through his pyjama top, his ribs feel hardly more substantial than chicken bones. Tomorrow is Christmas Eve. He should be warm, asleep in his bed and dreaming of Santa. Not here, in an unheated caravan, with a twenty-year-old loser incapable of looking after him.

'Listen,' I say. 'I know you won't remember this. I know, when you're older, you won't remember me. You probably won't even realize this happened unless he tells you – and I can't ever see him doing that – but I'm glad we got to spend some time together. And read *The Gruffalo*.'

He lifts his chin, frowns. Then I hear what he's already noticed: voices, drifting out of the forest. Men.

'Daddy,' he says, looking up at me.

I grin. Mainly because I don't know what else to do. 'Close your eyes, kiddo,' I whisper. 'Go back to sleep.'

Abandoning my perch, I switch off my torch and return to the window. Carefully, I lift a corner of the blackout sheet.

A man steps out of the forest. No features. Just a silhouette.

Fear curdles my guts, shortens my breath. I raise my Celestrons for a better look and see him gesture with two curled fingers.

Three more figures slide from the trees. They move towards the other caravan, their torch beams like scalpel blades slicing open the dark. They examine its front door, shine light through its windows.

I clench my teeth, wondering who betrayed me. The first taxi driver? The second? I tipped them both well, in the hope they'd keep quiet. Maybe they did. Maybe we were spotted on the train. Or by CCTV.

A low, black shape separates from the treeline. It trots around the caravan opposite like something from a nightmare. I watch it sniff the entrance, lose interest. When it pads into the clearing, the moonlight reveals its breed: a black-furred German shepherd. It thrusts its snout into the stag's hoofprints, snuffling and chuffing. Then it lifts its head towards my window. Its ears flatten and it growls.

Immediately, one of the torch beams arcs across the clearing. I drop the blackout sheet just in time.

I'm blind, now. Trapped in the dark.

Our caravan's rear window swings open from the top, an obvious escape route, should I dare to use it. But I don't – not with a toddler to protect and a trained German shepherd prowling around outside.

There are two large knives in the cutlery drawer – but that's another thought best left alone. I've had enough of blades and blood. Closing my eyes, I recall a scene from two years ago: a lake house; a dead woman; a red baby clapping hands bright with her blood.

Then, like now, I wasn't alone long.

Claws rake the caravan's front door. My eyes snap open. I see torchlight bleeding through gaps in the damaged seal. The dog starts to bark: frenzied, savage sounds – as if our scent has driven it wild with hunger. I get to my feet, imagining the damage its teeth could do to young flesh. My legs press against the cutlery drawer. My fingers twitch.

'OK, *now*!' a voice shouts.

With a bang, the door bursts off its hinges. My eyes burn with light.

'Get *back*!'

I try to stitch meaning from what I'm seeing: human shapes, moving fast, glimpsed behind the brilliance of their torch beams. A hand shoves me in the chest. I fly backwards. My skull strikes a cabinet, filling my head with sparks. I stagger into the lounge area and collapse on to a window seat.

My assailant holds his torch high, brandished like a club. I want to raise my arms, protect my head from further trauma, but I daren't give him another excuse to strike me. He's hard-looking, grim-faced. Maybe he won't *need* an excuse.

I hear commotion behind him, from the direction of the bedroom – then a woman's voice, scratchy with excitement: 'It's him. He's alive.'

In snatches of torchlight I see her squeezing his tiny arms, his tiny legs. She's checking for injuries, signs of abuse.

It angers me, that. Clearly, it upsets him too, because he starts to cry. His wails bounce off the walls.

'Keira Greenaway?' demands the man.

I shake my head. 'Keira Greenaway is dead.'

He blinks, stares at me hard, decides that I'm lying. 'Keira Greenaway, I'm arresting you on suspicion of child abduction. You do not have to say anything—'

'I *want* to say something.'

He sets his jaw. 'You do not have to say anything, but it may harm your defence if—'

'Don't take him back there,' I tell him. 'Please, it isn't safe.'

He pauses, just for a moment. Then he steps closer, shining his light right in my face. 'You've some fucking nerve.'

THREE YEARS
LATER

ONE

It's night when we first meet. You should know – here at the end of things, or perhaps at the beginning of their ending – that I mostly live after dark. There are Day People and Night People, and I am absolutely the latter. Long before all this happened, I counted myself among the Day People. But while you can change once, you can't go back to what you were. It's lonelier at night, but at least it's safer.

Of course, to be *completely* safe, you must also avoid other Night People – but then there'd be no chance to make a difference. And a person who doesn't strive for that is hardly a person at all.

I notice the puncture to my trike's front wheel halfway between William the Navigator's place and Home Alone Jacob's. There's no pop and hiss of escaping air. No violent decompression. At first I feel a squishiness to the steering, a reluctance to turn into bends. Pretty soon I'm grinding along on the wheel rim. That's when I have to stop.

Five years since my brain injury and I still can't ride a bike. My balance issues and recurring dizziness mean I need a stabilizing wheel. Still, I've improved a lot from where I was. There's a chance, even this late in my recovery, that if I keep up my exercises I'll make further gains.

My ride, this past year, is a Jorvik electric mountain trike; black wheels, black handlebars, cherry-red frame. At night, its forty-five-mile range offers me the freedom of Cranner's Ford. It'll happily go off-road – once, it even took me to the top of Pincher's Mount, the hill that overlooks my adopted town. Coming back down was scary, though. I wouldn't try that again.

The Jorvik's oversized tyres are puncture resistant. Yet somehow, tonight, a nail has penetrated. When I crouch over the wheel and shine my torch, I see the culprit embedded in the rubber.

I've rolled to a stop on Copper Beech Lane. No streetlights, no road markings, no lights from nearby homes. Past midnight, the humidity is merciless. For six long weeks, we've had nothing but record-breaking temperatures, gasping heat.

The moon is newly risen, silvering the hedgerows and overhanging oaks. Close by, something is lumbering around in the undergrowth. It sounds huge but is probably little more than a badger. Out here, no living thing can harm me. Not unless I cross paths with another human.

Abruptly, the lumbering thing senses my presence. With a grunt, it crashes deeper into the thicket. I climb off my trike, unzip the rear cargo bag and sort through it: binoculars, rattle can, tray of geraniums, rucksack, screwdriver, vintage Walkman, bag of mix tapes, claw hammer, knife.

No puncture-repair kit. No hand pump.

How can that be?

I'm too far from town to push my ride home. And I can't leave it here until morning, at the mercy of any thief who might happen by. Besides, I'm Night People. Vampiric. I only venture out after dark.

Think!

Could I drag the trike to Home Alone Jacob's and ask to leave it there? I've got to know Jacob well this last year, but he's never met me – nor knows that I even exist.

The world starts to spin. I plant my feet, but it's too late. My stomach clutches. Around me the moon-silvered trees blur, then multiply.

Without warning, the road surface stands upright. It wallops me across the back, punching the air from my lungs. I lie there like a flipped woodlouse, limbs flailing. If a car comes round the corner, it'll see me far too late to stop.

Somehow, I get an elbow beneath me. Then I roll on to my side and vomit. Not a lot – I didn't eat before I came out. Still, it clears my head. Another minute and the worst of the vertigo has passed.

Returning to my Jorvik, I disconnect the motor cable, loosen the bolts and slide out the wheel. With the front forks supported, I ease the machine into a ditch.

From my cargo bag I retrieve the Walkman. It's a WM-102, from 1987. Busted when I found it. A few hours with a toothbrush and a head-cleaning cassette brought it round.

I like to fix stuff. Especially stuff that others have thrown away. Mainly because it's sad to see things become unloved just because they no longer work as well as they once did. In the last three years I've taught myself how to solder, test circuits, do all sorts of repairs. I know it doesn't make sense. VHS players and SodaStreams and old Walkmans don't have souls – nor do they feel sad once they're discarded – but I can't help myself.

I like to fix stuff, but I *love* to fix people. In the twelve months since I moved to Cranner's Ford, it's become something of an obsession. Not that I've turned out much good at it. (Fixing people, I mean. Obsession I do pretty well.)

Removing my cargo bag from its rack, I hide it beneath a bush. The flap I leave unzipped so my geraniums can breathe. The screwdriver I slip into my pocket.

A mile back along Copper Beech Lane is a Texaco. Officially, it's open twenty-fours. That's not always the reality, but it's still my best bet.

I don my headphones and press play. A few seconds of tape hiss, then Randy Crawford's 'Street Life' fills my head.

Clutching the punctured wheel, my gaze fixed on the moon to aid my balance, I retrace my route towards town.

TWO

I'm in luck.

The Texaco is lit up like a visiting UFO – or one of those gaming machines I sometimes glimpse through pub windows. Its neon-red canopy stands on four glowing white pillars. Light pools on the forecourt from the overhead spots.

Through the kiosk windows I see Tariq. He doesn't know me, but I know him. I've memorized the faces and name tags of all the Texaco's late-night cashiers. I know their shift patterns and plan my visits around them. This is one of the places I buy groceries – either for me or for someone I think might need them – and I don't want to be remembered. They're a rare breed, these night workers – not Day People or Night People but a bridge between the two. Guardians, I call them. They have a heightened awareness, an instinct for danger that Day People usually lack.

I turn off my Walkman and carry my wheel across the forecourt. This late, no vehicles are filling up. Three youths, out of Tariq's line of sight, are leaning against the compressed air pump. Skateboards are parked at their feet.

I see this trio around town all the time: Dragon Back,

Greasilocks and Wisp. My names for them aren't kind and I feel a tiny bit bad about that. Similar to Guardians, they exist on the periphery. Like all teenagers, they're feeling out their futures, deciding which side of the dividing line they want to fall.

Their conversation dies at my approach. I feel their eyes on me, but I don't look, immediately conscious of what I'm wearing: white T-shirt, dungaree shorts, oxblood Doc Martens.

Dragon Back mutters something as I pass. Greasilocks and Wisp snigger.

Blushing, I push open the shop door. It's chilly inside. Goosebumps break out across my flesh. Partly because of the aircon. Partly because of the CCTV cameras trained on my face.

Tariq, behind the counter, is flicking though an *Auto Express*. He sells me a puncture-repair kit, a Dr Pepper and a pack of grape-flavoured Bubblicious without comment or eye contact.

Back outside, one of the fuel pumps is now occupied: a vintage VW camper, white and mint-green, the driver filling up. Around me, the forecourt feels oddly disconnected, as if it's existing in two separate realities and I've planted a foot in each.

This happens sometimes – a side effect of my condition. It's far more frightening than the vertigo. I want to speed-walk out of here, but I don't have that choice.

On a well-lit patch of concrete I crouch over my wheel and find my screwdriver. It takes me a minute, breathing deep, to lever the tyre partway off its rim. I pop out the nail, apply rubber cement to the inner tube and affix a patch. It'll need a while to cure before I inflate it. I just hope the bond is strong enough.

'Looks like somebody's night went a little flat.'

Two hyena yips greet the comment. Glancing up, I see the three amigos looking over. Dragon Back – named for the red-scaled dragon on his jacket – basks in the appreciation of his peers.

My stomach flops. Somehow, I manage a grin. Emboldened, he pushes away from the air pump. Greasilocks and Wisp follow. Moments later they've formed an arrowhead around me.

'Lemme guess,' Dragon Back drawls. 'While trying to escape from the circus, you rode your unicycle over broken glass . . . aaaaaaaand *pop*.'

More hyena yips from his friends. I laugh, too – but my attempt sounds desperate. I tell myself they're just teenagers having fun. Even so, their sneers have me worried. I'm not sure where this is going.

A forecourt CCTV camera hangs above Dragon Back's head. Is Tariq watching us? Or is he still nose deep in his *Auto Express*? I don't want more attention, however sticky this might get.

'Hey, nice – Dr Pepper.'

Dragon Back scoops up my bottle. He twists the lid and takes a long swallow. His belch echoes across the forecourt.

'Oh, *dude*,' Greasilocks says. 'Brutal.'

Dragon Back flips the bottle and catches it, the drink fizzing up inside. 'You think I should've asked? I'm sorry, Mamacita. Do you mind?'

'Finish it,' I mumble. 'It's no problem.'

I'm not sure what *Mamacita* means. Possibly, the word is uglier than it sounds. I *do* know Dragon Back is taunting me to impress his friends.

'You got a cigarette?'

I shake my head. 'Don't smoke.'

'You want to buy us some?'

'I don't . . .' I begin, and hesitate. I was about to say I don't have any money, but that would be a lie, and lying is something I avoid. Honesty's always the best policy.

'You don't what?' he asks.

'I don't know.'

'You don't know what?'

More cackles. My blush fills my cheeks. Why am I letting them frighten me?

Wisp jiggles his foot. 'Dude, you should tell her to come with us up Rycroft Hollow.'

'I can't,' I tell him. I might be a recluse, but I know people go up Rycroft Hollow for two reasons only: to get high or get laid. 'I have to go home.'

'Supercool,' Dragon Back shoots back. 'We'll walk you.'

'That's really kind, but—'

'This time of night, all kinds of sharks out hunting. You live alone?'

'I . . .'

He steps closer, tilts his head. 'Shit, I think I *recognize* you.'

If I was nervous before, now I'm frightened. All my senses are screaming: *Leave the wheel and run!*

But I can't get my trike home without it. And without my trike I have nothing. No link to those I watch in Cranner's Ford. No ability to help anyone who might need it. No purpose.

To his friends, Dragon Back says, 'Check it out. You know who I mean – chick on the red tricycle.'

My diaphragm has locked. No air in. No air out. I press a hand against the forecourt to steady myself and realize my entire arm is shaking.

Greasilocks tilts his head. Then his eyes widen. 'Dude, I think you're—'

'Trivia question,' says a voice. 'Who's playing?

THREE

Dragon Back, Greasilocks and Wisp glance up. The voice came from behind me so I scoot around to face it.

A few metres away, backlit, stands the guy who was refuelling the campervan. I hardly noticed him earlier. Now, he fills my world.

Perhaps it's my relief at a possible escape route, but in my entire life I've never seen anyone so mesmerizing. It's as if he's producing his own gravity, sucking in light and attention.

He's older than me. Whiter teeth, darker hair, sharper cheekbones. His green eyes are so bright that I flinch away when they examine me – and yet seconds later I've sought them out, wondering what they see: my pale skin, no doubt; my home-cut hair; my pinched nose and wide mouth.

He'll have certainly noticed my eyes – one brown and one blue. Heterochromia, the doctors call it. Some people are born with the condition. Others, like me, acquire it more violently.

His clothes fit so well they look tailored: white jeans;

slim-cut silk shirt with a psychedelic print; vintage leather bowling shoes in red, white and navy blue. From a cord around his neck hangs an enamelled yin-yang pendant. When his gaze moves to the three amigos, I find I can breathe again, if only lightly.

Campervan Guy tilts his head. A half-smile hovers on his lips. 'How many skaters does it take to fix a puncture?' He waits a beat, then adds: 'In this skatepark, none. So how about you boys bid us goodnight?'

Dragon Back glares at him. 'Whatever, dude. Since when did you start renting our space?'

At this, Campervan Guy smiles. Those teeth really are very white. He steps closer, speaking directly into Dragon Back's ear. I can't hear the words, but I witness their effect. Never have I seen the colour drain so quickly from some-one's face. Finally, he pulls back, giving the youth the full benefit of that million-watt green gaze. A soulful serious-ness has replaced the smile. 'Look at me carefully. You see what I mean?'

Dragon Back swallows, nods. He turns to me, ashen. 'Sorry for being a dick.' Then, to his friends: 'Come on – we're out of here.'

They must sense something in his tone. Moments later, all that's left of them is the sound of their skateboard wheels rolling down the road.

I don't feel much relief. Because now that green gaze has settled on me.

'You OK?'

'Just kids being kids,' I mutter. 'They didn't mean any harm.'

'Probably not. But it can be scary, this time of night. They might want to be more aware of themselves.'

Crouching while he's standing feels awkward. As I get to my feet the forecourt rolls beneath me. I stagger, manage to compensate. Rarely do I have two episodes back to back like this. Is it stress from the encounter? The fact I haven't spoken this much in weeks? Just as I think I'm safe, the concrete tilts again and the petrol station pirouettes – but I don't hit the ground, because somehow Campervan Guy has closed the distance between us. His hands are gripping my bare arms. His skin on mine. Flesh against flesh.

Human contact.

I squirm, teeth squealing. Those green eyes swim far too close.

'Steady,' he says. 'I've got you. You want to sit? Or can you stand?'

'Please. I'm OK.'

He releases my arms gently, as if balancing me on a tightrope. And honestly, that's how it feels. Like there's a chasm beckoning on both sides and I'm an atom's breadth from toppling in. My skin burns from our brief contact. My blood effervesces beneath the surface.

'I'm Louis,' he says, raising his hands. 'I'm sorry if I startled you. I didn't want you to fall. If you want me to leave you alone, I—'

'*HEY! LADY WHO RIDES RED TRICYCLE! YOU NEED POLICE?*'

The voice seems to be everywhere – and yet it sounds like it's seeping from a tin can: Tariq, I realize, addressing me via the forecourt loudspeakers.

This is deteriorating by the moment. I spot Tariq through the window, shake my head. The last thing I need is him phoning the police. I have to engage this Louis in conversation, however brief – prove to my Guardian that I'm OK.

'I think my night went a little flat,' I say, stealing Dragon Back's line. 'But it's a lot better, now – I am, I mean. I am a lot flatter. Better.'

Louis studies me closely. Then he laughs.

Who could blame him? I sound ridiculous. Like a malfunctioning speaking toy. And now I remember something else. I was sick, earlier. I'm probably huffing my deadly breath all over him.

Digging in my pocket, I pull out my pack of Bubblicious and stuff gum into my mouth. Louis stares at me as if I'm utterly insane. 'Grape flavour,' I explain, around a mouthful. Then, because it would be weirder if I didn't offer: 'You want one?'

'I try not to accept sweets from strangers.'

I nod, silently masticating. Or as silently as I can manage. Louis's half-smile does something funny to my insides. When he raises his eyebrows, I understand his meaning. 'Mercy Lake,' I tell him, relieved that all those hours of practice paid off – that when it counted I sounded natural.

Sort of natural.

'Mercy,' Louis says, taking some gum, and I shiver at the sound of that name on his lips. Lifting my wheel, I roll it towards the compressed air pump.

'Wait,' he says, behind me.

I grit my teeth and ignore him, rolling the wheel faster.

'It's your choice, obviously. But that's an old-school pump. Unregulated, high pressure. Use it on your tyre and you'll likely burst your inner tube.'

I freeze, examining the machine. Slowly, I turn to face him.

Louis reaches into his pocket. He retrieves a rubber ball, coloured like planet Earth. From it hangs a chain and a single key. 'Do you ever get the feeling,' he asks, 'that what at first seems random is actually something more mysterious?'

I plant my feet. Every one of my senses feels super-charged. I notice symbols melded into the pattern of Louis's shirt. They look vaguely astronomical. I don't recognize them, but somehow they feel significant. 'What do you mean?'

He points at the parked VW camper. 'Simply that I have a hand pump in the back of that old bus. If you wanted to borrow it to inflate your tyre, you could do so fully confident of my good intentions.'

My heart thumps. At the back of my throat, I taste grape juice and vomit.

Louis blows a bubble. Its pop echoes across the fore-court. Despite the bright lights of the petrol station, and Tariq and his *Auto Express*, I feel, suddenly, like we're the only living creatures in the entire world, the entire universe, perhaps, and that everything that came before did so purely to bring us to this moment – me and him, Mercy and Louis – and that I need to get out of here right now, before whatever has begun to sprout beneath this neon-red canopy is given the slightest chance to develop leaves.

FOUR

Instead, I say, 'Just the pump. And then I go.'

Louis tosses his key fob into the air and catches it. Turning, he walks towards the campervan. He seems one hundred per cent confident that I'll follow.

What are you doing? What are you risking? Have you completely lost your mind?

I don't know the answers. But if I want to get home before sunrise, what choice do I have? I use the short trip across the forecourt to study Louis more closely, safe from those unusually attentive eyes. Walking behind him, rolling my deflated wheel, I smell fresh soap overlaid with a citrus and sandalwood cologne. There's the faint aroma of leather, too, plus hops, dry-cured bacon, strawberry sherbet, ripe banana, peppermint, basil – as if someone is making the world's most confusing cocktail.

I'm not *really* picking up all these scents – it's just my stupid old brain, up to its stupid old tricks. Much of the time I have the olfactory mojo of a brick. Other times, like now, the severed things inside my head collide, a scent cannon detonates and my nose fills with crazy combinations.

The campervan is spotless, as if it just rolled off a 1960s production line – but its muscular look can't be original. It sits low on chrome wheels, hunched down like a predator about to strike. Inside, the mint-green and cream leather seats appear bespoke.

Louis rolls open the side door. I see chrome fixtures and panelled wood, a polished mahogany steering wheel and a chequerboard vinyl floor. There's a sink, a hob, a fridge and an expensive-looking sound system.

'Mercy, meet Eleanor,' Louis says, climbing in. 'Eleanor was born in 1963. She enjoys rusting, overheating and full engine rebuilds.'

When I rest my hand against the doorpost, I think I feel, just briefly, the hum of something sentient. It surprises me so much that I snatch away my fingers.

Louis clambers out, handing me a pump. 'You want some help?'

I shake my head.

First, the tyre needs to go back on the wheel rim. While I get to work, Louis plants his behind on the chequerboard floor. He stretches out his legs, resting his bowling shoes on the forecourt. 'How are you feeling now?'

For a moment, I don't know what he means. And then I recall the spectacle I made of myself earlier – how I staggered into him like the boneless no-hoper I am. 'Better.'

It's not quite a lie. Nor is it entirely accurate.

'Has it happened before?'

'I'm used to it.'

'Does it have a name? I mean, a medical one?'

'Probably.'

He nods. 'Zip your mouth, Louis. Take a hint when it's offered.'

I pop the tyre back on the rim. My fingers are black with wheel grease; my dungarees are similarly stained. The contrast between us could hardly be starker.

From his pocket, Louis withdraws a pristine white handkerchief and blots perspiration from his forehead. 'This heat,' he says. 'It doesn't let up, even at night. There's no way of escaping it.'

'If you climb high enough, you can escape,' I tell him, focusing on my wheel. 'Get up closer to the stars and you can breathe easier too. It's what I do almost every night.'

With the pump attached, I inflate the inner tube. I feel Louis's eyes but don't meet them.

'So,' he says. 'The tannoy guy mentioned a tricycle. If you arrived with just the wheel, I'm guessing you got the puncture too far away to push the tricycle here, too.'

Instead of replying, I pump harder. The silence stretches to breaking.

'I'm kind of torn,' he continues. 'I'd be happy to drive you back there if you asked, but I don't want to be the kind of creep who'd offer. On the other hand, you don't seem too steady on your feet. Is there someone you can call to pick you up? Or I'd happily pay for a taxi.'

I press my thumb into the tyre wall, testing its firmness. Louis has said nothing sinister. In fact, the very opposite. And yet my urge to escape has become all-consuming.

I don't have anyone I can call (cue the violins). But I don't *need* anyone (cancel the violins), so I shouldn't feel sad about it. And, most of the time, I don't.

Nor do I want Louis to call me a taxi, because that would put me in his debt. Then I might have to see him again – and that isn't something I can risk.

'It's very kind,' I hear myself say. 'You're obviously a

kind person. But I don't have far to go and I'm feeling much better now, thank you very much. And I do like the night air this time of year.'

Earlier, I'd started to sound vaguely human. Now, I'm back to malfunctioning robot. I can feel the burn of Louis's attention. Deliberately, I keep my eyes averted.

The wheel has enough air to get me home. I disconnect the pump, grit my teeth and stand.

The world shimmies. The forecourt lights pulse. But my Doc Martens remain firmly planted. I'm an oak tree, now, not a daisy.

I hand Louis the pump. When he takes the end, completing the circuit, I feel a snap of electricity between us so bright it feels real.

Releasing my grip, I mumble something tragic in farewell. Then I pick up my wheel and start walking, carefully placing my feet. I'm still on that tightrope, but safety is in sight.

Behind me, following my progress, I sense Louis, Tariq and the forecourt CCTV. Breathing deep, I step on to Copper Beech Lane. The night smells of lavender, coconut, pineapple, aniseed and ginger.

Illusory scents.

Comforting, even so.

Like a memory, I fade into them.

FIVE

Twenty minutes later, my wheel is reattached and my trike is out of the ditch. Overall, the puncture stole an hour of darkness. I'm just glad it didn't steal more.

Climbing on to the saddle, I concentrate on the night. For a moment I think I hear a far-off sound, like rattling metal tools, dimming and swelling. But when I turn my head, I see no headlights anywhere close.

I need to calm down, reset. My heart is still racing from what just happened. I'm not worried about the three amigos. I'm much more concerned about Tariq, the Texaco Guardian: *HEY! LADY WHO RIDES RED TRICYCLE!*

I buy groceries at the petrol station quite often, but I've been careful to go unnoticed – at least, that's what I'd thought.

My red trike *is* memorable. And yet tonight I went there without it. So how did Tariq recognize me? Surely my home-cut hair isn't *that* noteworthy. Perhaps it's my mismatched eyes. Maybe I should wear sunglasses next time I shop – although at night they might draw as much attention.

Still, the Tariq problem is solvable with a little thought.

It's Louis who fills my head. How he looked at me. How his eyes felt on my skin. I recall the fizz of my blood as our bodies touched; the crazy aromas blooming in my nose.

Was Louis Night People, like me? Day People, simply out late? Could he have been a Guardian? Might he even—

Stop!

My muscles ache. I need to rest. Tonight has delivered a month's worth of adrenalin in one hit. Less than two hours of full darkness remain. I don't have time to finish all tonight's planned visits. I need to prioritize – and there's one destination I simply *can't* miss.

Another ten minutes and I'm gliding up Abbot's Walk, at the base of Pincher's Mount. Our local paper calls this Millionaires' Mile. The higher it climbs around our famous hill, the more luxurious the homes. Each residence is set far back from the road, shielded by oaks, rhododendrons and glossy-leaved laurels.

Of them all, Arcadia Heights boasts the highest elevation and the most extensive grounds: broadleaf woodland, mainly, except for its swimming pool and its rectangle of perfect lawn. A hydraulic gate flanked by security cameras bars the main drive. From it, in both directions, runs a tall drystone wall. Fifty metres north, a fallen tree has demolished a section. That's both my access point and the hiding place for my trike.

It's far darker inside the woods. Still, the tree trunks make useful handholds for a person prone to toppling. I move from silver birch to alder to ash, steadily approaching my target.

The Raffertys have lived here eighteen months. A year earlier, they bought Arcadia Heights for 2 million, spending another vast sum to upgrade it.

Ahead of me, the trees thin out. There's the Raffertys' pool, green-lit by underwater spots. As always, I imagine how it would feel to strip off and swim a length. I'll never get the chance, of course – these days, for me, deep water isn't a great idea. Instead, I pick my way through a perfectly landscaped border to my vantage point behind the filtration pump.

Beyond the pool looms the house, monstrous and alert – a power statement of concrete, glass and steel formed into haphazard geometric shapes. If a prison colony for wealthy entrepreneurs were built on Mars, Arcadia Heights would be the blueprint.

Tonight, the building's ground floor is awash with light, spilling over with it, no blinds or shutters drawn across the floor-to-ceiling glass.

One thing I've learned, since my old life ended, is that the rich and powerful are far less likely to cover their windows at night. They don't fear the darkness like the rest of us. Maybe because they expect to be feared right back.

I spot Simon Rafferty in the cinema room. He's sitting on the floor, legs outstretched, his back against a white leather sofa. An empty wineglass stands beside him. His focus is on a MacBook balanced across his lap.

Simon's a tall man, deeply tanned, graceful in poise and economical in movement. Sometimes, watching him, I convince myself that his every muscular contraction is weighed and considered ahead of time. Three days ago, he turned forty-one, but he looks far younger. You'd never think eighteen years separate us.

I don't see Nadia Rafferty, Simon's wife. Probably, she's already in bed. Rarely do I visit the family this late.

Really, I shouldn't be visiting at all. Their restraining order against me still has three years to run. If I go within thirty metres of the couple – or five-year-old Ollie Rafferty – I face jail. Even stepping foot inside these grounds is a violation.

A wall-mounted CCTV camera monitors the pool area. A second camera, fixed to the orangery, covers the patio. There's a blind spot, though. It allows me to get within a few paces of the orangery's doors. With the lights on inside, I'll be invisible to anyone looking out – so that's what I do, closing the remaining distance as stealthily as I can manage. Then I sit on the flagstones, legs outstretched, perfectly mimicking Simon's pose.

We face each other in silence, one of us aware, the other oblivious. My heart rate is a bazillion beats per minute, but that's OK. I need to do this.

'*I see you,*' I whisper.

Simon closes the laptop. He picks up his wineglass, takes a long sip and stares at me through the window.

Right at me.

The muscles of his throat contract as the wine goes down. He continues to stare. I continue to hold his gaze. An artery in his neck pulses steadily. Glancing at my watch, I begin to count. A minute later I have my answer. Fifty-eight bpm – proof that Simon hasn't *really* seen me, even if that's how it might look. He's contemplating his reflection, unaware of what lurks behind it.

Still, the longer we share the silence, the more my discomfort grows. I'm Night People, attuned to danger. Right now, my instincts are flashing red. I feel eyes on me from somewhere – and not Simon's. When I glance around at the darkness, my stomach grips.

Finding my feet, I retrace my steps to the filtration pump. From there, I survey the unlit glass cubes, separated by concrete plinths and glass walkways, that form the building's upper levels.

Is someone up there awake? Foolish of me to sit outside the orangery when I don't have eyes on Simon and Nadia together. Tonight's puncture – and what happened at the Texaco – has seriously messed with my head.

Teeth clenched, I weave back through the trees to the section of toppled wall and clamber on to my Jorvik. Dawn is a way off yet, but it won't be long before a zombie grey-ness infects the sky. I can feel the Earth turning, threatening to reveal the sun. All that light and heat and pain.

Just the thought of it makes me feverish. I imagine my skin crisping, my eyeballs shrivelling in their sockets – the sun transforming me from a living, thinking human into a dead and desiccated husk. I need to be inside before the sky even *thinks* about twilight. But first . . . Laurie.

Beautiful Laurie.

Smart, creative, kind, calm.

And screwed.

SIX

Naked in her bathroom, right foot braced against the vanity top, Nadia Rafferty moisturizes her skin.

This room, with its sunken bath and black granite walls, was meant to be her sanctuary, but the look is far too masculine for her taste. In hindsight, she should have paid closer attention to the designer's plans. The installation cost, as with everything else in this house, was extraordinary. For a woman who grew up north of Pleven, in Bulgaria's poorest region, it crossed the line into immoral. So Nadia is stuck with the design, even though Simon would readily change it. At least the candles flickering around the bath somewhat soften the harshness.

One wall, entirely of glass, offers an incredible night vista of stars – except where the impenetrable mass of Pincher's Mount blocks the sky. Nadia took a long time to get used to that – particularly after what happened at the last house. Even now, eighteen months since moving in, she sometimes feels eyes on her while she bathes. The police promised she needn't worry, but only fools trust the words of strangers. And in recent days Nadia has had something new to worry about. Something that's consumed her since the moment she discovered it.

Her right leg finished, Nadia moisturizes her left. On the vanity top beside her foot lies the Clearblue pregnancy test. She examines it a final time. Then she shoves it to the bottom of the waste bin, blows out the candles, spritzes herself with Guerlain Mitsouko and wraps herself in a towel. Barefoot, she walks to the master suite.

It's her third test in as many days – and the third positive result. If her hunch is correct she's seven weeks pregnant, suggesting a due date sometime in March.

In front of a wall mirror, dropping the towel, Nadia examines her stomach. It's as toned and as flat as a boxer's, but she wonders how much protection it offers the tiny life inside her. The floors in most of these rooms are diamond hard. One slip and she could miscarry. Perhaps she should gorge herself on cakes and pastries – add layers of insulation and padding. Pulling on a robe, she walks to the bedroom window.

There it is above her, that colossus of earth and rock: Pincher's Mount. Nadia can *feel* its presence even if she can't see it.

At her grandfather's farm in the mountainous Stara Planina where her parents took her each Christmas, wolves sometimes crept down from the slopes at night to kill sheep, dogs – anything they could find. The old man had a saying: *When the wolves begin to multiply, expect misfortune.* These last three days, Nadia has sensed wolves all around.

Picking up her phone, she scrolls through her contacts and dials a number. When it's answered, she gives her name and asks for Detective Inspector Marius England.

A minute later he comes on the line. 'Mrs Rafferty?'

'Thank you for taking my call.'

'Of course. It must be a year since we last spoke. How are you? How's Ollie?'

'Ollie's good,' she says. 'And I'm OK, too.' The distinction is subtle but intentional. 'Are you still playing rugby?'

'Mrs Rafferty, is something wrong? Are you calling about anything specific?'

Nadia winces. The conversation has moved on faster than she'd have liked. He's given her no time to work on him. 'I know it's been a while. I just wanted to ask if you've seen her recently.'

'Keira Greenaway? Not since the trial. Afterwards, responsibility passed to the probation service. But you know this, Mrs Rafferty. Last time we spoke, I—'

'Is she still living at her parents' place?'

'I have no idea.'

'Can you check? Ask one of your officers to visit?'

'Has something happened?'

'Not exactly, but—'

'Look,' England says. 'I completely understand why you might be anxious, even after all this time, and I really don't want to sound like we're prioritizing her freedoms over yours, because we aren't, at all. But unless you have something specific, I'm afraid the answer's no.'

'Can I speak to her probation officer?'

'I'm sorry, Mrs Rafferty, you can't. Keira Greenaway complied with all the terms of her suspended sentence. She attended all her rehabilitation programme appointments. She does now have a right to privacy. If it helps put your mind at rest, there's no indication she might reoffend. Considering her various ailments, I'd say the chance is unlikely.'

Nadia returns to her mirror. She watches her reflection show its teeth. 'They didn't stop her before, did they?'

The detective pauses. 'Mrs Rafferty, if anything specific happens – anything at all – I want you to know that you can call me day or night.'

'I will,' Nadia lies, and hangs up. Because if she can't rely on the police for a single basic check, best not rely on them at all.

Abandoning the mirror, she crosses the hall to Ollie's room. The boy is lying on his mattress, his summer duvet kicked to the floor. Nadia doesn't cover him up – it's far too hot and he looks comfortable. Instead, she perches beside him and watches him sleep. She's protected this child for almost as long as she's known him – save for those three days of hell when Keira Greenaway walked into their old house and snatched him away.

Ollie's hand is curled around a toy. Nadia eases it from his fingers and sweeps his hair across his brow.

Will she ever recover from those seventy-two hours of horror? How Greenaway avoided a custodial sentence, even with all her issues, Nadia will never know.

She turns over the toy in her hands. It's the size of a quail's egg, with a small LCD screen. She remembers these, from the late nineties. Tamagotchis, they were called – for a few years they were everywhere. Ollie's has taken a battering, the plastic scratched and sun-faded. Checking the screen, she sees that his virtual pet is sleeping. Placing it on his side table, she leaves the pair in peace.

Back in her bedroom, Nadia scrolls once again through her phone. Her influence on the detective might have faded. Not so her influence on Konstantin Tapia. That is, if the teenager she knew in Gulyantsi is still alive. It's been a decade, maybe more, since she last spoke to him – but the bond they formed is unbreakable.

Asking Konstantin for help would be a last resort – like lobbing a live grenade into the air and chancing to fate where it fell. Konstantin was damaged goods, even back then. God knows how the last ten years might have twisted him.

Nadia finds his contact details. Then she goes downstairs to her husband.

SEVEN

Laurie – beautiful, smart, creative, kind, calm – owns Gimme the Dough, an artisan bakery in Cranner's Ford. It must take guts to open your own business. So that's something else to admire about Laurie: her tenacity.

I haven't watched her as long as I've watched the Raffertys – unlike them, she's not the main reason I'm here – but I've got to know her fairly well. It helps that she keeps a baker's hours. Even in summer, she's often awake before sunrise.

Unfortunately, despite Laurie's manifest good qualities, she has a world of hurt coming her way. Before it hits, I'm preparing her the best I can.

Gimme the Dough stands on Bartholomew Street, between a Chinese takeaway and a nail bar. I park at the head of the alley that runs behind them. I won't spot Laurie through the bakery's front windows. Right now she'll be around the back.

The alley's so dark I can't even see my Doc Martens. I edge past the Chinese, right hand extended. Another couple of metres and I'm behind Gimme the Dough. Here, finally, there's a little light. The fire door is a single steel slab, featureless except for a push-button security lock. The bakery's rear window is long and thin, set high in the wall. An empty pallet offers me a step-up.

And there's Laurie. Radiant. Surrounded by stainless-steel worktops and aluminium trays.

I can tell from her expression that she's deep in thought. Her eyebrows are gathered in a frown. Beneath them her blue eyes seem unfocused. For a moment I wonder if she's fretting about what's coming to her, but how could that be? Unless she knows more than I realize.

Laurie's blonde hair is tied back. On her nose is a smudge of icing sugar so cute I just want to lick it off. Her forehead shines with perspiration – probably due to the ovens coming up to temperature. And, of course, her weight.

Unlike me, Laurie's no shapeless whelp. Her upper arms judder as she works; her belly strains against her apron. Despite her size, her movements as she cuts the dough are those of a dancer. She's a baking Venus and I love her to bits – which is why watching her makes me so sad.

Fishing in my dungarees, I draw out what I brought along: a silver chain, slippery as water, that once belonged to my grandmother. From the links hangs a pendant I purchased especially for Laurie.

It's a hammer. Not like the claw hammer I was taking to William the Navigator's nursing home before I got my puncture. This is a tiny representation of Mjölnir. Archaeologists have dug up pendants just like it from burial sites all over Scandinavia. Mostly, from women's graves.

Laurie's hammer is inscribed with runes from the Elder Futhark. If ever she chooses to transcribe them, she'll read a personal message from me.

It's not the first symbol I've sent her as a warning. Two months ago, Laurie left her car unlocked overnight. On the passenger seat lay the woollen poncho she wears on chilly mornings. Opening the door, I removed it. Oh God, the *smell* of her. The goodness and the richness and the heady notes of her perfume.

It didn't take me long to figure out which part of the garment lay across her heart. That's where I fixed the pin: a vintage Navajo arrow, hand-stamped in silver, a cabochon of green turquoise on the shaft. If Laurie researched it, she'd understand the meaning.

A week before I pinned the Navajo arrow over Laurie's heart, I posted an envelope through Gimme the Dough's front door. On it I'd stencilled her name, along with a Chinese symbol I copied from a tattooist's website. Inside the envelope was the silver ring I'd bought her: a wraparound Chinese dragon with malachite eyes and tongue.

That morning, before sunrise, I hid across the road while Laurie unlocked the bakery. I watched her pick up the envelope and examine it, front and back. She removed the ring, turning it over and over.

Try it for size, I urged her. *Slip it on*. And after a moment, Laurie did. I imagined the dragon's tail coiling tight around her finger and extending up her arm. But nothing like that happened and moments later Laurie took off the ring. She held it up to the lights, looking inside the band. Then she dropped it into her apron. I haven't seen her wear it since.

I could stand here for hours, watching Laurie preparing her cakes and loaves. But the darkness won't last much longer. Not with a gazillion tonnes of burning plasma about to burst over the horizon.

Kissing Laurie's hammer, I hang my grandmother's chain over Gimme the Dough's fire-door keypad.

Good luck, Laurie.

You'll need it for what's coming.

Back at the alley entrance, I check I'm still alone. For a moment I think I hear the clatter of skateboard wheels. A coldness spreads up my spine, as if something undead just licked my skin.

It's beyond late. The Earth is still turning. I need to get inside – and fast.

Climbing on my trike, I glide into the dark.

Home. Mine is the basement flat of a converted Georgian townhouse. Surprising what an inheritance can buy, once you decide how to spend it. When the Raffertys bought Arcadia Heights, and moved in a year later, I started looking for a place in town.

I couldn't follow them to Cranner's Ford immediately. At the time, my two-year suspended sentence still had six months to run. That meant staying where I was and meeting regularly with my offender manager. I also had to attend counselling. For my phobia, they said – and my occasionally obsessional behaviour. When the two years were up, I changed my name and moved.

The air is cool inside my flat. I go from room to room, fixing my home-made panels to the windows. They're cardboard covered with black fabric, held in place with Velcro tabs. Once they're up, I pull down my blackout blinds and close the curtains. Then I unfurl floor-to-ceiling wall hangings over each window space, completing an unbroken circuit. Each room features a different wraparound scene: in the living room, a tropical beach; in the kitchen, snow-covered mountains. My bathroom is an underwater reef. My bedroom lies inside a forest glade.

Only when my artificial world is ready do I switch on the daylight lamps, scrunching up my eyes while they adjust. There, on a shelf, where it's least useful, I see my pump and puncture-repair kit.

Top marks, Mercy. Ninja-level skills.

In the living room, against a backdrop of palm trees and Thai fishing boats and turquoise ocean, hangs a huge street map of Cranner's Ford. The town is hourglass-shaped, squished between two hills: Pincher's Mount in the west, crowned by its stone-built Gothic folly; Old Cobb in the east, with its tourist road right to the top. The River Gunn runs north to south, separating the Georgian buildings of Old Town, clustered around Pincher's, from the newer developments near Old Cobb.

Paper flags, attached to cocktail sticks and affixed to the map by Blu Tack, highlight areas of interest: my flat in the heart of Old Town; the Rafferty place up on Abbot's Walk; the Gimme the Dough bakery; the Tall Pines nursing home; Deevis Farm; the drive-thru where I meet Lost Travis; Ollie Rafferty's new school.

There are flags for the people I watch, too: Lovesick Linda, Home Alone Jacob, Raj the Reborn, Cold Hand Carl, Unproud Tina, Edward Gropey-Hands, Roaring Mary; plenty of others.

From my workbench I grab a spare flag. On it I write *LOUIS* and affix it to Copper Beech Lane.

Only then do I approach the fireplace and tell Mum and Dad about my night. Their teal-coloured urns, inlaid with tiny silver leaves, stand at either end of the mantelpiece.

I'm too exhausted to exercise. Kicking off my DMs, I'm too tired even to eat. I crawl on to my bed inside my artificial forest and command my smart speaker to fill the trees with birdsong.

Sleep falls over me like a cloak.

EIGHT

Despite all my precautions, I open my eyes to daylight –
and a five-year leap back through time.

I'm on the lake, a hundred metres from shore. The Italian summer sun isn't just bright but excoriating in its
sharpness. On the water float a million razor-blade reflec-
tions. There's no wind. No respite from that white-hot
mass overhead.

The heat is fierce, yet I don't feel it. My bare shoulders
are as cool as when I closed my eyes. My tanned legs,
stretched out before me in the rowing boat, are supple and
well defined – certainly the best they'll ever look; nothing
like the pale grubs they've become.

From the shore in all directions, close-growing pines
climb the slopes. The lake is shaped like a kidney – or an
embryo after one month's gestation. Here at the tail, I can't
see the entire shoreline. Nor can I see any other evidence of
humanity: no craft except my own; no jetties thrusting out
across the water; no dwellings or power lines, no rising
smoke; not even a jet trail bisecting the sky.

Above me, the sun is about as high as it can reach.

Weird, how calm I am, how detached. I rub the back of my skull, feeling its smooth curve of bone. Less than a centimetre's protection for every memory or hope I've created. Everyone has a weak point. This is mine.

From over my left shoulder, I hear it: a clattering of wings like distant gunshots. I turn in time to spot a flock of ravens taking flight from the trees. Then comes the honking of geese from a part of the lake I can't see. Moments later I spot them banking hard and flying low across the water towards me. They part before my bow, so close that I feel the turbulence from their wings as they pass.

I bend forward to grab my oars. And see that my hands are gloved in blood. It runs down my elbows, drips on to my thighs, splashes on to the wooden hull.

I glance again at the shoreline, searching for the outcrop that obscures the lake house. When I re-examine my hands, I see that the blood has entirely disappeared.

I angle the bow towards my destination. Then, grimacing, I begin to row.

NINE

Saturday night.

I hide my trike in brambles beside the Monk's Brook, tiny tributary of the Gunn, and splash through the shallow water towards Pincher's Mount. This time of year, I'm granted only seven hours of darkness. I need to make every minute count.

I woke mid-afternoon and spent the early evening fixing my latest skip find – a Little Professor toy from 1977. All it needed was a new LED display. Now it's as good as the day it left Texas Instruments. I know a little boy who'll love it, if I can figure out a way to get it to him.

It's another warm night. I'm sweating within minutes of starting up Pincher's. I don't climb to the top – my Cele-strons won't reveal anything useful from that high. Instead, I find my usual vantage point – a scooped-out bite a third of the way up where I can rest my back against grass. From here, Cranner's Ford is a jewelled map laid flat. Above it hangs a moon so plump it belongs in a fairy tale. All around me, field crickets conduct their night chorus.

I zero in first on the Texaco. From there I skip north,

bouncing from one landmark to another until I find the drive-thru. Outside, on litter patrol, I spot Lost Travis. Hopefully, he's discovered my latest gift.

From the drive-thru I travel to Chaplin Row. There's Lovesick Linda's sad maisonette, still with its broken porch light. Linda's bedroom is brightly lit. Guaranteed she's alone in there. Probably scrolling through dating sites. For a minute I linger at her window, but she doesn't reward me with an appearance.

Linda's my next project. No one should have to live a life like hers. Soon, with any luck, nor will she.

From Linda's I head over to Sycamore Row, where I find Raj the Reborn's townhouse. His windows are still covered with newspaper, preventing me from looking inside. Raj, I fear, may not be much longer for this life.

My lenses travel east, to the shabbiest part of town. On Prospect Avenue, the windows of Cold Hand Carl's shared flat are dark. Carl is Night People, like me. I can't say what drives him, but the *Cranner's Ford Gazette* regularly reports his crimes. Astonishing, really, that no judge has locked him up. Still, he's not the only one to have benefited from a lenient court system.

I drop south. My lenses slide along Abbot's Walk at the base of Pincher's Mount, location of the town's most expensive homes. A few hundred metres below my hollow, I find Arcadia Heights, its glass-and-concrete architecture rising proud of the surrounding trees.

Steeling myself for what I might see, I sweep my binoculars across its floor-to-ceiling windows. Unlike last night, the house lies mainly in darkness: just a few lamps on downstairs; an oval of flickering candles in one of the upstairs rooms.

The doors to the orangery stand open. Outside, the

Raffertys' pool glows a futuristic green – like the birthing tank of some alien species. Simon Rafferty is pacing up and down beside it, phone clamped to his ear.

At a nearby patio table sits Hugo the Shade. Hugo is the managing director of Sheergen, the clean energy start-up Simon founded a decade ago. The company builds, leases and repairs onshore wind turbines. These days it's a major player in renewables, both here and all over Europe.

Since Simon and Hugo relocated to Cranner's Ford, their influence on the local landscape – and local landowners – has been clear to see. From this slope I can count five Sheergen turbines, their sails silently turning.

Abandoning the two men for now, I return to the upstairs cube and its oval of yellow candlelight. The room is vast, clad entirely in black granite. At the centre of the oval is a sunken bath. In it, water lapping at her like oil, lies Nadia Rafferty.

My chest thrums like a plucked string.

Elbow balanced on my knees, I keep watch while Nadia bathes. I'm no voyeur. I take no sexual satisfaction from our encounter. This is a ritual we've shared many times previously. When she rises from the water I don't avert my gaze. Instead, I track her to the vanity top. Her head drops as something captures her interest. A blemish? A phone message? From this angle I can't be sure.

Nadia leaves the bathroom and appears, moments later, in the master suite. Before a floor-length mirror, she presses her fingertips to her belly and turns on the balls of her feet, studying herself from different angles.

A coldness spreads out from my own belly. My Night People instincts, I wonder? Or something more fundamental?

'I see you,' I whisper. *'What do you see?'*

Moments after I speak, my skin begins to itch, as if hidden eyes are crawling over me from somewhere deeper inside the house.

I lower my binoculars, take a breath – but the prey-like feeling persists. And then, with horror, I realize it's justified. Because I *am* being watched. And the danger is far closer than I'd anticipated.

TEN

Sound first, then movement.

The sound is scuffed stones and breathing. The movement is a black shape flowing up the slope towards my hollow.

I've no chance of escaping to higher ground. I'm a slow climber, unsteady on my feet. Instead, I press my spine into the grass. My claw hammer is in my cargo bag with my knife, a few hundred metres down the slope. Up here, all I have are my Celestrons.

Just like last night at the Texaco, the once-solid dimensions of reality feel like they're tearing. Even worse is my sense, inescapable, of shadow things crouched in those unstitched spaces: nameless horrors whose attention has now turned upon me.

A doctor who hadn't experienced this once told me it's a by-product of my condition – just another wonky connection in a brain chockful of them. It must be nice to live in a world unpopulated by demons. I've completely forgotten what that's like.

Teeth clenched, I watch the approach of that liquid

black shape. And then, against all my expectations, it turns its back and sits, not five metres below my hollow.

Down in Cranner's Ford, people spill from pubs. Cars negotiate lamplit streets. No one lifts their gaze to Pincher's Mount, where a spectre has climbed the slope to find me.

My muscles have locked. My head is buzzing like a faulty dimmer switch. Slowly, the ripped fabric of my reality knits together. But it doesn't banish the spectre, which means it isn't illusory. When, finally, it speaks, blood surges in my arteries.

'You said if I climbed high enough, I could escape,' Louis says. ' "Get up closer to the stars and you can breathe easier, too." That's what you told me, and it's true.'

I hear a rustling in the grass and imagine a serpent gliding up the slope, fangs bared. But the rustling is just my leg, twitching like something possessed. I grip my Celestrons harder, feel the carry cord bite my neck.

Louis sighs. 'It's so *different* at night. I feel like we're in touching distance of outer space. Don't you?'

Incredibly, I find myself nodding. Because that's *exactly* how I feel on nights like this, when clear skies reveal the heavens.

The silence stretches like a wire. My nose fills with wild scents: jasmine and gunpowder, honeysuckle and barbecue smoke. I need to unstick my tongue, say something. 'Did you follow me?'

Louis turns his head, revealing his profile in silhouette. 'I was worried you'd think that. If you want to be alone, Mercy, I'll climb down this hill right now and you'll never see me again.'

A breeze licks the grass flat. My arms pucker into gooseflesh.

Another minute passes, each second an aeon. Finally, Louis adds: 'There's another option – something to consider before you decide. I could sit here and you could sit there, and neither of us would have to get any closer, and if we both felt like talking we could do that. And if one of us didn't, that would be OK, too.'

Just like at the Texaco, I'm struck by both his confidence and his serenity. Doubtless *his* heart isn't beating faster than a kingfisher's wings. He's doing his best not to frighten me, I think. Like a vet comforting a broken bird – or a socially awkward twenty-something with a debilitating fear of daylight.

Louis turns his head towards Cranner's Ford. Now, I smell sea air and rotting fruit. My leg resumes its jumping. I clamp my hand around it, examining myself and what I'm wearing: the same white T-shirt and grubby dungaree shorts from last night; the same oxblood DMs.

Below me, Louis nods. In a single fluid motion, he stands. 'Goodbye, Night Eyes,' he says. When I don't respond he moves off, picking his way down the slope. All too soon, his silhouette merges with the darkness. Suddenly, it's possible to believe he really *was* an illusion.

I frown, trying to think back to the exact moment I stopped being terrified. Or, more accurately, when I stopped being certain of what I wanted. I squeeze my knees together, my buttocks. And then I call out for Louis to wait.

ELEVEN

Two minutes later and I can't believe this is happening.

Louis is sitting beside me in my hollow and I'm still doing all the things a human might do – like breathing, or blinking – although I have to concentrate hard not to make a mess of it.

He hasn't said a word since joining me. I wonder if he's waiting for permission. It's been so long since I talked to someone who isn't a doctor, a police officer or a probation officer that I've forgotten some of the rules. At least the silence gives me a chance to list all the things I *could* say but shouldn't – not only for my own safety but for fear of looking moronic.

I sneak a glance at Louis. Gone is the silk shirt from last night. Likewise the white jeans and vintage bowling shoes. Tonight he's all in black: polo shirt, trousers, boots.

When he turns to face me, I reel away.

'You OK?' he asks.

I clench my teeth, shrug. Even with my mouth buttoned I can reliably act like a bimpus. My breathing's too loud. I sound like I'm trying to give birth, or pass a really big poo.

Louis is studying me with what can only be pity. And yet when he speaks, it's not to query my nonsense but something else.

'Have you lived in Cranner's Ford long?'

I prise apart my lips. 'Have you?'

'It's certainly a nice place to be.'

I nod. Conversation without information. Nothing learned and nothing revealed. This I can handle – just about. 'Why'd you call me Night Eyes?'

'Sorry. I do that sometimes. Give people different names. Ones I think suit them.'

I think of Lovesick Linda, Raj the Reborn, William the Navigator, Cold Hand Carl. 'You don't have to apologize. I do it too.'

'Really?'

'All the time.'

Louis grins. I grin right back.

The moment is a connection between us – tenuous and short-lived, but a connection nonetheless.

'A lot of Koreans believe in *saju*,' he says. 'Have you come across it?'

I shake my head.

'It's the concept that a person's destiny is linked to the exact moment of their birth. If someone's birth name is in conflict with their *saju*, it's a sure-fire recipe for bad luck. In Seoul you can visit a *saju* tent and for a fee a fortune teller will give you a new name – one that's balanced with your destiny. Thousands of Koreans do it every year.'

'Have you been there?'

'I lived in Seoul for a while. In China, where I went next, they have a strict taboo against writing names in red ink. In Japan, that's frowned upon, too. The naming of a thing is far more powerful than most people realize. An act of creation. Human magic, if you like – or trickery.'

From the ground he selects a pebble and holds it up to the moon. 'This is no longer just a pebble,' he says. 'This little guy is Otto. Want to meet him?'

I hesitate, then hold out my hand.

Louis reaches over – but at the last moment he flings Otto up and out into the night.

I gasp. My heart nearly leaps from my chest. For a moment I'm appalled by his cruelty. And then, shaking my head, I remember it was just a pebble.

'The magic of names,' Louis says.

Steadily, I recover my breath. 'So, why Night Eyes?'

'Because your eyes are what I remember most from last night. How . . . well, just how astonishing they are.' He gestures at the night sky. 'Like something you might find up there.'

I need a moment to process that. I think – although I'm not certain – that he was trying to pay me a compliment. 'It's called heterochromia,' I tell him. 'A few hundred years ago I'd have been burned as a witch. Back then, people thought eyes like these could see into the underworld. It creeped them out, made them reach for the firewood. Say what you like about modern society, but at least we've stopped burning each other quite as regularly.'

'These days we have Twitter.'

I nod as if I know what he's talking about. 'Central heterochromia is when you have different colours in the same eye. Complete heterochromia is when each eye is different. Ugly word, don't you think?'

'I think I prefer Night Eyes.'

'Me too.'

'I brought something,' Louis says. 'Just in case I found you again. I hope you won't mind.'

He rummages in his bag. I hear a pop, then a fizz of bursting bubbles. Seconds later, he offers me a flute of what I'm guessing is champagne.

'I don't know what made me seek you out,' he says. 'I don't know if this is the last time we'll see each other, whether it's the start of something or the end. But I knew before I came up here tonight that finding you again – even just once – would be an event important enough to mark.

'I don't believe in coincidences. Maybe once, not now. What happened last night at the Texaco – me, you, those skaters – all in the right place at exactly the right time. I don't think that was chance. I believe we live in a universe that brings people together for a reason, Mercy – one that seeks equilibrium wherever possible. Light to balance dark. Order to balance chaos. Good to balance evil. Each of us is a weight on the scale. It's up to us what we choose, but only by following our intended path can we reach our true potential.'

He pauses, chews his lip. 'You're looking at me weirdly.'

I shake my head, accepting the champagne flute. 'It's just my weird eyes.'

He laughs. I laugh. We are laughing.

This is insane.

Louis clinks his glass against mine. 'To weird beginnings.'

'I don't . . .' I begin, and hesitate.

I don't drink, I was about to explain. Because when you're the Leaning Tower of Pisa's two-legged cousin, alcohol is best avoided.

I believe we live in a universe that brings people together for a reason, Mercy – one that seeks equilibrium wherever possible.

Light to balance dark. Order to balance chaos. Good to balance evil.

To Louis's words, I dare to add a few of my own: *companionship to balance isolation.*

I smile, heedless of my mismatched eyes and home-cut hair; my grubby dungaree shorts and dusty knees. I'm up here on Pincher's Mount with another human – and it feels like just about the most dangerous thing I've done in my new life, and also one of the most thrilling.

'Cheers,' I mumble. And for the first time in six years I'm drinking champagne, and my tongue is alive with bubbles and the taste is *glorious* – woody and fruity, with the fragrance of white flowers.

Louis tops up my glass, then his. 'This is Louis Roederer Cristal. They don't produce it every year. Only during the finest vintages, when the grapes have achieved perfect maturity.'

I feel a burp pressing at my throat. 'Well,' I say, 'it beats the hell out of Dr Pepper. Although I hear they make that all the time.'

'Who were you watching?'

My stomach twists like a dishcloth. 'Me?'

'The binoculars,' Louis says. 'I'm guessing that's what you were doing. A pair like that isn't much use for astronomy.'

'Do you like stargazing?'

His mouth twitches. He's seen straight through my deflection. 'Now and then. But I find people far more interesting. Don't you?'

'Maybe.'

'Who were you watching?'

The moon, swinging violently in the sky, is a lifebuoy I fail to catch. My head lolls. The chirping of the field crickets increases in pitch. Suddenly, their song feels like the prelude to something awful awakening – as if the entire hill is about to unfold from sleep and rise on granite legs. The thought makes me dizzy, sick. I dig my fingernails into sun-crisped turf, fearful I'll be thrown loose.

If Louis notices my distress, he gives no sign. 'Mercy,' he says. 'Pretend, a moment, we're not just alone up here on this hill. Pretend we're alone on this entire planet, floating through space with only comets and asteroids for company. Just the two of us. No judgements, no baggage. Whatever we choose to talk about stays between you and me, because – just for this one evening – you and me is all there is.'

Louis's words ease the moon's pendulum swing. Strange, but right now I can't see a single car moving on the streets below. Nor a single figure. It's almost possible to believe we *are* the only ones left – that the residents of Cranner's Ford, and everywhere else, have spontaneously winked out of existence.

My skin furs up. The idea is terrifying and half delicious.

No more doctors or parole officers or police. No more Day People, Night People or Guardians. Would that make me free? Unshackled from the night? What would I do with my time? What would be the *point* of me?

What's the point of you, now?

I don't like that voice, so I ignore it. I want to hug my knees, but I'm still gripping my champagne flute.

'Is it someone you know?' Louis asks. 'Or a stranger?'

My toes curl like autumn leaves. The answer, of course, is neither. Because it's not just one life but a collection. What began with the Raffertys has grown to include many others. I collect lives – and intervene in them – the way others collect Pokémon cards, perfume bottles or parking fines. Until now, I've never considered how creepy it must seem.

Beside me, Louis waits for my answer. Even *I* can see we've reached a turning point. What I say next will change my life. For better or worse, I don't know.

Honesty's always the best policy.

And yet what I do isn't honest. I'm not ashamed of it, but it isn't that.

My champagne flute is empty again. I twirl it in my fingers. If I want this conversation to continue, I need to offer Louis *something*.

In the end, honesty doesn't decide me but a sudden appalling loneliness. It's a feeling I usually keep buried, so perhaps honesty decides me after all. I think of everyone I could introduce, all those stories playing out. And then I settle on one.

'Her name's Linda,' I say. 'And I watch her because I think she needs help. A release from all her pain.'

TWELVE

Louis refills his champagne flute. Then he leans over and refills mine. 'Lonesome Linda,' he says.

I shake my head. 'Lovesick Linda.'

'Lovesick?'

'Long story.'

'I like long stories. Especially love stories.'

'Actually, it's not that long, or lovely. Just sad.'

'Does it have a happy ending?'

'Not yet.'

'Is that where you come in?'

I lick my lips. Already, I've shared more than I'd intended. 'Linda's a problem I'm not sure how to fix.'

'How do you know her?'

My toes are curling again. This time, Louis must sense my discomfort, because he abandons the question and asks another. 'What's our Lovesick Linda up to tonight?'

'I'm not sure.'

'You haven't checked in?'

'Yes, but I didn't see her.'

He looks down at Cranner's Ford. 'Which one's her place?'

'You know Chaplin Row?'

'Not really.'

'See the drive-thru? And that row of maisonettes to the east? Linda's is the one with the broken porch light.'

'Can I borrow your binoculars?'

My fingers become claws. It takes all my willpower to unstick them. Shakily, I hand him the Celestrons.

Louis seeks out the maisonettes, fiddling with the focus wheel. 'Looks like someone's home, all right.'

'She'll probably be online around now.'

'Internet dating?'

'How'd you guess?'

'Home alone on a Saturday night. What else might our Lovesick Linda be doing?'

'She doesn't learn from her mistakes.'

'She was wounded before?'

'The worst offender is her ex-husband. He beat her, I think, before their divorce. And since the split he just won't leave her alone.'

'That's rough. Everyone has the right to forge a new path. Is it just Linda you watch?'

'Yes. No. I mean . . . I just . . .'

I sense Louis's eyebrows climbing. It's what my eyebrows would do, if I heard this gobbledygook from someone else. But it's not easy making decisions at warp speed. The difficult questions come just when I'm least expecting them. My brain is struggling to keep up.

'Remember, Night Eyes,' Louis says. 'Tonight it's just you and me. No judgements, no consequences, no reproach. No need to share anything difficult or personal. Anything we do talk about stays strictly between us.'

I nod. A little of my tension ebbs away. It's an unguarded

moment and my tongue takes full advantage. 'There are others,' I say. 'Quite a few, actually.'

Louis lowers the binoculars. I wish I could read his thoughts. The silence between us is excruciating – again, my tongue hurries to fill it. 'I know how that must sound. But the people I watch . . . some of them, they have no one else. They need somebody to see their lives for what they are. They need somebody to . . .'

I flail around, hunting for the right word.

'To what, Mercy?'

'To intervene.'

I wonder if he can see how much blood has rushed into my face. Or if he feels the heat radiating from my cheeks.

Louis lowers the binoculars. 'Tell me about someone else. If you want to, I mean.'

Despite the warm evening, I've started to shiver. I cast another look at Louis. Here we are, perched on a planet turning inexorably towards the sun, and I find I don't want the moment to end. Whatever nonsense I've spouted, however awkward my behaviour, I'm here, at least, and this is happening, and it's an event to file away and keep. I'm starting to grasp how exhilarating it is to be scared witless of something, when it's something you're quite enjoying.

While we've been talking, the distance between us has shrunk. Have I drawn closer to him? Or have we drawn closer to each other? When I breathe, my lungs fill with scents of gardenia and wet stone. 'I can tell you about William the Navigator.'

Below us, in the scrub surrounding the Monk's Brook, the nightjars begin their warbling.

THIRTEEN

I've been watching William the Navigator so long that it's easy to forget why I started. My intentions back then were misguided – and I certainly won't share them with Louis.

Tall Pines, where he lives, is the most exclusive nursing home in town. Beneath its glossy veneer lurks a distressing truth: high fees don't always mean quality care.

William's ground-floor room is around the back. I can see into it from up here if his blinds are open – luckily for me, few Tall Pines staff ever bother closing them. Usually, though, I keep watch from the landscaped garden outside his French windows.

I don't know if William has visitors during the day – or if he ever leaves his bed. Whenever I check in on him, he's lying on his back alone, face angled towards the sky. One night in March, I witnessed him lie there for twelve hours straight, without a single carer to turn him or offer company.

His room is clean but spartan. Above the bed are his air-force medals, collected in a frame. They're the only personal items on display – and positioned in the one spot

William can't see. I took a photo of them once, shining in a torch while he slept. Later, I did a bit of detective work. The ones awarded for gallantry are worth quite a bit.

For months, I've wondered how to end his long days of boredom. Last night's puncture stopped me just as I was hoping to intervene.

There's another scent now, over the gardenia and wet stone. Primal. More urgent. I can't tell if it's Louis or me or something entirely imagined. It excites me, unsettles me. It dances cold fingertips across my stomach and along my thighs.

Before I fully realize what I'm doing, I hear myself telling Louis all about William and his medals, and how no one should have to live out their last days alone.

'Lately, when I see they're neglecting him, I ride to a payphone, call the front desk and tell them to get their act together. They hate it, but at least someone always checks on him afterwards.'

'Which one's his window?'

I direct Louis towards it.

'The blinds are open,' he says, 'but the lights are off inside. You can't see much from here.'

'Sometimes they leave his side lamp on and you get a better view.'

'It's good of you to watch over him.'

My cheeks flush with blood. Not because what he said is true – but because he thought it. If he knew my original motive, he'd no doubt be appalled.

Louis returns my binoculars. Then he takes my champagne flute and puts it into his bag. 'You're an enigma, Mercy Lake. One of a kind. You've given me lots to think about, that's for sure.'

'You're going?'

He looks at me square on. My toes curl so hard that one of my Doc Martens squeals.

'I don't want to crowd you,' he says. 'I get the feeling that this – just sitting here talking, I mean – isn't something you do a lot. You might need a while to get used to it. So let me give you a little space. And then, if you want, maybe I'll see you some other time.'

'Like when?' I ask, and cringe. Even *I* know you should never appear too keen for company.

'Will you be here Thursday night?' Louis asks.

'Around midnight.'

'Who's first on the watchlist?'

'I don't know. William, probably. Just to check up.'

'OK, Night Eyes,' he says. 'With any luck I might see you then.'

I nod. Those ghost fingers walk my skin again, probing and teasing. Digging in my pocket, I bring out my grape-flavoured Bubblicious and pop a chunk into my mouth.

Louis smiles. Then he climbs to his feet and dusts himself down. Only once I'm alone again do I realize that I never offered him any gum.

Loser. World's biggest.

Me.

FOURTEEN

Nadia Rafferty's fruitless conversation with the detective has developed, twenty-four hours later, into a sore she can't leave alone. Each time she recalls his little speech, she grows more incensed.

Keira Greenaway complied with all the terms of her suspended sentence. She attended all her rehabilitation programme appointments. She does now have a right to privacy. If it helps put your mind at rest, there's no indication she might reoffend. Considering her various ailments, I'd say the chance is unlikely.

Bullshit.

Bull*shit*.

Nadia's not going to go through the next seven months of her pregnancy worried about Keira Greenaway's whereabouts, or what she might do next.

Admittedly, in the three years since the court case, the woman has been wholly absent from their lives. Nor, until a week ago, had Nadia thought of her that often.

The pregnancy has changed everything. If yesterday's conversation with the detective is a sore, the knowledge that Greenaway is out there somewhere – loose and unobserved, free to turn her broken mind to whatever new obsession comes calling – has grown into a pus-filled canker the size of a bus.

Yes, her story is a tragic one, but that's not Nadia's concern. Life isn't a fairy tale. It can be cruel; random. You can work hard, make all the right choices and still have everything snatched away: a train leaves the tracks; an aircraft plunges from the sky; cancer pulls your name from a hat.

Keira Greenaway made all the wrong choices – and then she made even more, her freakish obsession with Simon gradually transferring to his son.

Right now, Nadia's chief concern is the life growing inside her. That means understanding all the threats to its safety. Keira Greenaway is a threat, so Nadia needs to find her – and somehow keep an eye on her.

Clearly, the police won't help. And she refuses to put her faith in a stranger. Nor does she want to involve Simon – mainly because then she'd have to tell him about the pregnancy, and she isn't quite ready to reveal that. Four years of marriage haven't dulled her feelings for him – she wants the moment he learns he'll be a father again to be one of joy unsullied by past tragedies. Also, somewhat irrationally, she fears that by telling him she'll make the danger more immediate.

This morning, forgetting it was the weekend, Nadia phoned their security service to request an upgrade to their home system. She'll try again on Monday, when the sales staff are back in the office.

Lying in her bath, surrounded by candlelight, she scrolls through her phone contacts for the name she sought out last night.

As a teenager, Konstantin Tapia was different to the

boys Nadia knew. For a start, he never tried to sleep with her, nor signalled any interest in doing so. That aroused her curiosity, because in her home town north of Pleven – if you discounted pulling crusted shit from the woolly backsides of sheep – there wasn't much else to do. Thanks to her looks, Nadia received a lot of attention, and as she didn't much like sheep's backsides, she sometimes deigned to reward it.

Konstantin, by contrast, seemed utterly indifferent. It frustrated Nadia, that. Tormented her. She resolved to make an impression.

His parents owned a farm a few miles east of their school. One afternoon, she followed him home. Konstantin went into the house for a while. Then he visited one of the barns, where he stayed until it grew dark.

The next afternoon, Nadia rode her bike over there before Konstantin arrived home and sneaked inside the barn. In its loft she discovered a jar full of cigarette ends and a crate full of magazines. The magazines weren't the kind she was expecting but copies of *Vokrug sveta*, the Russian geographic magazine, and *Nauka i Zhizn*, the science journal. Many were very old. Some were even pre-Soviet. She also found Spanish-language editions of *National Geographic*.

Konstantin's collection had been carefully curated. Most of the cover stories featured the same subjects: volcanoes, wildfires, supernovas, nuclear-weapon tests, coronal mass ejections. Along with the magazines, she found a book on the Tunguska explosion of 1908, the largest asteroid strike in recorded history. According to the back cover, it killed reindeer and flattened trees across an area of Siberia the size of Moscow.

Nadia put everything back where she'd found it. Then, slipping off her underwear, she sat on the crate and waited. When Konstantin appeared on the ladder, his face showed no surprise at her presence. He stared at her for a while, unblinking. Then he climbed into the loft.

Nadia's heart raced with the excitement of something new. She'd invaded his territory, violated his privacy. How was he going to react?

Konstantin took out his cigarettes. He lit one, sucked hard. Still, he didn't speak.

Slowly, deliberately, Nadia rucked up her dress and opened her legs. 'If I told you that today, here in this barn, you could do anything you liked with me – once and never again – what would you choose?'

Konstantin took another drag, blinked. '*Are* you telling me that?'

Nadia worked up some moisture, wetted her lips. 'Yes.'

'*Anything* I liked?'

She saw the pulse flickering in his neck, nodded.

'Did you open my crate?'

'No.'

'Are you lying?'

'No.'

'If you're lying, I'll know.'

'I'm not lying.'

'Take off the rest of your clothes.'

A minute later, Nadia lay naked on the loft's dusty floor. Konstantin, still fully dressed, sat beside her.

'Will it hurt?' she asked.

'Are you scared?'

'No. Will it hurt?'

'Of course.'

'Where do you want to do it?'

'Here,' he said. With his index finger, he touched the inside of her right thigh five centimetres from the top. At the moment of contact, her entire leg twitched.

'Do it,' she whispered.

Konstantin took the cigarette from his mouth. He held it above the spot he'd indicated. For over a minute he gazed into her eyes. Then he pushed the glowing tip into her skin.

The pain was instant, brutal, and it kept building – a super-heated needle, lancing her flesh. Nadia clenched her teeth, her fists, but she didn't cry out. She'd give him something, but she wouldn't give him that.

Konstantin's pupils flared, then contracted. He dropped the extinguished cigarette and lit another. Nadia smelled tobacco smoke, burnt skin.

'Well?' he asked.

'Well, what?'

'You'll let me carry on?'

'I said so, didn't I? Twice, but no more. And nowhere obvious, where people will see.'

Konstantin touched the same spot but on her left thigh. 'Here.'

Nadia grimaced.

'Are you scared?'

'No.'

'Are you lying?'

'I'm not scared.'

This time, the pain was *far* worse. Like before, she refused to cry out, but she couldn't hold back the tears.

Konstantin grunted when he saw the burn develop: a

weeping white bulb. 'In future years,' he said, 'any man who opens your legs will see that I was there before him. It'll drive him mad with envy.'

Nadia shivered. In hindsight, she'd given him far more than she'd intended. But it was done, at least. She'd kept her word and she hadn't let him see her pain.

'Fire burns, but it also protects,' Konstantin said. 'As I will now protect you.'

Nearly two decades later, lying in her bath, Nadia stares at his number and wonders what would happen if she dialled it and he answered.

He'd be here in a day – no doubt about that – but there'd almost certainly be a price. And once he arrived she might not control the situation for long.

She raises her left leg clear of the bath water and touches the pea-sized circle of scar tissue on her inner thigh. Time has smoothed it flat.

Holding her breath, Nadia dials.

FIFTEEN

I take longer than usual to climb down Pincher's Mount. Mainly because my legs are misbehaving and won't do what I tell them.

I'm not drunk. At least, I don't think so. I'm just uber-sensitive to anything that could affect my balance. It's a relief to climb on my trike and grip the handlebars, but I'm too wired from my encounter to go straight home. Also, I need to eat. At this time of night, there's only one place.

The drive-thru is lit up brighter than the Texaco, as if it's touting for business passing through from outer space. Two cars filled with hungry earthlings are queuing at the order window. Inside the restaurant, a couple of Just Eat riders are grabbing their last deliveries. Outside, by the bolted-down tables, I see Lost Travis operating his trapdoor dustpan.

It *obsessed* me, that device, when I first saw it. I ordered one for my flat and spent an entire weekend dropping things on the floor and sweeping them right up. Who needs friends when you can clean up your own peanut shells without bending at the waist?

I wait for the cars and the Just Eat gophers to collect

their food. Then I ride up to the speaker and give Whiplash Becky my order. Becky's the nightshift manager and Lost Travis's boss. She's nearly always angry and I've never found out why.

I order a cheeseburger, fries and a strawberry shake. Then, as an afterthought – and because I'm super-hungry – I add an apple pie. For reasons unknown, this irritates the hell out of Becky. Fortunately, the speaker unit converts her response into a series of whistles and shrieks.

I ride to the pick-up window and collect my sack of shame. Then I loop around to the front and park. I'm two bites into my cheeseburger when I hear a familiar voice.

'Hi, Merdy.'

I look up and there's Travis. He's huge – a big-boned giant with floppy hair, trusting eyes and a fuzz of blond stubble. His blunt-tipped fingers are curled around his dustpan handle.

'Hey, Travis. New shoes? Very cool.'

He grunts, pleased that I noticed. 'Merdy gotta milk-shake.'

'I have. *And* a pie. Greedy, eh? I'll get fat.'

He sniggers at that, rocking on his heels. Then he reaches under his shirt and pulls out a leather necklace. From it hangs a silver lightning bolt pendant. 'Found,' he says. 'Merdy left for me.'

'I did. You approve?'

'Lightning,' Travis replies. 'Crash-bang.'

'That's right.'

'Becky said dumb thing to have around neck.'

'She did?'

'Lightning's a bad omen, Becky said. Means trouble coming. Punishment. But I don't care. I wear it nice.'

'I'm sure Becky's right about a lot of things,' I tell him carefully. 'But lightning's also a sign for strength.'

'Travis strong.'

'I know you are. Strong as an ox. But soon—'

'Special Fried!'

Travis flinches so hard that for a moment I think he's been struck. He drops to a crouch, eyes roving like searchlights.

Becky calls out again, clapping her hands. *'Time's up, Special Fried! You get in here right now and mop this floor! I'm not hanging around all night.'*

'Gotta go,' he says.

'She's calling you Special Fried?'

But Travis isn't listening – at least, not to me. I watch him slope back to the drive-thru, head hung low.

Lightning's a bad omen, Becky said. Means trouble coming. Punishment.

That's the last thing I wanted him to hear. Has Travis mentioned me to Becky, I wonder? Until last night, he was the only person in Cranner's Ford who knew my name. Telling Louis was a terrible idea, but that's the trouble with isolation – it makes you do stupid things.

I look around the car park, checking I'm still alone. Then I screw up my burger wrapper, finish my shake and vamoose.

SIXTEEN

If there's a sound James Matthews likes, it's a small-block V8 sucking fuel through a Holley four-barrel carburettor, combusting it into music.

Idling, his 1966 Ford Shelby Mustang sounds like a pack of growling wolves. But tug on that carburettor and immediately those wolves howl. It's the sound of a lost era, an era James wishes he'd seen. An era when girls didn't blink if you slapped their backsides because at least you weren't a *communist* – and because if Ivan *did* drop the big one, a red handprint would be the last of anyone's worries. It's the sound of power, of freedom. Of confidence and unfettered masculinity. It's 4.7 litres of fuel and air, compressed and detonated inside eight monstrous cylinders. It's angry and violent, hungry and impatient, and to James Matthews it's even sexier than the creature currently occupying his passenger seat – although admittedly it's a close race.

The heel of her cowboy boot is braced against the dash. James could scream, seeing that, but he doesn't, even though he's post-coital and post-cigarette and post-giving-a-shit-what-she-thinks – because the angle of her leg means the folds of her khaki skirt have fallen perfectly, revealing a tease of sun-kissed thigh whenever they pass a streetlight.

Earlier, James thought he'd drunk his fill. Now he's not so sure. Still, he can't do anything about it while driving. Instead, he cranks the window.

The air inside the car stirs. James gets another hit of perfume. Yeah, definitely not sated. He drums his fingers against the wheel. They're on Liphook Avenue, approaching the crossroads with Bartholomew Street. He could turn around, cruise back towards Pincher's Mount. He never takes the Mustang to Rycroft Hollow, where the town's freaks and geeks go to bump uglies – he won't risk the loose gravel on his paintwork – but there's always the lane just below it. Still, he doesn't fancy the Twister-like contortions of in-car copulation twice in one night . . . and those cowboy boots are making him twitchy.

'So – I'm dropping you home?'

She turns, cocking an eyebrow. 'That's what you said.'

'Yeah. I mean, I could come in.'

Her lips swell when she grins. 'You're as thirsty as this car.'

'For you, permanently.'

It's not true. Still, when the moon is full, he's always horny as hell – as if a little werewolf blood kicks through his arteries with the testosterone, nicotine and motor oil.

Her grin fades and she winces. 'My housemate's home tonight. I promised her we'd goss.'

James has seen photos of the housemate. He's regularly entertained fantasies of a threesome. 'There's a bottle of Jim Bean under the seat,' he says. 'I could join you.'

'Oh, hon. Strictly girls only, I'm afraid.'

James is preparing a final pitch when something red barrels out of Bartholomew Street, right across their path.

He has no time to think. Fortunately, muscles fuelled by testosterone, nicotine and motor oil reliably function on instinct. He flicks the wheel, right foot dancing between brake pedal and accelerator. The Mustang kicks into a slide. James counter-steers, controlling the drift, a long shriek of rubber confirming the flat-spotting of his Cooper Cobra tyres. As he fights the tarmac, he realizes that the red something streaking towards his chrome bumper is an adult-sized tricycle – piloted by a crazy-looking freak in dungaree shorts and clumpy maroon boots.

For a moment he thinks he's going to bounce her, tricycle and all, right over his grille and across his bonnet, in a metal-shearing horror of destruction. But even as the restoration cost flashes through his head, the tricycle is already in his side window, and then his rear-view mirror, and then he's flicking the Mustang back straight while simultaneously blasting the horn.

Beside him, the girl rocks in her seat, cowboy boot skittering across his dash.

'Oh, sweet *Jesus*,' James moans. Suddenly, he just wants her out of his car. In those stacked leather heels she's simply too dangerous. Maybe he'll buy her a pair of Ugg boots, or insist in future she goes barefoot. Five minutes later, he pulls up outside her place.

'Sorry about coming in,' she tells him. 'I'm not trying to keep you a secret. Thursday night, instead?'

'Can't do Thursday,' he tells her brusquely. 'Got plans.' By which he means a twenty-eight-year-old estate agent called Dani.

'Next weekend, then? Maybe we could go out some-where, like a bar or something, rather than just . . . you know.'

She gives him a half-smile. In that moment he spots a vulnerability he hadn't suspected and realizes with a jolt that to her this is more than just sex – that she's actually started to care for him.

Remorse curdles his stomach, worse than a dose of food poisoning. *Sometimes*, he thinks, *you're really a prize bastard*.

She leans over and kisses him. He responds with a big, shitty grin. Despite his remorse, when she swings her cowboy boots out of the car and grazes the door, he can't help grimacing. Then he's accelerating away.

He stops at the first opportunity. Grabbing a penlight from the glovebox, he examines the dash. No damage, praise the Lord – her heel hadn't picked up any grit. He might be a prize bastard, but this time karma hasn't pun-ished him. It's enough of a reprieve to fortify his appetite and send him scrolling through his phone. Three voice-mails, two unanswered calls and one success later, he's pulling up outside 34 Greek Street.

Hazel Docherty doesn't own cowboy boots. Nor does she have a housemate who wants to goss. She *does* own a cat that makes James sneeze, but he keeps a couple of fexofenadine in the Mustang for precisely such an emergency.

Hazel's preparing a late supper when he arrives – something with onion and garlic that makes his eyes smart. It's hard to maintain sexual interest while watching her eat – especially when she feeds the cat little parcels of meat directly from her plate, or when she chokes on a parsley stalk and thumps her chest until it's dislodged. But he manages, just about, even after her tiny belch at the meal's conclusion. In her bathroom, pre-coitus, he discovers evidence of a rival male: two skull-and-crossbones cufflinks and a can of Dove Men deodorant. It's almost as off-putting as the belching.

The sex that follows supper is perfunctory, unsatisfying. James leaves Hazel rifling through her fridge for dessert. He drives home carefully, alert for red tricycles piloted by crazies in dungaree shorts and clumpy boots, or any other nutcases karma might throw at him. His earlier remorse has faded, the frustrating experience at Hazel's reminding him of a universal truth: that despite their soft voices and perfumed skin, women can be just as piggish as men, with habits just as base.

At home, he drives his Mustang into the garage and sits a while in silence. Then he lets himself into the house.

It's dark inside, and quiet. James patrols the ground floor, checking windows and doors before climbing the stairs. His hand glides up the handrail and he can't help feeling for tiny scratches, like those caused by cowboy heels ingrained with grit.

In the bathroom he showers, washing off all traces of tonight's women. Then he cleans his teeth and gargles. With the lights off, he tiptoes into his bedroom. His wife is a tightly curled lump beneath the duvet.

James watches the lump expand and shrink, listening to the steady hiss of its breathing. Asleep – he's almost certain. Men lie, but so do women, and James knows which sex is better at it. Recently, he's begun to suspect that his wife knows more about his late-night liaisons than she admits.

He slips under the duvet, careful to keep his distance.

He might be a prize bastard, but he's not a monster. And although his exploits might be viewed unfavourably by any stranger looking on, James knows his wife must take some of the blame. They don't have kids, so what other reason could she have for letting herself go? These days, the beauty products that previously crowded her dressing table have dwindled to a few supermarket basics. Their sex toys, once frequent bedfellows, are so grossly fugged through disuse that they'd probably cause an infection should he attempt to reintroduce them.

The mattress creaks. James concentrates. Has her breathing changed? Is she awake and just pretending? Her car was in the drive when he arrived home, but he hadn't tested the bonnet for warmth. She could have followed him to Pincher's Mount, watched his cowgirl rodeo and driven home while he was at Hazel's.

There's something darkly erotic about that thought. Gingerly, James whispers his wife's name. Her breathing remains constant: slow in, slow out.

Maybe he's just being paranoid. Maybe he's simply feeling guilty again, even though little of this is his fault.

He falls asleep thinking of a small-block V8 sucking fuel through a Holley four-barrel carburettor, but when he dreams it's of a girl wearing dungaree shorts and riding spurs perched on his bonnet, scissoring her legs so that the spurs rake deep gouges into his paintwork.

SEVENTEEN

Inside my flat, I follow my usual routine: panels up; blackout blinds down; curtains closed; and wall hangings unfurled.

I cross a tropical beach and snow-covered mountains and journey through forest greenness to my underwater reef. Not quite the real thing but good enough. Certainly the closest I'll ever get.

From the bathroom cabinet I grab two paracetamol, downing them with a glass of water. My head is thumping – whether from stress or champagne, I can't tell.

Back in my forest glade, I open my wardrobe and examine the contents. If I see Louis on Thursday night, I can't wear my dungaree shorts a third time, but it's far too hot for jeans and I don't own any dresses.

I *do* have a pair of stripey shorts, two pairs of leggings with holed knees and two more sets of dungarees in different shades of denim. Combined with any of my tops, the overall look is hybrid garage mechanic and circus clown.

The storage chest beside my bed represents my last hope. But when I turn towards it, the room upends.

Balancing on a floor that's ninety degrees to horizontal isn't feasible, even with arms flailing like hummingbird wings. I topple backwards, ricochet off the cupboard and pirouette towards the bed. Something strikes my knee. Then I'm falling in a different direction. I see the storage chest just before a corner strikes my face. Fireworks detonate behind my eyes. A tsunami of pain washes them away. I lie on my bedroom floor, stunned and gasping.

I should wait here a while and recover, but I'm far too stupid for that. Instead, I drag myself up and stumble back to my underwater reef. There, in front of the mirror, I assess the damage: an eye already swelling, a gash on my cheekbone like parted lips.

After twenty-four hours of chaos, it's a much-needed moment of clarity. I can't allow someone into my life. I just can't. Louis called me Night Eyes, brought me champagne, said all sorts of nice things. In a different world, that might be the start of something. Not this one.

Even if I *could* risk it, look at the state of me. Mismatched eyes, one of them bruised. Blood running down my cheek. Half the time, I can't even stand upright. Whenever I open my mouth, a steady stream of gibberish pours out.

Louis doesn't need me in his life. And nor do I want him in mine. It's not as if I'm alone. I have my conversations with Lost Travis, my visits to the Raffertys and others I watch in town. My life here might not be perfect, but there are moments of joy, plenty of them. Fretting about what *clothes* I should wear isn't joy. Far from it.

Louis knows nothing about me except the name I gave him – and that won't help him track me down. He saw me at the Texaco, but he doesn't know I shop there, just that I visited to fix my puncture. He *does* know to find me up on

Pincher's Mount, which means my world just got a lot smaller than it was. That'll be hard for a while, but it won't be for ever. When I don't show up Thursday night, Louis might give it one more shot. After that, he'll lose interest – and life can return to how it was.

Decision made, I clean up my face the best I can. Then I go to the living room and push back the sofa to the wall. I unroll my yoga mat and strap on kneepads, elbow pads and skate helmet. The helmet features Twilight Sparkle from My Little Pony. She offers me protection – although not always – from the demons of bad balance.

Last night I was too exhausted to exercise. I can't let that become a habit. Holding out my arms scarecrow fashion, I lift one leg and start to count. When I reach ten without incident – *Go, Mercy!* – I repeat with the other leg. Over the next twenty minutes, I cycle through the rest of my exercises. I fall over twice. Fortunately, I live on the lower-ground floor, with no one beneath me to complain.

Once my equipment is packed away, I go to bed. It's far too early for sleep. Still, I'm exhausted mentally and physically. Turning off my daylight lamps, I lie in darkness with my pulsing cheek.

I might have no downstairs neighbours, but I do have one overhead. Humpin' Honey, I call her. Honey's bedroom is directly above mine. Tonight, she has company of the birds, bees and booty kind. What starts as a muffled thumping steadily builds in pitch. It sounds like her bed is juddering across bare floorboards. Pretty soon, my cheek starts throbbing in unison.

Vertigo kicks in, a sudden rush. Even though I'm motionless, my mattress feels like an ocean wave has taken it. I clutch my duvet, try to anchor myself. Here I am, listening to my neighbour do the bad thing, while my bed heaves on a sea entirely imagined and my mind creates images I'd rather not contemplate.

'Hey, Google. Play "Tragedy" by the Bee Gees, volume ten.'

My virtual assistant obeys – albeit with a somewhat weary tone. The music is loud, but it doesn't drown out the sex pageant upstairs. Pretty soon, the thump of the bass, the pulse of my cheek and the knocking of Honey's bed are perfectly synchronized. I feel like I've been dragged, unwilling, into the world's unsexiest threesome.

When Honey's moans graduate into delighted screams, I wedge pillows either side of my head and sing through gritted teeth until it's over.

Afterwards, exhausted, I return to a place I'd rather forget.

EIGHTEEN

Sunlight. Azure sky. Razor blades on water – each one sharp enough to slice through flesh.

Like a bad home movie, the scene jump-cuts. Suddenly, I'm no longer on the lake. Behind me, the prow of my rowing boat rests on gravel shore.

My Converse All Stars are soaked. They squelch with each step, my feet forcing out water through the ringlets. At last I lift my head. And there, before me, stands the lake house: gabled roof, wooden porch, logs of honeyed spruce. A silver Mercedes is parked outside, between a black Porsche Cayenne and an aluminium boat trailer.

She's inside.

They all are.

My fists clench. Above me, the sun beats down with a ferocity barely comprehendible. Turning my head, I seek out an exposed patch on the dirt track to the main road. Afterwards, Italian police will spend hours photographing it, measuring it, sifting it. At one point, months later, determined to uncover the truth, they'll make me visit. For now

I just need to see it, acknowledge what will happen there. The main show lies ahead.

My body feels like a sack filled with something curdled; a dense liquid in which threads of congealed matter float like worms. I wish I didn't have to do this, but I do.

I make no attempt to conceal my approach. No one will see me through the front windows. Right now, they're otherwise engaged.

Again, the scene skips. I'm standing in the living room. Standing over *her*.

Bloody skid marks criss-cross the floorboards. They disappear into the hall, from where she dragged herself before rolling on to her back.

Her eyes – dark as antique wood – are fixed on mine. But they're sightless, now. My hands are gloved in her blood.

This is what obsession does. This is what *lust* does. And greed; wrath; pride. All the bad things wrapped up.

So far, the dream has been silent. Now, sound begins to leak through. I hear rustling, soft breathing. Turning my head, I see the baby. He's sitting upright beside the sofa, naked except for his white nappy. When our eyes meet, Ollie Rafferty coos and claps. His hands and feet are wet with his mother's blood.

NINETEEN

Tuesday, at noon, even with three fans blowing and the front door wedged open, the Glam It Up nail bar is unbearably hot. Its south-facing windows act as a giant magnifier, roasting the interior.

Nadia Rafferty vows to make this her last visit. Simon, ever hungry for positive PR, presses her to support local businesses where she can, but the place is so poorly ventilated, and the stink of acetone so thick, that she fears for the health of her baby.

Wanda, the nail bar's owner, is hunched over beside a daylight lamp. Her leopard-print halter gapes open, revealing the darkly tanned breasts of an oncologist's nightmare. The vinegary stink of her sweat suggests she spent most of last night drinking. 'Don't get much call for green,' she drawls. 'Ain't a popular colour, this side of Halloween. You got a fancy-dress party or something, babe?'

'Awards ceremony, Thursday night,' Nadia says. 'Green energy. My husband's company is shortlisted.'

Wanda hangs up her airbrush and slips Nadia's hand

beneath a UV drying lamp. 'Don't tell me he's the one been putting up all them wind turbines around here.'

'He isn't,' Nadia lies.

'Each one of them things,' Wanda says, 'kills fifty thousand birds. A *week*, you believe that? *And* they interfere with the internet. What's so wrong with global warming, anyway? This is the best summer we ever had.' She nods through the window at the street, where a black Range Rover Evoque is parked behind a mint-green and cream campervan. 'Can't say I ain't doing my bit. That thing drinks petrol like it's friggin' Chardonnay. Costs me a new mortgage each time I fill up. So where's this awards bash, babe?'

'London,' Nadia says. 'Soho House.'

'Well, now you got the claws for it.'

Nadia examines her nails: white tips feathering to a dark and leafy green. It's good work, despite the awkward small talk. She pays and goes outside, where a line of customers is snaking out of the door of an artisan bakery. Thinking of her flat stomach, and the minimal protection it affords her baby, Nadia joins the queue. She leaves five minutes later with a box filled with macarons, mille-feuilles, choux à la crème and a huge tarte tatin.

Putting the cakes in her car, Nadia crosses the street to a pharmacy. It's blessedly cool inside. In the pregnancy aisle, she doesn't see the stretch-mark cream she read about online, but she does find a vast range of alternatives, plus supplements, maternity pads, nipple balms, breast pads, perineal sprays, comfort cushions, sleep pillows and thermometers.

'A whole new world, isn't it?'

The guy who spoke is standing to Nadia's right, his

focus on the merchandise. She gives him a quick once-over, decides he's safe. When she returns her attention to the rack, he adds: 'Impossible to figure out which brand is best.'

Running her tongue over her teeth, Nadia double-checks her first pass. He looks wholesome enough – around her age, maybe a fraction older, dressed for the heat in linen shirt, shorts and white pumps. An enamelled yin-yang pendant hangs at his throat.

'Girlfriend sent me,' he says. 'Asked me to pick up a test. She thinks . . .' He shrugs. 'Well, fingers crossed.'

After an hour with Wanda, Nadia's in no mood for further chat, but she feels herself thawing regardless. 'I use those,' she tells the guy, pointing.

'Clearblue?'

'Works for me.'

He picks up a pack, turns it over. 'Hang on. You *pee* on these things?'

She laughs. 'If that freaks you out, I'd say you're in for a bumpy ride.'

The guy meets her gaze, grins. Not just wholesome, Nadia decides. He's straight-up attractive: strong jaw, good teeth, green eyes that could charm a cobra. Genes worth passing on.

He glances into her basket. 'You look like you've got it all covered.'

'Uh-uh. I'm a learner driver, too.'

'How many weeks?'

'Eight, I think.'

The guy's smile broadens. 'That's such good news.'

Nadia smiles too, can't help it. On her way back to the

car, she realizes with a jolt that he's the first person she's told.

She doesn't drive straight home. Instead, she takes the lane that climbs clockwise around Pincher's Mount to the woods on its eastern slope. Once parked, she slips on sunglasses and running shoes and climbs out of the car. Twenty metres inside the treeline she finds a place to sit: the trunk of a fallen oak, in a clearing with a view of the lane.

Her strappy dress offers little protection from the sun. If she stays out here too long, she'll burn. That wouldn't be a good look for the awards ceremony. Twenty minutes later, Nadia's shoulders are buzzing. She checks her phone, looks up. And there he is.

As an adult, Konstantin Tapia resembles little of the boy she once knew. He's a large man, fleshy and hairless, his scalp shaved perfectly smooth. His clothes are unsuited to the weather: a black wool suit and a black shirt buttoned at the neck. His bare head is red with sunburn. Sweat has run down his temples and darkened his collar. Staring at him, Nadia feels breathless, curiously weightless. When she begins to get up, Konstantin shakes his head.

'Tell me everything,' he says. 'Miss nothing out.'

Nadia starts talking. She tells him a lot, but not all. Some parts – questions she hasn't answered, suspicions she's previously ignored – she doesn't want to share, even with him. *Particularly* with him. Because she knows he'd seek out the answers regardless. She wouldn't be able to rein him in.

Konstantin examines her closely. 'Why now?' he asks. 'After all this time. What's got you so spooked?'

Nadia swallows. Her fingers twitch and she sits on them, worried she might touch her belly. She *definitely* doesn't want him to learn about that; doesn't know how he might react. 'Just a feeling,' she says. 'A *watched* feeling. You know how it is. Will you help?'

Konstantin tilts his head towards the sun. He takes out a pack of cigarettes and lights one, taking a long drag. The tobacco crackles as it burns. 'Take off your clothes.'

Nadia's stomach flops. Strangely, the feeling isn't entirely unpleasurable. She glances through the trees to the lane, but it's an isolated spot. Since her arrival, she's seen no other vehicles passing by.

'I'm married, now,' she says.

'Yes.'

'I'm just – nowhere obvious. OK?'

Konstantin shrugs.

Nadia stands, slips out of her dress.

TWENTY

Thursday night.

New adventures, new dangers, new opportunities to live a better life. Before I leave the flat, I pack my cargo bag: claw hammer, rucksack, fairy costume, Little Professor toy, rattle can, grape-flavoured Bubblicious.

Friday's puncture seriously curtailed my evening's activities. Saturday night's encounter on Pincher's Mount delayed me further. Bad enough that I've neglected Raj the Reborn, Home Alone Jacob and others I've been watching. But there's one place I can't avoid – one person I *must* see – even though I risk everything by visiting.

My hair is tied back, secured with a net. Over it I'm wearing a neon-pink wig cut into a fringed bob. Combined with my heavy make-up, I look like someone from a William Gibson novel – although the transformation isn't yet complete.

At the door to my flat I hesitate. Thoughts of my destination have furred my skin. I'm Night People, attuned to danger, and I've learned to trust my instincts. Returning to the kitchen, I rummage through a drawer for my bear spray. It shoots a burst of concentrated capsicum up to ten metres. Anyone catching a faceful is going to be maximum sad I used it. The stuff is illegal in the UK, but you can find it with the right search-fu.

Ten minutes later I'm on Abbot's Walk, beside Arcadia Heights's crushed boundary wall. I hide my trike in undergrowth. Then I clamber over the fallen stones, breaching my restraining order for the second time inside a week. I pick my way through the trees, emerging at my usual spot beside the pool's filtration pump.

Tonight, just like on Friday, the building's ground-floor windows are ablaze. Despite that, none of the rooms appear occupied. I'm pondering Simon and Nadia's whereabouts when I spot movement in the orangery. A young woman enters: dark hair, mid-twenties, flawless physique. She's barefoot, wearing camo leggings and a pink crop top. Not Nadia, but I've seen her here before: the couple use her for babysitting. Daisy Double-Take, I call her – because she won't have escaped Simon's eye. As I watch, she unrolls a yoga mat, gets down on all fours and extends a leg.

Perfect. (Not the leg, although it's fabulously sculpted, and I *would* like to watch her exercise – Daisy's movements are so graceful and well balanced that I might learn something useful.)

Perfect because it means Simon and Nadia aren't home.

My gaze rises to Ollie Rafferty's first-floor bedroom, one of the cubes furthest from the pool. If this were any other house, I wouldn't be able to reach it. Access is possible thanks to Arcadia Heights's unique design: from poolside to grass slope; along concrete plinth to mid-floor deck; up side steps to terrace; over glass balustrade to Ollie's balcony.

It's not without risk. And for me, the dangers are magnified. Still, none of the potential falls are more than a metre. Apart from striking my head on concrete, the greatest danger is that I black out somewhere exposed and lie there prone until discovered.

Of course, the jeopardy doesn't end there. Two CCTV cameras fixed to the house keep constant watch. If I stray into their field of view, or leave any other evidence of my visit, the consequences will be devastating.

In the orangery, Daisy Double-Take transitions from pistol squat to crescent lunge. I've probably got thirty minutes before she takes a break.

Still wearing my Doc Martens, I strip to my underwear. Then I unzip my rucksack and put on the outfit I brought along: lavender corset; matching sleeves; layered skirt with jagged hem. There's a wand somewhere. Found it.

This is foolish. Worse than foolish. It's dangerous, indulgent, destined to end in calamity. But this is how I reintroduced myself to Ollie Rafferty and earned his trust. I've no choice but to continue the charade. Reports of a stranger outside the boy's window would doubtless ring alarm bells. Sightings of Tinker Bell, on the other hand, might go unchallenged.

I shrug on my fairy wings and don a silver plastic tiara. Then, with a final check on Daisy, I emerge from safety.

TWENTY-ONE

Seven minutes later and I've almost completed the assault course. My muscles are aching. My palms are slick. It'll take me far longer to climb down than up. If I'm discovered now, I won't escape. At the balustrade separating Ollie's balcony from this one, I pause for breath. Gripping the rail with both hands, I pull myself over.

The glass wall of his bedroom is as black as the surrounding night. Two panes along the top are open for ventilation. I step closer, reminding myself that I'm Tinker Bell. Then, breath fluttering like the fairy wings strapped to my back, I tap five times on the glass.

It's late. I realize that. Ollie's probably asleep and he probably won't wake. It won't stop me delivering my gift, but I'd give anything to see him.

A vision swells in my head. I imagine lights winking on inside the room, revealing all those I watch in Cranner's Ford gathered together; their eyes on me, instead of the other way around.

It's such a disturbing thought that my stomach turns over. The balcony rolls with it. Just as I think I'll lose my balance, a face materializes behind the glass. Ollie Rafferty knuckles away sleep and squints up at me. His eyes widen. His mouth drops open in wonder.

Oh, God. I love this.

For a magical moment I really *am* Tinker Bell, my wings no longer refurbished skip finds but the real thing, ready to carry me moonward should I desire it. My imitation plastic wand is capable of casting all the spells I might need.

Abruptly, Ollie disappears from view. I wait while he switches on his bedside lamp. When he scampers back to the window, I flutter my eyelashes and smile.

He's wearing Minions pyjama bottoms and nothing else, his chest a cage of fragile ribs. He's blond, like his mother, with the same smattering of freckles. His eyes, in contrast, are all Simon's.

For a while we stand motionless, contemplating each other in the lamplight. The handle to his sliding door is inches away, but I daren't touch it, even though I'm sure it must be locked – because if I found it wasn't, I might lose all self-control. I might slide the door open, gather him up . . .

. . . and then what?

We all know how that finished last time.

Instead, I place my palm against the window, fingers splayed. Ollie stares, transfixed. Then he mirrors my gesture.

My heart thumps like a tribal drum. I feel its echo pulse down my arm to my fingertips, and through the glass to Ollie's hand.

This is a moment in my life and his. An experience that belongs, exclusively, to us. Tears swell in the corners of my eyes. To disguise them I lean forward and make myself monstrous, curling back my lips and baring my teeth.

Ollie flinches, whipping away his hand. Then, recovering, he puts his face to the glass and snarls. I cower in pantomime terror. His laugh – audible through the open top panes – is like falling water.

From the waistband of my skirt I remove the refurbished Little Professor. Earlier, I attached a length of ribbon. Standing on tiptoes, I post the toy through the open glass and lower it to Ollie.

He unties the bow and turns his prize over in his hands. Then he looks up and smiles.

Immediately, the wooden balcony starts tilting again, as if I'm on the deck of Captain's Hook's *Jolly Roger* and we've just hit bad weather.

I grit my teeth and ride it out. Luckily, it's not a nasty one – perhaps my fairy wings are helping – but it *is* a warning to get going. I point at the Little Professor and press a finger to my lips. Ollie's room overflows with toys. Unlikely that this one will stand out, but I'd still prefer him to keep it hidden.

The boy nods, solemn-faced. When I wave my wand in goodbye, his chest quivers and his eyes shine. Retreating to the rail, I make my escape.

TWENTY-TWO

Midnight. Pincher's Mount. My familiar scooped-out bite.

Saturday night I made a decision, vowed not to come. And yet somehow, after leaving Ollie, this is where I ended up. Now that I'm here, I'm trembling so hard my teeth are clattering inside my mouth.

Did I visit Arcadia Heights because of its proximity to the mount? In truth, I don't even remember climbing up here, nor the ride over from Abbot's Walk.

It's more than a little frightening. As always, what I fear most is a new symptom – proof that my brain injury isn't healing but worsening. These last five years I've come a long way, or so I keep telling myself. Trouble is, I've got no one's word except my own.

I won't return to hospital. I can't face further surgeries. And I've had my fill of speech and language therapists, occupational therapists, neuropsychologists and TBI specialists.

I'm grateful for every single thing the medical profession has done for me. I'm in awe of every doctor, every surgeon, every nurse. But if I'm dying, I don't need to hear it from a stranger wearing a sad face. I have my exercises and I'll keep doing them. If something explodes in my head, so be it. Until then, I'll try to make each day count.

From my hollow I pick out Ursa Major and Ursa Minor. Am I really doing this? Am I really going to sit here, hug my knees and wait for Louis? I recall the snap of electricity that passed between us at the Texaco; that sense of something dangerous about to sprout.

I'm jeopardizing everything, and for what? Some people might think my life is worthless, but I don't. What just happened outside Ollie's room wasn't worthless. Neither for him nor for me. And while Ollie might be the reason I moved here, there are plenty of others in Cranner's Ford I'm doing my best to help.

Admit it, Mercy. You're here because you're lonely to the point of desperation.

That's *not* true. It really isn't. I have Lost Travis and Home Alone Jacob. I have Laurie, my baking Venus. And, of course, I have Ollie.

Looking at my watch, I see it's ten past twelve. Busy people can't always be punctual. I recall Louis's words, Saturday evening, when I told him I'd be here around midnight:

OK, Night Eyes. With any luck I might see you then.

In hindsight, that wasn't anything like a commitment. The more I think about it, the more I realize Louis promised absolutely nothing. Somehow, my hamster brain has inflated a throwaway nicety into a vow of grail knight solemnity.

Yeesh, what a human tragedy.

My nose fills with petrichor – the scent of rain falling on dry soil. Although the hillside is parched, no clouds have opened above me. The petrichor is just another olfactory hallucination. Another reminder of my messed-up head.

If Louis doesn't show, it's a crisis averted, not cause for disappointment. I don't need to be sad. Cranner's Ford is full of marvels, stories and adventures. I'm already amply blessed.

At seventeen minutes past midnight, I resolve that Louis really isn't coming, and that it really is OK. After all, I knew almost nothing about him. His number plate, which I memorized, threw up no search results. And I could hardly google his first name. During our conversation I revealed far more than he did, mainly because I failed to ask any questions. Small talk, even in my old life, was never my strong point.

He called me an enigma. One of a kind.

I let myself feel pleased about that, even though they were just words. Steadying my jaw, I recall our final exchange: about where I'd be tonight, at what time, and whom I'd be watching first.

I find my Bubblicious and shove a chunk into my mouth. The intense grape flavour karate-chops my self-pity. A bit of noisy mastication and I can think again.

My binoculars are round my neck. Raising them, I zero in on the Texaco. I see two cars filling up. No campervan and no Louis.

From the Texaco I pan south to the back of Tall Pines – and notice, immediately, that something's not right. This late, William the Navigator's room is usually in darkness. Right now, though, it's brightly lit.

My stomach plummets. I rotate the focus wheel, sharpening the image. If the bed is empty, it can mean only one thing. But there's William, lying motionless beneath his covers. And there, at the open window – inside the room rather than outside it – stands Louis. He's holding binoculars of his own. They must be trained on the mount, because moments after I spot him, he raises a hand and waves.

TWENTY-THREE

Never have I moved so fast, or with such little care for my condition. By the time I've descended to the Monk's Brook, I've taken too many tumbles to count. I'm scratched, scuffed, bruised. Covered in dirt and dust.

Splashing through water to the far bank, I climb on to my trike. The moment I hit open road, I push the Jorvik to its limit. How could Louis have seen me? Unless his binoculars are infrared? Up on Pincher's Mount, I should have been invisible, a tiny figure against a pitch-black slope.

Of course, that isn't the main question. Not even close. *What was he doing in William's room?*

I swerve across the road and rocket up Tall Pines's drive. Just before the main building I hit the brakes, skidding to a stop behind a rhododendron.

When I clamber off the Jorvik, my world upends. Falling backwards into a rhododendron isn't as painful as hitting tarmac, but it still hurts. Above me the silhouetted pines rotate like pointy-hatted figures around a cauldron.

I roll on to my side, find my feet. Checking my bear spray is still inside my waistband, I crash through the undergrowth. When I reach the tree closest to the building, I wrap my arms around it.

William's room is dark.

I take a moment to process that. Then I stumble to the window. I cup my hands to the glass and see William asleep in his bed. Alone.

My strength goes. I sit down hard.

Did I *imagine* what I saw? Might I have confused Louis with one of the Tall Pines carers? Perhaps I hallucinated the entire thing. Now *there's* a scary thought.

A scratch on my forearm is leaking blood – whether from the rhododendron, the Monk's Brook brambles or some other forgotten event, I don't know. Recovering my breath, I pick grit from my palm.

Since I'm here, I shouldn't waste the opportunity, even if I'm still rattled. Friday night, a puncture interrupted my plans. Right now, though, the coast is clear. Returning to my Jorvik, I unzip the cargo bag and retrieve my rucksack and claw hammer.

Back outside William's room, I approach the glass and freeze. Because the night air, now, is laced with sage and mint and cedarwood. I turn from the window and find, behind me, Louis.

It's a knockout-level shock, stomach-shrinking and horrible. How I keep my balance I can't say. I do take a step back, but my foot lands squarely. My hips remain level, my spine straight.

The moon has turned Louis's skin to milk. His eyes have become obsidian dials. Even now, I'm struck by his beauty; his fine bone structure and full lips. But I'm struck even more by his expression – a puppy-dog eagerness wholly at odds with the situation.

'*You.*' My voice comes out as a super-dramatic hiss. It hardly matters – I'm fully expecting Louis to dissolve into smoke-like threads. When he doesn't, I hear myself add: 'I thought I was hallucinating, imagining things. It *was* you in there. Why? What were you doing?'

Louis blinks. For a moment I see something utterly alien in his expression. It's gone before I can get a proper handle on it – leaving me wondering if I saw it at all. In its absence, the puppy-dog eagerness changes to hangdog sheepishness.

'Acting on impulse,' he says, visibly cringing. 'And on the worst idea in the history of worst ideas. I should have checked with you first. I'm sorry, Mercy, this was . . .'

His voice trails off. I realize his gaze has fallen to my claw hammer. It's an awkward moment, made worse when I slide the hammer behind my back.

'Did you bring that in case . . .' Louis begins. Now, the hangdog sheepishness collapses into dismay. 'You think I'm a monster.'

'What?'

'You brought a hammer to protect yourself.'

'No, I—'

'I don't blame you. I . . .'

He frowns, takes a forward step.

I match him with a backward one.

'Are you . . .' Louis shakes his head, as if a wasp has flown into his ear. 'Are those wings? Are you wearing angel wings?'

I scowl, angry with myself and with him. 'Fairy wings.'

'You've ripped one.'

'Well, damn it – then I guess I won't be able to fly.'

For the first time, I've spoken without thinking. And actually, I'm reasonably satisfied with the results.

Louis opens and closes his mouth.

'What were you doing in William's room?' I demand.

'His name isn't William.'

'What?'

'His name's Sidney. Sidney Cottam. But you're right about one thing. He *was* a navigator. Forty-four Squadron – they flew Avro Lancasters. I'm guessing you gleaned everything from his medals except his real name.'

Now it's my turn to look sheepish. Still, there's one thing I know that Louis doesn't, and one thing further I can deduce. Simon Rafferty installed his great-grandfather at Tall Pines not long after moving to Cranner's Ford. If the old man's surname isn't Rafferty, the pair must be related through Simon's mother.

I glance through the window and get my next shock. Because the framed medals above the bed have vanished. When I twist back towards Louis, the moon swings wildly in the sky. 'What did you do with them?'

'That was meant to be the surprise. I couldn't stop thinking about what you said. About how he didn't seem to have any belongings except his medals. And how even those had been placed where he couldn't see them. I thought I'd fix that.'

It takes me a moment to understand. Returning to the window, I cup my hands to the glass – and can just about make out the framed medals, hanging from the wall opposite the bed.

'You . . . How did you manage it?'

'I just walked in. After you showed me the place from our hilltop, I knew I could find his room. Then it was just a case of tapping in a nail without disturbing his sleep.' Louis pulls a hammer from his belt and raises it. Then he shrugs, tests out a smile. 'You're not the only one around here with one of these.'

'Nobody stopped you?'

'Not a soul.'

'You didn't see anyone?'

'The front desk was empty. The main doors slid open when I walked up.'

'That's crazy.'

'Sometimes, the universe speaks clearly,' he says. 'So, your hammer really wasn't for me?'

'It really wasn't.'

'Then what?'

I hesitate, hunting for a distraction, but I've been caught red-handed. 'What I was intending to do Friday night, before the puncture.'

'Which was?'

My cheeks are burning. Because it now seems so stupid. Sliding the rucksack off my shoulder, I pull out the bird-house. 'I thought it might give William something to look at, while he's stuck in bed all day.'

If Louis believes me foolish, he doesn't show it. 'You made that?'

'Rescued it from a skip. Rubbed down the wood and gave it a new coat of varnish.'

'Can I see?'

I hand it over, rubbing my arms while he examines it. My toes are curling again. I wish they'd stop doing that. 'I added the hooks myself,' I tell him. 'I've got some feeders in my bag to hang from them. Fat balls and pumpkin seeds.'

'It looks great.'

I scrunch up my nose. He's trying really hard – which is wise, considering he walked into Tall Pines uninvited, broke into William's room, banged a nail into the old man's wall and repositioned his medals. Still, when it comes to invasions of privacy, I can hardly sit in judgement.

'Can I ask about the fairy wings, now?' he asks. 'And the hair and make-up?'

Oh. Em. Gee.

The hair and make-up.

I can't remove the wig – beneath it, my hair is gelled to my scalp. My eyes are shadowed in violet and feathered to turquoise. My lips are a glossy pink. Glitter dusts both my cheeks. Worse, not only am I still wearing the fairy wings but also the silver plastic tiara. I snatch it off my head and stuff it into my pack. Then I tear off the wings and stow them. Louis was right. One of them needs mending.

I changed out of the layered skirt before climbing Pincher's Mount, but not the lace-up corset. Pointless to ask *why* I forgot to take off the rest of my costume following my turn as Tinker Bell. Right now, I'm wearing only one part of the outfit I scraped together to avoid a third outing of my dungaree shorts – a woollen miniskirt in red tartan, horribly pilled, rescued from the storage chest my face tried to mate with on Saturday night.

Stripped of my wings and tiara, but still in my white tights and oxblood DMs, I'm more Harley Quinn than Tinker Bell. At least the ridiculous make-up hides my blackened eye and gashed cheek. Yay for silver linings.

When Louis sees my discomfort, he abandons his question and indicates the birdhouse. 'You're going to nail this up?'

'Right there.' I point to the nearest pine. Then, because my head's a mess and I'm not thinking: 'You want to help?'

TWENTY-FOUR

The birdhouse goes up, and it looks good. William – I can't think of him by another name – will get a perfect view when he wakes. I just hope it attracts some wildlife.

Louis and I fixed it to the tree together. I still can't quite believe that. We stood side by side, working in harmony – and during that time I felt nothing and I felt everything. The craziness in my nose spread to my tongue, lighting a fire of different tastes: tamarind pulp, dark chocolate, Roederer Cristal champagne.

'Where next?' Louis asks, examining our handiwork.

The sensations in my mouth ebb away. 'What do you mean?'

He looks at me, raises an eyebrow. 'You didn't plan on going somewhere after this?'

Hands on my hips, I feel the curve of the bear spray cannister inside my waistband. I could whip it out, blast him with concentrated capsicum, get out of here before he recovers. But the answer's no big secret. 'Raj the Reborn is my next stop.'

'You want company?'

I take a breath, blow it out. I can't say yes, because I can't let Louis discover more about my life in Cranner's Ford – and certainly nothing of what came before. But nor do I want to say no.

I can't meet his gaze for long – the experience is too intense. Instead, I focus on the moon-dusted garden behind him. 'Friday night at the Texaco. What did you say to that boy? To make him leave me alone?'

Louis shrugs. 'I told him to imagine it was his mother kneeling on the forecourt instead of you. I asked if he'd want a passer-by like me to stick around and help her out – or allow her abuse to continue. And finally I explained that karma isn't a human concept. It's real. The universe keeps a tally and it always finds a way to push back.'

'Judging by his reaction, I guess he loves his mother.'

'As all boys should.'

'You really believe this stuff? That the universe is somehow . . . watching us?'

Something passes across Louis's face when I ask that. Not a shadow, exactly. Nor what I thought I glimpsed earlier. A flicker of pain, perhaps, or regret.

'I think the evidence is all around us,' he replies. 'The universe engineers situations, presents us with choices. I'm convinced that's what was happening at the Texaco, Friday night. I'm convinced that's what pulled us back together. We can choose to be its agents – restore balance, preserve it. Or we can choose an alternative path.'

'Which is?

'Chaos. Disorder. Entropy.'

My scalp shrinks. I raise a hand, touch the back of my head, feel its uneven indentation. Louis's words are difficult to accept. And yet why did I come to Cranner's Ford, if not to restore balance; to seek absolution for an old sin? I might not have managed it, but that hasn't stopped me trying.

'Why are you here, Louis? When there are so many other places you could be?'

'You don't feel it?'

I think of what I felt at the Texaco, after Dragon Back, Greasilocks and Wisp disappeared – the sensation that he and I were the only living creatures left in the world, in the entire universe, perhaps, and that everything that came before did so purely to bring us to that moment. 'I can't explain what I feel.'

'Well,' Louis says, 'I'd be surprised if you weren't feeling uneasy. You might be feeling awe. That's exactly how someone *should* feel when they first start to grasp what the universe intends of them. You're being tested, Mercy. *We* are being tested.'

I force myself to meet his eye, hoping he doesn't notice the yo-yoing of my throat. 'What do you think we're being asked to do?'

TWENTY-FIVE

We travel in convoy through sleeping streets.

With the VW's headlights at my back, a monstrous shadow of me rides on the road ahead. It makes me ponder which version of myself I'm showing Louis. And which version of himself he's showing me.

Sycamore Row, where we end up, is notable for its lack of sycamores. This is the part of Cranner's Ford where the go-getters live before they've earned the serious money. The residences are modern interpretations of Old Town's Georgian townhouses.

I lock my Jorvik to a lamppost. Louis swings in behind me. 'So,' he says, climbing from the campervan, 'Raj the Reborn.'

My history with Raj dates back to last February's cold snap. I don't recall what dragged me up Pincher's Mount on a frozen Sunday night. I'd expected to have the hill to myself and for a while I did, until a slipping and a scrabbling announced the arrival of another climber.

Raj didn't see me, even though he passed within a few metres of my position. Back then, I didn't know his name, merely what I saw: a spry Asian man lugging a crowbar. He was muttering incoherently. In his wake he left sour threads of whisky breath.

Only once before had I ventured to the top of Pincher's Mount on foot, and never in winter. But I couldn't just sit in my hollow. Emotional men and night summits aren't natural companions. Or perhaps they're too natural.

Despite the whisky, Raj set a brisk pace. I never came close to catching him. And when I reached the top, I found no sign.

Trivia dump: our town's landmark hill took its name from Edwin Pincher, an aristocrat and astronomer who once owned much of Cranner's Ford. Pincher built an observatory on his estate, but he did much of his stargazing from the mount. In 1786 he crowned the summit with a folly. Starcase, he named it. The stone-built Gothic tower, fifty metres in height, raised Pincher even closer to the heavens. These days, its grand oak doors are locked by a huge iron key kept at the town hall, but only a thin padlock protects the rear servants' entrance. A determined intruder would face no difficulty defeating it.

Raj seemed to be exactly that kind of intruder. I found his discarded crowbar beside the busted padlock. The servants' door hung open, revealing a triangle of perfect black.

No way was I going inside – I'd seen enough horror movies to know how *that* scene might unfold. I retraced my steps to the front facade and peered up at the stonework. There, right at the top, balanced on the parapet with his boot tips protruding over the edge, stood Raj. As I watched, he raised his arms ninety degrees. When I opened my mouth to shout, the sound died in my throat.

'*DO IT!*' Raj raged, fifty metres above me. '*WHAT ARE YOU WAITING FOR, LOSER!*'

Vertigo battered me like a heavyweight boxer throwing head shots. Suddenly I was rolling, spinning, out into space, as if Raj and I had swapped places and *I'd* stepped off the ledge and was tumbling towards my death.

The stars rotated, then exploded. Mud was in my mouth. Blood, too. As I lay there gasping, I heard boots clattering down the stone steps. Raj appeared – moaning, cursing, wild with anguish. Again, he stumbled past me unaware. Winded and speechless, I watched his descent. A minute later, I found my feet and followed.

Now, pushing away the memory, I focus my attention on Louis. 'The Reborn thing is wishful thinking,' I tell him, finishing my story. 'Raj didn't kill himself back in February, but he didn't recover. He's Day People, so our worlds don't always collide. Still, I've seen enough to know there's a limit to how much I can help him. Not that I should stop trying.'

'Day People?'

'Doesn't matter. Come on – this isn't a place you can linger long without drawing attention.'

'What's the plan?'

Unzipping my cargo bag, I pull out a rattle can. 'Home improvement.'

I noticed the graffiti on Raj's front wall three weeks ago and assumed that either he or the council would remove it. But the abusive message stayed up.

In December last year, he acquired fleeting fame when a pupil at Beacon Hill announced she was pregnant by him. The *Cranner's Ford Gazette* picked up the story and ran with it.

Raj owned a successful accountancy business, sat on the parish council and volunteered weekly at the school, where he provided extra maths tuition. The girl turned out to be a fantasist whose story quickly fell apart, leading police to exonerate Raj long before he climbed the Starcase.

And yet his business continued to haemorrhage clients. His friends and neighbours still shunned him. Raj resigned his council seat and abandoned his volunteering work. He stopped going out. He piled on weight.

'What happened to the girl?' Louis asks, as we walk. 'Did she face any consequences?'

'A session with a youth-offending team, I think.'

'For wrecking a guy's life?'

'We don't know her history. If you ask me, most people who do bad things have had bad things done to them. Everyone deserves the benefit of the doubt.'

'Regardless of what they've done?'

'Pretty much.'

I walk a few steps more before realizing that he's no longer by my side. When I turn, I find him standing on the pavement. I can't decipher his look.

Louis examines me a moment longer. Then he laughs – fortunately, not the way someone might laugh at a platypus. 'I know I told you already, but you're an enigma, Mercy Lake. I can't emphasize it enough.'

His expression turns my insides to a shivery mess. If there's a word for what I'm experiencing, I don't think I've learned it.

Sycamore Row is well served with streetlamps. This is the best look I've had of Louis since the Texaco. There's a poise to him that's almost balletic. His features are so symmetrical they make my teeth hurt. Meeting his gaze has grown no easier. It's like holding my hand against a just-boiled kettle. I can manage half a second, maybe three quarters at best.

'You said this wasn't a place to hang around?'

He's right. I did. I almost forgot that I'm standing on Sycamore Row, brandishing a rattle can. Quickly, I get to work. My spray paint doesn't blend well with the white wall, but it covers the graffiti, and that's the main thing. I'm just finishing up when a door bangs open. A woman's voice shouts, 'Smile, bitch, you're on doorbell cam. Now get the *fuck* away from my Range Rover.'

I glance up so fast the world jibber-jubbers on its mountings. I feel like all the cars will slide down the street. Fortunately, they don't, and when the wrinkles in the world pull taut, I spot Raj's neighbour in her doorway.

Her name's Wanda. She owns the Glam It Up nail bar a few doors down from Gimme the Dough. She's fearless, utterly – the human equivalent of a wrecking ball.

White Knuckle Wanda, I call her. Frequently, around town, I've seen her stumble out of a bar and clamber into her Range Rover. Once, driving home drunk, she swerved across the street and nearly mowed me down.

Tonight, she's falling out of a thigh-length kimono in raspberry silk. In her hand is a glass of amber liquid, ice cubes clinking inside. Advancing on to her front step, Wanda cocks her hip and bares her teeth. 'You hear me, freak?'

Already, lights are coming on in neighbouring houses. Grabbing Louis's arm, I tow him back down the street. Reaching my Jorvik, I fumble with the lock. Doubtless, someone's called the police. I can't let them find me in

Cranner's Ford. I just can't. They'd want to know what I'm doing. Worst of all, they'd warn the Raffertys.

'Mercy?' Louis asks, as I stuff the lock inside my cargo bag. 'You've done nothing wrong. This is a public street.'

The stench of burning hair fills my nose, as foul as if it were real. Gripping the handlebars, I swing a leg over the seat.

'You don't need to run,' Louis says. 'Covering up graffiti is hardly a crime. You're safe, here. With me.'

Gulping for air, I shake my head. 'You can follow – but I'm leaving.'

Then, battery power dialled to max, I get out of there.

TWENTY-SIX

The awards ceremony, for Nadia, is unbearable. Not because Simon's company doesn't win – it does, handsomely – but because of the table plan.

She's trapped between Hugo Jepp, Sheergen's managing director, and the woman he's brought along. Hugo is loud, brash, aggressive. Nadia dislikes him immensely. The woman, she suspects, is an escort. An expensive one, but an escort nonetheless.

The rest of the table is little better. Marcie and Patrick Lockheart currently lease two giant Sheergen wind turbines on their farm outside Cranner's Ford. Simon only invited them in the hope of placing a positive PR piece into the local press. It certainly wasn't because of their wit.

Nadia knows she's being a bitch, doesn't care. What makes the evening even more uncomfortable is the pea-sized blister on her right buttock.

She tries to disguise the fact she isn't drinking by taking only tiny, occasional sips of wine – a plan the waiters sabotage by constantly refilling her glass. She wonders whether Simon, flanked by his executive directors, has noticed; and whether he has any sense, preternatural or otherwise, of the life he so recently helped to create.

It's a relief to crawl into their chauffeur-driven cocoon for the three-hour journey home. That is, until they pass through Arcadia Heights's front gates. Looking through the rear window, Nadia sees another vehicle following behind. 'Who's that?' she asks Simon, with weary resignation. 'Please don't tell me you invited Hugo and his hooker for an after-party.'

'Don't call her that.'

'If he's paying for her services, she's a hooker. Come on, Si – it's 2 a.m. What're you doing?'

'I'm celebrating,' he snaps. 'In case you don't remember, we won big tonight – *Sheergen* won big – and Hugo was instrumental in that success. It's only right that we acknowledge it.'

Nadia winces, realizes she's being selfish – knows how long and how hard the two men have worked to achieve success. She touches Simon's leg in apology.

'They won't stay long,' he says, in a softer tone. 'Smile, be nice, and before you know it, it'll just be me and you.'

Inside, he pays the babysitter while she slips upstairs to check on Ollie. Tonight, the boy has fallen asleep with a different toy in each hand.

Nadia crosses the room to the window. It's late enough that the moon has swung right over Pincher's Mount, illuminating its western flank. For a moment, she thinks she sees a glimmer of reflected light up there, like two flashing eyes – and recalls the wolves that stalked her grandfather's farm in the Stara Planina.

When she tests the door to Ollie's balcony, she's surprised to find it unlocked. Thumbing the lever, she secures it – and notices, on the glass, the boy's tiny handprint. The fragility of it, the sheer impermanence of Ollie's mark, raises within Nadia a fear she cannot fully explain.

In her bedroom, she stands before the mirror and examines her reflection. Since her first positive test result, eight days ago, the entire world has changed. What had felt familiar now feels alien. What had felt safe now bristles with danger.

Back downstairs, she walks into the cinema room to find that Simon didn't just invite Hugo Jepp and his hooker. Marcie and Patrick Lockheart are here too, and obnoxiously drunk. Worse, Hugo is carving out a line of white powder on one of the glass coffee tables.

She stares at him, incensed. 'Who gave you permission to do that?'

He rolls his eyes. 'Grow up, Nadia. We're all adults.' The hooker chuckles.

On a side table stands a neoclassical bronze of the Three Graces. Nadia wants to smash it over Hugo's head. Instead, she leans over the sofa and puts her mouth close to his ear. 'Don't talk to me like that in my own house. Don't talk to me like that ever again.'

Hugo turns his head, examines her contemptuously. 'How about you help Simon with the bubbly?'

Nadia's fury is made white-hot by her impotence – because if there's one night she can't eject Hugo, it's this one. Cheeks burning, she stalks out. In the kitchen, Simon is popping the cork on a bottle of Pol Roger. 'They're doing *coke* in there,' she hisses.

He starts filling a champagne flute. 'Sorry.'

'Is that all you have to say? Your *son* is upstairs.'

'*My* son?' Simon frowns. 'Nadia, what's wrong? You've been uptight all evening. In fact, all week. Here.' He hands her the flute. 'Why don't you relax a little?'

Appalled, she upends the champagne into the sink. 'I don't *like* him. I've *never* liked him. He's a misogynistic prick and I'd like him to stop coming here.'

Simon's jaw tightens. 'Then you're going to be disappointed.'

Nadia slams down the empty flute. She touches her stomach, snatches her hand away. Eight weeks pregnant, and she's dealing with *this* shit – Hugo Jepp doing coke with his whore and two drunken landowners while Simon merrily plays host. She needs this house to feel *safe*. After what happened to Simon's first wife, she'd have thought that'd be his priority.

Nadia thinks of the wolves that used to creep down from the hills to prowl around her grandfather's farm at night. She thinks of the eyes she thought she saw earlier, peering down from Pincher's Mount.

When the wolves begin to multiply, expect misfortune.

What is Hugo Jepp, if not a wolf?

'In the morning I'm having the alarm system upgraded,' she says, veering off topic. She'd called the security company again on Monday. Tomorrow was their earliest slot.

Simon blinks at her. 'Why?'

'I've been meaning to do it for a while. This place is wide open. We need better protection. New tech.'

'Has something happened?'

'No.'

'Are you sure? Because if it has—'

'It really hasn't. It's just . . .'

Nadia's about to say more when she notices something in his expression. She can't define it, but it's there. 'What about you? Have *you* noticed something?'

He shakes his head a beat too late.

'Simon, don't lie to me.'

'Just a weird thing, last week. It's nothing. Nothing I can put my finger on, at least.'

'You didn't tell me.'

His gaze moves to the black windows. 'As I said, there's not really anything to tell.'

'You think it could have been her?'

'No. God, no. Nothing like that. It was more a feeling than anything tangible. A weird sense of someone walking over my grave.' He scoops up four flutes fizzing with champagne. 'Look, you're right. Upgrading our security is a good idea. Now come and join us. Make your peace with Hugo.'

'I'd rather slit my throat.'

'If you hide away in here, you let him win.'

'I'm not hiding from anyone. I'm going to bed.'

Upstairs, her phone is buzzing on the dresser.

'I asked you to tell me everything,' Konstantin Tapia says, when she answers. 'You didn't even tell me half.'

'I told you what I could.'

'Keira Greenaway no longer lives at her parents' old place.'

'What?'

'She moved out a year ago. Almost to the day she completed her suspended sentence.'

Nadia's shoulders prickle, as if a host of tiny claws has sunk into her skin. 'She's here. Isn't she? In Cranner's Ford.'

'Too early to say. But if she is, I won't need long to find her.'

'Do it,' she tells him. 'Please.'

Konstantin rings off. Nadia steps out of her dress. Her hand moves to the blister on her right buttock. She touches it, winces. Then, clenching her teeth, she drives a green-painted fingernail deep inside the wound.

TWENTY-SEVEN

Speed and distance – that's all that matters. I'm Night People, attuned to danger, and my instincts are screaming at me to run.

The Jorvik drags me through deserted streets, no vehicles or pedestrians to slow my progress. Traffic lights turn green at my approach, as if the town has come alive beneath my wheels and has chosen to open a route. I hum through junctions unimpeded, the humid night air drawing tears from my eyes.

God knows what I must look like. Pink hair; fairy make-up; lavender corset; ratty tartan miniskirt, white tights and clumpy boots. And now, completing the horror, even the make-up is running – eyeliner mixing with glitter and oozing down my cheeks.

My head is bursting with worries and what-ifs. More than that, it's bursting with *Louis*. The feel of his eyes on my skin. The feel of his arm when I grabbed it. Real flesh. Real bone. Not the gossamer threads of make-believe I'd half expected.

I don't trust the part of me that unlocked the door and

let Louis in, because it doesn't seem concerned about the danger. I created this life from the wreckage of another. If I ruin it, there won't be a third. In truth, I didn't deserve a second. And yet I'm starting to wonder if what I've built, here in Cranner's Ford, is any kind of life at all.

I hear the watery clatter of Louis's campervan at my back. As before, its headlights paint a grotesque silhouette of me on the road ahead. I'm heading east towards Pincher's Mount – but I can't ride past the Rafferty residence twice in one night. Instead of turning right on to Abbot's Walk I swing left, climbing our famous hill clockwise. When the road forks, I take the steeper route. It terminates at a gravel car park tucked into a dell on the northern flank.

This is the place the locals call Rycroft Hollow. It's where Dragon Back, Greasilocks and Wisp wanted to take me on Friday night. It's where people my age go to get high or get laid. I've never come here for that – although it's where I appear to have brought Louis.

Woods either side of the car park offer a windbreak. A footpath climbs through them to an observation point. On weekends, Rycroft Hollow might host a couple of steamed-up cars, one or two motorcycles, perhaps a few drunken dancers howling at the moon. But this is a school night. Right now, the hollow is deserted.

I ride across the car park and stop beneath the trees. Louis pulls in beside me and kills his lights. I listen to the tick of the campervan's engine as it cools.

OK, Brainiac, what now?

On my hip is the bear spray. In my cargo bag is a kitchen knife honed to wicked sharpness.

My breath is in my throat again. My nose is full of scents: gravel dust, boot polish, freshly baked scones. I lift my wrist and inhale, but I can't detect the fragrance I sprayed there before coming out. Perhaps my ancient bottle of Issey Miyake has finally lost its aroma. Perhaps adrenalin has totally fried my senses. It's well past midnight and I'm at Rycroft Hollow with a man I barely know. This is what Day People do for kicks. I wonder if they ever feel anything like this. When I climb off my saddle and stand beside my Jorvik, every muscle in my body seems to be jittering.

Louis's door opens. He appears on the gravel beside me. My eyes haven't adjusted to the dark, but I can see he's holding something. I hope it's not more champagne.

'There's a viewing platform,' I mumble. 'Up that path through the trees. A place to sit.'

'You want to check it out?'

My fingertips are tingling. Now that I'm here, I don't know what I want. And because honesty is always the best policy, I tell Louis exactly that.

'If it helps,' he says, 'I can tell you what I want.'

'It might.'

'I want to understand why the universe is throwing us together like this. I want to figure out its purpose. Just think of everything that had to align, Friday night, to bring us to this moment: your puncture, my empty fuel tank, those skaters, your throwaway comment that allowed me to find you again. I know it wasn't random chance. I was drawn to that Texaco. I think you were drawn there, too. The question I couldn't answer earlier is why.'

'You think you can now?'

'Now that I've seen what you do, I have an inkling.'

'Which is?'

'I suspect I was sent here to help you.'

His words are too much to take in. Hackles raised, I begin to walk. Louis keeps pace at my side.

The trees retreat. The sky opens. I see the viewing platform: two park benches along a path cut into the slope. Twenty metres below it lies the lower fork of the lane we took to get here. Cranner's Ford sparkles to the west, but the main view is north across a spine of hills.

I choose a bench. We both sit.

'So,' he begins. 'Do you—'

'Please. I've already told you lots. More than I've ever told anyone. You've told me virtually nothing.'

'You're right,' he says. 'What do you want to know?'

I keep my gaze on the moon-touched hills. I had a million questions and now I can hardly think. 'Your full name might be a start.'

OK, so that wasn't one of the million, but it'll do.

'Louis Carter.'

I nod. It's a nice name, with a nice weight. It feels balanced. 'Is Louis Carter from Cranner's Ford?'

'He isn't. Is Mercy Lake?'

I shake my head. Then I remember that *I'm* meant to be asking the questions. 'Do you live in town?'

'I don't live anywhere.'

I glance over, just to check he's being serious. 'Meaning?'

'Exactly that. Eleanor's my home. Has been for a while. Really, though, she's more than just a place to sleep. Eleanor's become a kind of motorized divining rod. I climb behind the wheel and find out where I'm meant to go.'

I think of my basement flat, its blackout panels – the very antithesis of what Louis is describing. 'How long have you been doing it?'

'Six months, give or take. Before that I was a year in

India, two years in Southeast Asia, eighteen months in South America. Looking back, I was on a journey long before I ever realized it.'

'You must have seen a lot.'

'There's still so much to discover.'

'How did you end up in Cranner's Ford?'

'Friday night, on the motorway, I needed fuel. Usually, I'd stop at the services. Instead, without really thinking, I took the next turn-off. I'd never been here before. Never even heard of this town. I drove for a mile, pretty much on autopilot, rolled on to that Texaco forecourt. And then *you* appeared.'

I shiver. It's an enjoyable shiver. 'Spooky.'

'That's one word for it.'

'So where have you been staying?'

'First few nights, I found rest spots in the lanes around these hills. Monday, I checked into a campsite just outside town.'

'The Seven Crosses?'

'That's it.'

'If you spend your life travelling, how do you support yourself?'

'A long time ago,' Louis says, 'I was employee number three.'

'What does that mean?'

'A tech start-up. I was third on the books. The guy had no money, so I took stock options as payment. When he took the company public, I bought up my shares at a fraction of their value. Then I cashed out, tuned out, dropped out.'

'So you're rich?' I ask, and immediately clench my teeth. 'Sorry. Rude question. Please don't answer that.' I sneak a look, worried I've offended him. 'I'm not used to this. Talking, I mean.'

'Don't apologize. You say whatever comes into your head, and I like that. If everyone did more of it, humanity might not be in such a mess. Yes, there was money. Probably far too much. If I'd stayed longer, even more. Money makes a huge difference when you have none, but if you're already comfortable – not so much.'

'You could give it away. Some of it, at least.' I gesture at the lights below us. 'A lot of people down there need help. I'm sure that's true everywhere, but I *know* it's true here.'

Louis turns his own gaze towards town. 'How many do you watch?'

My stomach cramps. Annoying how it does that, every time he asks a question. But he's been open with me. I feel like I owe him the same courtesy. Before I can change my mind, I trap my hands between my thighs and say, 'A dozen, give or take. The number goes up and down. It's hard to justify. Nobody likes a snoop. But I'm not a sex pervert or anything – and it isn't just nosiness. I only watch people who have problems they can't seem to fix, and where I think there's a chance I might make a difference. Once you get to know someone, even just a tiny bit, even if they don't know you back, you end up wanting the best for them. That's inbuilt in all of us, I think.'

'You're like a shepherdess,' Louis says. 'The Angel of Cranner's Ford.'

I glance at him again, convinced he's mocking me. But when our eyes meet, I see only sincerity.

'Of those you watch, how many have problems money alone would solve?' Louis asks.

'Some, definitely.'

'Not William the Navigator. Not Raj the Reborn. And from what you said last night, not Lovesick Linda either.'

Holy Crapoli. Have I really shared all these names? I watch a pair of headlights crawl along the lane below us. My head is starting to ache. It's the effort of all this talking – all this *thinking*. Because although I want to be honest, there are things I mustn't share.

'In my experience,' Louis says, 'most people's problems aren't caused by money. They're caused by other people.'

Down in the lane, that car rolls past. As I watch, its rear lights flare a deeper red – like eyes that have registered my interest. 'I'd say most people try to do good deeds rather than bad ones. Most people just want to be loved.'

'Is that what you want, Mercy?'

I shut my eyes tight. If I had a chalkboard, my fingernails would be squealing across it. No way can I handle a conversation this intimate.

'That was clumsy, I'm sorry,' Louis says quickly. 'Here, I brought you a gift. Something I think you'll like.'

When I open my eyes he offers me what he's been cradling – a shoebox-sized plastic case.

'What is it?' I ask, forgetting my manners. 'I mean – thank you very much. What is it?'

Louis laughs. 'Go ahead. Open it.'

There's a metal clasp, which I pop loose. Then I raise the lid.

Inside lies the largest and most expensive-looking pair of binoculars I've ever seen.

'They're Steiners,' he says. 'From their military range. Eighty-millimetre lenses, twenty times magnification.'

They look like some kind of futuristic weapon. I'm

almost too afraid to touch them. 'Louis, you can't just . . . These are—'

'Weren't you just suggesting I give away my money?'

I look at him, aghast. 'I didn't mean to *me*.'

'I'm teasing, Mercy. Please, I want you to enjoy them. At least try them out.'

Carefully, I remove the binoculars from their case. They're much heavier than my Celestrons. I can't hold them as easily.

'You'll need a tripod for extended viewings,' Louis says. 'I got you one of those, too.'

I pop off the lens cups and figure out the focus control. Then I zero in on the Texaco. The image is extraordinary. Not only can I see which Guardian is working the till – Hasseem right now, rather than Tariq – but the magazine he's reading. With the tripod for stability, I might even pick out the cover story.

'It's like standing right outside,' I tell Louis. 'Actually, it's more like standing *inside*.' I swallow, my throat tight with emotion. 'There aren't enough words. I don't know how to thank you.'

Below us, in the lane, the car stops. When its engine dies, those red eyes wink out. With a lurch, I realize who's down there.

Beside me, Louis says: 'How about you tell *me* something?'

I drop the binoculars into their case as if they're scalding hot. Honesty's always the best policy, but secrecy's a pretty close second. Too late now. I nod, braced for what's coming.

Louis looks at me, deadpan. 'What's with the crazy outfit?'

Oof.

I blow out my breath in relief. But I'm not off the hook yet. No way can I tell Louis about Arcadia Heights and my visits to Ollie Rafferty. Humiliation feels like my only option. 'I was worried what you'd think if I wore dungaree shorts three nights running.'

Louis tilts his head. 'Why would I care about that?'

'I don't know. I'm not very good at this stuff. Not very experienced, I mean.'

I tug down the hem of my ratty tartan skirt. If the world squirming championships were being held on this bench, I'd win it, no contest. 'God. That's not what I meant to say, even if it's what I was thinking. Anyway' – I gesture at my clothes – *'voilà.'*

Louis flashes another smile. 'I'm flattered you made the effort. I've got to say the pink hair was a surprise. And the fairy wings.'

'You weren't meant to see those.'

'Can I ask about them?'

'I'd rather you didn't.' Needing a distraction, engaging my mouth before my brain, I say, 'You want to meet another Cranner's Ford resident?'

'I can think of nothing finer.'

With a flourish, I indicate the car in the lane below us. 'Louis Carter, may I present Edward Gropey-Hands.'

TWENTY-EIGHT

Like a couple of kids – or one kid and his pink-haired Poundland pet fairy – we creep down the slope. The moon-bleached grass tickles my thighs. At least we'll have some cover, should we need it. I just hope there are no snakes.

This was Louis's idea, not mine. But after my over-the-top introduction, I can hardly fault his curiosity. My attempt to distract him – or more likely show off – has backfired.

Despite the moniker, there's nothing at all funny about Edward Gropey-Hands. My overriding feeling is of revulsion. Most people I watch in Cranner's Ford are victims of some kind, whether of poverty, grief, isolation or abuse. Others, like Edward, are active spreaders of misery. There's nothing I can do to stop him, but I *can* try to help those he dupes. That, if nothing else, is a good enough reason to keep tabs.

We descend the slope until we're level with Edward's roof. He's twisted around in the driver's seat, his window lowered a few inches. I hear the bass murmur of his voice and the higher-pitched responses of his passenger. From past experience, I doubt their conversation will last long.

Louis pulls me into a crouch. 'Give me the scoop on Edward Gropey-Hands.'

'He's married, that's the first thing. Second thing – his wife almost certainly isn't in that car.'

'Is there a third?'

I nod. 'Whoever he's with, she probably thinks she's the only one. But he brings plenty of others up here.'

Below us, the car rocks as the occupants reposition themselves. I didn't think this through. If we stay here much longer, the action will start. It's enough of a cringefest on my own. Watching it with company would be unbearable.

As if to troll me, a woman's wedge heel appears in the driver's window, tapping like a beak against the glass.

'They're not messing around,' Louis says.

'They kind of are.'

He chuckles softly. Briefly, the tension dissipates. Then that wedge heel arcs across the window. I begin to hear noises that would make a movie censor sit up straight.

'This is kind of awkward,' Louis mutters.

'It kind of is.'

A few moments later, he adds, 'Kind of tragic, too. That guy swore an oath – and there he is, desecrating it. A one-off mistake is just about understandable. Not this.'

Louis is right. What we're witnessing is betrayal of the very worst kind. If I've learned anything these last few years, it's the sanctity of human relationships – and the consequences when we choose to violate them. But I've also learned not to judge. 'We don't know Edward's history,' I say. 'All kinds of bad things might have happened to make him like this.'

'Bad things happen to everyone. It doesn't give him a free pass.'

That's true too, I guess. While I won't judge Edward's actions, I can't defend them.

Louis turns to face me. 'I have an idea,' he says. 'Do you trust me? Think about it. Only answer if you're certain.'

'Yes, but—'

'Great. Then wait here.'

Before I can quiz him further, he retreats up the slope. Within seconds I lose sight of him among the trees.

I draw up my knees and hug them. I don't know what Louis is planning, or whether I feel scared or excited, or both. I *do* know I'm about to become part of something – even if I'm not sure exactly what.

A few metres below my hiding place, Edward's car creaks on its springs. The sounds of physical pleasure escalate.

Louis returns. When I see what he's carrying, my cheeks grow hot. I want to say something, but my words – just like my breath – are lodged in my throat.

As I watch, he creeps down the bank to the lane. The car's occupants are far too preoccupied to notice.

TWENTY-NINE

When James leaves the house, his wife is already asleep. At least, she's lying in bed and making all the right sounds. Impossible to know if she's *genuinely* asleep, but James is reasonably sure. He saw her eyes flickering behind their lids. Only a complete psychopath would fake that.

The moon rides in his side window as he crosses town, an ally and a hunting partner in his never-ending carnal quest. In one of his wife's magazines he read about its influence on female sexual desire. During a full moon, more women ovulate than at any other time. Their hormone levels spike, fuelling their libido.

Cruising Cranner's Ford's streets, James can *feel* all that pent-up tension, all that unreleased sexual energy. If only there were a way to pinpoint its location. An app would be great – Google Maps overlaid with glowing red dots, like unexploded bombs. James would pay a *fortune* for that. He might even sell the Mustang.

At least, tonight, he has the location for *one* of those red dots. Right now, Google Maps would show it blinking away furiously inside Cave 173, a self-consciously stylish wine bar in Old Town. James finds a parking spot right outside.

Full moon or not, Dani Whitaker won't be tempted into his Mustang without plenty of Veuve Clicquot lubricant. As a result, he wastes an hour at the Cave, sipping Diet Coke through clenched teeth and cringing at Dani's laugh.

It's not all bad. Counterbalancing her champagne habit and hyena cackle is a body that proves, irrefutably, the value of a good personal trainer. Dani is soft where she's meant to be and firm everywhere else. Tonight, she's squeezed herself into a white minidress that hugs her like a rubber glove. Her skin is tanning-shop gold, her teeth whiter than piano keys. Her nails are *killer* – yellow flames licking back from the tips on a background of perfectly lacquered pink. James wonders at their sharpness and what they might do to his skin – or to his Mustang's vinyl upholstery.

Soon after leaving Cave 173, they reach the lane circling Pincher's Mount. Dani's perfume and natural musk heats James's blood and quickens his heart. Past the fork for Rycroft Hollow, he finds a layby.

Jesus titty-fucking Christ, he's horny. Sometimes he thinks nature messed up, that he should have been born one of the polygynous species, where each alpha male maintains a faithful harem. He could have been a red stag, or an elephant seal. Perhaps even a hamadryas baboon with a raw, overworked, pink—

'I'm not a seal,' Dani says, peering through the side window.

James reels away from her. 'How did—'

'We're not here to perform,' she continues. 'This ain't that dogging site, is it?'

He exhales. 'You mean the hollow, where the kids go? That's further up the slope. From what I've heard, it's strictly a weekend thing.'

'You're sure?'

'Listen to that silence,' he says, feigning patience. 'Guaranteed we're the only ones here.'

Dani nods. Moments later she's pressing her mouth against his, hissing instructions and tugging at his clothes.

James responds, greedy with his hands, an hour of tedious small talk finally rewarded. A thought intrudes and he grimaces, tries to ignore it, but it knocks against his brain like a moth against a light.

'Shoes,' he mutters, teeth scraping Dani's. In the bar he checked her footwear, mindful of Saturday night's cowgirl incident. The soles of Dani's cork wedge heels looked like they were harbouring all kinds of nasty, scratchy shit. 'Take them off.'

Dani removes a hand from his crotch to undo them. James hisses with frustration. She gets one shoe off but has trouble with the other, and it takes all his self-control not to swear – or shriek like a hamadryas baboon. In desperation he helps out, tugging at the shoe strap, his fingers bumping against hers, the two of them getting in each other's way like they're performing a farcical, pornographic version of Cinderella that's playing in reverse.

At last, the shoe thumps into the footwell. But now the Mustang's steering wheel is in the way. James nearly splits a tooth. 'Do you . . .' he begins. 'Shall we—'

'What?'

'Like this.'

He slaps Dani's thigh, indicating a flip. Understanding,

she twists around until she's on all fours. With a few more adjustments, they're going at it.

The Mustang creaks. Its vinyl seats squeal against flesh. Another thought-moth flutters inside James's head. He gropes in the back for a blanket, which he tries to drag across the passenger seat.

'What,' Dani says, between gasps, 'the hell is that?'

'Fingernails,' he tells her. 'To protect the—'

'No. That *smell*.'

With the blanket in place, James doesn't care. His nose detects nothing but her perfume and her sweat. Both are driving him crazy.

'Smells like . . .' Dani says, grunting as he thrusts harder. 'Like fuel.'

And then James notices it, too. When he pauses his exertions he thinks he hears something outside – the scrape of a shoe on tarmac – and catches movement through his side window, a grey streak in the blackness.

Fear loosens his guts. He pulls out of Dani, stuffing himself back into his trousers. His nose, now, is smarting with that chemical stink. Some kind of solvent or accelerant.

In a blink, his fear blossoms into terror. Every horror story from childhood floods back, every urban myth – couples stranded on lonely highways; severed heads beaten against car roofs; horny lovers immolated in flagrante by mask-wearing loons.

The rasp of a match will mean it's too late. James can't stay in the Mustang, but nor does he want to face a puritanical fanatic intent on castrating him. In that moment he wishes he was anywhere but here – in bed with his wife, perhaps – and regrets every betrayal of the woman he once loved enough to marry.

His hand hovers on the door release. Beside him, Dani corkscrews in her seat. 'What is it?' she hisses, tugging down her dress. 'Is someone fucking *out* there?'

The panic in her voice decides him. James throws open his door, staggers out. He twists around, night-blind, swinging his arms to defend himself. But his fists meet no resistance, and as he comes to a halt in the middle of the lane he realizes he's alone. No severed heads. No mask-wearing loons. No puritanical fanatics wielding scalpels or scissors.

James pants for breath, his heart still hammering – because he *knows* he didn't imagine that grey streak folding into the night, nor the chemical stink in his nose. Someone *was* here. Someone *was* watching. And they've left evidence of their visit.

The Mustang's passenger door opens. Dani climbs out, barefoot. She's shivering, despite the humidity and heat. James leans inside, retrieves his penlight. He pans its beam across the car.

'You've got to be kidding me,' Dani whispers.

James stares in horrified disbelief.

THIRTY

We're driving.

Louis is behind the wheel. I'm sitting beside him.

I thought I'd never climb inside another vehicle – certainly not with another human. I expected to feel trapped, claustrophobic to the point of panic. Instead, it's scary-heebie-jeebies glorious.

My Jorvik, stowed behind us, is *nothing* to the freedom Louis's campervan represents. If Eleanor had blackout curtains – and I knew how to drive – the possibilities would be endless.

As we cross the bridge into Cranner's Ford, I can't believe how different everything looks. Maybe it's the new perspective from the VW's passenger seat. Maybe it's my own new perspective.

I sneak glances at Louis whenever I can. The street-lamps swing light and shadow across his face. One moment it's amber-hued; the next it's wreathed in darkness. The more I look, the more I *want* to look. I know I'm obsessive, but this is freakish even by my standards.

I keep returning to what just happened – what we just

left behind. Each time, I find it harder to contain myself. Finally, the dam breaks. I snigger, then I guffaw. I'm not used to laughing, especially not in company. I sound like a honking cow, and the thought of *that* makes me lose it completely.

Louis grins. And then his own composure dissolves. Pretty soon we're both howling. When he drapes his arm across my seat I realize that the last traces of my fear have entirely melted away.

Again, I rerun the memory. The Mustang, rocking to the rhythm of its occupants. Louis, wielding the rattle can he took from my cargo bag. The soft hiss of aerosol, almost drowned by sounds of passion. The slow reveal of his handiwork, progressing across the Mustang's bonnet.

C . . . H . . . E . . . A . . . T

Then: Louis's hasty retreat; the car's sudden quiet; the clunk of a door opening; Edward Gropey-Hands staggering out and pirouetting across the lane; his slow, stunned return.

And over it all my exhilaration at the thought that Louis might have achieved something I never managed, nor even considered: the gentle nudging of Edward towards a less destructive path.

OK, *gentle nudging* is a stretch.

Gentle terrorizing, maybe.

Maybe just terrorizing.

'I feel bad about his car,' I say. 'About the cost of fixing it, I mean.'

'Don't. No one driving a Shelby Mustang has money problems, I promise you. For our friend, it's an inconvenience. Not a disaster.'

We're through Old Town, now, and heading up Old

Cobb. Pincher's Mount isn't the only hill overlooking Cranner's Ford, just the tallest. Old Cobb forms the town's western boundary. It's a gentler ascent, with a road all the way to the top.

Tonight, the summit is ours. I'm struck, yet again, by how different the town looks. This last year, it's been a place of marvels, stories and adventures, but right now it feels doubly so. Perhaps this is what life is like, once you've found someone with whom to share it.

With the engine off, the campervan seems far smaller. I try to hold on to my euphoria but already my anxiety is seeping back. Louis must sense the change, because he switches on the music player and throws open his door. 'Come on.'

'Where . . .' I begin, but he's already climbed out. The bassline to Jackie Wilson's 'Higher and Higher' starts to thump from the speakers. Impossible to feel anxious, hearing it.

Louis appears in front of the VW's headlamps, spot-lit. For the first time tonight I see his outfit – a linen suit of pale sage, paired with white pumps. At his back, the night sky forms the perfect backdrop. He looks like an actor in a movie scene. I cannot tear my eyes away.

Louis peels off his jacket, revealing a floral-print shirt that wouldn't work on anyone else. He hangs the jacket on a wing mirror. Then, hand outstretched, he invites me to join him. Without thinking, I open the passenger door.

It feels like reality is fracturing again, that by climbing from the van I'm stepping into a dimension where the normal rules don't apply. When my feet touch the ground it seems solid, dependable – utterly alien. I feel as if I could lift my arms and twirl without any risk of falling, a human gyroscope free to experience the universe as the universe intended.

Louis smiles. Clearly I *am* in a different reality, because I go to him without hesitation, gasping when he takes my hand.

'Shall we?' he asks, placing his free hand against my back.

I respond with a sound like a kid choking on a gobstopper. Because even in this alternative universe it seems I can reliably disgrace myself. Clearing my throat, I point out the obvious: 'I can't dance.'

'Tonight you can,' Louis says. And then he begins to move. I have no choice but to follow, and no option but to hold on. With the possible exception of tightrope walking, I can't think of an activity more unsuited to my condition.

And yet somehow I don't stumble. I don't tangle myself in Louis's legs. Nor do I drag him down on top of me. No one could reliably describe what I'm doing as dancing – but I'm moving in tandem, at least, and the world is staying upright, even as it rotates.

Suddenly, my ratty tartan miniskirt doesn't matter, nor my streaked Tinker Bell make-up or my stupid pink hair. Because I've found a moment, here on this hill, one I'll be able to replay long after Louis has lost interest and moved on.

The lights of the town and those of the night sky sharpen to a jewel brightness, then explode in prismatic beauty. My nose bursts with scents; rolling, cascading, intertwining; too many and too fleeting to name. Jackie Wilson gives way to Marvin Gaye. Marvin Gaye gives way to Dusty Springfield.

'Night Eyes,' Louis murmurs, his movements slowing.

Then he takes my chin between thumb and forefinger and gently tilts it. 'Your cheek,' he says. 'Did you injure it?'

I grin, embarrassed. 'Tiny argument with some furniture. We shook and made up.'

'You fell again?'

'More like an emergency landing.'

'Your doctor . . .' he begins, but I cut him off with a shake of my head. As Dusty Springfield gives way to Mitch Ryder and the Detroit Wheels, we climb back into the van's front seats.

'You're an agent of the universe, Mercy Lake,' Louis says, contemplating the night sky. 'Whether you know it or not. It blows my mind what you do – how you try to help people, for no other reason than they need helping. People you don't know. People you haven't even met.'

I look over, surprised at his words, even more surprised at the emotion etched into his face. I want to reach out, take his hand. Of course, being an awkward loser, I do no such thing.

'You bring light where there's darkness,' he continues. 'Compassion where there's neglect. Take William the Navigator, stuck in that room with nothing to break the monotony. You saw it and you *did* something. Without any expectation of reward. Without even any hope of acknowledgement.'

My cheeks are reddening. I can't sit here and bask in unjustified praise. Particularly in regard to William. When I started watching Simon Rafferty's great-grandfather, my intentions were far from altruistic. If anything, I wanted the old man dead. Thankfully, I'm in a better place now than I was.

'That birdhouse was just a skip find,' I say. 'Somebody's else's junk. It wasn't worth anything.'

'I'm sure it'll be worth something to William. And I'm not just talking about him. What about Raj? You saw that abuse sprayed on his wall and you went out of your way to remove it. Any of his neighbours could have done the same thing, and yet they didn't. You might not think what you did was important, Mercy, but it'll be important to him. It *should* be important to this whole town.'

'Honestly,' I say, 'you're making this sound more than it is. All I do is fiddle around the edges. There are far more people in Cranner's Ford I *haven't* helped – like Edward Gropey-Hands's wife. In one night, you've probably done more for her than I could do in a lifetime.'

Louis shakes his head. 'That situation isn't fixed, Mercy. Not even close. A guy like Edward doesn't start behaving himself just because someone graffitied his car.'

'We don't know that. He could be home right now, vowing to change his ways. Even if he isn't, I bet he'll think a lot harder next time he's tempted to go behind her back.'

'Small chance.'

'*Big* chance. And what about William the Navigator, seeing as you brought him up? You walked inside Tall Pines and moved those medals without a second thought. You do things I'd never even dream of, because I'm far too scared of getting caught.'

Louis chews his lip. This time, when he looks at me, his expression is different. 'You know what I think?'

'Yes,' I say, then blink. 'Actually, no.'

'I think the universe is revealing its plan. I think we have work to do in this town. I think, together, we'll be unstoppable.'

'You do?'

'We're two sides of the same coin, Mercy. Like yin and yang.'

I grin. 'Like fish and chips?'

'Like thunder and lightning.'

My knees press together. This won't last. It *can't* last. Not just because it feels like a fairy tale and fairy tales aren't real, but because even though honesty's always the best policy, there are things that Louis must never know. 'I should probably head home.'

'I'll drive you.'

I shake my head, indicating my Jorvik. 'Never waste a good hill. Especially when you're at the top of one. That's a strict rule.'

There's another reason, too. I don't want Louis to find out where I live.

'Can I call you?' he asks.

'I don't have a phone.'

'Email?'

'I prefer an analogue life.'

'OK,' Louis replies. He drums his fingers on the gear-stick. 'OK.'

'We could meet somewhere,' I say.

'How about lunch, Saturday?'

Negative buzzer sound. 'I don't do lunch,' I tell him. 'At least, not when most people do lunch. In fact, I don't really do day. How about Saturday night?'

'It's a date,' Louis says. 'Just name the place.'

THIRTY-ONE

James drops Dani at her flat and drives home. At least the streets are quiet. No one to point and laugh. No one to read the *goddamned abuse* on his bonnet.

If he catches the culprit, he can think of six ways to skin them. Trouble is, he doesn't know *who* followed him up Pincher's Mount and defaced his Mustang. Dani didn't know either, but it didn't stop her assigning blame.

'Was that your fucking *wife*?' she'd demanded, standing in the lane and staring at those spray-painted letters.

'I don't—'

'Christ, James. The woman's a fucking *psycho*, you hear me? We need to get out of here, right now. She might still be prowling about.' Back inside the car, Dani continued to freak. 'The doors weren't even locked. She could have reached in, slit our throats. She could have poured in petrol, *incinerated* us.'

'Look—'

'No, *you* look. What are you going to do about this? You should report her to the police. You know what? Maybe *I* should.'

Listening to Dani's anger, James knew the evening was ruined – that he wouldn't convince her to finish what they'd started, even if he found another layby. And by then he'd lost all enthusiasm. Dani's voice – and her whining – had started to needle him.

Now, a few houses from home, James stops the car and unbolts the bonnet. It's a hassle to carry, but he manages, just about. Inside his garage, he wraps it in two soft blankets and leans it against the wall. Then he brings in the Mustang.

The house, when he enters, is dark. In the kitchen he finds evidence of his wife's evening: a plate dotted with crumbs, a knife smeared with butter. It makes him sad, seeing that. And then he thinks of the malicious damage to his Mustang. His hands make fists. One of his knuckles cracks.

Instead of going to bed, James opens the front door. He stares at his wife's car, sitting on the drive. Not a thing of beauty. Like most things in her life, it's strictly functional. He crosses the tarmac and places his hand on the bonnet.

Warm.

Did she say she was seeing friends this evening? In all honesty, he can't remember. Most of the time, when she speaks, he tunes out.

Silent, James climbs the stairs. He uses the bathroom and cleans his teeth. Then he opens the bedroom door. Just like on Saturday night, when he last played away, his wife is a tightly curled mass beneath the duvet. This time, though, a gap in the curtains admits a triangle of orange streetlight. James stands there, motionless. Had she been watching for his return?

The doors weren't even locked. She could have reached in, slit our throats. She could have poured in petrol, incinerated *us.*

Despite her perfect body and killer nails, maybe it's time he saw less of Dani. He'd certainly save a fortune in champagne.

James undresses. Thanks to the streetlight, he can see an odd assortment of trinkets on his wife's side table. They seem to be her new fad, like the quilting she did for a while until he explained – sensitively – that she was no good at it.

Tonight, as well as a dragon ring, and a brooch shaped like an arrow, he sees a silver chain attached to a tiny silver hammer. The violence implicit in those objects triggers in him a flicker of unease.

Christ, James. The woman's a fucking psycho.

Just imagine if that were true. Just imagine how utterly goddamned *terrifying* that would be.

He slips naked into bed. Beside him, his wife sighs and turns over. Her hand reaches out and finds his chest.

Rigid, James concentrates on her breathing.

Is she awake? *Was* she in the lane? *Did* she spray *CHEAT* on his car?

Beneath her dormant fingers, his heart beats wildly. He wonders how loudly he'd scream if she whispered into his ear that single word of accusation.

She doesn't, but still James cannot sleep.

THIRTY-TWO

I can't ride straight home. I'm too jittery with adrenalin. Too worried and excited and confused. After freewheeling down Old Cobb, I head east back through town, without much thought for where I'm going. Only when I arrive at the foot of Pincher's Mount do I realize it was my destination all along. A short climb later and I reach the place where I often sit.

Overhead, the stars seem brighter than usual, the mysteries of the heavens more inscrutable. For the first time in my life, I find myself wondering: am *I* being watched, from somewhere up there? The thought is so unsettling that my skin breaks out in goosebumps. Tonight, Louis spoke with such conviction that his words are difficult to shake off:

Just think of everything that had to align, Friday night, to bring us to this moment: your puncture, my empty fuel tank, those skaters, your throwaway comment that allowed me to find you again.

Earlier, I told myself that what's happening between us can't last, because there are things Louis must never know: not just that I'm watching the Raffertys, or that three years ago last winter I snatched Ollie, but what happened two years prior.

What if – just what if? – everything Louis told me is true? That our meeting at the Texaco *wasn't* coincidence. That we found each other for a reason? I don't believe that, not for a moment . . . but what if?

I know it wasn't random chance. I was drawn to that Texaco. I think you were drawn there, too. The question I couldn't answer earlier is why.

You think you can now?

Now that I've seen what you do, I have an inkling.

Which is?

I suspect I was sent here to help you.

When I close my eyes, I recall this evening's visit to Arcadia Heights: Ollie Rafferty, standing behind the glass in his Minions pyjama bottoms; the handle to his sliding door, mere inches away; my terror that if I touched it and found it unlocked, I'd lose all self-control; that I'd slide the door open, snatch him up.

Unbidden, a scene starts playing in my head. Louis and I, in the campervan's front seats, driving along a coastal road somewhere hot. Sunlight is pouring through the windows. Somehow, I'm unafraid. He grins at me, and I grin back, and when I turn my head I see, sitting behind us—

Flinching, I open my eyes, breathe deep.

In my lap are the binoculars and tripod Louis gave me at Rycroft Hollow. I set up the rig, put my eyes to the lenses and seek out Arcadia Heights. The resolution is so clear, the magnification so extraordinary, that I pull back for a moment, shocked. Then I take a second look.

In the kitchen, Simon Rafferty is standing at the island, removing foil from a bottle of champagne. He's wearing a tux, the jacket discarded. A bow tie hangs loose around his neck.

In the cinema room, Hugo the Shade sits on one of the white sofas. He's dressed just like Simon. At his side is a woman I don't recognize, beautiful in a silver sequinned dress. Another couple sits opposite.

I pan across the house, but I don't see Nadia. When I linger on the dark windows of Ollie's room, I think I see movement, just briefly, behind the glass. A minute later, a light goes on in the master suite.

There she is. Platinum-blonde bob, perfect physique, stunning emerald dress. The clarity of what I'm seeing robs me of breath. Never before have I had such a close-up view of her bedroom.

Nadia goes to her mirror. She studies her reflection for a while. Then she draws the fabric of her dress taut across her stomach, turning from side to side.

I feel a flickering in my own stomach – a stirring of something wholly imagined. Disturbing, but not as disturbing as what I think I'm watching. This is a repeat of what I saw on Saturday night. Surely there can be no doubt, now, about its meaning.

In her bedroom, Nadia Rafferty continues to study her reflection. Thanks to my new binoculars, I feel like I'm standing right behind her – that if I wished, I could reach out, touch her neck, feel the jump of her pulse through my fingers.

A mother's pulse; beating strong. And yet so incredibly fragile.

THIRTY-THREE

By noon, Saturday, it's thirty-seven degrees in the shade. On the street bench where Konstantin Tapia has been sitting this last hour, it's far hotter. The crown of his bald head, angled towards the sun, sizzles like meat on a griddle.

Tapia exalts the heat, worships it. If a control dial existed that he could manipulate, he'd rotate it to the highest setting. He'd watch the grass blacken, trees burst into flame, people ignite like candles before melting into liquid tallow.

Tapia knows these thoughts are unconventional. Over the years, he's learned to conceal them. At night, when the Earth has turned from the sun, he fortifies himself with footage of atomic explosions. He bathes in the white flash, the swelling orange, the conflagration produced by a truly seismic event. If reincarnation exists, Tapia plans to return as a desert lizard and to sunbathe on a nuclear test stand until the fires of hell accept him.

His bench is a few metres from the road. The property he came here to see – a converted Georgian townhouse in the heart of Old Town – stands a dozen or so metres to his right. If his information is correct, Keira Greenaway lives in the basement flat – although, considering the heavy curtains he saw pulled across the living-room window, *hiding out* might be a more accurate description.

A paper bag on Tapia's lap contains three Bhut Jolokia chillis. He reaches in and takes one, biting off the fruit at the stalk. One chew and his mouth fills with agony. Not quite a nuclear heat, but close. Still, he gives no outward sign.

From here, he can't see the basement flat but he has a full view of the main entrance. If Greenaway comes out, he'll spot her.

Beside him on the bench are a couple of sealed parcels. On top lies a *National Geographic* – the Vesuvius issue. Tucked inside it are two newspaper images of Greenaway taken during her trial.

The fire in Tapia's mouth swells until it's almost unbearable, but he controls it. Over one million SHUs on the Scoville scale – and, ultimately, a disappointment.

Standing, he picks up his parcels and crosses the street. He walks up the townhouse's drive, climbs the front steps and presses all the intercom buttons except one.

Leaning over the balustrade, he has a far better view of the basement flat's front window. Visible around the edges of the curtains are what look like custom-made blackout panels.

When a voice answers the intercom, Tapia says, 'Amazon.'

The door buzzes and he pushes through.

To his right, a row of metal post-boxes hangs above a console table messy with restaurant flyers. Printed on the box for flat one is a name: *M. LAKE*.

Stairs to his left lead up. Past a door at the end of the hall, a second flight leads down. Tapia follows them. At the bottom, a motion-activated light comes on overhead. It illuminates the basement flat's entrance and a pair of oxblood Doc Martens on the mat.

Tapia presses his ear to the doorframe.

Silence.

Is it true silence, he wonders? Or the silence of bated breath? Might Keira Greenaway be standing on the other side, her head cocked at the same angle? He could break down the door, find out, but that's not his style. Instead, he puts his eye to the spyhole and confirms that it's dark inside.

'Are you in there, little fish?' he whispers. Running his tongue around his gums, he tastes the last traces of heat from the Bhut Jolokia chilli. On his way out of the building, he dumps his empty parcels on the console table.

Two streets away, he unlocks his hire car. The midday sun has turned it into a furnace. Swinging into the leather seat, he feels like a naan slapped against a tandoor's clay wall.

The steering wheel is too hot to touch. Tapia grips it tightly regardless, relishing the pain. Then he takes out his cigarettes and lights one. He stares at the glowing tip, remembering the smell of Nadia's burning skin.

Closing his eyes, he recites the first lines of his favourite poem by Robert Frost: 'Some say the world will end in fire, Some say in ice.'

Tapia prays it's the former.

THIRTY-FOUR

Saturday night. Just over a week since the Texaco.

I'm on Bartholomew Street, crossing the junction to Liphook Avenue, when I spot White Knuckle Wanda's Range Rover parked a few doors down from Cave 173. Two nights ago, the nail-bar owner yelled at me while I was covering the graffiti outside Raj the Reborn's. No doubt she's inside the wine bar, downing a last drink before her boozed-up journey home.

I ride past, lamenting my usual inaction – and then, before I'm even fully conscious of what I'm doing, I turn around and pull up behind her car.

Climbing off my Jorvik, I unzip my cargo bag and grab my knife. Right now, the street is quiet – but it won't stay like that for long. If I'm to do this, I'll have to be quick.

Buzzing with adrenalin, I sneak up to the Range Rover's rear wheel and plunge my blade into the tyre.

It deflates far more explosively than I'd anticipated – with a sound like the air brakes on a bus. I retreat to my Jorvik, stow my knife and scarper.

Five minutes later, I'm at a window seat in the

drive-thru. Beneath the table my knees are knocking like conkers. It's so *bright* in here – like a laboratory, or the inside of a space station. I'm contemplating my nearly empty milkshake when Louis slides into the opposite seat.

'Boo,' he says, shooting me a grin.

I flinch, hunting for a clever reply, but my brain flatlines – and when I try to mumble something I choke, causing Louis to ask if I'm OK.

I nod, slurp milkshake, force a grin. I think about telling him what I just did. Instead, I indicate the nearby touchscreens. 'You want to get something?'

He glances around the restaurant, his nose wrinkling. 'I'm good.'

Two nights ago, Louis suggested I pick the location for our next meet-up. It's beginning to dawn on me that normal people probably wouldn't choose a drive-thru. I'm about to apologize when a familiar voice says, 'Hi, Merdy.'

I look up, grateful for the distraction. Lost Travis, gentlest of giants, is leaning over us.

'Hey, Travis. What's up?'

His big brown eyes study Louis. 'Merdy gotta new friend.'

'I do.'

Awkwardly, I introduce them. Travis bows solemnly before returning his attention to me.

'Lightning,' he says. 'Crash-bang.' He reaches under his uniform and pulls out his pendant. 'Bad omen. Means trouble coming.' He's about to say more when his eyes widen. He retracts into himself like a turtle into its shell.

Turning, I spot Whiplash Becky striding towards us. Her expression could melt the scales from a snake. '*Off* the floor,' she hisses, passing Travis without slowing.

He reacts as if to gunfire, ducking his head and bolting for the staff door. It's horrible to watch.

'Trouble coming indeed,' Louis mutters. 'One of yours?'

'Travis is the most innocent, most trusting guy you could hope to meet.'

'Is he why we're here?'

'No, although I'm glad you saw what just happened. Don't look now, but there's a guy by the ketchup station. Adidas tracksuit, grey baseball cap.'

Louis's eyes remain fixed on mine. 'The neckbeard? Early thirties? Broken nose and dirty fingernails?'

My mouth falls open. 'You didn't look.'

'Spotted him on the way in.'

I slurp the last dregs of my milkshake. 'Are you a secret agent?'

'Maybe. Tell me about Neckbeard.'

'You mean Cold Hand Carl.'

'I guess I do. Tell me about Cold Hand Carl.'

I glance around the restaurant. Right now, only half the tables are occupied. I hunch forward and speak quietly, even so.

I can't say Carl Edward Sergeant is the most accomplished housebreaker in Cranner's Ford – but he's likely the most prolific. Unusually for a burglar, he operates exclusively at night. Entering occupied homes doesn't seem to faze him. If anything, I think he enjoys it.

I first encountered Carl nine months ago, when he tried to burgle Arcadia Heights. Back then, the Raffertys hadn't installed CCTV and I was still using my old hiding place – behind the pizza oven on the far side of the pool. Carl emerged from the treeline and crept up to the kitchen's bi-fold doors. The shock nearly gave me a heart attack. Still, there was no way I was sharing the Raffertys with anyone. I lobbed a stone, hitting the glass. Carl fled, but the cracked window alerted Nadia. The security cameras went up the next day. When Carl's path crossed mine a second time, I started watching him.

He's a creature of habit. His Saturday nights always start at the drive-thru. From here he walks the streets, seeks out new targets and monitors those already marked. He watches a property three weekends consecutively before committing. Some, he abandons. Most, he enters.

It's a ruthlessly efficient system, albeit surprisingly easy to predict. If the police spent as much effort following Carl as they once did prosecuting me, the crime rate around here would plummet.

Carl steals from widowers, pensioners, families and young professionals. Anyone with something he wants. Small, highly valued items are his favourite: money, jewellery, laptops; things that fit into pockets or a rucksack.

The first house I watched him burgle was on Copper Beech Lane. Home Alone Jacob's place was the perfect target: a large plot surrounded by woods; a resident with poor hearing, in the early stages of grief; no neighbours in earshot; no alarm system or barking dog.

I still feel sick that I let it happen. Admittedly, I didn't know Jacob Creese back then. I had no idea of his recent bereavement; that he'd loved his wife with an intensity most people never experience; or that the couple had raised no children with whom Jacob could share his grief. Not that it should have made a difference. In my defence, I'd wanted to see how Carl operated so I could protect future victims.

That night, he roamed the house for eleven minutes

unchallenged. According to the *Gazette*, which reported on what happened, Carl escaped with Jacob's late wife's wedding band and engagement ring, plus the music box in which she'd stored them.

I don't tell Louis about the Rafferty incident, but I do tell him what happened at Home Alone Jacob's.

'So,' he says, once I'm finished. 'You didn't intervene back then. What about since?'

My knee knocks the table. I take a deep breath. And then I describe the notes I've started delivering to the houses I see Carl scouting, all with the same message:

> Your home is being watched by someone who breaks into places after dark. Please be extra careful and <u>stay safe</u>.
> THIS IS NOT A JOKE.

'Does it work?'

'Hard to say. So far, there's at least one place he didn't burgle after I posted a note. The homeowner put up a couple of Nest cameras, too.'

'Then it probably worked. Have you gone to the police?'

I shake my head.

'Why not?'

'They probably wouldn't do anything.'

'Then again, they might.'

'I guess.'

Louis tilts his head. I squirm beneath his gaze. Suddenly, the lights feel even brighter. The restaurant sounds louder. Fortunately, Carl chooses that moment to abandon his table. We wait until he's outside. Then we follow.

THIRTY-FIVE

Tapia loves the heat, but he cannot abide humidity.

Heat purifies; it destroys infection, burns away disease. Humidity encourages rot – and it's been climbing steadily since sunset. An hour before midnight, it's close to saturation.

The back of the van's a swamp. Sitting on a deckchair, Tapia's wet with sweat. He's already soaked two beach towels, but he won't lower a front window or crack the rear door. Important that the van looks like it's been left for the night. If anyone shines a torch through the windscreen, they won't see him through the partition.

He bought the vehicle earlier this afternoon. Eyeholes drilled through the bodywork offer good all-round views. On the exterior, signage advertising a now-defunct dog-grooming service disguises the modifications.

Across the street stands the townhouse he visited at lunchtime. Because of the basement flat's blackout blinds, Tapia can't tell if Keira Greenaway is home. In the five hours he's been watching, no one vaguely resembling her has entered or left the building.

'Don't be a shy fish,' Tapia mutters. 'I might hook you, but I won't gut you. Not tonight.'

From a paper bag he retrieves a Carolina Reaper chilli and bites into it. Heat, then pain, then agony. When he swallows, the fire in his mouth travels down his throat. It feels like layers of tissue are burning away. Tapia gasps, delighted. He takes another bite – and sees a young woman emerge from the townhouse's front entrance.

Keira Greenaway pauses beneath the porch light and looks straight at his van. She's an unusual specimen. Ragged hair, uneven features, wild look. Tapia's ears itch as he studies her. She's wearing dungaree shorts and the same oxblood Doc Martens he noticed outside her flat. She's so *pale* – like a rare white truffle dug from the soil.

Carefully, as if she's had too much to drink, Greenaway descends the steps. She unlocks a storage shed and wheels out a cherry-red electric trike.

'Let's find out where you're going, little fish,' Tapia says, climbing into the front seat. When Greenaway heads off, he waits a few moments, then follows. Five minutes later, he's sitting in a drive-thru car park, watching his little fish through the restaurant's front windows. She looks nervous. Maybe because of her weird act of vandalism committed en route. When a man slides on to the opposite seat, Greenaway flinches, then offers him a timid smile.

So – his little fish has a little buddy. The buddy looks smart, perceptive, alert. But no big deal.

Tapia watches them, motionless. The more he thinks about Keira Greenaway's pale, moon-touched flesh, the hungrier he grows. The burn Nadia granted him in the woods, although intimate, was little more than a palate cleanser. If anything, it's made him more ravenous.

When the couple step outside the drive-thru and load the trike into a campervan, Tapia starts his engine.

THIRTY-SIX

Randall Road. Anyone living here is doing all right. The homes are detached, double-fronted and widely spaced, with landscaped front gardens and two or three cars to each drive.

In the last ten minutes, Cold Hand Carl has walked down this street twice. On his second pass he hopped a front wall and ducked behind a huge leylandii, from where he's studying the property opposite. Louis and I are two houses along, crouched beside a wheelie-bin shelter.

I've never followed Carl here before. I suspect this is another scouting mission. In one of the first-floor windows of the place he's watching, a lamp glows behind white shutters. The rest of the house is dark.

In the pocket of my dungarees is an envelope containing my pre-written message. But I won't get to post it tonight – because Carl vaults the wall and crosses the street. Within moments, he's through a wrought-iron side gate and out of sight around the back.

'Well,' Louis says. 'There he goes.'

I stare at the house, dismayed. Thanks to the street-lamps, there's plenty of ambient light. On the front porch, two partially deflated balloons hang from a wall-mounted carriage lantern. Beneath the balloons, a pink scooter leans against the porch wall.

So, another Cranner's Ford family is about to fall victim. That this one just celebrated a birthday feels particularly cruel. I try to imagine what's happening behind the house. Has Carl gained access? Is he already rifling through the family's belongings? Perhaps he's slipped off a ledge and impaled himself on railings. Or sliced open his jugular climbing through broken glass.

I blink, flinch.

These aren't my usual thoughts.

Scents bloom in my nose: butcher's sawdust, wet metal. I clutch on to the shed and grimace. Across the road, I think I see something in one of the ground-floor windows – torchlight flickering through shutter slats.

'He's inside,' Louis mutters. At least his focus is on the house and not the malfunctioning mess beside him – but then he touches my arm. 'You're having another attack.'

'It'll pass.'

'You want to sit?'

'No. This is good.'

'There are kids in that house. Innocents.' Louis is silent a moment, before adding: 'Wait for me.'

He's halfway across the street before I've even registered his departure – and by that point it's too late to call him back. Louis walks up the driveway without breaking stride.

There's a roaring in my ears like wind, as if I'm falling

through turbulent air. When I let go of the storage shed, the world yo-yos. I have no choice but to grab back on.

This isn't why I brought him. This wasn't the plan.

What did you think would happen? Did you imagine he'd stand here and do nothing?

When Louis disappears through the side gate I can't suppress a moan. This is all my stupid fault. I abandon the shed and manage five strides towards the house before the world runs away from me. The ground strikes my side like a swung baseball bat. My head cracks against tarmac. The world shrinks, then disappears.

When I lurch back into consciousness, I have no idea how long I've been out. I scissor my legs, sit upright, think about being sick. Somehow, I find my feet. The road is a surfboard on which I balance with great difficulty. Ahead, the house which swallowed Louis and Cold Hand Carl fractures in two. Neither option looks promising, but I pick the closest and shuffle towards it.

The sloped driveway is another puzzle for my misfiring brain. Somehow, I zigzag up it and push through the wrought-iron gate. I'm breathing hard, using the side wall as a crutch. I feel my way past a glass-panelled door, nearly trip over a concrete step. My hand bumps around a plastic downpipe and along a window ledge where a few garden hand tools have been left. I knock one loose, wincing as it clatters on to the paving stones.

How will Cold Hand Carl react if challenged? He's a big guy, brutish, certainly bigger than Louis. What if the homeowners hear something, call the police? I can't afford to get caught.

So go! Now! Get out of here!

But nor can I abandon Louis.

I reach the corner of the house and pause until my twin perspectives merge. Opposite, I see a set of wicker furniture arranged around a firepit. A timber-built climbing frame stands on an extensive lawn.

To my left I have a view along the back of the house: utility room, kitchen with bifold doors, dining room with French windows, all dark. One of the French windows hangs ajar.

Glancing up, I see no lights above me. Two of the first-floor windows are plastered with stickers, toys crowding their sills.

Holding my breath, I rush past the kitchen's doors, praying I don't fall, knowing I'll be visible to anyone inside. I think I glimpse movement – darkness twisting inside shadow – but then it's gone. Arriving outside the French windows, I step through them.

I've still no idea how long I was unconscious. A minute? Five? Clearly, not long enough for a passing car to run me over, but there are few clues in that – this time of night, these residential streets are quiet.

It's far darker inside the house. My eyes take a while to adjust. I see the outline of a rectory table, eight chairs; the silhouettes of a sideboard and what might be two display cabinets.

A doorway to my left leads to the kitchen. From somewhere close I hear vague, confusing sounds: mouse-like squeaks, clicks and drips, sibilant and disjointed breathing.

Overhead, a floorboard creaks. I recall the windows I saw on the first floor: two kids' rooms; a staircase window; a fourth window of mottled glass.

A toilet flushes above me, masking the softer sounds I

heard earlier. Pipes rattle inside the walls. A cistern gulps and refills.

I reach the doorway and lean against the frame. The room beyond isn't just a kitchen but a combined living space – island, a couple of sofas, a huge expanse of tiled floor. A figure is slumped against the island, legs splayed. There's something wrong with its head.

THIRTY-SEVEN

Within minutes of leaving the drive-thru, Tapia discovers something curious: his little fish and her buddy are engaged in a hunt of their own.

That piques his interest, but it does present challenges. Ahead, the campervan drives erratically, pausing at the roadside for short periods before accelerating to the next junction. Tapia is forced to hang back and do the same. By the time the couple park up and climb out, he still hasn't seen their target.

Abandoning his own vehicle, he trails them along a residential street. When they take cover behind a structure on one of the driveways, Tapia does likewise behind them.

For the next ten minutes, he waits and watches and eventually spots the focus of their attention – a guy in a baseball cap and tracksuit, surreptitiously scouting the houses, who eventually ducks out of sight behind a tree. A few minutes pass. Then the guy breaks cover. He crosses the street and walks up the driveway of a house.

Moments later, the buddy fish follows. Shortly afterwards,

so does the little fish – but she only manages a few steps before she collapses.

Tapia considers her prostrate form. He really doesn't know what's happening here. It makes him all the more determined to find out. Silently, he closes on the campervan.

The interior is spotless, nothing on display to indicate anything of the driver's personality. The van itself, however, has attitude. Tapia has the weirdest feeling that it's aware – and sizing him up. He shakes his head. Some strange side effect of the Carolina Reaper, perhaps.

From his pocket he removes the tracker he ordered online. It's a plastic box, smaller than a pack of playing cards, featureless save for two neodymium magnets. He's already synched it to his phone. Its associated app uses the Google Maps system along with nine alternative interfaces. It'll show the campervan's position in real time, recording locations visited and duration.

A shame he doesn't have a tracking device small enough for the trike. An Apple AirTag dropped inside the frame might work, but it would take time to install – and the AirTag's functionality isn't great. The vehicle tracker is a far superior solution. Tapia crawls halfway under the campervan and attaches it. A quick check of the app confirms a signal.

In the street, his little fish begins to stir. Before she can recover fully, Tapia crosses the street and walks up the driveway to the house.

THIRTY-EIGHT

On the floor I see an irregular run of dark spots. Unlikely it's blemishes in the tiles. Far more likely it's blood.

So far, I've seen no movement from the figure by the kitchen island – but as I watch, its chest fills. I'm so sick with fear I need a moment to gather myself. When I do, I realize that a second figure is sitting on one of the sofas.

Upstairs, the cistern moans and the water shuts off. Now, all I hear is my breathing. I slide my hand along the wall. When I find a switch plate, I clench my teeth hard and fill the kitchen with light.

The figure slumped against the island is a man. I recognize him by his clothes but not his face – because his head is entirely wrapped in clingfilm.

For long seconds, the discovery is too confusing to process. When I turn to the nearest sofa, I see Louis. His face is angled towards me, eyes shining beneath two banks of LED spots.

'What's going on?' I hiss.

'I've been having a heart-to-heart with Carl,' he replies. 'I've explained that we're unhappy with his behaviour. And

Carl, to his credit, has promised to explore alternative career options.'

I glance at the burglar's clingfilm-wrapped head. A small hole has been punched through the plastic around his mouth. It's offering him enough air to breathe, but he's having to work hard for it. The clingfilm compresses his face on each inward breath, ballooning as he exhales. Blood from his nose is spreading beneath the layered wrap. It's like watching a chrysalis in the final stages of pupation.

'You'd agree with that assessment, wouldn't you, Carl?' Louis asks.

The sound issuing from the blood-flecked hole is hardly a word at all: 'Ysch.'

'We've even discussed a few avenues. Why don't you name one for my friend? Prove that you've been paying attention.'

'Divree,' the plastic-wrapped head splutters. 'Divree duvver.'

'Delivery driver, that's right,' Louis says. 'For Amazon, perhaps. Or UPS. A far better career choice than burglar. You've seen the people who live here, Carl. They look nice. They don't need Carl Edward Sergeant in their lives. They certainly don't deserve the trauma of a home invasion conducted while they were asleep. You agree, don't you?'

'Ysch.'

I wonder how Louis can know anything about the people who live here. Then I spot the photo canvas on the far wall. It's a family shot, taken near the climbing frame. Mum and Dad look like science types, geeky and full of energy. Their daughter is a blonde-haired imp. Her arm is slung around an older brother whose face bears the classic features of Down syndrome. His smile suggests he's unlocked the secret to everlasting happiness.

Rarely have I seen four people so obviously radiating love. At that moment, my heart hardens against Cold Hand Carl. I know he'll have faced difficulties in his life, but I also know how he operates. He'll have scoped out this house at least twice before entering it. He'll have peered through those bifold doors and seen the faces smiling from that canvas. Just now, he'd have seen the balloons hanging from the carriage lamp.

'Oh, damn,' I say, because suddenly it's all too much. And because I just worked out something important.

Louis shoots me a look. 'What's wrong?'

'I'm going to be sick.'

'Are you sure?'

'Pretty sure. I don't think I can—'

'Sink.'

I'm already moving. Fortunately, I reach the kitchen island without stumbling, and then I'm throwing up sixteen hundred gallons of strawberry milkshake into the porcelain sink. Gasping, I rinse it away with cold water. Then I swill out my mouth and spit.

'OK?' Louis asks.

'Fabulous. Really enjoyable. Can we get out of here now?'

'We can—'

He stops, and I know why. Because I heard it, too: the creak of a floorboard somewhere deeper in the house, followed by the sound of a staircase flexing under someone's weight.

'Lights,' Louis says.

I stumble towards the wall, hitting the switch with my

palm. Overhead, the LED spots wink out. In an instant we're blind, the darkness far worse for us than for whoever is creeping down the stairs.

I hear a final squeal of wood, then silence. Impossible to tell if our visitor is standing at the bottom of the flight or walking across a solid floor towards us. Far too slowly, my eyes readjust. I see Louis, Cold Hand Carl and, through an arch in the far wall, the silhouette of a girl a few years older than the photo canvas imp.

She pauses in the arch, sniffs. I think of the sixteen hundred gallons of strawberry milkshake I vomited up. I'm guessing the air must be foul with it.

Finally, the girl moves. Her bare feet slap against the tiled floor. I hear the squeak of a cupboard hinge, the scrape of a glass. She walks across the kitchen, somehow avoiding the blood splashes. At the sink she fills her glass, drinks deeply and sighs.

Carl is sitting to her immediate right. Mere inches separate them. If he moves, even slightly, she'll hear him. And then she'll scream and her parents will come running. If she takes any other route back to the arch, she'll trip over his legs, with the same result.

The girl yawns, rubs her eyes. Then, dumping her empty glass, she turns her back on Carl and slopes out of the kitchen. I hear the staircase creaking, the floorboards overhead flexing, the *thunk* of a bedroom door.

Immediately, I hit the lights. I know it's a risk, but I need to see what's happening. Louis is already on his feet. 'We're leaving,' I tell him.

'Agreed.'

'We've got to get rid of that blood.'

He opens the cupboard under the sink. Finding a cloth,

he dampens it and starts to mop up. 'They'll never know we were here. Carl, stand up, keep quiet, avoid further punishment.'

The larger man struggles to his knees, then his feet. For the first time, I notice the clingfilm binding his wrists. His head moves left and right, as if he's trying to make sense of his surroundings.

Louis picks up Carl's rucksack and stuffs the bloodied cloth inside. I switch off the lights. Then, leading our burglar like a tethered goat, we leave the same way we entered, closing the French windows behind us.

Outside, the street is still quiet. We walk to the junction, where foliage spilling from someone's garden offers a patch of shadow.

'Sit,' Louis says.

Cold Hand Carl complies.

'Raise your hands. I'm giving you back your phone.'

Again, Carl does as he's asked.

'Excellent,' Louis tells him. 'You really are very good at this. As I explained to you earlier, for far too long you've been an agent of chaos. From now, you're an agent of order. You're going to listen to what the universe is telling you, and you're going to act in accordance with its wishes. Aren't you, Carl?'

'*Ysch.*'

'You just gained a couple of very observant followers – fellow seekers of order, just like your good self. We'll be watching you, Carl. We'll be following with great interest your choice of new career path. I know you're going to impress us, but here are a few ground rules. They're non-negotiable, so pay attention. For the next month, don't let us catch you outside past sunset. And don't, whatever you do, attempt to leave town. Because wherever you went, Carl, we'd find you. And you wouldn't like what came next. Tell me you understand.'

'*I yunnershan.*'

'Excellent. We'll leave you, now – allow you some space to think. I've set a timer on your phone. When it rings, you're free to go. Rucksack's at your feet. Stanley knife's still in the side pocket, should you have difficulty with the clingfilm. Be careful not to cut yourself.'

'*Kay.*' Carl takes a heaving breath, shudders. His Adam's apple bobs. '*Shankoo.*'

'You're very welcome.'

Gently, Louis puts his arm around my waist. I don't flinch. In fact, I feel strangely euphoric. Together, we walk down the street.

THIRTY-NINE

Old Cobb's summit. Me, Louis and a topsy-turvy world where the rules are for us to decide.

We're sitting in Eleanor's front seats. In my lap is a vintage Speak & Spell I fished from a skip we passed en route. On the radio, the Temptations are singing 'The Way You Do The Things You Do'. Great music, but oh Lord, my head's a *mess*. I'm scared, shocked, appalled, incredulous. I wonder if I'm falling in love. I've certainly never felt this way before.

'How's your stomach now?' Louis asks.

'Feeling ashamed of itself.' Fishing out my grape-flavoured Bubblicious, I load up my mouth with gum. This time I remember to offer it, but Louis shakes his head. 'You think it'll work?' I ask. 'That he'll just stop?'

'Tough call. But I actually think he might.'

I chew my gum and consider that. I think of all the people Carl burgled while I shoved envelopes through letterboxes. I was so *pleased* with myself. I even boasted to Louis about it.

Thanks to him, that family on Randall Road will wake

to nothing worse than the ghost waft of my sick. If tonight's intervention works long term, how many other families might be spared? Cold Hand Carl's clingfilm-wrapped head was horrible to behold, utterly nightmarish. But in this case, might the end justify the means? I feel my strange euphoria returning.

'I almost forgot,' Louis says. 'I got you something.'

I look at him sideways. 'Another present?'

'Three, actually. Just a few things I thought you might like.' He reaches behind him and hands me a tissue-paper-wrapped bundle.

I place it on my lap and tuck my hands beneath my thighs. I want to savour the moment, soak up every detail. Because this is more evidence that I've crossed Louis's mind while we've been apart, that I've made an impression on his world. I know how cringey that sounds, how lacking in self-respect – but until just over a week ago, my social contact was limited to a few snatched conversations with Lost Travis. In eight short days my life has changed utterly.

'Go on,' Louis urges. 'Open it.'

When I tear through the paper I discover a summer dress, letter-box red, printed with tiny white flowers.

'It might not be your style,' he says. 'And that's totally OK. It was a spur-of-the-moment thing, really. I saw it yesterday and thought you'd look cool in it. Then I remembered how worried you were the other night about your current wardrobe.'

I smooth my hands across the red fabric, marvelling at its feel. 'I love it,' I tell him, because I do. 'Honestly, it's perfect. You think I could wear it with my Doc Martens?'

Louis smiles. 'I think you could wear it with wellies and still look good.' He reaches into the door well and hands me a gold iPhone. 'There's this, too. Again, I *really* won't be offended if you don't want it, but I programmed it with my number, just in case.'

The phone wakes at my touch. On its screen I see an image of Pincher's Mount at dawn, the sun a ball of orange fire. It's enough to make me shudder – a full-body spasm. Fortunately, Louis doesn't seem to notice. I turn the phone over in my lap, hiding the screen.

'I figured it might give us options,' he says. 'Allow us to meet without relying on the drive-thru.'

'In hindsight, that was an awful choice.'

'At least I got to meet Travis – and see the place where you drank all that milkshake you threw up.'

'Oh God, stop.'

'Are you ready for your last present?'

'Louis, I—'

'Same deal as before.' Twisting around, he grabs a white box so long it has to sit across both our laps. 'OK,' he says. 'I have to admit I'm a tiny bit excited about this.'

When I raise the lid, it takes me a moment to figure out what I'm looking at. Then my breath goes. On a bed of crushed velvet lies a pair of folded wings. But these aren't the cheap fancy-dress kind, like the ones I found in some-one's rubbish and mended. Nor are they the wings of a butterfly.

These are feathered, anatomically accurate, an impos-sibly opulent cascade. They look like an exhibit from a museum of the fantastic – appendages torn from a genuine angel. Reaching into the box to touch them, I almost expect to find severed muscles and dried blood. Their ivory col-ouring reminds me of old piano keys. Antique lace.

My fancy-dress wings are for Ollie Rafferty's benefit,

but I've long dreamed of the real thing. When balancing on two feet is a daily challenge, it's easy to fantasize about flight.

'I know they're not fairy wings,' Louis says. 'But they felt appropriate.' He pauses, then says: 'Mercy Lake, Angel of Cranner's Ford.'

If I wasn't still wearing my seatbelt, I'd be in danger of floating through the open window and up into space. I can't believe the amount of *thought* that went into these gifts. When I turn towards Louis I realize we're in a moment – the kind with a capital M. On the radio, a new song starts: 'Happy Together' by the Turtles. Now, it's not just the M that's capitalized but the whole word, formed of giant lightbulbs and blinking like an emergency beacon.

To his credit, Louis doesn't make the first move. I do. We close in on each other like two wilting plants, like the Dragon capsule docking with the Space Station, like tectonic plates, like—

Shut up, Mercy, and kiss him.

At last, I do just that. My eyes close, our lips touch. It's a new experience, stupefying in its intensity. Unforgivable, really, that I forgot about my gum.

'Sorry,' I say, pulling back. I spit the Bubblicious into my palm and become, again, a wilting plant, a Dragon capsule, an idiot girl incapable of metaphors – with mismatched eyes and home-cut hair and a feeling in her heart of unparalleled joy.

It can't last, I know it can't, but I do enjoy the kiss.

FORTY

Konstantin Tapia takes the road that climbs Old Cobb with his headlights doused. Halfway up he pulls over, hiding his van behind a pipe stack destined for some future drainage project. He continues on foot to the summit.

There's the campervan, parked on gravel near Old Cobb's sharpest face, its nose pointed towards town. The windows are down. Music is playing. Overhead hangs a moon so round and beautiful that, staring at it, Tapia recalls his favourite lunar story.

A year after the Soviets launched *Sputnik*, the US was losing the space race. It needed something eye-catching – a giant dead cat. Its air force came up with Project A119: a plan to fire a nuke at the moon. Money was spent. Carl Sagan was brought in to work the maths. Tragically, the project was cancelled before humanity could enjoy the beauty of a lunar blossoming.

Tapia sighs. What has brought this pair to the summit on a hot and humid Saturday night? He can think of no reason except one, but after the madness he witnessed inside that house on Randall Road, they could very easily surprise him.

He drops below the ridgeline, skirting the summit until he's directly opposite the campervan. Carefully, he lifts his head.

Inside the cabin, the couple are wearing expressions he only ever sees on the faces of new lovers. As he watches, they lean into each other and kiss. It's tentative, delicate, achingly sweet. It might even be the first time.

Tapia's skin prickles.

The more he learns about Keira Greenaway, the more he fantasizes about burning her. He knows Nadia won't ask him to do that, even if she might desire it. She has no clue how his appetite for fire has developed in the years since her first barn visit, nor the lengths he has gone to satisfy it.

If not for Nadia, of course, he may never have explored it at all. For that, Tapia fluctuates between hatred and idolatry, a conflict that one day he knows he'll have to resolve. In the last decade, he's set alight four people and watched them burn. No greater intimacy can exist between two humans, he's discovered, than when witnessing the first seconds of a person's combustion. A spark transforms into pillowing orange; rolling, velvet heat. Eyes become windows. In them he's glimpsed the edges of revelations; tantalizing mysteries. Sometimes, he's even seen ecstasy. On all four of those occasions, Tapia didn't bring death so much as perfection distilled from imperfection, via the medium of fire.

Closing his eyes, he visualizes Keira Greenaway tied to a stake at the top of one of these hills, her mushroom-white flesh glistening with ethanol, her ragged hair dripping with it. He imagines the stiffening of her limbs as she senses what's about to happen, her rabbit-eyed terror.

Tapia still has one Carolina Reaper chilli left. He bites

into it and feels his mouth, his throat and his scalp ignite with heat.

With pain comes an epiphany; an extension to his vision.

Now, he sees not just Keira Greenaway soaked in accelerant but also her little buddy. He pictures them tied to separate stakes a few metres apart, facing each other across the hilltop but unable to touch. He sees himself standing between them, brandishing a flaming taper.

In those transformative first moments of fire, he'd share the enormity of their loss; and the beginnings of their separate journeys into the unknown. He'd witness their shock and their agony – and, ultimately, their release. For them, a singular experience. For him, a moment of nirvana.

Saliva floods Tapia's mouth. He opens his eyes, watches the couple continue to kiss, summons the sensation of their lips on his.

Shivering despite the evening's warmth, light-headed despite his sobriety, Tapia steals back down the slope.

FORTY-ONE

Tuesday night. Seventy-two hours since Louis and I parted.

My new phone hasn't rung, not even a chirp. Still, Louis wouldn't have bought it had he never intended to contact me, so I'm not worried.

OK, I'm not *frantic*.

But I *am* desolate.

Last night, waiting to hear from him, I stayed home for the first time in months. I swept up peanut shells with my trapdoor dustpan. I strapped on my Twilight Sparkle helmet and did my exercises. I paraded around in my red dress and startled myself with the stranger I saw in the mirror. I even tried on my angel wings.

But as the night wore on I grew disconsolate. I ordered new underwear from an online shop. I read the *Cranner's Ford Gazette*. I dismantled and reassembled the Speak & Spell I found in the skip on Saturday night. Only when I was reinstalling my blackout panels near dawn did I realize how much time I'd wasted, how many visits I'd missed.

I won't make the same mistake again. Better to do something useful than sit around mooning. After a last check of my neon-pink wig, I zip up my rucksack and carry it out to my Jorvik.

Ten minutes later I'm on Abbot's Walk, crouched inside the grounds of Arcadia Heights. A stone's throw from my hiding place, the Rafferty pool glows an unearthly green.

From here I have a perfect view of Ollie Rafferty's balcony, as well as my usual route up to it. In my backpack, along with my Tinker Bell outfit, is the refurbished Speak & Spell. I haven't decided if I'll give it to him. It's far larger than my previous gifts – far harder for Ollie to hide. Still, I won't have to decide tonight. Certainly not unless I'm content to wait. Firstly, because three freshly installed security cameras have joined the original two and I cannot easily see a way past them. Secondly, because right now the pool is occupied by a swimmer.

Nadia Rafferty – bronze skin, platinum bob, diamond-cut cheekbones – glides through the water like a seal. In recent days I've seen her twice from Pincher's Mount, but this is the first time for a while up close.

Physically, she's without flaw, silicone and collagen providing the enhancements that yoga and genetics could not. The overall effect is unsettling, chilling even, yet undeniably compelling. I feel like I'm watching an android swim perfect lengths, oiled servos beneath the skin driving a system of advanced hydraulics.

For a short period, six months ago, I grew obsessed with Simon Rafferty's second wife. I cut my hair into the same bob, bought the same yoga mat, blitzed myself the same smoothies. I even ordered some of the same outfits.

But the more I tried to copy her, the more I emphasized my own shortcomings. Put us side by side and you couldn't fail to spot the counterfeit. Looking back, I see my behaviour through a clearer lens. I was trying to get inside Nadia's head and see what it contained. As if by dressing like her, looking like her, I'd be able to learn her secrets. Of course, she may not *have* secrets. In fact, it's likely she doesn't.

Nadia completes a length and turns to begin another. Beyond the pool, the doors to the orangery swing open. On to the patio steps Simon Rafferty.

I wasn't ready for this, wasn't expecting it – and because of that I haven't prepared myself. In an instant I'm breathing through clenched teeth, fighting to keep my balance.

Tonight, he's wearing a white linen shirt over pastel boardshorts. The shirt is open, revealing a hairless chest. In one hand he holds a whisky snifter containing a double measure.

Hard, now, to believe how I once felt about him. Before Ollie's birth, I thought Simon Rafferty represented everything one might want in a partner: kindness, humour, intelligence, good looks.

Of course, that was before Sheergen launched publicly. Before the *serious* money rolled in. Before Simon started to attract engineered perfection like Nadia.

I don't blame her. Not any more. She wasn't the first, and I doubt she'll be the last. If anything, I worry for her future. When that android body develops faults, when time and gravity defeat silicone and collagen, I suspect she'll find herself obsolete. I just hope she can move on from it. The last thing I need is an android crouched beside me on the grass, watching its upgrade perform laps of the pool – and dreaming up ways to cripple it.

Just for clarity, I have no intention of crippling Nadia Rafferty. I have no intention of crippling anyone.

Simon crosses the patio. He swirls his scotch, eyes on his wife as she shuttles through the water. I see, just briefly, his look of smug satisfaction: the pleasure of a man who can afford expensive toys, enjoying his favourite acquisition.

Until three days ago, Simon Rafferty was the only man ever to kiss me. I'm so glad that's no longer true.

When Nadia notices him, she abandons her length and stands. Water drips from her platinum hair. It glimmers, green and gold, against her perfect skin – pearls of android lubricant.

Behind me, towards the road, I hear the snap of a branch, followed by the sound of a night creature scurrying through the undergrowth.

I tense. Simon lifts his eyes to the spot where I'm hiding. It feels like we're looking directly into each other's eyes.

'Inside,' he says.

My heart freezes mid-beat. Simon can't have seen me. Nor can I be the target of his demand. Still, I find myself unable to breathe until he drops his gaze to Nadia and says it again.

'What is it?' she asks.

'Not out here.'

Something unsaid passes between them. Effortlessly, she emerges from the water. Simon hands her a towel.

I watch them head into the house. Nadia's feet leave wet prints that fade like ghosts. I look again at Ollie's balcony, and then at the three new security cameras covering sections of my old route. Given time, I might figure out a way to evade them, but my Night People instincts are flashing red. Tonight wouldn't be a good time to try.

I'd love to sneak closer, eavesdrop on Simon and Nadia's discussion. When they stepped inside the orangery, they didn't lock it. But I'm not Louis. And a false step at Arcadia Heights would probably be fatal.

My leg starts vibrating. Except it's not my leg – it's my new phone. Thank God I switched it to silent before I came out. When I answer, Louis says: 'Can I pick you up?'

His voice – so casual after our seventy-two hours apart – throws me into a tailspin. With a last glance at Ollie's room, I hurry back through the undergrowth. 'Sure.'

'Where are you?'

I can't tell him I'm at Arcadia Heights. Nor even on Abbot's Walk. Arriving at the crushed section of boundary wall, I climb on to my Jorvik. 'You know Marlborough Avenue?'

'I'll satnav it.'

'Great. I'll see you there.'

I hang up, gasping. No lies told. Honesty still intact. All good.

FORTY-TWO

Ten minutes later I'm clambering into the campervan's passenger seat while Louis lifts my Jorvik into the back. When he joins me up front, we lean in and kiss. My toes perform familiar paroxysms.

He pulls back, eyeing my neon-pink wig. 'I'm guessing you have a plan.'

'Deevis Farm,' I tell him. 'Near the old quarry.'

'I don't know it. Can you direct me?'

'Like a boss.'

He puts the VW in gear and we drive. On the radio, Aretha Franklin is singing 'I Say A Little Prayer'. As I listen to the lyrics, I think about Nadia Rafferty swimming perfect laps of the Raffertys' perfect pool – and Simon Rafferty's look of satisfied ownership. Then, deliberately, I turn my thoughts to what lies ahead.

Will we change the world tonight? Beyond the windscreen, Cranner's Ford teems with opportunity: situations that need improving; people who need fixing; and, just possibly, thugs who need educating.

'I've been thinking,' Louis says. 'This weekend – how about a road trip? Weather's meant to be good. We could drive Eleanor to the coast, take a boat out. Have a barbecue on the beach.'

My face twists. 'I can't.'

'You've got something on?'

'Not exactly.'

He glances over. 'Too soon?'

'No. It sounds lovely. It's just . . .'

When Louis doesn't follow up, I feel compelled to fill the silence. 'You remember last week? When I said I didn't do lunch? And that I didn't really do day? Well, I meant it. Literally, I meant it.'

'You don't do day?'

'More accurately, I don't do daylight.'

Louis laughs. 'Do you sleep in a coffin?'

That stings, but I try to ignore it. 'I know it's pretty weird.'

He glances over. 'When was the last time you saw the sun?'

Turning away, I stare through the side window. Now he's asked the question, I can't avoid it, but I'm terrified of his reaction.

'Mercy?'

'Five years.'

'Five—' Louis inhales. 'You haven't seen daylight in five *years*?'

'It's not that bad. I take vitamin D. And I have daylight lamps at home.'

'But still . . . *five years*, Mercy? How can you live like that?'

'I live the same as anyone else,' I tell him. 'I just live at night, that's all. I'm sure I'm not the only person in the world who does.'

This time, Louis remains silent. I wish I could read his thoughts. Eleven days ago, at the Texaco, I was shaken by a notion that he and I were the only living creatures on the planet, in the entire universe, perhaps, and that everything that came before did so purely to bring us to that moment. Terrified, I fled into the dark, determined that whatever had begun to sprout between us wouldn't get the chance to develop leaves. Eleven days later, and I've failed utterly. The seedling has pushed out roots and unfurled flowers. I let it grow without appreciating its fragility – and now I'm terrified of losing it.

'Do you drive?' Louis asks. 'Do you have a car?'

I shake my head.

'So how do you get around? I mean, to places outside Cranner's Ford.'

'I don't.'

More silence. I sense the flowers of our strange creation wilting – its roots shrivelling in the soil.

'Have you seen anyone about it?' Louis asks. 'Like a therapist?'

'Don't want to. Not any more. I'm used to it, now. Resigned to it.'

'You can't have darkness without light,' he says. 'Not indefinitely. Just like you can't have winter without it eventually turning to summer.'

I don't know how to respond to that. It didn't *sound* like a rebuke – more a statement of fact. Louis doesn't look as repulsed as I'd feared, but his pitiful expression is almost as bad.

'If there were a magic pill,' he asks, 'and it could cure you, no ill effects – would you take it?'

'Do you have one in your pocket?'

'I'm being serious.'

The vision I tried to banish on Thursday night at Pincher's Mount swells again in my head: me and Louis, driving along a coastal road, sunlight sparkling off the ocean; and, sitting behind us, Ollie Rafferty.

'I'd bite your fingers off,' I tell him. Then I sit up straight. 'Turn left and pull over. We can walk the rest of the way from here.'

FORTY-THREE

Deevis Farm. A place of horror, hiding in plain sight. If anywhere could shake my belief in humanity, this would be it.

Half a mile along Mullpenny Lane we find a padlocked gate and climb over. It's very dark. The farm's outbuildings are silhouettes against the night sky. High overhead, the blades of two Sheergen wind turbines quietly rotate. Beneath our feet lies a battleground of cracked earth. We cross it in careful silence. More than once I've spotted torchlight out here after dark. In these fields, trespassers are most definitely not welcome.

The farmhouse stands to our left. A lit bulb over the back door offers the only evidence of human occupation.

I lead Louis between two huge, open-fronted storage sheds. We reach a fork and turn right. The track takes us over a rise. Now, we're out of sight of the farmhouse; out of sight of the road. Ahead, I can just make out the silhouette of a single-storey shed. As we draw closer, our need for silence diminishes. The ruckus coming from inside is loud enough to mask our voices: a baying and a howling – how I imagine hell would sound, should it exist.

'What *is* that?' Louis asks.

We close to within twenty metres. The stink of dog faeces and putrefaction reaches my nose. Real, not imagined – so thick it's as if I've ingested it.

I crouch behind a rusted tractor and examine the shed. Windowless timber walls support a corrugated-iron roof. No light leaks from beneath the door. A wheelbarrow parked outside wasn't there on my last visit.

I need to do this before I lose my nerve – or my stomach. With a final scout around, I climb to my feet, pulling Louis across the rutted ground to the door.

Here, the smell is so awful I start gagging. It's too dark to see inside the wheelbarrow but its contents are clearly the source. I hear what sounds like maggots boiling inside a carcass.

The door, set on steel rollers, slides open without complaint. Immediately, the baying intensifies. I wonder if the shed's occupants are expecting food, and curse myself for not bringing any along.

Once we're inside, I switch on my torch. It illuminates a scene ripped straight from a nightmare. Either side of us, haphazardly stacked cages form rows the length of the shed. Through the bars I see eyes. Hundreds of them.

Some of the cages house individual puppies; most contain full litters. In their haste to reach the light, they scrabble over each other. Those too weak to move squeal beneath the weight of stronger siblings.

It's appalling, heartrending. Beyond shocking. And far worse than what I witnessed on my last visit. Some of the puppies are in such dreadful condition I can't even guess the breed. Fur that should be soft and glossy is soaked with urine and matted with excrement. Faces untouched by daylight are sallow with misery and suffering. Faecal matter floats in the water bowls. It clings to the rotten bedding.

Hard to imagine how any of these creatures could be cleaned up well enough to dupe a buyer – but I guess that's what happens. Even if only half of them survive long enough to find owners, the profits will still be huge. There's certainly little cost in maintaining conditions as rank as these – other than a moral one.

Behind me, Louis's breathing changes. I angle my torch towards him and see his chin thrust forward, his jaw set. He's peering into a cage containing what might be four lab retriever pups. Three of them look close to death. The fourth is just about strong enough to stand. It quivers beneath Louis's gaze, tail between its legs. When he pushes a knuckle through the bars, it tries to suckle.

'This is unconscionable,' he says. 'More than that. It's pure evil.'

He's right. Really, there's no other word. Even this late at night, the air in here is stifling. Temperatures during the day must be hellish.

'You've reported this?' he asks.

'To the council six times. To the RSPCA three times.'

'The police?'

'Crimestoppers.'

'And nothing's been done?'

'I can't say what's been done. Maybe not nothing.'

'Mercy,' he says, 'I'm not suggesting for one minute that you're complicit.'

I wipe my eyes, unable to stop my tears. Because whatever Louis says, humans caused this misery and I failed to stop it. 'I thought, if I showed you . . . Maybe we could do something about it.'

He turns, meets my gaze. 'You feel that?'

'Feel what?'

Louis's eyes shine. 'The universe – posing its question through your lips. We're being tested, Mercy. *Right now*, we're being tested.'

His words are so hypnotic – delivered with such conviction – that they're impossible to resist. My breath, suddenly, is in my throat. My belly feels like it's full of hatching eggs.

'I had a puppy when I was a kid,' Louis says. 'Just for a short while. One night it peed on the carpet after my dad rolled home drunk. It didn't survive what came next. What's worse is that I stood by and let it happen. I was young and I was scared, but that's no excuse.'

He glances around the shed. 'You know what? This feels like an opportunity to finally put that right. Let's rinse out the water bowls and refill them. We'll figure something out and come back.'

FORTY-FOUR

I hadn't expected Deevis Farm to affect Louis so deeply. Nor had I anticipated that story from his childhood. Tonight's the first time we've revealed anything significant from our pasts. It feels like we've hit another milestone, almost without noticing.

From the farm we drive back to Cranner's Ford. Two streets before Chaplin Row, I ask Louis to stop.

'Roaring Mary,' I tell him. 'I'll only be a minute.'

I climb out of the campervan, crunch across Mary's gravel drive and grab the two wheelie bins parked near her wall. Best to do this confidently, regardless of the noise. I drag the bins to the pavement, where all the others are lined up. Then I rejoin Louis.

'Roaring Mary has dementia,' I explain. 'Bins are one of the things she forgets.'

'She roars?'

I shake my head. 'The first few nights I ran into her, she was walking the streets with a broom. Said she'd seen a lion prowling about and needed to protect the local children.'

'There was no lion?'

'If there was, I haven't seen it.'

'Where next?'

'Chaplin Row.'

'Lovesick Linda?'

'You remembered.'

One street from Linda's maisonette, I climb into the back with my trike. From my cargo bag I retrieve my new binoculars, along with two lightbulbs. 'Her porch light,' I explain. 'It's been broken for weeks. I don't know if it's a screw bulb or a bayonet, so I brought both.'

'The Angel of Cranner's Ford,' he says. 'Bringing light to all who desire it.'

My nose wrinkles. I still don't like him calling me that – but it's a sign, at least, that he's recovered a little from the horrors of Deevis Farm.

'You want to help a girl out?' I ask. 'First time I tried this, I couldn't reach the fitting. I've been debating a stepladder.'

'Possibly unwise, considering the balance thing.'

'One of the reasons I've been delaying it.'

Linda's maisonette is towards the middle of the row. From street level we can't see into her first-floor living room – not unless we walk south, where the elevation is higher. The porch light is recessed into a wood-panelled ceiling. Louis unscrews the dead bulb and shows me the fitting. I hand him the correct replacement. When he rotates it into place, light floods the porch. We retreat before anyone spots us. Then I lead Louis back up the hill.

It's been a while since I saw Linda. I want to check she's OK. At the top of the street we arrive at a kids' playground enclosed by chain link. The gate isn't locked, so we go inside. I sit on a swing and train my binoculars on the living room.

There's Linda, curled on the sofa with her laptop. She's wearing thigh-length pyjamas, candy-striped in turquoise and white. They make her look even more vulnerable than usual. I feel like I'm watching a young girl trying to imitate a woman living alone – and not quite pulling it off.

'Tell me about Linda.'

'Late thirties,' I say. 'Recently divorced. She spends seven nights a week in that room, except the odd occasion she has a date. She's desperate to find love – I'll bet you anything she's on a dating site right now – but Linda's one of those women who always attracts idiots and always gets hurt.'

'Edward Gropey-Hands?'

'Not yet. But that's exactly the kind of guy I mean.'

'Can I borrow those?'

I hand him the binoculars. While Louis watches Linda, I watch Louis. It's easier when his attention is diverted. Those green eyes don't miss much. I worry they'll see the parts of me I prefer to keep hidden.

'She looks sad,' he says, after a while.

'Yes.'

'This phobia of yours. Is it connected?'

I grip the chains of my swing. 'Connected?'

'To the balance thing,' he replies. 'The fainting. And the heterochromia.'

'You can have heterochromia from birth.'

'And sometimes an external event triggers it.' He lowers the binoculars and studies me. 'I looked it up. I hope you don't think that's a betrayal.'

'No,' I tell him, and ask myself if I'm being honest.

'Five years ago, you'd have been, what?'

'Eighteen.'

'Did something happen back then, to cause all this?'

'Quite a lot happened when I was eighteen. But I'm not . . .'

Not the person I was.

I lift my gaze skywards and watch the flashing lights of a plane passing high overhead.

'Tonight, before we met up,' Louis says. 'Where were you? What were you doing?'

I grip the chains even harder. 'Why are you asking?'

He shrugs. 'I just want to make sure I'm getting the full Mercy Lake story. Not some kind of sanitized version.'

I think of my visit to Arcadia Heights, earlier this evening: the new security cameras; Simon Rafferty telling Nadia to get out of the pool; the branch snapping behind me, startling something in the undergrowth.

'What were *you* doing, earlier?' I ask. 'Just before you phoned me?'

'I was at the campsite. Wondering if you'd answer if I called. Wondering what tonight would bring if you did – what the universe might ask of us, and how we might respond.'

He pauses. 'Your turn.'

I take a deep breath. Then I blow it out and take another, because honesty is always the best policy, and I'm about to tell him my first lie. 'I was at home.'

Louis stares at me, blinks. The moment feels frozen – as if I've just stepped off a precipice into empty space and gravity hasn't yet caught up.

He holds my gaze a while longer. Then he turns back to the maisonette and says, 'Looks like Lovesick's got company.'

FORTY-FIVE

I recognize the car parked outside Linda's maisonette – and also the man climbing out. I stand up far too fast. The world swings violently.

'Problem?'

'*He* is. Come on. I need to hear this.'

We cross the playground, opening the gate carefully so it doesn't squeal, and hurry down the street. Linda's visitor walks up the path and leans on the bell.

'Hugo Jepp,' I mutter, pulling Louis behind a car parked opposite. 'Aka the Shade.'

'Hugo's the ex-husband?'

'Affirmative.'

I don't tell him that Hugo is also the managing director of Sheergen, the company Simon Rafferty founded. Nor that I last saw him Thursday night, as he sat in the Raffertys' cinema room with the woman in the sequinned dress.

A panel of privacy glass flanks the maisonette's front door. I see a light go on, then Linda's silhouette flowing down the stairs. Through the glass she says something I don't catch.

'Really?' the Shade shouts. 'You're going to make me

stand out here and yell through a closed door? Force all your neighbours to hear our business? I really don't want to do that, Linda. But I will if that's what it takes.'

Silence for a three-count. Then the door opens.

'Hey,' Hugo says, with false geniality. '*There* you are. That wasn't so hard, was it? I was just passing – thought I'd say hello.'

Linda folds her arms tight. 'You said you wouldn't do this any more.'

'Do what?' he asks. 'Check up on you? Make sure you're OK?'

'I'm OK, Hugo. But it's late and I'm tired.'

The Shade puts one hand on the doorframe. 'New nightwear. Or do they call that playwear? Either way, Hugo says woof. Are you alone up there?'

I sense Linda's unease from across the street.

'Please,' she says. 'Don't do this.'

'Let me come up. Just for half an hour.'

'Hugo—'

'Let me come up.'

'Please, I—'

'Are you seeing someone?'

'No.'

'Is anyone up there?'

'No.'

'So what's the problem?'

'It's late, like I said. And I'm tired. And I've got work in the morning, and you—'

'Oh, *fuck* off,' Hugo spits. 'Fuck . . . *off*. You think I'm going to put up with this shit? You think you can *discard* me like this?' He clenches and unclenches his fists. 'OK. If that's how you want to play it. Give me the TV.'

'What?'

'The goddamned *TV*, Linda. I bought it. I *want* it. *Now*.'

'Can we just—'

'Actually,' he says, 'you can give me the microwave, too. You're so grown up – you can buy your own appliances, same as everyone else.'

'Hugo, they're virtually the only things I *kept*. I could have asked for half of everything. My solicitor said I was crazy. She wanted—'

'Fine, in that case give me half the TV. And half the microwave. Up to you which halves you keep, but I'm not leaving without my share. So either you go and get them or I'll come in and help myself.'

'Hugo, that's—'

'I'll count to three, Linda. Then I'll tear this door off its hinges if I have to. Your choice.'

I'm still holding Louis's arm. I feel his biceps flex beneath my fingers. Just as I think he'll shrug me off and intervene, Linda steps back. The Shade follows her inside and slams the door.

I only realize I've been holding my breath when I release it.

'People like Hugo,' Louis says, 'are great at recognizing weakness. But the only thing they understand is strength. I don't think your friend is strong enough to stand up to him.'

My stomach twists. 'I think she was strong enough, once. But the divorce, living alone, the fact she hasn't found love with anyone else – it's all been too much.'

'You want to help her? You think that's what we're being asked to do?'

I look up at Linda's first-floor window, try to imagine

what's happening inside. 'Yes. Maybe. I don't know. I don't know how.'

'Sometimes,' Louis says, 'there's really only one solution to a problem. I love your creativity, Mercy – the ideas you dream up. But birdhouses and porch lights can only take you so far. Sometimes you have to tackle a situation head on.'

In my head I hear whistling like a distant train. These are uncomfortable truths, hard to face. In a blink, I'm back inside that house on Randall Road. Cold Hand Carl is slumped against the kitchen island, clingfilm compressing his bloodied face.

I recall how I felt in the hours afterwards, viewing Cranner's Ford from Old Cobb. My shock, my jubilation. My sense that the rules were ours to decide. I recall what Louis said to me at the time: *I think the universe is revealing its plan. I think we have work to do in this town. I think, together, we'll be unstoppable.*

Lovesick Linda's front door bangs open. Hugo Jepp emerges with a huge TV. A corner scrapes a gash along her wood-panelled porch. He dumps the TV inside his car and returns to the maisonette. Linda stands helpless in the doorway, a mouse frozen with fear. A minute later Hugo carries out a microwave, its plug bouncing along behind him.

I could find her another one, I suppose. Clean it up, leave it on the step. Finding a TV would be harder, but I have money in my account. I could order a replacement. I could even give her mine.

'I think we're being tested, here,' Louis says. 'In fact, I'm convinced of it. But the decision rests with you. If you want us to fix this, just say the word.'

Hugo returns to Linda's front step. He stands before her, breathing hard.

'You got what you wanted,' she says. 'Please, leave me—'

The slap comes out of nowhere. The sound of it ricochets like a gunshot. Linda staggers backwards. She collides with the door, bounces off.

'God*damnit*,' Hugo hisses, shaking the burn from his fingers. 'Why would you make me do that? *Why*, Linda? I didn't want *any* of this. To say that I did is a lie.'

He marches to his car. Linda, nursing her bloodied mouth, stares after him.

'OK,' I say. 'I want us to fix it.'

FORTY-SIX

For a short spell on Wednesday afternoon temperatures in Cranner's Ford touch thirty-eight Celsius – one degree higher than last week's record.

For Konstantin Tapia, consumed with such things, the milestone is particularly satisfying. Thirty-eight is over a hundred on the old Fahrenheit scale. It's still a long way off the temperature at which human flesh will combust, but it's a big, clean number, nonetheless.

He spends the morning shirtless, getting a good roast on his skin. At lunchtime he visits a Mexican restaurant in Cranner's Ford, where he dines on caldo Xóchitl soup, corn tacos stuffed with beef, and marinated lamb steamed inside banana leaves. He requests a side bowl of El Yucateco green sauce, the hottest on the menu. When the waiter spots his disappointment at its trifling heat, he brings over a chilli-based condiment served in a hand-grenade-shaped bottle. For the rest of the meal, Tapia loses himself in agony and ecstasy – and leaves a huge tip, despite his desire to be forgotten.

Outside, he checks his tracking app. The campervan is still at the Seven Crosses campsite, where it's been for the last four hours. Tapia visited yesterday and saw it parked on a gravelled pitch. He ordered a beer from the onsite eatery and sat outside in blazing sunlight for two hours, but the vehicle's owner never appeared.

Tapia knew that Keira Greenaway would be holed up in her basement flat, where she'd doubtless remain until sunset. After four days of watching her, he's steadily learned her routines. It seems that what he read in the news reports is true: the brain injury she suffered five and a half years ago triggered a lasting phobia of daylight. When he looks up at the sun and feels its unrelenting heat, he can barely imagine the horror of her torment. No one, regardless of past misdemeanours, deserves that. If, in some unguessable future, Tapia *does* set her alight, he knows he'll bring her peace.

The coffee shop Nadia proposes for their meeting is little more than a service hatch above a glass chiller, open to the street. He waits for her on one of the pavement stools, burning his tongue on unsweetened Americano. On the countertop before him lies his copy of *National Geographic*.

Nadia appears, taking the adjacent seat. He wonders if she chose the apple-green trouser suit because of how much of her skin it covers. He wonders if she chose the coffee place because he couldn't burn her on the street. Her nails are green, he notices. Maybe *that's* the reason for the suit.

'Last night you had a visitor,' he says.

Nadia stiffens, meets his eye. For a while, she's silent. 'Was it her?'

He nods. 'A section of your boundary wall is damaged. That's how she got in. She didn't stay long. Also, you should know she's found herself a buddy.'

'There were two of them?'

'Not exactly. Greenaway arrived on her own. He showed up soon after, followed her inside. I don't think she knew he was there.'

'Who is he?'

Tapia shrugs. He turns a page of his *National Geographic*, revealing an image that startles him. The photograph, taken at night, is of Mount Etna. The volcano's silhouette is revealed from the surrounding darkness only by the bright magma rolling down its slopes. He sees rivers of molten rock. Fire and smoke. A moment both of creation and destruction. It's stunning. Perfect.

'Tell me about him,' Nadia says.

'Early thirties. Dark hair, good teeth. I imagine you'd find him pleasant to look at. He's staying at a campsite just outside town.'

'You have a photo?'

'No.'

'Could you get me one?'

Tapia eyes her trouser suit. When he thinks of the smooth flesh hiding beneath it, his fingers twitch. 'I could.'

Nadia shifts on her stool, crosses her legs. 'I don't care what it costs, Konstantin.'

His eyes narrow. 'This was never a financial relationship.'

'I wouldn't insult you by suggesting it was. You know what I'm talking about – gifts offered freely. Will you do it?'

'Of course.'

Nadia nods, leans forward, examines him more closely. 'Your scalp is starting to burn. You might want to invest in some Piz Buin. Or a hat.'

'Thank you for the advice.'

FORTY-SEVEN

Wednesday's relentless heat continues well into the evening. Overhead, the stars are of a clarity I've rarely seen. We're driving through Old Town. On the radio, Creedence Clearwater Revival are singing about a bad moon rising.

Since Louis picked me up, he's been pretty quiet. Hopefully, he isn't mulling over more questions. I'm starting to regret the lie I told him last night, about being at home just before we met, rather than at Arcadia Heights. I have a horrible sense he knows the truth – although if he did, that would indicate something even more disconcerting than the exposure of my dishonesty: that he'd been watching me without my knowledge.

Again, I recall what happened yesterday evening: Nadia Rafferty rising from the pool; the brief commotion in the undergrowth; Simon Rafferty staring directly at my hiding place. As if he *knew*.

'Are you ready for this?' Louis asks.

Aware of our destination, I glance over, smile at him, nod. My Doc Martens are tightly laced and double-knotted. In one pocket is my bear spray. In the other, my phone.

'It won't be pretty,' he continues. 'But I'm hoping it'll be effective.'

'If it works . . .'

'You don't have to watch. In fact, I'd rather you didn't. There's another task, if you'll agree to it. Just as important in the scheme of things. Particularly for what comes afterwards.'

Ten minutes later we're past Old Town and driving along country roads. No streetlights, no other vehicles. When we reach Mullpenny Lane, Louis slows and eases the campervan into a ditch beside the hedgerow. He switches off the engine, then the headlights. 'Remember – if something goes wrong . . .' he begins.

'I start walking and I don't call you until I'm out of there.'

'If something *feels* wrong, anything at all . . .'

'Start walking, don't call until I'm out of there.'

'Kiss?'

I lean forward. Our lips touch.

'OK, Night Eyes. Let's do this.'

FORTY-EIGHT

Marcie Lockheart doesn't scare easily.

She's lived in this old farmhouse long enough to know that it wakes at night. Wooden beams, swollen by summer sun, creak as they contract. Pipes tap and knock. Sometimes, the ghosts of former residents walk the rooms – and choose to leave evidence of their visits. Downstairs, she'll discover the shards of a vase knocked over while she slept; or a hat flicked from its hook. Weird, but not frightening. Not if those are their best moves.

Marcie blinks in the darkness, wondering why she woke. She doesn't need to pee. The house, right now, is silent.

Her mouth feels dry, gummed up – legacy of last night's booze. When she reaches for Patrick, her hand finds cool sheets. Did she leave him downstairs when she came to bed? Her memory of how their evening ended is fuzzy.

Marcie rolls over. She caterpillars her hand across her side table, hunting in vain for glasses and phone. Either she didn't bring them to bed or the ghosts have been playing tricks again. Patrick has an old-fashioned clock radio on his side of the bed, but from this angle Marcie can't see the glowing red numerals.

She hears something shift, in the furthest corner of the room.

Not a sound of settling, that. Nor does she think it was a mouse scratching around inside the walls. Something about the bedroom doesn't feel right.

Marcie sits up straight. Around her the air seems heavy, as if it contains a presence. Maybe this isn't the ghost of a past resident. Maybe it's a ghost from Marcie's past. One of her family, perhaps. Her mother.

'Get the fuck away from me, you dirty old bitch,' she hisses. She didn't put the old woman in the ground only to see her rise up. But the presence doesn't announce itself, and Marcie doesn't *really* believe her cancerous old mother could come back. What the hell was in that small-batch gin to spook her like this?

Outside, a fox shrieks.

She slides her legs out of bed. Patrick keeps a baseball bat in the wardrobe – protection against any gypsies who might break in before he can reach the gun cupboard downstairs. There's also a ten-inch hunting knife.

Marcie searches her side table again, this time for her lamp base. Squinting to protect her eyes, she snaps the switch. Nothing.

She thinks of Patrick's clock radio – the red numerals now dark. Her heart rate kicks up a notch. More than just a blown bulb, then.

Is that where he's gone? To check a fuse? If he'd suspected a break-in, he'd have woken her. She thinks of all the cash hidden around the house – and how often she's warned Patrick against complacency. Just because someone's always home, and the gun cupboard is fully stocked, that doesn't make them safe. Especially when the guns are downstairs and Marcie is up here and Patrick has pulled a disappearing trick.

She stands, breathes deep – thinks, for just a moment, that she detects a man's cologne. When she moves towards the wardrobe, the floorboards protest with a creak. Why is it so damned dark?

Another shuffling step and Marcie touches the wardrobe. She opens the door and reaches past Patrick's clothes. As her fingers close around the baseball bat, a fist drives into one of her kidneys.

The pain is stunning. She can't even cry out before a hand grabs her by the hair and swings her towards the bed. Her shins crack against the wooden frame and then she's on her front – and a *monster* is astride her back.

Marcie puffs and blows. She tries to fill her lungs through a mouthful of rucked bedsheets. When she manages to suck in a breath, she spits out one word: *'Fucker.'*

Her temerity is rewarded with further violence: another fist, this one into the back of her neck. It's a devastating blow, hard enough to do serious damage. She squeals out the breath she just won, feels her hands being duct-taped behind her back.

When the pressure on her face recedes, Marcie takes her chance. She lifts her chin, fills her lungs. Before she can scream, a strip of duct tape seals her mouth.

The tape confuses her, brings down the shutters on her thoughts. A hand grabs her hair again, a solid fistful. It yanks back her head, exposing her throat, straining the tendons to breaking. One slash and her ruptured arteries will hose the mattress with blood.

But that, it seems, is not her assailant's plan. Instead, the duct tape winds three times around her skull, blocking her mouth and nose. Now, Marcie *really* can't breathe. She bucks, kicks, writhes beneath her attacker's weight. Abruptly, the downward pressure vanishes. She's alone on the bed, rapidly asphyxiating, her eyes swelling in their sockets.

'You can keep struggling,' says a man's voice, close to her ear. 'Use up the last of your air. Or you can roll on to your back and lie still – be a *good* girl. Maybe then I'll let you breathe.'

In thirty-seven years, Marcie hasn't submitted to anyone. But never has she been so close to death. That voice is chillingly calm. Mocking, even.

She rolls over, hands mashed beneath her spine. Marshalling all her willpower, fighting every instinct to struggle against her bonds, Marcie forces a stillness into her limbs, adopts a calmness she doesn't feel, lies limp and tries to control the pressure building in her chest.

'Careful, now,' says the voice. 'I'd hate to slice off your nose.'

Marcie makes fists, begins to shake. She hears two pops and suddenly she's snorting like a walrus, drawing in air through twin punctures in the tape.

Able to breathe again, her focus switches to a new horror. She's wearing nothing but a T-shirt. During her struggles it's ridden up around her waist. She doesn't know what this freak wants, but if it's *that* . . .

A hand grabs her right ankle, winds tape around it. If he forces her legs apart, tethers them to different bedposts, she'll be helpless.

Marcie's terror ignites into fury. She twists her hips,

kicks out her legs, but her assailant is stronger. He catches her left foot. It takes her a moment to realize that he's taping her legs *together*, not apart.

That changes things – means the assault she was dreading isn't his plan. But if not that, what? Moments later, a pillowcase goes over her head.

'I'm treating you like an animal,' the man whispers. 'Is that what you're thinking?' He twists the pillowcase, raising her head closer to his lips. 'But this is nothing to how you treat *them*, is it, *Marcie*?'

In an instant, she realizes what this is about. Not gypsies stealing farm equipment. Not burglars raiding their cash.

This is a reprisal. This is about Patrick's golden goose, *their* golden goose. It's about the windowless shed on their land that pumps out a steady stream of riches.

Maybe the guy's a PETA fanatic. Maybe he's a lone wolf. Either way, her situation is far worse than she first feared.

Abruptly, the stranger releases the pillowcase. She hears him leave the room and go down the stairs. The back door slams.

Silence.

Marcie flips on to her front. Getting her knees beneath her, she drags her head back and forth across the mattress until the pillowcase comes off her head. Working her hips and shoulders in tandem, she slides off the bed to her knees.

Outside, a diesel engine starts up. Marcie pauses, cocks her head. That's their excavator. She hears it trundle across the yard, tracks squealing.

Dropping to her belly, trying not to panic, Marcie worms across the floor. A short distance from the farmhouse, the excavator begins to dig.

FORTY-NINE

I hear the dogs the moment I crest the rise. As I pick my way down the slope, their baying climbs in pitch. I wonder if they've sensed my presence.

Deevis Farm was part of tonight's agenda from the moment Louis picked me up. We just had to wait until it was late enough to visit.

As I pull open the shed door, the stink of putrefaction rolls out, hot and ripe. Bile rises in my throat. Something died in here, recently – and then bloated up. My torch picks out familiar horrors: dogs scrabbling over each other to reach the light; pregnant bitches and nursing mothers turning away from it. Everywhere, clinging excrement.

One element of our Deevis Farm intervention hinged on whether or not this shed – and its inhabitants – still existed. My task was to confirm it either way.

In a corner I see three sacks of dry food. Working quickly, I distribute the contents. Sweat runs down my forehead and into my eyes. I should have left already, but I can't ignore the suffering. I feel like opening all the cages and letting the puppies escape. Louis's suggestion is far better.

As I'm leaving the shed, a singularly pathetic sound cuts through the darkness. I point my torch at the source and illuminate a pair of eyes steeped in misery. The puppy – I can't even tell its breed – is the only living creature in a cage of lumpen forms. When I push my fingers through the bars, it quivers but doesn't retreat.

I can't supress a sob. Next thing I know, I'm fumbling with the latch. I lift out the puppy, appalled at its meagre weight, incredulous that it was strong enough to attract my attention. 'OK, little guy,' I mutter, blinking away tears. 'OK.'

He's a boy. Sole survivor of what might be six or seven siblings. I doubt he'll last much longer. Taking him with me is futile, sentimental. But he deserves a chance, however small.

When the other dogs realize I'm leaving, their baying intensifies. Again, I resist the temptation to unlock their cages. *Help is coming*, I promise them. *Help is coming.*

Maybe it's the fresh air after the shed's cloying stink. Maybe it's my emotions or the frayed connections inside my head. But as I step outside, the night fractures.

Two white moons hang in the sky above the rise, forming a pair of frowning eyes. The stars are a silver blizzard. I push through the storm, unsteady on my feet.

Little Guy's heart flutters against my fingers. A minute ago our paths hadn't crossed. Now they feel inextricably linked.

The blizzard intensifies. I clench my teeth, set my shoulders, stumble up the slope. 'Sometimes,' I tell the pup, 'life is kind of confusing. Kind of scary, too. But if you keep pushing forward, it mostly works out OK.'

Little Guy squirms in my grip. I pause as a wave of dizziness hits.

Beyond the rise, I hear the clank of something mechanical. My nose fills with competing scents: wet straw, cinnamon, burnt coffee. The world shrinks to a round dot inside a black tunnel. Clenching my teeth, I force it to expand. This is the worst attack I've had in months. Maybe the worst in years.

At last, I crest the rise. And my breath goes completely.

A short distance from the farmhouse, a collection of cars and trucks has formed a shallow semicircle around a huge pit dug into the earth. Their headlights are aimed at its heart. It seems like there are a lot, until I remember to divide them by two. Near the pit, a yellow beast with two necks takes twin bites from the earth.

Gradually, the two realities slide together, forming a single image. As I watch, the yellow beast's neck straightens. Its maw, filled with soil, hangs directly over the pit.

When I realize what lies beneath it, I can't stay upright. As I crash to my knees, and then to my side, my overriding thought is of Little Guy – how I mustn't crush him as I fall.

And then the curtain drops.

FIFTY

Lying on her back, hands digging into her spine, Marcie Lockheart lifts her feet to the edge of her bedroom door. Bending and unbending her knees, she saws her bound ankles against the latch. It's hard going. The door wobbles; the latch pops in and out. Marcie's thighs burn with the effort of her contortions. But slowly, painfully, she makes progress.

Outside, the excavator falls silent. Earlier, she heard cars starting and recognized the engines: her Volvo; Patrick's Discovery; Janek's Qashqai; even the two farm pick-ups. Initially, she figured they were being stolen, but each was driven only a short distance before stopping.

Marcie's thigh muscles are spent. She takes a breather, waits for the burn to subside. Then she lifts her feet and resumes her sawing. She feels the fibres of the duct tape beginning to sever. She's not free yet, but it's working.

Her assailant didn't take the baseball bat hidden in the wardrobe. He didn't find the hunting knife. If she frees herself before he returns, she'll have a surprise waiting.

With a sound like ripping meat, the tape's last fibres

split apart. Marcie takes two full breaths. Then she scrabbles to her knees. She gets one foot beneath her, two.

Downstairs, she hears movement – a door banging open. Adrenalin fizzes through her arteries. Turning around, she saws her bound wrists against the latch. It's easier standing up. She can brace the door with her ankles.

Torchlight flickers up the stairs. Marcie saws faster. She gouges her wrist against sharp metal. Feels the wound but not the pain.

Footsteps, breathing, white light in her eyes. Then a hand, yanking her by the hair. 'Good,' says the voice. 'You freed your legs. That saves me a task.' The pillowcase drops back over her head. 'Let's go.'

He leads her out of the bedroom, down the stairs. Beneath Marcie's feet, the hall's bare floorboards surrender to kitchen lino. Moments later, she's outside. Concrete gives way to sun-cracked earth. Through the pillowcase she smells freshly turned soil. She recalls the excavator she heard earlier. Lights are shining, somewhere close.

The ground changes. She's climbing a slope that didn't exist before tonight. Next, she's slip-sliding down the other side. Clay oozes between her toes, sticks to her soles. There's so much adrenalin in her system it feels like her chest might burst.

'Stop,' says the voice, behind her. 'Don't move until I tell you.'

Earlier, Marcie's instincts told her to fight. Now, they're screaming at her to run. But she's blind, bound and barefoot. There's zero chance of escape.

A hand rips away the pillowcase. White light dazzles her. Marcie squints, tilts her head, tries to decant meaning from madness.

She's standing at the bottom of a huge pit dug by the excavator's bucket. Five vehicles are parked with their noses facing down the slope, headlights switched to full beam.

It's a difficult sight to process. Beside her, Marcie sees something even more confusing: the red-painted cage that usually sits outside their feed shed – lockable storage for the farm's propane cylinders. Inside, instead of propane, she sees her husband.

Patrick's lying on his back, mouth taped and hands bound. He's wearing jeans, nothing else. His immense belly gives him the appearance of a pregnant toad.

Patrick's eyes are terror-stricken, wider and whiter than she's ever seen them. Despite suffering no obvious injury, he's writhing in agony. Considering him, Marcie feels disgust. She's never needed a man to protect her, but she damned well expects them to try; Patrick looks like he'd rather cower in her shadow than fight.

Beside him lies Janek, their Polish farmworker, naked save for his ludicrously tight briefs. Janek is bound, too – and clearly in just as much pain – but at least he has the decency to look furious about it. The murder in his eyes makes Marcie glad she fucked him. He might be as dumb as half a pig, but his balls are ten times larger than her husband's.

Abruptly, their assailant appears in front of her. She blinks, tries to pick out his features, but the headlights have made him a silhouette.

Not everything is obscured. Marcie sees she was wrong, earlier, about the baseball bat. Because he's holding it.

Oh *fuck*.

When she peers back inside the propane cage, she

notices something she missed earlier: Janek's kneecaps have ballooned to twice their normal size. Patrick's knees, beneath his jeans, look similarly deformed.

Suddenly, it's hard to fill her lungs. She snorts air through the punctured duct tape, wonders how much worse suffocation might be than whatever else is coming.

If she could *speak* to the guy, reason with him, she knows she could talk her way out of this. Trouble is, with her mouth taped shut, she can't negotiate.

Surely he won't kneecap *her* over a shed full of damned dogs. Patrick and Janek, maybe – but not her.

'Far more cash in that house than brains to hide it,' the stranger says. 'Seriously. The toilet cistern? The freezer? I found seven grand taped behind the piano.'

Marcie bristles despite her situation. The seven grand was hers – fresh-start money, should she ever need to get away. She feels the burn of Patrick's stare, ignores it.

'I had a dog when I was a kid,' the guy says. He steps to the side and for the first time she sees him clearly. Younger than her. Black hair, green eyes, white teeth. His expression is mild – and yet somehow utterly merciless. 'That is, until someone killed it.'

Marcie hums frantically behind the tape.

'Oh, you want to speak?'

'Mmm.' She nods. '*Mmm!*'

'OK,' he says. 'Let me just break one of them, and then you're free to talk. Deal?'

Marcie squeals, furiously shaking her head. And then the guy swings the bat and shatters her right kneecap.

The pain is a nail bomb exploding inside her flesh. The sky rotates and she goes down hard. Her breath bursts so forcibly from her mouth that her taped lips tear open.

The agony keeps climbing – too much to take. Marcie's back arches. Her skull drums against clay. There's blood in her mouth and fire in her splintered knee. A roaring inferno.

'Wow,' the man says. 'I mean, that looks bad. Not as bad as a cage full of shit and death, but within sight, certainly. How much does a lab retriever cost these days, out of interest? That's what I had. How much do you make off a full litter? The ones that live?'

Marcie grunts like she's in labour. She straightens her good leg, levers herself backwards. It triggers fresh agonies, but anything to get away from him.

'Not going to answer? In that case here's another question, because I've always wondered: when someone breaks your kneecaps, which one hurts more? The first? Or the second?'

He lifts the bat. Marcie closes her eyes. She hears a crack like a gunshot – the sound of her left knee splitting. The pain is a tsunami, sweeping her up. Her brain scrabbles to comprehend its enormity. Her teeth grind together. She's going to vomit – and then, because of the duct tape, she'll drown. Perhaps it's better that she does. Dying can't be worse than this.

The guy grabs her by the hair and tows her across the pit. She's blind with agony, now. Consumed by it. She feels the metal lattice of the cage floor against her back, hears the door clang shut, the snick of a lock.

'Well,' he says. 'The jailors become the jailed. If this isn't the universe pushing back, I don't know what is. What's it like – being on the inside, looking out? Does it give you a new perspective?'

Marcie blinks until her eyes are clear. Through the bars

she sees him, baseball bat slung over his shoulder – a demon-black shape in the headlights.

'Hey,' he continues. 'Here's an idea. Maybe you should sleep outside tonight, the three of you. What do you think?' He pauses, waits for an answer he knows isn't coming, then shakes his head. 'But it's not as toasty-warm as that shed of yours, is it? Maybe I should tuck you in.'

He turns his back and climbs out of the pit. Marcie watches him walk around the perimeter. He reaches the excavator and jumps into the cab. When the diesel engine fires up, her insides boil like they've been microwaved.

The excavator's arm swings down. Its bucket takes a huge bite of clay piled up from the pit. With a hiss of pneumatics, it angles up, swings directly overhead.

Maybe I should tuck you in.

When Patrick and Janek start screaming beneath their tape, Marcie joins them.

FIFTY-ONE

The world comes crashing back; a sound like air rushing into a vacuum; a sensation like popping candy sprinkled on my brain.

Fireflies dance before my eyes. Only when I clench my fists and concentrate hard do they resolve into streetlights, headlights, illuminated road signs flashing past. Music is playing: 'Time Is On My Side' by the Rolling Stones, a track I've always liked.

'There you are,' Louis says, beside me. 'Where'd you go?'

I sit up in the campervan's passenger seat, rub my eyes. 'The Emerald City? I don't know. Was I . . . Did I—'

'You want some water?'

'No.' I shake my head. 'Thanks.'

'Gum?'

'Louis, what happened back there? How'd I—'

'You don't remember?'

What *do* I remember?

'I remember two moons.' I hiccup, glance at Louis, wrinkle my nose at my nonsense. It's been a weird night, but that's no excuse. I sound like an apprentice witch doctor.

Beneath the two moons I recall a pit dug into the earth, a yellow beast with two necks, and, in my arms—

Violently, I lurch forward. The seatbelt cuts across my chest. 'We've got to go back.'

'We can't.'

'But Little Guy . . .'

'Little who?'

'Oh, no.' I raise my hands, clutch my head. 'I was taking him *out* of there. He was my responsibility. If he dies, it'll be my fault.'

Louis gestures behind him. 'You mean *that* little guy?'

I twist in my seat. And there he is, curled on a towel and looking even more pathetic than earlier: two round eyes in a ball of miserable fur.

I moan with relief, grateful to Louis, to the universe, to anyone else I can credit. Reaching around, I lift Little Guy on to my lap.

'It's OK,' I tell him, although it's really not. His fur reeks. He looks incredibly unwell. To Louis, I say, 'We need to get him some food. Milk, I guess. Although I don't know what kind.' I pull out my iPhone and start searching. 'There's a recipe here for orphan formula,' I say. 'Goat's milk, egg yolk, full-fat yoghurt, corn syrup or something similar. We can get a lot of that from the Texaco, but I don't know where we'll find a bottle.'

'There's a twenty-four-hour supermarket outside town,' Louis says. 'We can grab it all there.'

I nod, worried we won't make it in time, worried about a whole mountain of different things. When I think of the pit I saw at the farm, and those vehicles with their headlights shining down, my anxiety spikes.

'Louis?'

He glances over.

'Deevis Farm. What did I miss?'

'We took care of it.'

'We did?'

'They won't do it again.'

'In that shed – there was so much death. Little Guy was the only one alive from his litter.'

Louis takes his hand off the steering wheel. He strokes the pup with one finger.

'Did you make the call?' I ask.

'Just before you woke.'

On the music player, Mick Jagger launches into a new song: 'Sympathy For The Devil'. Louis turns it up, puts his foot down. Eleanor ferries us across town. We see few other vehicles on the road, save for two police cars that pass us with lights flashing.

At the all-night supermarket, Louis shops while I stay with Little Guy. How I'm going to look after a puppy, I have no clue. The more I read, the more freaked out I get.

Louis returns with everything on my list. We leave the supermarket and head north towards Old Cobb. At the summit, I clamber into the back and mix the orphan formula.

Little Guy doesn't take much. Still, some is better than none. Afterwards, we heat a kettle. A saucepan serves as a bath. We change the water four times before something recognizably puppy-like emerges. I dry Little Guy's fur and wrap him in one of Louis's shirts.

It's late. Or early. I'm not sure which. I do know I need to get home. Already, I can sense the sun climbing towards the horizon. I shudder, turn to Louis – and find him watching me from the driver's seat.

'You're getting twitchy,' he says.

'I need to go home.'

'Stay, both of you. In the van with me. We can close the curtains, block out the dawn.'

'I can't. I know it's crazy, but it's not enough. I've got to get inside. Blackout blinds, the works. Sorry. Really, I am.'

He nods. Our eyes remain locked.

'We could do it the other way,' I suggest. 'You could come home with us. With Little Guy and me, I mean. That is, if you wanted to.'

Louis's throat bobs as he swallows. Mine does the same. Before I can change my mind, I blurt out my address.

FIFTY-TWO

Weird, how bringing another human into my flat makes me see it as if for the first time. And Holy Guacamole, what a freaky geek I must seem.

Louis makes no comment as I put up blackout panels, pull down blinds, arrange the wall hangings. His eyes move over my workbench, my rolled-up yoga mat, my Twilight Sparkle skate helmet. He checks out my hydroponics tent filled with plants, my red dress on a hanger, my angel wings strapped to a dressmaker's mannequin. Going to my bookcase, he tilts his head and reads the titles. Fortunately, his eyes roll past my scrapbook without slowing.

Never did I expect anyone to see inside this flat. Never did I intend to share it. When Louis approaches my map of Cranner's Ford and checks out the flags, I can't breathe. Many of the locations we've already visited, but a few crucial ones remain. Arcadia Heights and Ollie Rafferty's school are the two I'm most concerned he'll see.

'Hey,' Louis says. 'This one has my name on it.'

'The Texaco,' I explain, grateful for the distraction, if not the cringe. 'The night we met.'

His eyes meet mine. He grins. Then he goes to the fireplace, lifts my dad's urn, removes the lid and peers inside.

I'm so stunned that I can't move. I didn't have time to warn him and now it's too late.

The colour drains from Louis's face – a clear indication that he's just figured out what he's holding. 'I'm sorry,' he mutters, replacing the lid and returning the urn to its spot. 'Wow, Mercy. I don't . . . I'm so sorry. What am I doing?'

My stomach flops. 'It's fine,' I say. 'Really. You couldn't have known. Most people don't keep their parents on a shelf.' Appalled, I slap my hand over my mouth. Why did I just say *that*?

Louis's gaze moves from my dad's urn to my mum's. He takes a faltering step back. Then he sits down hard on the sofa, looking as if he might faint. 'I'm not good with death.'

Talk about a mood killer. But rather than changing the subject, I hear myself trying to explain. 'They always wanted their ashes scattered on the ocean. I haven't been able to do that, and I guess . . . I've kind of got used to having them both here.'

It's super-awkward. Extinction-event-level awkward. I make a nest of cushions for Little Guy. Then I stand by the door, rubbing my hands like a supervillain. 'I know,' I say. 'I'll put on some music.'

Louis looks up at me. 'OK.'

'I mean, shall I? Would you like that?'

Erk. What am I doing? It feels like there's a tiny clown inside my head, furiously writing bad lines – except the tiny clown is me.

Louis nods. 'Sure.'

'Right. I will, then.'

I go to my smart speaker – and I'm so embarrassed to

converse in front of Louis with what's essentially a robot that I lower my voice and whisper, and of course it misunderstands me and starts reeling off facts about the Pyramids, and then I get flustered and shout at it to stop.

'How about a drink first?'

'Whisky would be good,' Louis says. 'Maybe with some ice.'

I feel myself starting to sweat. 'Sorry. I don't have any.'

'Just neat, then.'

'No, I meant, "Sorry, I don't have any whisky."'

'You have ice?'

'No. Actually, I have neither whisky nor ice.'

'Beer?'

'I can . . . I have Dr Pepper.' I swallow. 'Or Lucozade. Or I have milk, if you want milk. Semi-skimmed milk. I'll probably have Dr Pepper, myself. I don't really drink alcohol. That stuff we had on Pincher's Mount was the first I'd drunk in *years*, which is why I don't have any in the flat, generally, although to be quite honest I could probably do with a shot of something right now, stop me babbling, maybe even a tranquillizer, one of those they use to bring down eleph—'

'I'll have milk, please,' Louis says. 'Cold, no ice, just a glass. Look – Mercy. I know this is weird for you. I know it's stressful. If you want me to go, just say. It won't change anything. This is your home.'

I'm breathless. Why am I breathless? I flee to the kitchen, where I lean against the fridge and pray that the tiny clown has run out of ink. Once I've recovered, I deliver Louis his milk. Then I make up some formula for Little Guy. I keep coaxing him with it long after I know he's full because I'm so scared of what will come next. Eventually, though, I can stall no more. Louis has finished his milk. I've spluttered my way through my Dr Pepper.

It feels, now, like every step of this journey has been leading us to this moment. From the Texaco to Pincher's Mount. To places all over Cranner's Ford. To my living room's tropical beach, to my bedroom's forest glade, to Louis and me and no one else.

That first night, sensing danger, I took my wheel and ran. Multiple times since, I've tried to repeat the feat. But it's hard to turn down companionship when you have none. A life lived in solitude is bleak, even when you're accomplished at pretending it isn't.

We sit on my bed, then lie on it. Artificial birdsong fills the artificial trees of my artificial world. Beneath those artificial boughs I find a new experience, new meaning. And, for a time, solace.

But when I close my eyes, I sleep.

And when I sleep, I dream of bloodshed.

FIFTY-THREE

A blade of sunlight pierces the lake-house window and cuts the living room in half. Dust motes dance within it, stirred by solar energy into brief and glorious life.

Beside the sofa, the red baby coos and claps.

The blade of sunlight is a barrier separating us. I imagine it vaporizing my flesh as I step through, my clean white skeleton collapsing in a heap of bones on the other side. But that's a terror for future years. Here, in this moment, I have no phobia of the sun.

Time slows, then stops. Before me, the dust mites suspend their dance. Ollie Rafferty sits frozen, his hands and feet bloodied, his eyes fixed on mine. In them I read an accusation: *Look at what you did. Look at what you took.*

My gaze moves to Phoebe Rafferty, lying beside him. They share the same eyes, those two. Antique mahogany or dark honey.

Phoebe died in a frenzied crosshatch of blood – proof to anyone who discovers this scene how stubbornly she held on to life, how grudgingly she relinquished her grip.

Averting my gaze, I look around. I need a moment's solace – a respite from blame and blood.

The room is beautifully appointed. They've been used to luxury for a while. Around the inglenook fireplace stands a couple of greeting cards.

To my darling wife, on our anniversary.

You're my favourite husband so far!

There's no way back from this. And probably no way forward. But I can't remain frozen. I have to act.

Dropping to my knees, I search through Phoebe's jeans. I hear myself muttering – it sounds almost like a prayer. But my words aren't directed to any God. Because no right-minded deity would intrude here.

To my darling wife, on our anniversary.

I recall his lips on mine. His hands on my shoulders. To him, I was just meat. A quick and squalid distraction.

To my darling wife.

Phoebe's pockets are empty. I climb to my feet and cross the room.

When I step through that curtain of golden dust, it doesn't strip away my flesh. I pass the red baby and enter the kitchen. Here, blood streaks the work surfaces. It decorates the cabinets. Not Phoebe's, this time, but his.

From here, I see only legs and feet. The central kitchen island hides the rest. One foot is bare. The other wears a blood-stained espadrille. I bought him those for his birthday. He said they were the comfiest things ever.

I start to shake. Somehow, I summoned the courage to search Phoebe. But I can't go near *him* – even though I should probably confirm he's dead.

On the nearest worktop, a Jimmy Choo handbag lies

beside a baby monitor and two bunches of keys. The handbag is Phoebe's, unfathomably expensive. I know because I looked it up online. As I move towards it, blood crackles like gum beneath my Converse All Stars. Lights flicker on the baby monitor. Static issues from its speaker. Ghost warbles.

The return of sound and movement is a signal. Time, no longer frozen, spools forward. I grab Phoebe's handbag, yank it open. Purse, cosmetics, hairbrush, portable charger, mobile phone. No bubble-gum wrappers. No lint. No screwed-up vouchers or fast-food receipts. None of the gross compost that collects in my own cheapo bags.

I pull out the phone, try to concentrate. My head's a mess. I can see, hear, react – but I'm finding it difficult to think.

In my hand, the phone wakes. When I see the screensaver, my stomach clutches. Because it's a family shot – Simon and Phoebe cradling Ollie. I swipe away the image, bring up the keypad.

Outside, summer sun beats down with a savagery almost unimaginable. Hard to fathom why the forest doesn't combust, why the pine needles don't ignite into flame. On the shore of the lake I see the prow of my boat, just visible past Phoebe's Mercedes. I'd tried to keep my approach hidden. It looks like I mostly succeeded.

With my palm I strike my forehead, kickstarting my brain into action. It works, just about. I dial a number, stare at the baby monitor, wait for the call to connect.

A man's voice, then: *'Qual è la sua emergenza?'*

FIFTY-FOUR

Thursday morning, Nadia's in the kitchen making a smoothie when the front gate's intercom starts buzzing. Whoever's outside holds their finger on the button far longer than necessary.

She goes to the newly upgraded security panel and checks the screen. When she sees Hugo Jepp's face, she scowls and activates the mic. 'What is it?'

'Let me in.'

Nadia bristles. 'Try again.'

'OK, let me the fuck in.'

'Last chance, Hugo.'

Simon sweeps into the kitchen. He reaches past her and hits the button for the gate. 'No games,' he says. 'Not today.'

Onscreen, the front gate swings open. One of Simon's office phones starts ringing. Moments later, another one joins it. 'Don't answer them,' he tells her. 'And don't speak to anyone.'

'Has something happened?'

'Understatement.'

'Want to share?'

'You remember that pair of pricks we hosted at the awards night? It seems they've been running a side hustle.'

'The Lockhearts?' she asks, but Simon's already turned his back. Nadia follows him to the entrance hall, past the bag packed for his Salerno trip, and watches him open the front door.

Hugo Jepp glares at her as he steps inside the house.

'In every one of those press images,' Simon tells him, 'there's a Sheergen turbine in the background. The fact that we only leased them makes no difference. That place *looks* like a Sheergen site.'

'I'm flying out to Italy in a few hours. We need to draft a statement, have the reputation management guys OK it before release. And we should start legal action against those idiots, even though it won't stick.'

'If someone hadn't already kneecapped them,' Hugo says, 'I'd be at the hospital doing it myself. Put me in a room for ten minutes with Marcie Lockheart and I guarantee she'll never have babies.' He follows Simon into the office and shuts the door.

Nadia stares, revolted by Hugo's words, half imagining they were a taunt, a coded threat. That can't be true, of course, because he can't possibly know her secret.

Returning to the kitchen, she carries her smoothie out to the pool. Overhead, the sun is a white scorch mark in an otherwise blue sky. Nadia opens her phone's browser and types in *Sheergen*. The first five hits are news stories about Deevis Farm.

Konstantin Tapia rings as she's finishing the first piece.

'Meet me,' he says. 'This afternoon. I have something you want.'

Three hours later, she's sitting in Cave 173's walled garden, sipping sparkling mineral water as Konstantin shakes tabasco into his tomato juice.

'Well?' she asks.

He pushes a magazine across the table. It's a copy of *Nauka i Zhizn*. On its cover she sees the rising fire of a nuclear detonation, ringed by condensation clouds.

'What's that?'

'Beautiful, no? You wanted to see Greenaway's friend.'

'I don't understand.'

Konstantin continues to spike his tomato juice. 'Page forty-three.'

Nadia snatches up the magazine. Inside, tucked firmly into the gutter, she finds three photographs taken in sequence. The first, a night shot, shows two people on the steps of an imposing Georgian townhouse. One of them, Keira Greenaway, is clearly recognizable. The next photographs show a man emerging from the same building, this time into daylight. When Nadia sees his face, she gasps. Because she recognizes him.

'I took the first one last night,' Konstantin says. 'The other two this morning. That's Greenaway's place on Greek Street.'

Nadia is barely listening. She picks up her drink, dismayed at how violently her hand is shaking. Last week, at the pharmacy, the man in the photographs had struck up a conversation. For some crazy reason, she'd revealed her pregnancy. She still remembers his grin, and what he'd said.

'You want to guess where those two were last night?' Konstantin asks.

'Will I like the answer?'

'You know that farm they keep showing on TV?'

'Deevis Farm?'

'Quite the news story developing there today.'

'You're telling me *they* did that?'

'I didn't follow them past the gate. But I can't imagine what else they'd have been doing. Can you?' Realizing that the tabasco bottle is empty, Konstantin puts it down. 'These last few days, I've been doing a lot of reading. Specifically, what happened to your husband's first wife.'

Nadia's hand is still shaking. She slips it beneath her thigh and adjusts her weight. While her memories of Italy haven't faded, she's grown increasingly adept at suppressing them. She has no wish to revisit that day – certainly not with Konstantin.

'The police investigation that followed,' he says. 'It sounds like a mess, start to finish.'

She swallows, shrugs.

'It seems they never suspected Greenaway because she was pretty much comatose by the time they turned up. But *they* weren't the first to intercept her that day, were they? *You* were.' Konstantin pauses. 'You and Simon, I mean.'

Beneath his gaze, Nadia feels naked. She takes a careful breath. 'By the time we arrived, Keira was barely conscious.'

'Talking?'

'Yes.'

'And yet she nearly died in the ambulance. The back of

her head was staved in. Catastrophic injuries to her cerebellum. Was she like that when you first saw her?'

'What?'

'Let me put it another way: did you leave Simon alone with her at any point before the police turned up?'

'I don't recall. Why is that even—'

'I'm wondering why, when Greenaway came out of that coma, she accused you both of trying to kill her. And why she still might bear a grudge.'

'It's obvious, isn't it? She's crazy. Two years after that, she abducted Ollie. She's obsessed with Simon. With all of us.'

'Was there ever anything between them?'

'Simon and Keira? Of course not. Back then, she was barely eighteen.'

'If there had been, you could argue she had a motive for killing Phoebe Rafferty. Or, if she was crazy like you say, maybe she didn't *need* a motive. And if Simon knew that . . .' Konstantin leaves the sentence unfinished. Then he tilts his head. 'Were you sleeping with him, back then? At the time of his wife's death?'

'I was *working* for him. Italy's Sheergen's biggest market. That's why I was in Salerno.'

'That's not what I asked.'

'I know it isn't.'

'Well?'

'Yes, I was sleeping with him.'

'Were *you* alone with Keira at any point before the police arrived?'

Nadia blinks. 'No.'

Konstantin sips from his tomato juice. Then he presses a finger against the magazine and the images it contains. 'If you ignore this, it won't go away. You've built a good life here, but don't trick yourself into believing it's safe. If anything, you're living Phoebe Rafferty's life, before you. This will get worse if you let it.'

Nadia feels something shift inside her, a featherlike tickling in her stomach. Not the baby – far too early for that. She recalls the guy from the pharmacy, his piercing green eyes, the enamelled yin-yang pendant at his throat.

How many weeks?

Eight, I think.

That's such good news.

Konstantin leans forward. 'They're coming for you, these two. They may not have realized it yet, but they'll come.'

Watching him, Nadia thinks of an episode from her childhood. She'd biked over to see Konstantin one afternoon when his parents were out. He wasn't in the barn. Outside, the air was foul with the stench of rendered pig fat. Following her nose, Nadia arrived at a dirt clearing, where she found Konstantin sitting on a log. Beside him stood a dented metal jerry can. Nearby lay the blackened carcass of a sow, still throwing off smoke.

'Impromptu barbecue,' he said, without looking up. 'Think I went a little heavy with the fuel.'

Nadia didn't know much about barbecuing, but she was pretty sure you didn't use petrol. For ten metres around the clearing, hoofprints and burn marks criss-crossed the dirt. She looked once and closed her mind to them.

Now, in Cave 173's walled garden, Konstantin says, 'I could fix this for you. I'd *like* to fix this for you. And no one would ever know.'

Nadia feels the fresh burn on her buttock begin to throb.

FIFTY-FIVE

Saturday night.

Three revolutions of the Earth since the events at Deevis Farm. In that time, I've lost my virginity and gained a puppy. I can't figure out which is more life-changing.

Little Guy survived his first night beyond the shed – and the following two. In the last twenty-four hours, I've switched from my homebrew formula to a tub of Royal Canin Protech.

It seems, from the photos I've found online, that he's some kind of poodle mix: a cockapoo, perhaps, or a labradoodle. Probably around four weeks old.

When I'm not researching puppy care, I'm scrolling through news articles about Deevis Farm. What started as a local story quickly went national. The reporting has been varied: from the sombre to the jocular. Some journalists focus on the caged dogs and caged humans. Others concentrate on me and Louis – who we might be, and whether our actions were justified. An online poll ended sixty-seven per cent in our favour. Callers to three phone-in radio debates reflected a similar split.

The headline writers have been enjoying themselves endlessly.

HOWL DO YOU LIKE IT?

RUFF JUSTICE

TABLES TURNED ON TERRIERISTS

HELL HATH NO FURRY

Three hundred and eighteen dogs were discovered at Deevis Farm. Shih-tzus, bichons, chihuahuas, Pomeranians, Rottweilers, huskies, lurchers, pugs, salukis, many more. Their injuries and infections were as shocking as they were diverse. Right now, our local sanctuary serves as a hub for a nationwide rehousing effort. A guy who volunteers there launched a crowdfunding drive that just hit six figures.

What I hadn't realized, until I read the coverage, was what Louis did to the people who lived there. I knew he meant to scare them, but not hurt them. Not break their bones.

I had a puppy when I was a kid. Just for a short while. One night it peed on the carpet after my dad rolled home drunk. It didn't survive what came next.

Perhaps that's why Louis reacted as he did. Or perhaps the people at the farm attacked him and he fought back. Whatever the reason, it doesn't make me feel any better. The violence has another consequence: the police are far more motivated to identify us. If they figure out my connection, it's all over. The Raffertys will learn of my whereabouts. My visits to Ollie will cease.

Poring through news sites and newsprint, I hunt for nuggets on the investigation. I made mistakes at the farm – opening Little Guy's cage without gloves, opening the dry food and distributing it. I know from my old life how easy it is to leave a trace. Thanks to my conviction, the police database still holds my fingerprints and DNA.

I'm worried, too, for Louis. He went inside the farmhouse, operated that excavator. What evidence might he have left? What trail of breadcrumbs for investigators to follow?

Tomorrow's a special day, for which I spend some time in preparation. Afterwards, I pack my cargo bag. My phone rings as I'm leaving the flat. Fifteen minutes later I'm inside the drive-thru, eyes glued to the car park, lips glued to a straw. Despite a steady stream of vehicles, I don't see Louis's van.

When he slides on to the opposite seat I'm so freaked out I can't help spraying milkshake. Apologizing, I swab the table with my napkin.

Louis shoots me a grin. 'Stressed?'

'A little.'

'Don't be. You look stunning, by the way.'

'I feel like everyone's staring.' Still, his closeness is reassuring. I sense the worst of my paranoia beginning to lift. 'Have you seen the news coverage?'

'Some. I thought we came out pretty well. How's Little Guy?'

'Better than he was. Listen, those people at the farm . . .'

'I know. I should have told you.'

I lean forward, keep my voice low. 'Louis, you *hurt* them. *Badly.*'

He nods. 'And now, just maybe, they won't do it again. You know the average sentence for animal cruelty, Mercy? Even if they're charged, convicted, they'll likely be out in no time. That's no deterrent. Sometimes, you have to fight fire with fire.'

Louis reaches across the table, squeezes my hand.

'Merdy got the *love* eyes. Merdy wearing a *dress*!'

I glance up. When I see Lost Travis beaming down at me, the last of my unease evaporates. 'You're right, I am. What do you think?'

'Travis likey-lotty. Merdy look like a *Disney*!' He turns to Louis. 'Don't she?'

'She does. I think red's her colour.'

Travis nods enthusiastically. 'Red like a fire engine. Like a letterbox.'

'Hey, Travis,' I say. 'You want to see something special?'

'Merdy got a secret?'

'I do. Here, have a look.' I lift the flap of my bag.

Travis peers inside. Then he screams, clasping his cheeks. '*OH, LOOK AT THAT! LOOK AT IT, LOOK!*'

The entire restaurant turns in our direction. Alarmed, I hide Little Guy from sight.

Travis, utterly overcome with excitement, steps backwards and collides with the recycling station. Trays and paper cups bounce across the floor. He twists around, knocking over an empty high chair.

Whiplash Becky appears. She apologizes to the nearest diners, shows Travis her teeth. Then, in a move so subtle I almost miss it, she sinks her nails into his triceps.

Travis is too frightened to cry out, but I see the pain register on his face. As Becky tows him through the staff door, his eyes flood with tears.

I turn to Louis.

'I saw,' he says. 'We'll fix it. In the meantime, check out the drive-thru queue.'

I turn towards the window. Two cars from the front, I see Edward Gropey-Hands's Mustang. There's no sign of damage to his bonnet. He must have already had it resprayed.

I recall what Louis said at the top of Old Cobb: that a guy like Edward doesn't start behaving himself just because someone graffitied his car. Turns out he was right. Because the woman in the Mustang's passenger seat definitely isn't Laurie, my baking Venus.

The car rolls forward, out of my line of sight. 'He's doing it again.'

'Give me a minute,' Louis says.

Before I can respond, he leaves through the sliding door and disappears around the corner. Thirty seconds later, he's back.

'What was that about?' I ask.

'Tell you later. Want another milkshake?'

'I don't think I can be trusted.'

'Shall we get out of here?'

'Do you have a plan?'

'A good one.'

'Going to tell me about it?'

'You're part of it.'

'I don't think I can take much more excitement.'

Louis grins. 'We'll see.'

FIFTY-SIX

A minute later, we're sitting at the fold-out table in the back of his campervan, curtains closed for privacy.

'Have you counted it?' I ask.

'Twice.'

'How much is there?'

'Give or take, around eighteen grand.'

'And this was just . . . lying around the farmhouse?'

'They'd hidden it, but not particularly well.'

'So you just took it?'

'Would you prefer them to have it?'

I shake my head. 'What are you going to do with it?'

Louis pushes it across the table. 'This is your test, Mercy, not mine. Close your eyes, reach out, listen to what you're being told. There's a plan for that money. You just need to identify it.'

I stare at the cash. Knowing how it was earned, I'm not even sure I want to touch it. But what if we spend it on something positive? Perhaps we can counteract cruelty with kindness.

'You remember the twenty-four-hour supermarket outside town?' I ask.

'Where we bought Little Guy's food?'

'That's where we're going.'

Ten minutes later, we're pushing a trolley along the aisles. This late on a Saturday night, the place is pretty quiet, particularly the home-entertainment section where we start our shopping. Afterwards, we load up the campervan with our purchases and drive back to Cranner's Ford.

Our first stop is Dalton Way, in the most neglected part of town – home to Unproud Tina and her nine-year-old daughter. Tina cleans for the Raffertys during the day. Weekday evenings she works shifts at a pizza place and on weekends she serves coffee at a soft play. And yet financially she's still drowning. After rent, fuel, heating and food, there's never anything left.

We leave four bags of groceries outside Tina's back door. Into one of them I tuck three thousand pounds and a note assuring her she can spend it freely.

From Tina's we visit seven more families I know are struggling. Each gets an envelope stuffed with cash, along with a handwritten note from me.

At Lovesick Linda's, we carry a brand-new TV and microwave to her front door, ring the bell and jump back inside the campervan. As Louis accelerates away, I glance through the rear window. On the porch I see Linda, staring at the boxes.

'All gone?' Louis asks.

'Every penny spent.' I glance at him from the passenger seat. 'That was a good thing we just did.'

When he grins, I grin back. My knees press together,

my thighs. I think of our intimacy on Wednesday night and find myself wanting more – but our evening of interventions isn't over quite yet. 'Left here,' I say. 'It's number fourteen.'

Louis peers through the side window as we roll past the house. 'No Mustang.'

'If he's home, it'll be in the garage.'

We turn right at the end of the street and pull over. 'Back soon,' Louis says, killing the engine.

'No way, Jose. I'm coming with.'

'Someone should stay with Little Guy. Doesn't he need another feed?'

Darn it, he's right. As Louis disappears around the corner, I climb into the back and mix up some formula. Little Guy takes his bottle like a champ. Afterwards, he submits to a tummy rub.

While I wait, I think about what happened at the drive-thru: Lost Travis's jubilation when he saw Little Guy; his pain when Becky sank her nails into him; Edward Gropey-Hands in the drive-thru queue, with a woman I didn't recognize. Finally, I think of Laurie, my baking Venus, and wonder if Louis will see her inside the house.

Sooner than I expected, he's back. He fires up Eleanor and we vamoose.

'Well?' I ask, re-joining him up front.

'All good.'

I snort. 'Pretty cryptic.'

'You trust me, right?'

'Of course.' I pause. 'Did you see her?'

'The wife?'

'Uh-huh.'

Louis looks at me. 'I did.'

'Really?'

'Truly.' He holds my eye a moment longer. 'You want to see?'

I frown. 'What do you mean?'

'I took a photo.'

'Stop it.'

'Stop what?'

'You're teasing me.'

'You don't believe me?'

'Of course not.'

Louis digs in his pocket, brings out his phone. Steering one-handed, he opens his photo library. 'There you go.'

When I see the screen, I feel like my stomach's been tossed off a cliff. Because Louis *isn't* teasing. Not one bit.

I take his phone and hunch over it. The image is grainy and low contrast, suggesting it was captured in near darkness.

It's a close-up shot. To get it, Louis must have leaned right over Laurie's bed. Her face is slack, her eyes closed in sleep. She looks so *vulnerable*.

My stomach boomerangs. I feel nauseous – complicit in something that can't be undone. Because this is a grotesque invasion of privacy. Indefensible.

'I know how much you wanted to get close to her,' Louis says. 'I figured this might be the next-best thing.'

'Right.'

He looks at me quizzically. I take a moment to breathe.

'Mercy?' he asks. 'What's wrong?'

'Nothing. Thank you. It's nice seeing her up close.' When he takes back the phone, I hug myself.

'Sure you're OK?'

'Absolutely.' Keeping my tone light, I add, 'So what else did you do in there?'

'Edward Gropey-Hands intervention, level two.'

'Level two?'

'Level one didn't work. So we escalate.'

I roll my tongue around my teeth. 'We escalate?'

'To level two.'

He's making it hard to pursue this. 'What exactly is level two?'

'I thought you trusted me.'

'I told you I do.'

'You *told* me you do?'

'I told you because I meant it.'

'You'd tell me if you didn't?'

'There's no need to worry.'

'There isn't?'

'Louis . . .'

I don't know what else to say, how to finish what I started, so I close my mouth and say nothing. We cross the bridge into Old Town and drive past the Ferryman. The riverside pub is lit up inside, music thumping out. I guess they finally won their late licence. When I spot a familiar vehicle in the car park, I ask Louis to pull over.

'Got any matches?' I ask.

He indicates the glovebox.

'Two minutes,' I tell him, opening the door and slipping out. After what I saw on his phone, I need some air, and this is the perfect opportunity.

White Knuckle Wanda's Range Rover stands in the darkest depths of the car park. I bet she won't be drinking mocktails inside the Ferryman – and I bet she isn't planning on getting a taxi later.

Still, she won't be driving home. Not tonight.

Circling the Range Rover, I drop to my knees. Tonight

I don't have my knife, so I unscrew the valve cap on the driver's side front wheel, take a match from Louis's box and jam it inside.

With a hiss, the tyre begins to deflate. It's loud, but not as loud as the one I punctured outside Cave 173. The music blasting from the pub helps to mask it. I'm inserting a match into the driver's side rear tyre valve when a hand grabs my shoulder and yanks me backwards. I tumble across the gravel, scuffing my knees and cracking my head.

'Showtime, *bitch*,' Wanda hisses.

Before I can recover, she's on me, stinking of booze and cigarettes. I raise my hands to fend her off, but I can't react fast enough. Her fist drives the air from my lungs. Her nails slash open my cheek. She puts her hands around my throat, starts to strangle me. I grab her wrists, but I'm not strong enough to prise her loose. My temples throb. I feel my eyes swelling in their sockets.

And then Wanda's head snaps back.

Behind her, Louis pivots, swinging her around by her hair. Wanda's face crunches into the driver's side door, leaving a huge dent in the metal.

I open my mouth to shout, but I haven't recovered my breath. As I try to sit up, Louis slams Wanda's face into the car door a second time. Then, dragging her backwards, he smashes his knee into her nose. She collapses on to the tarmac, choking on blood. He steps back, kicks her in the ribs. Once, twice, three times.

'*Wait*,' I say. '*Stop!*'

But my words are less than a whisper. And either Louis doesn't hear me – or he chooses not to listen. Calmly, he steps over Wendy and rains down more blows on her face. I hear the steady impact of his fists.

On all fours, I crawl over and grab Louis's leg. 'Leave her!' I gasp. '*Leave* her!'

He turns on me, eyes like sequins. For a moment I think he'll strike me too. But then, abruptly, his demeanour changes. He blinks, turns back to Wanda, leans in close. 'It's a woman,' he says.

As if she could be anything else.

Wanda's face is a red mask, her mouth a mess of broken teeth. She scissors her legs, rolls on to her side. '*Gitch*,' she groans, a blood bubble forming and bursting on her lips. '*Ucking gitch.*'

Louis pulls me to my feet. 'You OK?'

I nod, stunned, unable to take my eyes off Wanda.

'I left you for a minute,' he says. He glances at the blood-spattered gravel, then up at the pub. 'We need to go.'

'*Ucking gitch, I'll gill you.*'

Before I can object, Louis leads me back across the car park. And then we're riding away into the dark.

FIFTY-SEVEN

Saturday evening at his hotel, Tapia takes a shower and waits for the last of the day's light to die. To fortify himself, he watches a YouTube documentary on the Tsar Bomba, the most powerful nuclear weapon ever detonated. It exploded with ten times the force of all the munitions used in the Second World War. The mushroom cloud climbed sixty miles. The shockwave raced three times around the Earth.

How fearlessly mankind illustrated its destiny that day. How tragic that the feat remains unsurpassed. Tapia fantasizes about a chain of Tsar Bomba detonations encircling the Earth – so perfectly synchronized that they fracture the planet in two, releasing its core like yolk from an egg. The temperature of that molten mass pushes eleven thousand degrees – as hot as the surface of the sun. Tapia's muscles weaken in contemplation.

At 9.30 p.m., his phone vibrates. When he checks his tracking app he sees the campervan on the move. He watches it travel along Liphook Avenue, where it pulls into a car park serving a drive-thru. Probably, the couple are meeting there, like he saw them do once before.

Tapia leaves his hotel and walks to an Indian restaurant a few streets down. At a window table, he orders a blood-red lamb phall of such extraordinary heat it makes his nose bleed and his ears ring.

He eats, as always, as if it's his last meal. He watches his phone throughout, and imagines his little fish and her buddy tucking into burgers and fries, perhaps a few shakes.

It won't be *their* last meal, either, but there's a chance it might be one of them. On Thursday, at the wine bar, he offered to fix Nadia's problem. She declined, after a long pause.

Will she reconsider? He thinks there's a strong possibility. He recalls her discomfort when he questioned her about Italy; the shaking she couldn't quite conceal. Might she be more deeply involved than he first imagined? Not just in what happened to Keira Greenaway but what happened to Phoebe Rafferty, Simon's first wife? What does he really know about Nadia, other than her willingness to satisfy him?

For the intimacy she's granted him over the years, he's placed himself in her debt. Her culpability for past events won't change that. Nor is it any of his concern. If she reconsiders his offer, he'll deliver a solution without pause.

Afterwards, for the first time since childhood, they'd be square. Then he'd be free to reassess their relationship. His feelings towards Nadia have always been complicated. For a short while, she might rue what came next.

These thoughts arouse him. His sunburned skin throbs. He leaves the restaurant and climbs into his van, still monitoring the app.

For the last ten minutes, since returning from an out-of-town supermarket, the VW has followed a stop-start route around Cranner's Ford. Tapia decides to check up, just in case his tracker unit's been strapped to some pizza delivery guy's moped.

A simple drive-by will suffice. He plots an interception route and passes the vehicle while it's parked, his little fish and her buddy clearly visible in the front seats.

Satisfied, Tapia drives to Greek Street. He waits until he sees Greenaway's neighbour returning home. Then he follows her up the steps, smiling when she holds the door. She looks at him appraisingly, smiles back.

The neighbour goes inside her flat. Tapia takes the stairs to the lower-ground floor. Outside Greenaway's front door, he inserts a thin steel rod into the lock, followed by the needle of his lockpick gun. A few rapid pulls of the trigger and he's defeated the pin tumblers.

Inside, he flicks on a light switch and finds, to his astonishment, that he's standing on a tropical beach – or at least a disorienting approximation. Crossing it to a doorway, he discovers an underwater reef. In the kitchen he encounters snow-covered mountains. In Keira Greenaway's bedroom, he finds a forest glade.

Tapia goes to her bed. He kicks off his shoes and lies down on the mattress. When he turns his head, he smells her scent on the pillow, breathes deep.

How peaceful this is. How strange and unforeseen. He imagines the trees around him combusting, their branches crackling with fire. Why has he never thought to do this himself? He could sleep every night inside a volcano, lava running down the walls towards his bed.

Tapia thinks about switching off the lights and climbing under Keira Greenaway's covers – just for a while, just to see what it's like. But he doesn't want to fall asleep and have her find him.

Leaving the forest, he returns to the beach. There, he finds two teal urns. When he looks inside one of them, he finds ash – what he imagines must be incinerated human remains. He scoops up a handful and lets it trickle through his fingers.

In a corner, near the TV, he trails his hand over a huge pair of feathered wings hanging from a dressmaker's mannequin. When he imagines how brightly they would burn, Tapia can hardly catch his breath.

FIFTY-EIGHT

Home. Just Little Guy and me. I was going to invite Louis inside. And then I didn't.

It feels like we crossed a line tonight. I know that sounds insane, considering everything we've already done. But White Knuckle Wanda's beating in the Ferryman's car park was on a different level. And it's all my fault.

I step into the lives of Cranner's Ford's residents without invitation, I realize that, and I don't always get it right. But while good people can do bad things – bad people, just as importantly, can do *good* things. Can they make amends for past sins? Truthfully, I can't answer that. But they can try. *I* can try.

Until last week, when I spotted Wanda's Range Rover outside Cave 173, I'd restricted myself to positive acts – birdhouses, porch lights, notes shoved through letterboxes. Now, because of my choices, a woman has lost half her teeth.

At least she won't be driving home drunk.

I ignore that voice, because it isn't mine. I'm Mercy Lake, and I need to remember that. Instead, I replay tonight's events.

259

The Ferryman's car park was dark, especially where Wanda left her Range Rover. Was that a contributing factor? Did Louis not realize my assailant was a woman? Or that after his initial intervention, the threat was effectively over? Is that why he didn't stop attacking Wanda until I grabbed him?

Should I call the pub? The hospital? How can I check that she's OK?

Wanda's not my only worry. I can't stop thinking about the photograph Louis showed me, of Laurie asleep in her bed – and what a level-two intervention with Edward Gropey-Hands might have involved.

In the bathroom, I look at my slashed face – three red lines that start above my cheekbone and end somewhere near my jaw. No doubt my skin is trapped beneath Wanda's nails, full of the same DNA the police hold on their database; DNA that, if I'm unlucky, they might also find at Deevis Farm.

I go from room to room, putting up blackout panels and pulling down blinds and wall hangings. Usually, I find some comfort in the routine. Not now. Something about my flat seems different. It feels more like a bunker than a haven.

Before I seal myself off completely, I look outside at the street. No police. No parked vehicles except the dog-grooming van I first noticed last week.

I make up another bottle and feed Little Guy. Then I go online and search out the latest on Deevis Farm. Disturbingly, there's now an e-fit of Louis. Often, those things look comical – hardly like a person at all. This one's a perfect likeness.

I'm tempted to call and let him know, but I'm paralysed

by indecision. What started off as a grand, romantic adventure has developed into something horribly perilous, with three people already hospitalized – and now, presumably, a fourth.

In the living room, I find my scrapbook and take it to the sofa. With Little Guy curled beside me, I open the book in the middle and begin to flick through its pages.

I don't do this often. It's usually too hard to face. But tonight's events require a reminder – a warning of the consequences when obsession reigns unchecked. Read sequentially, the headlines tell the story:

FEMALE, 20, ARRESTED AT HOUSE TRESPASS
SECOND ARREST FOR FEMALE STALKER
RAFFERTYS SAY: 'SHE JUST WON'T STOP.'

But I did stop, for a while – because the next set of cuttings begins six months later.

TWO-YEAR-OLD BOY MISSING FROM FAMILY HOME
HUNT FOR OLLIE RAFFERTY INTENSIFIES
OLLIE RAFFERTY: POLICE SAY BOY SNATCHED FROM BED
RAFFERTY SUSPECT ARRESTED FOR TRESPASS LAST JUNE
OLLIE RAFFERTY FOUND AT CARAVAN PARK
PROSECUTION OUTLINES SORRY TALE OF OBSESSION
MENTAL HEALTH CLAIM IN RAFFERTY CASE DEFENCE
KEIRA GREENAWAY CONVICTED OF CHILD ABDUCTION
JUDGE SUSPENDS SENTENCE, CITES MENTAL HEALTH

Some of the articles show my image. Some show the Raffertys. When our photographs appear side by side, the contrast is stark: me, the wild-eyed child snatcher versus the respectable parents under siege. What was I thinking? How did I let things get so bad? Amazing, really, that I avoided jail.

The scrapbook's final cutting is two years old and comes from the *Cranner's Ford Gazette*: PLANNING PERMISSION GRANTED FOR ABBOT'S WALK MAKEOVER. An image shows Arcadia Heights as it looked before the Raffertys bought it.

They moved to Cranner's Ford six months later. I waited another six months before following. By then, I'd served the conditions of my suspended sentence: keeping my distance from the family and complying with my night curfew. My probation officer meetings had concluded. Likewise, my mandatory psychotherapy sessions.

Moving here was a risk bordering on insane, but I learned from my previous mistakes. My focus is no longer on Simon – the only man to have kissed me before Louis – nor on the woman he married before my trial. These days, my visits with Ollie are enough.

My life here isn't perfect. Sometimes I've slipped into old habits, destructive patterns of behaviour. My tendency to obsess hasn't subsided, nor my fascination with those around me. But, overall, I've felt things have been better, that I'm a mostly positive force – not just on Ollie but on others I've started to watch. What worries me now is my influence on Louis.

At first, I couldn't believe someone from the daylight world would so readily cross into darkness. In recent days, though, I've accepted what at first seemed impossible. Louis bought me champagne, a phone, new binoculars, a dress. And if that didn't signal his intentions, he even gave me angel wings.

What have I offered in return? Nights out chasing adulterers, puppy farmers, burglars, drunks and abusers.

I flick to the very start of the scrapbook. Then, clenching my teeth, I begin to turn the pages:

THREE BRITS FOUND DEAD AT ITALIAN LAKE HOUSE

SOLE LAKE HOUSE SURVIVOR IN COMA

LAKE HOUSE DEATHS: ALL VICTIMS RELATED

ITALIAN POLICE CONFIRM MURDER PROBE

LAKE HOUSE HORROR: MORE DETAILS EMERGE

'INVESTIGATION SHAMBOLIC' — EX-DETECTIVE

VITAL CLUES MISSED, HUSBAND CLAIMS

NO NEW LEADS IN LAKE HOUSE CASE, ITALIAN POLICE ADMIT

Many of the news stories feature photographs from a holiday brochure, of a place I well remember. And yet when I retreat to my woodland glade and lie down on my bed, it's not the lake house I dream of but a different property altogether.

FIFTY-NINE

Pendant lights, hanging over a granite kitchen island. From the hall, music and conversation.

I won't stay here long. Just long enough for the room to stop spinning. I'm no good at drinking, and tonight I've drunk a lot – mad and monstrous concoctions created by the party's private mixologist. The latest contained an olive. I *hate* olives – and I can't rid my mouth of the taste. Filling a glass with cold water, I drink it down. *Ahh* – blessed relief.

In the kitchen's bifold doors, I study my reflection. The clothes and the heels are borrowed, but I know that I look good. My skin is tanned, my legs muscled, my waist tight. The blue dress matches my eyes. I'm even wearing make-up: eyeliner and a touch of lipstick. I look like someone confident of her place.

In company, of course – especially at a party like this one – the illusion crumbles pretty fast. I blush when addressed, mumble when I speak, slavishly avoid eye contact. At least in private I can still pretend, so I cock a hip, make a gun of my thumb and forefinger and tell my reflection it's *smokin'*.

And then *he* comes in: confident, relaxed, effortlessly in control. He's carrying two empty champagne bottles, which he dumps on the worktop.

'Smokin', indeed,' he laughs. 'The party's best-kept secret.' And even though I shouldn't – even though I know he's only humouring me – I can't help but feel thrilled, despite my mortification at getting caught. His eyes linger on my hips, before travelling up my torso to my face. I feel a surge of something in my blood: alien, illicit, darkly pleasurable.

Simon Rafferty smiles. I gulp like I'm choking.

He opens the fridge and removes another bottle. 'Did Phoebe show you the wine cellar?'

I shake my head.

'You *have* to see it.' And before I can think up an excuse, he's disappeared through a door into a part of the house I haven't seen. We venture along a maroon corridor hung with monochrome prints of wind turbines – and down a steep flight of steps into darkness. At the bottom, Simon flicks a light switch. The cellar is revealed: row after row of empty wooden racking. It's cold down here, damp. My skin puckers into gooseflesh.

'Of course, I've now no option but to fill the damned thing with claret,' Simon says. 'First World problems, eh?'

He reaches out, touches my bare shoulder. I jolt as if hit by mains current. My head knocks against a beam.

Simon chuckles, steps closer.

'Sorry,' he says. 'Not sorry.'

With a wine rack behind me, there's nowhere to retreat. Simon tilts his head, examining me like I'm a strange new species of wildlife. Then he touches me again, tracing his finger down my cheek.

'Phoebe,' I tell him. 'My *sister* is—'

And then he kisses me.

I'm so surprised, I let him – and when his tongue pushes inside my mouth, I allow that too. He tastes of alcohol and privilege and something I can't even describe.

It's wrong, this, utterly – I've only just turned eighteen and my sister's about to have his baby – but it's the first time I've been kissed, the first time I've shared my mouth with anyone, and the sensation is so visceral that for a while I give myself up to it. By the time a light comes on in my brain, it's too late, I'm complicit. Worse, it feels like Simon's woken something inside me I didn't know existed – a wildness and a hunger and a casual disregard for consequences.

When I finally twist my head, expelling him from my mouth, I see that my perspective has changed. I'm no longer in Simon's wine cellar. Instead, I'm lying on the track outside his rented Italian lake house. My body is broken – a bloodied and pain-filled sack. My vision has started skipping, but I can still see the torque wrench gripped in his hand. Beside him stands a woman with sharp cheeks and a platinum bob. Nadia Sokolov works for Sheergen. I don't understand why she's here.

Simon bends over me. 'What did you do, Keira? Why did you come? Where's Phoebe? Where's my *son*?'

A flock of geese lands on the lake, kicking up jewels of water. I lift my gaze to the lake house. Simon and Nadia turn towards it.

They break into a run.

SIXTY

In the dream, James is eating a scorpion. Usually, for a human, this would be a bad thing. But James is a hamadryas baboon. *That* should be a good thing, especially as James is the harem male. But right now something is off with the females. And James cannot figure out what.

He bites off the scorpion's head and licks out the ichor. Around him, the females form a silent horseshoe. He feels their gaze, but he doesn't look up. Instead, he yawns, shows his teeth – a display of strength while he mulls their intentions.

One of the females lifts her head, chitters. James can't decode her meaning, but he suspects she might be mocking him. With his teeth, he decapitates another scorpion.

The female points, screeches. Then she raises herself on her haunches and turns her back. She's clearly in heat; her rear looks like a volcano mid-eruption. Still, the display feels more like an insult than an invitation.

Two other females start bouncing up and down. Their high-pitched gibbers resemble *laughter*. James flings the scorpion at them. He's the harem male, goddamnit. How *dare* they?

When they start pointing, too, he glances down at himself. His body hair, or fur – he isn't sure which – is silver-grey. It grows everywhere except between his legs. There, he sees nothing but a tiny pink stick. It's rigid, preposterously thin. When he looks up, he sees that his entire harem is laughing – and that his penis is the source of their mirth.

Are they idiots? Don't they realize that *all* baboon penises look like this? He opens his mouth to protest, but all that emerges is a shriek. The females laugh harder. One rolls on to her back.

James hears a buzzing sound, responds with another shriek. He sees movement to his right: two male baboons joining the horseshoe. They laugh, too. Their penises are *huge*.

More buzzing. And now music. Another three males sidle into the horseshoe. One of them begins to mate with Volcano Butt.

With a cry, James sits up in bed.

Morning daylight is streaming through the window. He scrunches up his eyes, knuckling away the dream. Ever since that nature documentary, he's fantasized about being a baboon. But the experience was more like a nightmare.

'James?'

He flinches, peers around the room. Laurie, in her dressing gown, is sitting in the chair opposite the bed. For a moment, he can't work out why she's there. Then he realizes it's Sunday and the bakery is shut.

He doesn't like the way she's looking at him. *At all*. He can't help recalling the harem females – their pointing and their shrieks.

'What's going on?' she asks.

James likes her tone even less than her expression. Throwing off the duvet, he stumbles to the bathroom and locks the door. He stands over the toilet and urinates, relieved to see that the awful pink baboon penis has gone, replaced with something more obviously human. Still, it doesn't ease his paranoia. *Something* is definitely up.

When he flushes the toilet and moves to the sink, the mirror shows him the answer. Across his forehead, in huge black letters, is a word:

TAƎHƆ

James stares at his reflection. Frantically, he replays last night's events.

Polly was a recent Tinder find: crass, filthy, energetic. After a few drinks in town, they drove to a nearby picnic spot. He nailed her outside, mainly because he couldn't stop thinking about something Dani had said, the night his Mustang was vandalized: *Was that your fucking wife? Christ, James. The doors weren't even locked. She could have poured in petrol,* incinerated *us.*

After the sex, he'd taken Polly to the drive-thru, where they'd collected a bag of cheeseburgers before he'd dropped her off. Then he'd driven straight home.

CHEAT hadn't been on his forehead at the bar in town. And he can't see how Polly could have scrawled it on him afterwards. That leaves only one option. Considering it, he recalls something else Dani said about his wife: *The woman's a fucking* psycho.

James's testicles tighten. Just now, Laurie had been watching him while he slept – sitting in her chair while his baboon harem humiliated him. He was defenceless, unaware of her attention. She could have done *anything*.

He turns on the tap, wets a flannel, scrubs his forehead. But Laurie must have used a permanent marker because the goddamned writing won't come off.

Later this morning, he's meant to be playing golf with her brother. It wasn't his idea, but Vincent's a captain in the Grenadier Guards – and kind of hard to refuse. James still remembers what the guy whispered to him at their wedding: *We're best buddies until you shit on her. Then I put my hands inside you and pull out all the important stuff.*

James scrubs harder, to no avail. Panicking, he turns on the shower. When the water's hot enough he strips off his T-shirt. And sees that Laurie's been busier than he'd first thought. Not content with his forehead, she's scrawled another message across his chest.

NEXT TIME, I CUT OFF YOUR COCK

However deeply James breathes, he can't fill his lungs. *Because his wife is clearly insane.* He needs to pack a bag and get out of here, right now, before her equally deranged brother arrives – or before Laurie swaps her Sharpie for scissors.

Turning off the shower, he opens the bathroom door. Laurie is standing outside.

James screams. He staggers backwards, trips over the bathroom scales and sprawls on his backside.

Laurie's gaze drops to his chest. 'James—'

'Stay away from me!' he shrieks. He finds his feet,

barges past her to the bedroom. She follows him inside while he's pulling on his jeans. He hops around the bed to avoid her. 'Jesus, I'm *SORRY, OK*? Please – just stay *away* from me!'

She stares at him, shakes her head. 'I think it's time you—'

'Fine! I'm a prick, whatever. There, I've said it. I screwed around. Repeatedly screwed around. But *this*,' he says, indicating his forehead, his bare chest. 'This is *abuse*, Laurie.'

'You think I did that?'

'Are you kidding me?'

'James, I think you might be having a breakdown.'

From somewhere, a bugle sounds a reveille. It's the WhatsApp notification on Laurie's phone – so absurdly and cartoonishly jolly that for a moment it robs James of thought. Beside the bed, his own phone buzzes. He snatches it up.

Laurie says, 'What do you mean, you screwed around?'

Ignoring her, he checks his messages. What he finds stops him dead. A memory surfaces from last night. He's sitting in the drive-thru queue with Polly, window down, elbow out. A guy comes over. Dark hair, white teeth. When Polly sits up straighter, James bristles. But the guy isn't a threat, he's a fan – a baboon supplicant offering fealty to the harem king. He checks out the Mustang, checks out Polly. Then he whistles, low and long.

'Seriously, fella. A genuine Shelby. You are literally living my dream.'

James inclines his head, acknowledging the compliment.

'You mind if I get a photo?' the guy asks. Then he rolls his eyes. 'You probably get asked that all the time. Probably drives you crazy, right?'

Polly squeezes James's thigh, requesting a display of charity. Reaching for his Oakleys, he flicks them open. 'No problemo, friend,' he drawls. 'Get some good shots.'

The guy takes out his phone, starts snapping. As Polly pushes out her chest and pouts, James cracks a smile just wide enough to reveal a dimple. Somehow, eight hours later, he's staring at the result.

It doesn't make sense. Suddenly, nothing makes sense.

'James?' Laurie asks. 'Who's that in the car with you? When was this?'

She angles her phone towards him. On its screen he sees the same photograph. He stares at her. Tries to think.

His phone buzzes, announcing the arrival of another photo. This one's from a week or two ago. He's in the Mustang with Dani, helping her remove her shoes.

James is still trying to process it when Laurie's phone sounds another bugle call. She brings up the new image, gasps. Their eyes meet.

Her expression stings his heart. Because although he sees Laurie's hurt, he also sees how quickly she recovers. He's been hurting her a long time. Not just the cheating. Countless little betrayals. Despite it all, she still loved him – and she's just received permission to stop.

Ironically, tragically, in the instant that James loses her he rediscovers the person he once loved. She's been there all along, hiding in plain sight. How inordinately stupid to have been blinded by a few pounds of extra weight – or a sex drive lower than it once was.

It's a bad moment, a horrible moment, but there's more to come. Because a few seconds later he hears the doorbell. When he looks through the bedroom window he sees his brother-in-law's Jeep Cherokee parked outside.

We're best buddies until you shit on her. Then I put my hands inside you and pull out all the important stuff.

'Well,' Laurie says. 'I guess Vince is early.'

James glances at the mirror. He sees that word written across his forehead. 'Please. Don't let him in.'

Shaking her head, a gesture more of pity than defiance, Laurie goes downstairs.

SIXTY-ONE

Sunday morning, Nadia Rafferty wakes alone, in a rarely used guestroom overlooking the front drive. It's inferior to the master suite in every respect except one: its west-facing outlook hides it from Pincher's Mount.

Simon flew to Italy Thursday lunchtime, after releasing a Sheergen statement reacting to the events at Deevis Farm. As a result, Nadia hasn't had a chance to talk to him face to face since her meeting with Konstantin at the wine bar. And she isn't naïve enough to reveal what she's learned over the phone.

She knows why he's over there – a contract signing to supply six government-green-lit wind farms – but she can't help suspecting a secondary motive: a desire to create physical distance between himself and the unfolding news story. That he's been gone three days, and isn't due home until tonight, lends further credence to her theory.

In her darker moments, Nadia considers an alternative explanation. She recalls her six-month stint at Sheergen's Salerno office while Simon was still married to Phoebe; his regularly invented reasons to visit her there; the passion and the intensity of their liaisons. Those memories seed a paranoia hard to dispel. Might he be cheating on *her*, the same way he cheated on his first wife? Even while she's raising his son from that marriage? Even while she's pregnant with his second child?

No. Nadia won't believe that. She's worked too hard and invested too much. Simon isn't a serial adulterer. Right now, she has more pressing problems than the paranoia of past transgressions. Because the lunatic younger sister of Simon's late wife, who once abducted Ollie and fled with him to some ghastly caravan park, has been visiting Arcadia Heights. Worse, Keira seems to have found herself a conspirator, a man to whom Nadia unwittingly confided her closest secret.

How many weeks?

Eight, I think.

That's such good news.

Downstairs, with morning daylight streaming through the kitchen's east-facing windows, she makes coffee and tries to ignore Pincher's Mount. Ollie joins her around eight. He slips, yawning, on to a breakfast stool.

'Feeling hungry, hombre?' she asks.

He nods, wrinkling his nose.

'Any special requests?'

'May we please have waffles?'

'You know what?' Nadia says, 'I think we may.'

Spurred on by Ollie's delighted grin, she roots through the cupboards for the waffle iron and plugs it in. As she assembles the ingredients and mixes up a batter, she looks him in the eye and says, 'Can I ask you something?'

'Is it about maple syrup?'

'It isn't.'

'Are we having maple syrup?'

'We are.'

'Are we having strawberries?'

'If you like.'

'And melted chocolate?'

'Don't push it.'

Ollie laughs.

Nadia laughs too, her mood brightening. She's been a mother to this boy since he was eight months old. No one – least of all Keira Greenaway – is going to come between them. Nor is her marriage to his father about to fail. Simon's in Italy to sign a contract – and that's all.

While the first two waffles are sizzling, Nadia decides it's time. 'Little man,' she says gently. 'Tell me about this.' On to the counter she places his beaten-up Tamagotchi.

Immediately, Ollie reaches for it. When Nadia slides the toy out of reach, he flinches. Their eyes meet.

And in that moment she *knows*.

'I had one of these when I was a little girl,' she tells him, keeping her tone light. 'I took mine everywhere. I fed it, trained it, cleaned up after it. I was so sad when it died.'

'What happened?'

'It got sick. And I didn't know how to give it medicine. Where did you get yours?'

Ollie's gaze moves to the Tamagotchi, to the waffle iron, then back to Nadia. His forehead creases. 'Found it.'

'You found it? Really?'

He opens his mouth, nods.

'OK. What about this?'

From her robe she removes the Little Professor calculator she found him clutching last night. An original, from 1976.

'I need you to tell me the truth, little man.'

The boy swallows. Then he whispers, 'It's the magic.'

Despite the summer daylight streaming through the kitchen windows, Nadia feels like she just stepped into a dream. Her skin tingles. 'The magic?'

He nods solemnly. '*Fairy* magic.'

The waffle iron sputters and hisses. Nadia opens a drawer, selects a knife. She tests its sharpness, unmoved when she sees a welling crimson pearl on her thumb. Turning to Ollie, sucking away the blood, she says, 'Tell me about the magic.'

SIXTY-TWO

I wake Sunday evening in sheets soaked with sweat. Last night's dream held me prisoner far too long.

Poor Little Guy. I missed his first feed. He's left a few small protests around the flat. I can hardly blame him.

As always, it takes my waking brain a while to boot up and figure out what day it is. This one, I realize, is special. I bottle-feed Little Guy. Then I decide to collect my post. I emerge from my flat, climb the stairs to the communal ground-floor hall and come face to face with Edward Gropey-Hands.

He's standing just inside the building's main entrance. As our eyes meet, my stomach rises into my throat. Quite a feat – for anyone's stomach. Behind me, down the stairs, the door to my flat clunks shut. I feel like a cowboy in an old-fashioned gunfight. Except in this stand-off I don't have a revolver, just my keys. Instead of cowboy boots, I'm wearing Twilight Sparkle slippers.

I could retreat, unlock my door, crash through it – but then I'd be trapped inside. Fortunately, Edward Gropey-Hands looks like his focus is far from a confrontation. In fact, it appears he already had one. Either that or a car crash. Or some kind of sky-diving accident.

His eyes are so dark and swollen he looks like a panda. His nose is definitely broken. Both his lips are split. Blood has spilled down his chin and stained his shirt. He's muttering to himself: a running commentary that includes plenty of grown-up language.

The hallway tilts. I touch one hand to the wall. Surely Louis didn't inflict those injuries last night. I can't see how he'd have had the time.

Edward has a laundry bag under his arm and a holdall over his shoulder. His elbow is hooked around the handle of a wheeled suitcase. To his chest he's hugging a paltry collection of sports trophies. The gold plastic head of one of them has come off. He's trapped it, somewhat awkwardly, beneath his bloodied chin.

As nonchalantly as I can manage, I slide along the wall towards him. Edward limps along the floor towards me. If this *were* a movie gunfight, it'd go down in history as the world's worst.

The distance between us shrinks – and then I see that Louis *must* have had some hand in this. Because scrawled across Edward's forehead, faded from repeated scrubbing but still visible, is the same word Louis sprayed across his bonnet.

I gasp, stop dead.

'*What?*' Edward snaps, noticing my surprise – and loses his grip on the trophy head. It slides out from his chin, bounces twice on the floor and rolls to a stop at my feet.

He glares at me expectantly. I bend down and retrieve the head. Then I wedge it back under his chin.

'Thanks,' he mutters.

'Any time. Tough day?'

'Like you wouldn't believe.'

He shuffles past me. I reach the front entrance and unlock my post box. Two battered envelopes lie inside: one white, one red.

Edward stops outside the ground-floor flat and pounds on the door. 'Hazel!' he yells. '*HAZEL!*'

I scoop up my post and close the box. So – my neighbour isn't Honey, after all. To be fair, we've never spoken. My only clue was a single item of post delivered in error. On the envelope: *H. Docherty*.

Returning to my flat, I shut myself inside. Upstairs, Hazel's door opens. I try to picture her reaction to Edward's battered and graffitied face.

At my workbench, I place the envelopes in front of me. I can't face opening them right now. Instead, I focus on the muffled voices I hear in the upstairs hall. At first, I can't make out what they're saying. Then the conversation escalates.

'*WHAT DO YOU MEAN? LOOK AT ME, CHRISSAKES! I'M DESPERATE!*'

Hazel, ironically, was the catalyst for this particular saga. Soon after I bought my flat, I learned that a Ford Mustang parked in the driveway usually led to Hazel's bed pogoing across her floorboards shortly afterwards. Initially, I didn't pay it much attention. Then, one night, I encountered the same Mustang parked below Rycroft Hollow – and witnessed Edward doing the bad thing with a passenger who wasn't Hazel. Feeling sorry for my upstairs neighbour, I followed Edward home. That's how I discovered he was married – and also how I met Laurie.

Infidelity on Edward's scale is hard to conceal indefinitely. I tried to prepare Laurie for what was coming with jewellery symbolizing strength. And yes – in hindsight, that was an uber-crap idea. My attempts to discourage Edward from visiting Hazel failed just as miserably: little gifts, left by her door, that I hoped she would keep and might indicate to Edward that he had a rival: male deodorant, cufflinks, a can of shaving cream.

I grab my phone and pick up Little Guy. Then I leave the flat. As I climb the stairs to the ground floor I spot Edward standing inside the main entrance, surrounded by his belongings, cursing as he scrolls through his phone. His head – the trophy head, not his real one – lies outside Hazel's door.

Hazel led me to Edward. And Edward led me to Laurie. Now Louis, via Laurie, has driven Edward back to Hazel. And Hazel has kicked Edward to the kerb.

Outside, there's a beaten-up Toyota Yaris on the drive. I walk past it to where Louis is parked. 'It worked,' I say, climbing into the campervan.

Louis leans over. When we kiss, some of my misgivings from last night melt away. 'What did?'

'Laurie threw him out, I think. And then *Honey* threw him out. Hazel, I mean.'

'Hazel?'

'My neighbour. Sorry. I call her Honey, but it turns out she's Hazel. I think Laurie kept the Mustang, too, because Edward's driving her Toyota. Oh, and someone gave Edward a beating. Please tell me it wasn't you.'

'It wasn't me.'

'Good.' I grin – a sickly one, but it's a start. 'They've released an e-fit of you, from Deevis Farm. I saw it on the news.'

'A what-fit?'

'A face they make from witness descriptions.'

'Those things don't ever look like anyone.'

'This one does.' I examine him, some of my unease creeping back. 'Louis, you need to take this seriously.'

He looks at me sharply. 'I take what we're doing here incredibly seriously.' Then his expression softens. 'Listen, I've told you before, but I'll happily repeat it: I believe in a sentient universe, one that presents us with choices, offers us chances to be its agents. I think you were working on its behalf before I arrived, even if you didn't realize it. I think I was brought here to help you succeed.

'I'll be honest, Mercy: I don't think you've told me everything. So far, I don't think we've even started to address what you're really here to do. Yes, we've taken risks. This is a small town – we can't keep intervening the way we have been for ever, which is why I need you to trust me and tell me where all this is heading.'

He's right – I haven't told him the main reason I'm here. So far, I've introduced him to nearly everyone I've been watching except the Raffertys. But there's a world of difference between installing a birdhouse at Tall Pines and delivering gifts to a five-year-old boy without his parents' knowledge. Besides, revealing my secret-squirrel relationship with Ollie Rafferty would reveal my conviction for child abduction – a difficult subject for any new couple to tackle successfully.

Unbidden, the same image forms in my head as last week: me and Louis driving a coastal road in bright sunlight, Ollie Rafferty sitting behind us.

I flinch. That's *not* my end goal, here. Nor would I ever consider it.

You've already considered it.

Twice.

282

'What's wrong?' Louis asks. 'You were shaking your head.'

'I was?'

He reaches behind him and deposits a gift-paper-wrapped parcel in my lap.

'What's this?'

'For you,' he says, pulling into traffic. 'Open it.'

Supporting Little Guy one-handed, I rip away the paper. It's dark in here without the interior light on, but the street-lamps reveal what looks like a leather vanity case. I unzip it and peer inside – and see a collection of expensive-looking cosmetics.

'Don't get me wrong,' Louis says. 'I'm not saying you don't rock the cyberpunk look. Or the tooth-fairy look. But they felt more like disguises than fashion choices. You seemed to like the dress. I figured you might like those, too.'

'Wow,' I say. 'Thanks. How did you know?'

I pull a glass bottle from the case. Nail polish, I think. In the orange glow of the streetlamps I can't tell the colour, but I can read the label: canary yellow.

'Know what?' Louis asks.

'That it's my birthday.'

He glances over. 'Today's your birthday?'

'Same day every year.'

'You're kidding me.'

'Nope.'

'I wish you'd told me beforehand.'

'Why?'

He jerks a thumb over his shoulder. 'I wouldn't have brought him.'

SIXTY-THREE

When I turn my head, I notice our passenger. He's sitting on the rear bench seat, hands zip-tied to his belt. A white cotton pillowcase covers his head. Considering his situation, he seems remarkably calm.

'Who's that?' I ask, cradling Little Guy, but I can already guess his identity. I recall last week's visit to Chaplin Row; the porch light we fixed at Lovesick Linda's; the confrontation we witnessed minutes later; and Linda, touching her bloodied mouth in the aftermath, as her TV and microwave disappeared down the street. I recall Louis's question and my answer:

If you want us to fix this, just say the word.

OK. I want us to fix it.

A week later and here we are: Hugo the Shade, managing director of Sheergen – and Simon Rafferty's closest acquaintance – hooded and handcuffed on the campervan's rear seat.

'Can he hear us?'

Louis shakes his head. 'He's wearing headphones. Right now he's about halfway through the *Frozen* soundtrack.'

I spot the music player clipped to Hugo's shirt – and the lead snaking under the pillowcase. 'Why's he just sitting there like that?'

'Maybe he's reassessing his position in the food chain. Then again, maybe he just likes the music.'

It's deeply inappropriate, but I can't help laughing. Weird, how, despite last night's dream, the Deevis Farm news reports and the violence at the Ferryman, I again feel so euphoric – and so invincible. Is it because of what I witnessed in the hallway of my building – Hazel's rejection of Edward Gropey-Hands? Or is it simply that I'm here with Louis? Perhaps it's because I have company on my birthday, for the first time in far too long. Perhaps it's all those things combined.

I switch on the overhead light and sort through the vanity case for a lipstick, tilting the rear-view mirror before applying it. The colour is called *Outrageous*. Right now, that feels appropriate.

'So,' Louis says. 'How many years on planet Earth are we celebrating?'

'Twenty-three. Or maybe twenty-four.'

'You don't know?'

I think about it for a moment, puckering my lips. 'Twenty-three.'

'Happy twenty-third birthday.'

'Thank you very much.'

'That colour looks good on you.'

'It does?'

'I knew it would.'

'What's our plan for the Shade?'

'You don't think the *Frozen* soundtrack's enough?'

'I *like* the *Frozen* soundtrack.'

'You do?'

'Let it go.'

I glance over, eyebrow raised, but Louis shows no appreciation for my comic genius. Damn it – the gag wasn't bad, either. Still, it helps settle my nerves. Because this is a whole new level of escalation.

I twist around in my seat for another glimpse at Hugo. He seems so placid, so *compliant*. Hard to believe it's the same guy I've watched abuse Linda. A few times, I've seen him abuse Nadia Rafferty, too. Not that I cared quite as much about that.

Looking through my side window, I realize we're passing the drive-thru. I think about what happened on our last visit: Lost Travis screaming with joy when I showed him Little Guy – and Whiplash Becky sinking her nails into his flesh.

'We'll get to her,' Louis says, as if reading my thoughts. 'We'll get to them all.'

I nod, replacing the lipstick. But of all those I watch, only the Raffertys are left.

This is a small town – we can't keep intervening the way we have been for ever, which is why I need you to trust me and tell me where all this is heading.

We're climbing, now, in a clockwise spiral around Pincher's Mount. When the road forks, we take the steeper route. Soon, we're crunching across Rycroft Hollow's gravel car park.

Sunday night, and the place is deserted. Louis swings into a spot beneath the trees and kills the lights. Darkness settles over us.

On the radio, Sam Cooke starts singing 'Bring It On Home To Me'. I'm half tempted to ask Louis to re-create our dancefloor from ten days ago. Maybe my coordination has improved since then.

Abruptly, something in my brain misfires. Scent explodes in my nose: Sharpie ink, blood-wet granite, smoke. My head lolls. Despite the darkness, images flash before my eyes. I see azure sky. Razor blades glinting on water. A wooden sign, its paint peeling like skin.

'Mercy? *Mercy.*'

Someone is touching me, shaking me. I hear Sam Cooke's voice, but the hands can't be his.

I jerk upright. The world rushes back. I'm in the camper-van's passenger seat. Louis's eyes are twin green pinpricks.

'OK?' he asks.

'I, uh . . .'

'Where'd you go?'

Digging through the vanity case, I find the bottle of nail polish, twist off the cap and inhale. The acetone flushes my head of rogue scents. No more Sharpie ink or blood-wet granite. No more smoke. On the radio, Marvin Gaye begins to sing 'Ain't That Peculiar'.

He's right. It is.

I am.

'Mercy, seriously. What just happened?'

'Delayed reaction,' I say. 'From the kiss.'

I force a smile, but I'm fooling no one, least of all Louis.

'Listen,' he says. 'This might not be the time. But do you remember what I asked you a while back? Whether, if we could fix your phobia, you'd want that?'

'Uh-huh.'

'You said you'd bite my hand off.'

'I said fingers, I think. No way could I manage a whole hand.'

Louis isn't smiling. 'You still feel like that?'

'Why?'

'Because,' he says, 'until you resolve it, you're trapped in Cranner's Ford.'

'I got here, didn't I?'

'So you'd leave?'

I stare at him. 'You mean, move away?'

'Think about it. If you had the freedom to go anywhere, where would you choose?'

A coastal road, bright sunshine. Ollie Rafferty, smiling at us from the back seat.

I laugh. I can't help it. Because that's not what I want, not even close. Because I tried it once, and it brought nothing but pain. And because if I had the freedom to go anywhere, I'd stay right where I am. 'What's wrong with here?'

'Nothing. But the world's a lot bigger than this town. Full of places we could explore, if we figured out how. That beach you created in your living room – imagine switching it for the real thing. Imagine showing Little Guy the sea.'

Hauling out my Bubblicious, I stuff my mouth with gum. I masticate nosily, listening to Marvin Gaye's lyrics.

Louis ducks his head, peering through the windscreen at the night. I follow his gaze, but all I see is black. 'What is it?'

'Nothing,' he says. 'Just a fox, I think.'

'Should we talk about this?'

Pursing his lips, he pulls his key from the ignition. 'Let's deal with dickhead first.'

SIXTY-FOUR

Dickhead, it turns out, isn't as compliant as I first thought.

The problems start soon after we get him outside. Louis reaches under the pillowcase and retrieves the headphones and music player. I wonder how far Hugo got through the *Frozen* soundtrack. His foot wasn't tapping, so he couldn't have reached 'Love Is An Open Door'.

Delving back under the pillowcase, Louis rips away a strip of duct tape.

'Ow. *Fuck* you,' Hugo hisses.

I'm guessing it hurt like hell. Maybe even more than Linda's mouth after he slapped it. As Louis tosses the headphones into the van, Hugo cocks his head. He's hunting for clues, I realize – using his ears and nose to try and identify his location. He'll hear the wind in the trees. He'll smell the dusty gravel and crisped grass. He'll notice the absence of traffic noise – the sound of a dog barking somewhere far below us. He'll work out that he's far from help.

Then again, perhaps he won't.

'*HELP!*' Hugo yells. '*SOMEONE CALL THE POLICE! I'VE BEEN ABDUCTED! HELP ME!*'

He twists left and right, anticipating a reaction. When none comes, he stops, cocks his head again, listens.

It's a weird display. Like watching a blind chicken that's just smelled a fox. I look at Louis. Louis looks at Hugo. 'Better?' he asks. 'Got it off your chest? Because—'

'*HELP! THEY'RE ABDUCTING ME!*'

'OK, look,' Louis says. 'This is getting—'

'*THEY'RE HOLDING ME AGAINST MY WILL! CALL THE P—*'

Louis punches him, hard, in the face.

Hugo staggers backwards. His head cracks against the campervan's side window.

'Consider that a warning,' Louis says. 'Ripped straight from the Hugo Jepp playbook. If you want to scream and shout, fine, but at least warn us first. Because there's no one else around to hear it.'

Hugo twists towards the sound of Louis's voice. 'You are so *fucked*. When this is over, I'm going to—'

Louis's second punch bursts his nose. Blood soaks through the pillowcase fabric, creating an instant Rorschach blot. I see two pigeons copulating. Or an old lady eating chips.

Hugo chokes on blood, splutters through it.

'In case you were in any doubt,' Louis says, 'that really does define the parameters of our relationship. So be a good boy, Hugo, and keep your good looks.'

Hugo starts to respond, thinks better of it – but something about his body language worries me. He doesn't seem cowed. Far from it. More like he's biding his time.

'Better,' Louis says, grabbing a bag from the van. If he's noticed Hugo's defiance, he shows no sign. 'Now, I'm going to tell you where to walk, and you're going to obey. Watch your feet. The ground's uneven.'

We cross the car park and climb the path through the trees. Hugo turns once or twice, spitting blood from beneath his hood. I step out of the way just in time.

Oddly, the violence I just witnessed barely troubles me. This is nothing like last night's incident at the Ferryman. When I recall Hugo bloodying Linda's mouth, then *blaming* her for what he did, adrenalin courses through me. I want him to taste what it's like to be a victim, for once. I want to scare him so badly he'll never go near Linda again.

'This is her work, isn't it?' he says as we climb. 'Short-sighted bitch. I'm *so* looking forward to discussing it with her. What a joke.'

Louis prods him in the back. Clear of the trees, the moon lights our way. We pass the viewing platform, where I introduced Louis to Edward Gropey-Hands, and begin our southerly ascent. Five minutes later, Hugo and I are breathing hard.

'Pincher's Mount,' he says. 'That's where we are, isn't it? Going up Pincher's, or maybe Old Cobb.' He trips over a stone, recovers. 'Definitely Pincher's – Old Cobb's not as steep. Whatever you're planning, it's not going to work.'

Hearing that, I feel a twinge of doubt. Because what if he's right? What if our intervention makes Linda's situation worse?

Ahead, Hugo's pace begins to slow. He's panting now. Climbing while hooded and bound must be hard work. I'm struggling, too. Not only with my fitness but with my balance.

'I just realized,' Hugo says. 'There's two of you – I can tell by the sound of your feet. Jeez, how fricking *brave* you are.'

Jeez, I wish he would *just shut up*. Above me I see the summit – and its moonlit folly rising into the night.

Without warning, the ground swings upright. My hands take the impact, then my chest. The breath whooshes from my lungs.

Louis crouches at my side. He waits for me to recover before helping me to my feet. I cling to him, limpet-tight. My palms are buzzing. Sharp stones have drawn blood.

'Serves you right, twat,' Hugo says.

Ugh, Linda. What did you ever see in him?

'Sorry,' I mutter to Louis. 'Talk about bad timing.'

'Don't be,' he says. 'We'll figure it out.'

And somehow, twenty minutes later, we find ourselves – one walking, one limping, one blind and bound – at the summit of Pincher's Mount. Louis guides me to the base of the Starcase, where I sit near the entrance steps, my back resting against stone. Hugo stands a short distance away, steadily regaining his breath.

It's a fine view. Really, I'd forgotten just *how* fine. Beyond the darkness surrounding Cranner's Ford I can see lights from other towns; little clusters of humanity; proof of a larger whole.

I think of the night I followed Raj the Reborn up here: how he broke into the Starcase through the servants' door; how he stood on the parapet and challenged himself to jump. I shared that story with Louis, the evening we removed the graffiti from Raj's wall. Clearly, he remembered it. Clearly, he intends to scare Hugo very badly indeed.

I no longer feel as euphoric as I did, nor as invincible. I don't want to be up here with the man I call the Shade. I want to be back in the campervan, cuddling Little Guy and pretending the world's a better place.

The trouble is, it isn't. One thing I've learned, these last few weeks, is that small acts of kindness are far less effect-ive than fear. Louis's interventions *work*.

It's a hard lesson. Being at the sharp end like this isn't pleasant, but sometimes – as Louis said, the night Hugo carted off Linda's TV – you have to tackle a situation head on.

He disappears around the building. One hand braced against the stonework, I struggle up. The world sways, then stabilizes. A minute later, Louis reappears. From his bag he removes a coil of rope. He ties one end to Hugo's belt.

'Did you get it open?' I ask.

'Yeah.'

'I'm coming up there with you.'

'Mercy, you can hardly—'

'I'm coming. I can't expect you to do this alone. I don't want you to.'

He glances at Hugo. 'It won't be pretty. I'm going to put the frighteners on this guy like he never imagined.'

'I know. I'm ready.' To prove it, I offer him a grin. 'Life can't always be birdhouses and porch lights.'

Louis licks his lips. He leans forward, kisses me. Then he nods. 'OK, then, Night Eyes. Let's do this.'

SIXTY-FIVE

Inside the Starcase, stone steps rise clockwise around a central chamber so tall it swallows my torch beam.

I go first. Louis follows. Hugo, attached to Louis's rope, brings up the rear. Only a thin metal guardrail protects us from the deepening chasm to our right.

The higher we climb, the sicker I feel. My thighs burn. Sweat rolls down my back. Below me I hear Hugo cursing and gasping. The sound of our scraping feet echoes through the tower.

I know from Wikipedia that two hundred and fifty-six steps separate the Starcase's viewing platform from the ground. Several times I have to stop, catch my breath, and my courage.

At the top, I expect to find a hatch. Instead, there's a wooden door, unlocked. I open it and step out, utterly unprepared for what greets me.

The viewing platform is smaller than a boxing ring, its protective stone parapet barely above knee height. The sky is *everywhere*, rolling away in all directions, unfathomable in its vastness. I see stars too numerous to count; the gleam of Jupiter and Venus; the dusky glow of Mars. In the east, the moon's half-closed eye keeps watch. I can't see any part of Pincher's Mount, below us. It feels like we're suspended in space.

My breath abandons me, spiralling into the night. The sweat on my back chills my skin. I clench my teeth, my fists. Is the tower swaying beneath my feet? Or is my balance going again? I want to crouch near the door, but there's no room – I need to let the other two pass.

Louis emerges, then Hugo. Immediately, the platform feels far too small – as if the slightest misstep could send all three of us plummeting over the edge.

'Well,' Hugo sneers. 'I guess we're at the top. Pincher's Starcase. How's the view?'

I scowl at him, even though he can't see. His fearlessness is infuriating, beyond baffling. Then it strikes me – a man who built a career in wind turbines might not be that afraid of heights.

Louis leads Hugo to the edge, then retreats. 'Here, take this,' he says, passing me the rope. Then he examines me more closely. 'You OK?'

I nod.

'Sure?'

I swallow. Nod again.

'You still want to go through with it?'

Third nod. Because we no longer have any choice. We're here, and it's too late to back out. Hugo's not stupid. Thanks to what Louis said after punching him, he's already guessed what this is about. He's wrong about Linda's involvement, but we'll probably never convince him.

Only now am I starting to grasp the depth of our dilemma. By involving ourselves in Linda's situation, we've made her safety our responsibility. If Hugo remains defiant, our only option is to escalate. So far – despite being bound, blindfolded and beaten, and dragged to the top of Pincher's Starcase – he hasn't yielded.

What if he's unbreakable? Fear might be more effective than kindness, but not if Hugo is fearless. How do we escalate then?

The moon bobs, as if tossed by an angry sea. The night swarms around me. 'I feel like I'm losing it,' I mutter. 'Is this thing moving?'

Louis kisses my cheek, shakes his head. 'You're doing great. Just stay here, by the door. Anchor yourself. OK?'

'You're kidding me, a fricking *woman*?' Hugo shouts. 'Jesus Christ, is this some kind of psychotic *date* night?'

My hearing goes: silence in my left ear, high-pitched whining in my right. Louis turns away from me, crossing the platform to Hugo's side. I see his lips moving, but I can't hear what he says. He grabs Hugo in a bear hug and lifts him on to the parapet. Then he steps up alongside.

My stomach yawns. My vertigo threatens to engulf me. I focus on Louis and Hugo, side by side against the night, one of them bound and anchored by my rope, one of them not. I feel the drop even if I can't see it: fifty metres of empty space.

Louis continues to talk. I watch as if through a vacuum. No sound except the shrilling inside my head. I press my back against the doorpost and slide down it.

When Louis stops speaking, Hugo cups his palms. It looks like a gesture of supplication, but I soon see its real purpose. Louis takes a rock from his pocket and places it in Hugo's hands. Hugo holds it for a moment, then opens his fingers and lets it fall.

The pair stand motionless, listening. I don't hear the rock strike the summit far below us, but I can identify from their reactions when it does – around three seconds of free-fall before impact.

Hugo tilts his head as Louis talks. He's building another map, I realize. The dropped rock told him what's in front of him. Now, he's focusing on Louis's voice and plotting his position.

I thump my right ear, try to restore my hearing. All my Night People instincts are screaming, but I'm deaf to what they're saying. I know this is an important moment – that we've reached a crisis point from which many possible futures branch.

In the end, I'm not sure who chooses the path. It all happens too quickly to be sure. I see Louis put his hand on Hugo's shoulder. I see Hugo twist violently towards him. There's movement, a coming together, a shocking and suicidal uncoupling. The world smears, wet paint across canvas. One moment, two men are on the parapet. Then, somehow, there are none.

SIXTY-SIX

Sunday evening, Simon phones from Italy to say he's been delayed. He apologizes, promising to return home on Monday night.

Nadia accepts the news with a stoicism she doesn't feel while offering assurances she doesn't mean. Bad enough that she's spent the last three nights alone. To have her isolation extended, just as she thought it was over, distresses her more than she wants to admit.

Once Ollie's in bed, Nadia checks the security interface and ensures that all the cameras are recording and the exterior alarms are activated. Then she decamps to the cinema room. Its floor-to-ceiling windows are the only ones in the house fitted with smart glass. At the flick of a switch, their liquid crystal cores form an impenetrable barrier.

The activated glass doesn't lift Nadia's paranoia, only heightens it. Although she can access the exterior camera feeds via her phone, she still feels blind. Eventually, she switches off the glass and sits in darkness, looking out at the night. Finally, she phones Konstantin.

He arrives within the hour. Nadia deactivates the alarms and leads him to the kitchen, where all the lights are blazing. She has no idea if Keira Greenaway is watching, but if she is, Nadia wants her to see this – because whatever the identity of Keira's conspirator, he's a *fucking minnow* compared to Konstantin Tapia; an arrogant and ineffectual child.

When she offers Konstantin a drink, he requests black coffee. She makes two espressos and carries them outside to a patio table beside the pool.

It's a clear evening. The moon is out, along with all the planets. Towering over Arcadia Heights, Pincher's Mount is a black mass against indigo sky. At its summit, the Starcase's solitary finger points heavenward.

Nadia's relief at Konstantin's presence doesn't last. He seems different tonight, restless. Several times, drinking her coffee, she catches his eyes roving over her skin. Foolish of her not to have changed her outfit. However she chooses to sit, her wrap skirt falls open at her knees.

Konstantin places a paper bag on the patio table. From it he takes a shrivelled black fruit and crunches it into flakes.

'How's your hotel?' she asks.

'More than adequate. Thank you for arranging it.'

When his gaze flickers to the shadows beyond the pool, Nadia's skin crawls. He must sense her unease, because he turns back to her and says, 'It's as if you've become Keira Greenaway's foil.'

'What do you mean by that?'

'You've grown as scared of the dark as she is of the light. It's sad to see.'

'I'm not scared,' Nadia lies. She points out the new security cameras, reels off the system's features. The longer she talks, the more confident she feels.

'A few cameras,' Konstantin says. 'To make you famous, once you're dead. Is it on? Right now?'

'No. Because you're here.'

'Where's the boy?'

'Upstairs. Sleeping.'

'If someone comes through the front door—'

'We'd hear them.'

'We would?'

Nadia swallows. 'The security company monitors the alarm system. If it's triggered, they call the police.'

'And how long do they wait – to see if it's a false alarm?'

'Under a minute.'

'Did they tell you the average response time to a reported burglar alarm around here? Do the police even respond at all?'

'The security company send their own people, too.'

'From how far away, Nadia? And who exactly shows up? How old are they? How fat? Are they armed with anything more than a torch and a cheese sandwich? I presume you asked all that?'

She hadn't.

Konstantin shakes his head. Scrunching up his paper bag, he pockets it and stands.

Nadia tenses. 'Where are you going?'

'It's late.'

'Please,' she says, hating the desperation in her voice. 'You've made your point. We're not safe. Simon's back tomorrow, but tonight it's just me and Ollie. Don't leave us here on our own.'

Konstantin breathes. His gaze drops to her split skirt and bare legs before returning to her face. Nadia's stomach rolls, but she doesn't break eye contact.

When he takes out a cigar rather than the cigarettes she was expecting, her spine arches.

SIXTY-SEVEN

How long the beat lasts – between Louis and Hugo's plummet from the ledge and my reaction to it – I can't say. It feels like a hundred years, a thousand. In reality, it's probably fractions of a second.

The world resumes. My ears roar with equalizing pressure. I hear the beginnings of a scream. I feel sudden, burning pain. My neurons fire, stitching meaning from chaos. I realize the rope is tearing through my hands, stripping my palms of skin. Another hundred years pass, or perhaps another microsecond. There's no time for thought. Only instinct.

My forearms bulge. My fists clench. An instant later my arms are yanked from their sockets – or so it feels. I slide across the flagstones, elbows knocking, knees cracking, head empty of anything except the rope and my grip on it, because the alternatives are simply too monstrous.

When I crash into the base of the parapet, my progress is instantly arrested. And yet there's confusion there, too. Because instead of hard stone I hit something yielding: a human torso and limbs. My vision clears and I see a face, inches from my own – *Louis's* face, impossible though that seems.

I choke, gasp for breath. I nearly lost him, and somehow I didn't. Two men fell from the parapet – one on either side.

The pain in my hands is extraordinary, the rope a heated wire in my flesh. My fists are trembling, my forearms and my shoulders. The tendons in my neck bunch with effort.

'I've got him!' I scream. 'Don't let me lose him!'

Louis's gaze drops to my hands. In his eyes I see a hardening. When he looks at me again his expression is different, as if he wishes I'd allowed Hugo to fall, but what follows is even worse, because he shakes his head and says, 'You haven't, Mercy. He's gone.'

When I look down I see he's right: my fists are clenched tight, but there's no rope.

I moan. It can't be.

My fingers uncurl. I stare at my ruined palms, unable to process the enormity of what's just happened. I look at the top of the parapet, above us.

He was right there.

He was *right there*.

'I'm going to be sick.'

'*No.*' Louis hauls me up, leads me back towards the door. 'You're not. Not here. You can't, Mercy.'

With a jolt, I realize why. I stare at him, nod. Right now, self-preservation is the last of my priorities, but I've no right to endanger Louis. Licking my lips, working up some moisture, I say, 'I can't go near the edge. Can you look? Can you check?'

Louis releases me. He returns to the parapet, leans out. He's silent for a moment. Then he turns to me. 'He's down there.'

The world is a tunnel. 'I killed him.'

'No.'

'I let him go.'

Louis's silence is all the confirmation I need: the very worst kind of indictment. Abruptly, I recall his instructions as he passed me the rope: *Here, take this. Anchor yourself.*

At the time, I didn't appreciate what he meant. But that's not his fault. I insisted on coming up here. I held the rope. I let go of it. The evidence of my failure is branded into my skin.

I'm not sure how we descend the tower's two hundred and fifty-six steps. Perhaps Louis carries me. Perhaps I walk. Outside, close to the entrance, I see the human wreckage that was Hugo Jepp. I force myself to look, to confront the truth of what I did.

Louis pulls a torch and a knife from his pocket and goes over. When he returns, he's carrying the rope, the burst zip-ties, the pillowcase. No more Rorschach blot – the entire fabric is soaked.

'We can't leave him.'

'We can't take him,' he says. 'I can make this look like a suicide, I think. Start walking. I'll catch up.'

'I don't want to be alone.'

'Mercy,' he says, tucking the campervan keys into my pocket. 'Start walking.' There's patience in his voice – certainly more than I deserve – but there's also an edge.

And so I do as Louis asks, stumbling down Pincher's Mount into a world changed once again from what it was.

Behind me I leave a dead man, a life taken. This wasn't meant to happen. This was meant to be a new start.

Later, I don't know how much later, I find myself at the summit of Old Cobb, on the opposite side of town. On the radio, Bob Dylan is singing 'Don't Think Twice, It's All Right'.

Little Guy, his belly full of warm milk, is curled up on the front seat. I'm in the back with Louis, holding out my palms as he bathes and disinfects them. The disinfectant is a screaming obscenity in my flesh, but I don't complain, don't pull back. Really, a little pain is the least I can shoulder.

'Listen to me,' Louis says as he bandages my hands. 'You're in shock. That's natural. But you need to understand one thing: you didn't kill him. Hugo knew where he was. Doing what he did was insane, but that was his choice, not yours. He rolled the dice on his life and mine. It could've been me at the base of that tower. The universe chose otherwise.

'I don't use bad language often, but you know what, Mercy? *Fuck* that guy. Let me ask you something: is Linda's life going to be better or worse without him in it?'

I know where Louis is going with this, but I can't bring myself to answer.

'Is what just happened a loss for the world or a benefit?' he presses. 'Is it a loss for the women Hugo might have met next? Or did they just dodge a bullet? *I* know the answer – and, deep down, so do you. So fuck that guy. Say it.'

I laugh, purely from shock.

'Say it, Mercy.'

'I don't—'

'*Say* it.'

305

'Fuck that guy.'

The words feel like a foreign language, foul in my mouth. But something changes as I say them.

Louis kisses me. I'm so surprised that I kiss him right back. Suddenly, his closeness is all that matters. His lips on mine. His touch and his feel and his heat.

We bump around the campervan's cramped interior, as awkward as we are hungry. I can't use my hands, can't undress myself, but I can give myself up to sensation. We just encountered death, and this is an affirmation of life, a rejection of our mortality.

Afterwards, we climb into the front seats and sit a while in silence. Little Guy snuggles in my lap. I stroke him with the backs of my fingers. 'How long before someone finds him, do you think?'

'Some time after sunrise, probably. A dog walker or a hill runner. We'll know soon enough.'

'I hate thinking of him up there all alone.'

'Then don't.'

My scalp shrinks. I sneak a glance. Did Louis mean to sound so short, just then? Staring at my bandaged hands, I ask, 'Where do we go from here?'

'Honestly, Mercy? I think that depends on you.'

I was right – his mood has definitely changed. And quickly, too. 'What do you mean?'

Louis puts his hands on the steering wheel, rolls his wrists. 'Do you know how many questions you've asked about my life since we first met? Virtually none. Why *is* that, Mercy? At the start, I presumed you weren't interested. Now, I'm starting to think it's because you don't like talking about the past – and asking about mine might naturally lead to questions about yours.

'You've told me nothing about why you're here in Cranner's Ford. Nor why you seem so frightened of being discovered. I don't know where you were before, where you grew up. About the only thing you *have* shared is that you've lived the last five years without daylight – which is, frankly, insane.'

I feel his gaze, but I don't meet it.

'I haven't pushed you,' Louis says. 'I'd hoped, given time, you'd open up. But you haven't. Before tonight, I could afford to wait. Now, I don't think I can. This life you're living isn't sustainable. Really, it doesn't seem much of a life at all. Darkness without light – that's no way to live. Honesty's the best policy – or so you keep saying. It's time to be honest, Mercy. With me.'

I listen to Louis's words in silence, my cheeks flushing with heat. I can't escape his gaze. Nor can I hide from his questions – and yet I can't answer them. I knew this confrontation was coming. I just didn't expect it tonight. It's too much. All of this is too much.

'Take me home,' I mutter. 'I can't do this. I'm sorry.'

Louis stares at me a moment longer. Then, shaking his head, he starts the engine.

We drive down Old Cobb in silence. I twist towards the side window, hiding my distress. My tears aren't for me but for Hugo Jepp; and for everyone who has ever suffered because of something I did.

When we pull up outside my flat, Louis keeps the engine running. He makes no move to kiss me. Understandable, really. What happens now is up to me alone.

'Wait here,' I tell him, climbing out. Inside my flat, I carry Little Guy through to the kitchen. Back in the living room, I go to my bookcase. Am I really going to do this?

Yes, I really am.

But if I think about it too much, I'll lose my courage, so I retrieve what I need and head back outside. When I tap on Louis's side window, he rolls it down.

'Here,' I say, handing him my scrapbook. 'This is my story. I'm sorry I didn't tell you sooner. I guess I didn't know how. But you're right – it's time to be honest. If you want to see me afterwards, you know where I am. And if you don't . . .'

I shrug. I can't finish that sentence. I guess there's no need.

Louis takes the scrapbook with a solemnity I didn't expect. He places it beside him with all the care of a historian handling an ancient text.

Head bowed, I retreat inside. By the time I reach the window, Louis's campervan has disappeared.

SIXTY-EIGHT

The first thing I do is feed Little Guy. With bandaged hands, it's not easy. Afterwards, I check the news. There's nothing yet about Hugo, but joining the Deevis Farm story, locally, is a piece about last night's violence at the Ferryman. White Knuckle Wanda suffered a skull fracture, an orbital fracture, a broken nose, three cracked ribs. She also lost six teeth. The sole positive is that there's no mention of a brain injury. In the accompanying photo, credited to Wanda's Facebook and showing her in a hospital bed, she's barely recognizable.

At 9 a.m. I see something new – a BREAKING banner on the *Cranner's Ford Gazette* site, along with a one-liner: BODY FOUND AT BEAUTY SPOT. MORE TO FOLLOW.

I take myself to the toilet and vomit. It's real now. Not that it ever wasn't – but suddenly it's inescapable. I wash out my mouth and swallow some painkillers. Then I stumble back to my laptop. I spend the next hour refreshing the page. When, finally, it changes, I see a library shot of Pincher's Mount. Another image shows two police cars at Rycroft Hollow, along with an officer putting out bollards. The story has been updated, the Starcase revealed as the location. So far, there's no mention of suicide or foul play.

At 11 a.m., the story develops further. Hugo isn't named, but he's described as a local man. A police spokesman is quoted: 'Formal identification has not taken place and investigations are ongoing.' I wonder how long the news will take to reach Lovesick Linda. I wonder how she'll react.

Early afternoon, I take more painkillers, Then I crawl into bed and sleep. I dream of a red baby – and a lake house reeking of death. I dream of Louis flipping the pages of a scrapbook, his hands growing slick with blood. I dream of a man with zip-tied hands falling through endless night.

I wake three hours later – nauseous, unrested, too frightened to check the news. The air in my bedroom is so heavy I can barely breathe, but I can't escape the flat. Daylight keeps me prisoner.

Instead I eat, throw up again, work up the courage to go back online. How quickly do the police contact a victim's next of kin? How quickly do they arrange identification and release details to the press? Answer, in this case: longer than twelve hours.

I wonder how far through the process they've got. I wonder how many people are grieving because of what I did. Linda might have divorced Hugo, but I bet someone else loved him. A mother, a father. A sibling.

The sun sets at eight thirty. An hour or so later, it's fully dark. At last it's safe to grab some air. On my workbench sit the geraniums from the night of my puncture. I pack them into my cargo bag with my tools, my bear spray and my torch. Then, swallowing yet more painkillers, I leave the flat.

Despite the humidity, it's a relief to be outside. Steering my Jorvik with bandaged hands is tricky, but I manage. I ride west along Copper Beech Lane to Home Alone Jacob's.

I carry the plants along an ungated driveway to the back garden. Here, the land recedes sharply, offering views across a wooded valley. A large deck supported by stilts extends from the rear of the house.

I kneel in front of a flowerbed. With my trowel, I begin to dig.

After Cold Hand Carl burgled the place, eight months ago, the *Cranner's Ford Gazette* reported what was stolen. It also described Harriet, Jacob's late wife. Before her passing, she'd been a keen horticulturist. The flowers and shrubs spilling from the terraces are all her work.

Since the burglary, Jacob's health has declined. He can't keep up with the maintenance and he can't afford a gardener. I know that upsets him – I've heard him talk to Harriet about it, the nights he appears on the deck. For the past seven months, I've secretly been helping him out.

I started off repairing the damage Carl caused when he visited. But the more time I spent here, the more I wanted to preserve what Harriet had created.

Now, grabbing a geranium, I lower it into the hole. Really, it's too late in the season for these little guys. Back when I started growing them, I was pretty clueless. At least, for a while, they'll add some colour. It takes me twenty minutes to complete the row.

I'm gathering up my tools when a door bangs open, somewhere above me. I stiffen, but the moon doesn't touch this patch of garden. There's little chance I'll be spotted from the house.

The suspended deck creaks. Jacob appears at the rail. For a long time our solitude united us, but then I found Louis – and Jacob is still alone.

'I was going through our old photos,' the old man says. 'Some of them got a bit damp in the back room. Bloody careless of me. I've rescued a lot, but the ones we took in Venice are past saving. You remember that trip? You remember buying this?'

Jacob digs in his pocket. He holds something up to the stars. 'Your Murano glass frog. God, I used to hate this thing. These days, I carry it everywhere.'

His laugh is half a sob. He puts the frog back in his pocket. 'I'm still alive, H. God only knows why. I don't want to be.'

My throat grows tight. His desolation is hard to hear. Bidding him a silent farewell, I creep up the slope to the drive. I wonder if I'll ever see him again.

Tall Pines is my next stop. On arrival, I spot a night carer at the reception desk. I wait twenty minutes until she leaves for a cigarette.

Now's my chance. Breaking cover, I cross the drive. The building's glass doors swish open at my approach. Inside, the air smells of citrus floor cleaner.

Instinct dictates my path. I follow a corridor, come to a door, try the handle, confirm it's unlocked. I step into darkness, wait for my eyes to adjust. Louis was right. The security here is a joke.

There's the bed. In it, asleep, lies William. It's weird, seeing him up close. On the far wall I see his framed medals.

This man.

If not for him, the man my sister married wouldn't

exist. I wouldn't have kissed Simon in that wine cellar. None of what followed would have happened.

I turn on the lamp beside the bed. This close, I can see every line on William's face, every pore. I can see the hairs inside his nose, the liver spots on his scalp. I can see his swollen knuckles, his yellowed nails.

Of course, I can't blame William. He had no hand in any of this. In a way, stuck here with no visits from his family, he's just as much of a victim.

I remain at his bedside a while longer. Then I place a feather, snipped from my angel wings, on his side table. I want to touch his hand, but that would be an invasion. 'Goodbye, Sidney,' I tell him. Important, if this is a parting, to use his real name.

Turning off the lamp, I retrace my steps to the main entrance. Outside, I climb on my Jorvik and head home. Back inside my flat, I lie on my bed and close my eyes.

I wake to a vibrating phone – and someone rapping on my window. Groggy from sleep, my brain takes a moment to catch up. Then I sit up so fast I overbalance, crashing from the bed to the floor.

There's that rapping again, violent and insistent. I check the time: 3.36 a.m. I think of the skin beneath White Knuckle Wanda's nails; my fingerprints on the food sacks at Deevis Farm; the evidence I may have left at the Starcase.

Am I about to be arrested? I climb off the floor and ease away a corner of my blackout blinds. I see no police vehicles parked on the street.

My phone continues to vibrate. When I check the screen, I see it's Louis. I accept the call and whisper, 'There's someone outside.'

'It's me,' he replies. 'Let me in.'

My relief is short-lived. Because now I have to face him. I pull on a vest and dungaree shorts. In the bathroom, I brush my teeth. When Louis comes inside, I can't read his expression. He doesn't ask how I'm doing. He's carrying the scrapbook, which he places on my workbench.

I hug myself, wait for his verdict.

'I don't know what to say to you,' he tells me. 'Will you come for a drive?'

'Where to?'

'Nowhere. Anywhere. Just a drive.'

Really, it's the least I can offer him.

We travel through streets so quiet it feels like a zombie apocalypse swept through Cranner's Ford while I slept. In the darkness, traffic lights blink secret codes from one junction to another. Soon, we're through Old Town and puttering up Old Cobb.

I can't look at Louis. I stare so hard through the windscreen that for a while I forget to blink. My tears make it look like I'm crying, when really I just feel numb.

We park at the summit and climb out.

'Let's walk,' Louis says.

'Where to?'

'Just down the slope a bit. Somewhere out of sight.'

I nod, traipsing behind him. It's dark, and I stumble, but we don't go far.

'This is good.'

Here on the eastern slope, the sun-crisped grass is tall and full of seed. It tickles my bare legs when I sit. I glance around us, wondering what's special about this spot. Below me I see Cranner's Ford's lights. Above us, an outcrop hides the summit.

Louis kneels beside me, dumping his rucksack. 'Drink?' he asks, retrieving an Evian bottle. When I decline, he spins the cap and takes a long swallow. I clench my teeth, waiting for the verdict I know is coming.

'What I read in that scrapbook,' he says. 'Shocking stuff.'

'Yes.'

'Hard to grasp, really. Not many people would understand. But you know something, Mercy – I think I do.'

When I realize I'm rocking, I force myself to stop.

'You probably shouldn't have come to Cranner's Ford. After what happened in Italy . . . and later, when you took the boy . . .' He sucks in a breath. 'Do you visit them?'

I open my mouth, close it.

'It's OK,' Louis says. 'You don't need to answer. Of course you visit them. All the others you watch – they're just window-dressing. The main focus was always Ollie Rafferty.'

I don't like hearing William the Navigator or Raj the Reborn described as window-dressing. Nor Lovesick Linda or Home Alone Jacob or Laurie. Nor Lost Travis, Roaring Mary, Unproud Tina. They're real people, whose lives I tried to improve.

'Was there ever anything between you and Simon?' Louis asks.

My stomach twists. 'Briefly. Very briefly.'

He nods. 'You came here to kill him.'

I reel away. 'No, I never—'

'You came here to kill him, Mercy, and take Ollie somewhere far away. You just never figured out how.'

I shake my head. I know what he's saying isn't true – I *know* it – but I'm too emotional to speak.

'This has to end, Mercy. Do you see that? I think I love you, but I can't stay here any longer, and nor can you. We need to move on.'

My brain's so scrambled I'm finding his words hard to process. The thought of living in Cranner's Ford without Louis – of returning to my solitary existence – is too agonizing to bear. But there's one thing I know above all else: 'I can't leave.'

'I realize that. I realize you *think* that. But you have no choice.'

'I can't leave.'

Louis takes another drink. 'I asked you, a while back, whether you'd take a magic pill to fix your phobia, if it existed, and you said that you'd bite my fingers off. Do you remember?'

'Yes.'

'Do you trust me?'

'Yes.'

'One hundred per cent?'

'One thousand per cent.'

'Because this magic pill, it's hard to swallow. For a while, you'll hate the person who supplied it.'

'I couldn't hate you.'

'I think you could.'

'Give me the pill.'

'You're sure?'

'A million per cent.'

'It's not a pill, Mercy. The pill's a metaphor.'

'I don't care. I don't care what it is. If it works, I want it. I don't want to be trapped any longer.'

'I told you I might love you. Did that mean anything?'

'Yes.'

'You didn't say it back.'

'I know.' I swallow. 'Louis, I . . . I don't know if I'm capable of love. Not any more. I know that sounds monstrous, but I can't lie. I'm capable of something. I'm capable of *this* – whatever it is we have. I can't promise more. Please, just give me the pill. *Fix* me.'

'OK,' he says. And before I fully realize what's happening, the world has turned upside down and Louis is sitting astride my chest, a club hammer in one hand and a metal stake in the other.

SIXTY-NINE

Monday evening, four days after flying out to Italy, Simon Rafferty arrives home. Nadia, monitoring the touchscreen security interface, watches the front gates swing open to admit her husband's car and feels a momentary lifting of her anxiety.

But when he walks into the house, he barely acknowledges her, going to his office and closing the door. Undeterred, Nadia follows. She finds him leaning over his desk, plugging in his laptop.

'Later,' he says, without glancing up. 'Sorry, but I've got a million problems, every one of them urgent – and in the meantime, Hugo's pulled a disappearing trick.'

'This can't wait until later.'

'*Nadia*,' he snaps.

She can't be bothered to argue. Instead, she lays down one of the photographs she received from Konstantin: Keira Greenaway, on the front steps of the converted townhouse.

Slowly, as if he's an inflatable from which air has begun to leak, Simon sinks on to his chair. For long moments he doesn't speak. Then, gingerly, he plucks the image off his desk. 'Where did you get this?'

'A friend.'

'When was it taken?'

'Last week. You want to know where?'

'Please don't say Cranner's Ford.'

'She's *living* here, Simon. Not only that, she's been visiting our *house*.'

Nadia places Ollie's scratched and battered Tamagotchi on the desk, along with the Little Professor toy and a vintage Major Morgan electronic organ she discovered this morning. 'I found these in his room. He says a fairy gave them to him; that she urged him to keep them secret. It gets worse, by the way. It seems Keira's recruited a helper.'

Simon blinks, slow and dumb. 'A helper?'

'Two weeks ago, in the pharmacy, a guy approached me out of the blue and struck up a conversation.' Beside the toys she places another of Konstantin's photographs. 'Here's the same guy, leaving Keira's flat. Don't tell me it's a coincidence.'

Simon reaches for the image, snatches back his hand. Unsteadily, he gets to his feet. He moves to the window, looks out. 'What did he want?'

'He didn't *want* anything. Other than maybe to check me out.'

'What did you talk about?'

Nadia opens her mouth, hesitates.

'Nadia?'

'Just small talk.'

Simon returns to the desk, stares at the two photographs. Then he takes her arms and kisses her forehead.

'I'm sorry,' he says. 'I should have been here. You've been dealing with all this alone.'

She closes her eyes, just briefly. His embrace has squeezed fresh agony from her right armpit, where last night Konstantin plunged a cigar. 'You're here now.'

'Did you call the police?'

'We always said, if this happened again, that we wouldn't rely on them. That we'd deal with the problem ourselves.'

'This friend. The one who got you the photos . . .'

'His name's Konstantin. I've known him a long time. He can help us, if that's what we choose.'

'Can he—'

A buzzing from the hall intercom interrupts him. Nadia frowns, checks her watch, wonders who could be visiting this late.

'Hugo,' Simon says. But when they step out of the office and check the hallway touchscreen, they don't see Sheergen's managing director.

'What the hell is *she* doing here?' Nadia mutters.

Shaking his head, Simon activates the gates. A minute later, he ushers Hugo's ex-wife into the cinema room.

A bruise is fading on Linda Galloway's jaw. A scab clings to the corner of her mouth. Her eyes are bloodshot. She's greasy with sweat.

'I'm just going to say it,' she whispers. 'Because right now everything's too surreal. I've been driving around for the last hour, wondering who I should tell.'

She pauses, twists her hands in her lap. 'Hugo's dead. He's . . . Earlier, I had to go and identify him. The police are contacting his parents, but you two have been friends a long time. I thought you deserved to know.'

In the ensuing silence, Nadia can hardly breathe. She looks at Simon, sees from his expression that he hasn't processed what he's just heard.

'They found him early this morning,' Linda continues. 'Up on Pincher's Mount. Pretty obvious from the state of him that he'd jumped from the top of the Starcase. Police aren't convinced it was suicide, but *I* know.

'He visited me, two nights ago. Didn't even ring the bell, just left a few parting gifts in the porch. A way of saying sorry, I think. For this.' She points to her damaged face. 'For everything.'

Quietly, she begins to weep. 'You know what's awful? We were married six years and the only thing I'm sad about is the fact I'm not devastated. What does that say about *me*?'

SEVENTY

What follows is a blur.

I know I fight. Certainly once I realize what's happening. I buck my hips, arch my back. I flail at Louis with my bandaged hands. I bite empty air and I spit. I don't want to hurt him. I don't even blame him for what he's doing. I just want to free myself.

But of course it's hopeless. Louis is heavier, stronger, more agile. Add the advantage of surprise and there can only be one winner. He pins me to the grass, knees pressed into my armpits – and in my craziness I think of other women before me, touched by heterochromia and ruined by it. Burned, most of them – although some died through even crueller methods.

As Louis lines up the metal stake, I rain blows on his chest. My bandaged fists bounce off him without effect. When he raises the hammer, I twist my face away. The head rings against metal and the stake goes deep. I gasp for breath. Louis strikes it a second time, a third. For a moment I think he's missed his target, that it's gone straight through my ribcage and into my heart, but then I see it to my left, standing proud of the grass – a monstrous-looking thing of galvanized steel, with an eyelet just below the hammer top.

From somewhere Louis grabs a length of rope. He tethers my wrist. Then he feeds the rope end through the eyelet, securing it with another knot.

'Please,' I moan. 'Not this. Please not this.'

But Louis doesn't respond, hammering in three more stakes. He tethers my other wrist, both ankles. Once he's finished, I'm spreadeagled on the grass. I twist my body, yank against my bindings with all the force I can muster.

Louis strokes my forehead, urges me to stop. 'Easy, Night Eyes. Easy. Those are mooring spikes, used for river barges. That rope has a breaking load of thirty-two kilonewtons. You can't get free, but you'll hurt yourself plenty if you don't relax.'

'Louis,' I gasp. 'You can't. Not this. Please not this, *please*.'

I'm crying, now. Panting for breath. Tears and snot run down my cheeks.

With a handkerchief, Louis cleans my face. Then he reaches into his rucksack and removes another bottle. When he flips the lid, I catch the scent of coconut, or pineapple, or some other crazy thing.

He squirts some of the contents into his hand. With his fingers, he applies it to my face. Now, I place the smell: suntan lotion. When he's done with my face and neck, he starts on my arms. 'I don't know if you've heard of flooding therapy,' he says.

'I've heard of it,' I hiss. 'But it's not done like this. *Never* like this.'

'I know it seems brutal. I know this is going to be hard.

But we don't have much time – and we can't let your phobia slow us down. We need you *whole*, Mercy.'

Louis climbs off my chest. I feel his hands massaging lotion into my knee. He works down to my ankle, back up to my thigh, then switches to the other leg.

I'm staked out on Old Cobb's eastern face. Obvious, now, that it isn't a coincidence. Already, a zombie grey has leached into the sky. When I raise my head and peer down the slope at Cranner's Ford, I see the emergence of roads and parked cars, the beginnings of houses and roofs.

How early is it? I've lost all track. I know the timings of sunset and dawn, and the grades of twilight that separate them. Astronomical dawn begins when the sun is eighteen degrees below the horizon. Nautical dawn arrives once the angle is twelve degrees. Civil dawn arrives at six degrees. At zero degrees, the sun starts to show.

This morning, civil dawn starts at one minute past five. Sunrise will follow thirty-eight minutes later. These are the numbers that rule my life and I know them intimately.

Mercy Lake won't survive daybreak. She'll sizzle and burn just like the girl she replaced. I simply can't let that happen.

'There's something I need to say,' I tell him. 'And you've got to listen. You've got to. I can't leave Cranner's Ford. I know you think I can, but I can't – which means even if this worked, it wouldn't make any difference. I know I said I'd bite your fingers off, but *this* won't fix me, Louis, it'll kill me. You might not believe it, but it's true.'

Louis listens without speaking. He grabs his Evian bottle, twists off the cap, brings it close to my lips. 'Lift your head. Drink.'

'Louis, you don't understand. You—'

'You need to drink, Mercy. Because I'm not staying. This is something you need to face alone.'

Hearing that, I *really* lose it. I grind my teeth, arch my back, thrash left and right. Louis forces my head against the grass, tilting the bottle until water gushes into my mouth. I have no choice but to swallow. I splutter and gulp until it's gone.

He looks at his watch, checks the sky. 'I love you, Mercy Lake,' he says. Then he stands. 'I'll be back in a few hours.'

'No,' I shout. '*No!*'

But Louis is already walking. A minute later, I'm alone.

SEVENTY-ONE

I strain against my bonds until I'm exhausted, until my wrists are raw and bleeding, until my ankles are a mess of flayed skin. And still I cannot tear myself loose.

Around me the world begins to change, the first hints of colour pouring like poison into my surroundings. Even worse, I sense the sun, that excoriating mass, now only a few degrees below the horizon. When its first rays touch my flesh, I'll crisp up, turn to ash.

There are Day People and Night People, and I am absolutely the latter. Five years ago, I counted myself among the former. But while you can change once, you can't go back to what you were. I tried to explain that to Louis, but he wouldn't listen. Maybe because he's Night People too.

Last night I killed a man, at the top of Pincher's Mount. Twenty-four hours later, I'm staked to the town's second summit. Maybe that's karma. Maybe it's the universe balancing the scales.

I can't escape my bonds, and I can't escape the sun. But perhaps I have one last option. I move my head left and right, scrubbing through the grass until I find hard ground.

Closing my eyes, I picture the delicate curve of skull that cups my brain.

I saw that part of me on an X-ray, once, during my long stay in hospital. An *after* shot, not one from before – the image showing an unnatural depression caused by blunt trauma. That injury heralded the arrival of so many different things: vertigo, heterochromia, an abiding fear of daylight.

An ounce more pressure, they said, and my head would have disintegrated, my brain squidged like a slug beneath a boot. Women's skulls are thicker than men's, by an average of five millimetres. That extra half-centimetre might have made all the difference.

If my hands weren't bound, I could reach up and touch the indentation that remains – and the scar tissue over which no hair ever grows. My vulnerable spot. My Achilles heel.

Right now, though, it might save me – at least, it might save me from facing the dawn. A coward's way out, admittedly. Beggars can't be choosers, but they can always be losers, as I've often shown.

Raising my head, I take a last look at Cranner's Ford. I search out my flat, where I've spent so much of this past year. I find Lovesick Linda's maisonette; the Tall Pines nursing home; Laurie's bakery; Wanda's nail bar.

Finally, I turn my gaze to Arcadia Heights; and, above it, the summit of Pincher's Mount, where last night a man lost his life. Then, summoning my courage, I slam my head against the ground.

It doesn't work – but it hurts a lot. My teeth snap together, lacerating my cheek. My brain pogos around my skull.

I pant for breath, tell myself to be brave, lift my head again, higher this time, screw my eyes up tight and . . . *slam*.

SEVENTY-TWO

Monday morning, Tapia drives to a chilli farm ninety miles north of Cranner's Ford, where he spends an hour talking to the proprietor and sampling the produce. He leaves with bags of Trinidad Moruga Scorpions, Naga Vipers and Red Savina Habaneros.

Despite their blistering heat, the chillis are a poor substitute for what he really needs. Yesterday evening at Arcadia Heights, he made Nadia scream for the first time in his life: a lit cigar pressed into her right armpit. He remembers the tendons standing proud in her neck; her angry, outraged tears. But most of all he remembers her scream. Rather than sating his hunger, it supercharged it.

Last night, he dreamed of Nadia and Keira Greenaway together, soaked in fuel and facing each other across the summit of Old Cobb. The experience felt real enough to be prophetic. When Nadia asks him to act – and he's convinced, now, that she will – she'll have no idea what she's unleashing. First, Tapia will hunt down and eliminate Greenaway's friend. Then he'll focus on the main event.

In a town close to the chilli farm, he visits an appointment-only S&M shop, where he buys three pairs of police-issue handcuffs and three sets of leg shackles. From there he heads twenty miles east. In a branch of Mail Boxes Etc. he collects an A4 padded envelope. From a nearby Amazon locker he retrieves a parcel. Tapia's always been a planner. He arranged these deliveries long in advance.

On his return journey, he diverts to a petrol station and fills a jerry can with fuel. His last stop is a DIY store, where he buys six litres of denatured alcohol. The alcohol will burn far cleaner than petrol, producing far less smoke. It'll allow him to see those he sets alight much more clearly through the flames. That is, until their body fat begins to burn. The petrol is for further clean-up once they've passed.

Back in his hotel room, Tapia opens his parcel. The shotgun he removes is German-made, impressively engineered. The accompanying cartridges are a mixture of buckshot and birdshot. Putting the weapon aside, Tapia tears open the envelope. Inside he finds syringes, needles, ampoules of lidocaine.

He hopes no one resists him. He really doesn't want to use the gun. Birdshot aimed at the legs probably won't be lethal, but it'll hurt – a lot. The pain would be a distraction, ruining the intimacy of their shared experience. The lidocaine is his solution if violence is unavoidable. Injected as a spinal block, it'll remove all physical feeling while leaving the mind unaffected. There's another benefit, too: complete paralysis below the waist.

Checking his phone, Tapia sees no missed calls from Nadia; no texts. The campervan is parked at the Seven Crosses campsite, where it's sat for most of the afternoon. Keira Greenaway is no doubt holed up inside her basement flat. It's a moment of calm. A stillness before the hurricane.

With his preparations complete, Tapia shaves his head and takes a shower, turning up the water to its hottest and scrubbing himself raw in the steam. Later, he goes out to eat. Breaking from his usual routine, he chooses bland fare: gnocchi, grilled chicken, buttered greens. Afterwards, he drinks two cups of peppermint tea and returns to his hotel.

The tracking app wakes him at 3.21 a.m. – a notification that the campervan is on the move. When he checks, he sees it heading south. Intrigued, Tapia throws on his clothes. Minutes later, he's trailing the signal through dead streets towards Greenaway's place on Greek Street.

He arrives in time to see the couple emerge from the building, get into the campervan and drive off. Tapia follows them west, through Old Town and up Old Cobb, the very same hill from his dream. As before, he abandons his van at the halfway point, climbing the remaining distance on foot.

Near the top, he hears something unexpected – a female voice, crying out. It's hard to pinpoint in the dark, but then he hears another sound: hammer strikes against metal. Steadily, he creeps towards the source. A few minutes later he spots the man heading back to the summit car park.

Instinct tells Tapia not to follow. Instead, he continues in the direction of the cry. Somewhere above him, the campervan's engine turns over. Ignoring it, he skirts Old Cobb's slope, where he discovers something remarkable.

Keira Greenaway is staked out on the grass, body angled towards the eastern horizon. When Tapia looks in that direction, he sees a low band of orange feathering to purple. The promise of sunrise elates him, but Greenaway doesn't share his enthusiasm. As the sky turns molten, her movements grow frantic. She contorts her body, thrashes against her bonds. Then, in desperation, she starts to slam her skull against the ground. When at last she goes limp, Tapia creeps closer.

Poor little fish. She's rubbed herself raw on those ropes. Her hands are bandaged, evidence of earlier injuries. Urine has soaked the crotch of her dungarees.

Her eyes are open but unfocused. Even in the sun's slanting light he can see they're different colours. Ghost eyes, he's heard them called. They offer the owner a view both of heaven and Earth.

Gently, Tapia trails a finger down her cheek. When he imagines her pale flesh combusting into flame, he can barely contain himself. What revelations will he see in those extraordinary, mismatched eyes, should Nadia give her consent? What secrets will he glimpse?

Convinced now that Keira Greenaway is a gift, a personalized message from the universe, he stays with her for twenty minutes, stroking and soothing, while her eyes are fixed on a different plane. Then he creeps back down the slope to his van.

SEVENTY-THREE

When I open my eyes I'm in a different place – at the beginnings of a different death.

Outside, Italian summer sun scorches the pines and scatters white-hot diamonds on the water. Inside the lake house, death thickens the air.

I blink, scrunch up my face. How cruel to flee a sunrise and wind up here, the worst of all places. Unless this is my purgatory. Unless I'm already dead.

Simon Rafferty never invited me to Italy, nor knew of my plans to fly out. It was meant to be just the three of them – him, Phoebe and Ollie – escaping for a week's solitude. A rented cabin beside a private lake. Luxury disguised as rusticity for a family who could easily afford it.

But that didn't stop me coming. And now I'm standing here gloved in Phoebe's blood, clutching Phoebe's phone.

'*Pronto*,' a man says, in my ear. He sounds so far away. A different galaxy.

Phoebe's handbag lies on the kitchen worktop where I dumped it – a dinky Jimmy Choo creation in vivid green snakeskin, fabulously expensive. The scales shine like emerald pearls.

Simon bought her that bag a few weeks after he kissed me at their housewarming – and after I rejected all his follow-up advances. At first, I thought it was because he felt guilty, a gift for my sister to salve his conscience. I hated myself for doing it, but I checked out that bag online, just to see how much I'd cost him, the monetary value of our kiss. The answer: over £2,000. Perversely flattering, in a way.

That was, until I recalled an incident a few months before, during my work experience placement at Sheergen. He'd caught me flicking through one of those glossy magazines Phoebe had left around his office. I'd started reading it during my lunch break – some dumb article about bags. When Simon leaned over my shoulder, I pointed a few of them out, scoffing at the prices and the idea that anyone would ever pay them.

Phoebe's bag wasn't a guilt purchase. It was a secret message addressed to me: *Look at what I can afford. Look at what you could have had.*

I *couldn't* have had it, of course, even if I'd wanted it, because I'd started watching Simon by then. I'd discovered the extent of his faithlessness – and my status as a bottom feeder in a tank stocked full of angelfish. The night of the party, Simon hadn't felt any attraction. I'd strayed across his path and he'd simply seen something he could take.

The Jimmy Choo bag was a taunt, then, but also a lie. A power play, pure and simple. Because power is what he's about. Power is *all* he's about.

As my snooping on Simon intensified, I uncovered more secrets. Not just his net worth, but also how contemptuously he viewed Phoebe, and how much he'd lose if they divorced. Despite all my research, when he rented the cabin I had no idea what he was planning. I knew he was a narcissist, but I didn't know he was capable of this.

'*Riesci a sentirmi?*'

The voice snaps me back. Beside the Jimmy Choo bag, the baby monitor's lights flicker green, as if the message really *is* coming from deep space.

I'm finding it hard to breathe, hard to think. I cannot grasp the full horror of what I've discovered – and how monumentally my life has just changed.

Through the window I see Phoebe's Mercedes, Simon's rented Porsche Cayenne, the prow of my rowing boat.

'*Aiuto,*' I reply. '*Aiuto.*'

That's when it happens.

Moments after I speak, the baby monitor lights spike. I hear a creak, then a thump, directly overhead. My eyes travel to the ceiling.

Phoebe installed the second baby monitor upstairs, in the room they've been using for Ollie's nursery. It just broadcast my words to the first floor.

Adrenalin tightens my muscles, drains my stomach of blood. My senses push out, interrogating every sound, tremor, vibration.

In my ear, far too loud, I hear: '*Dimmi cosa sta succedendo.*'

But although I can ask for help, I can't translate the response. Nor do I have the time. As I glance through the window at Simon's Cayenne, the baby monitor squeals with static. And then I hear him.

The house shakes. Thunder, on the stairs.

Phoebe's phone slides from my fingers. It hasn't even hit

the floor before I'm running. Out of the kitchen, into the living room, slip-sliding in my sister's blood.

There's Ollie, my red nephew, clapping at his dead mother, oblivious of the future his father just dealt him.

I skid past the sofa, my blood-soaked Converse All Stars carving fresh tramlines across the floor. I reach the porch door, burst through it. Inside the house, I hear the crash of something overturning. Through the glass I see movement. Leaping off the porch, I land in a shower of gravel. Simon Rafferty has an advantage over me in every possible sphere – except raw speed.

I blast past Phoebe's Mercedes and skid round its rear bumper. There's the lake, a bowl of razors. On the shore, my boat. I could push it into the water, leap in, grab the oars – but by then he'd be on me. Instead I swerve right and sprint up the track. Behind me I hear the porch door explode open. All around, birds launch from the trees.

I'm blowing before I've made a hundred metres. This track meanders through forest and open country for a mile before it hits the main road. Back home, I could cover that in six minutes without breaking much of a sweat. In this heat, with the sun beating down, I'll be lucky to do it in twice that.

I accelerate, feet kicking up dust. Despite my exhaustion, I know I've got more in the tank. I can process the horror later, deal with the unremitting tragedy of what I've seen. Right now, I just need to survive, get the word out. If I don't, he'll cover this up, escape justice.

Behind me, an engine turns over, then howls – Simon's Porsche Cayenne. Just like that, he snatches back the advantage. I glance over my shoulder as I run, see the Cayenne charge out of a boiling white cloud. It looks alive, sentient. A snarling, mechanical beast.

The track opens, cutting across scrub and pale rock. To my right the land climbs sharply. I think about scrambling up the bank, but on the slope I'll be slower, less agile. The 4x4 will tear up that gradient and mow me down.

The lake flanks me to the left. I scan it for boats, for anyone. But Simon picked his location well. He paid for privacy, and he got it. For a crazy moment I consider running full tilt into the water, swimming out deep where his car can't follow. But what then? Once I'm in, I can't get out. With the 4x4, he can circle the perimeter, wait for me to come ashore.

Gasping, I glance over my shoulder. Already, Simon's closed half the distance. The Cayenne is *flying*, bouncing over ruts, chewing up track, spitting stones in its wake. If it hits me at that speed, it'll kill me, no question, and yet there's nowhere to run and nowhere to hide.

I've seconds now, before it reaches me. The possibility that I'm about to die is so overwhelming – so *surprising* – that I almost pull up short. Instead, I feint left before jinking right into a dive, legs going over my head, rolling from shoulder to hip.

The Cayenne blasts past, sparing me by inches. Simon flicks it into a slide. The car machine-guns dirt and stones as it sloughs off speed. It rocks wildly. The wheels spin, then bite.

I'm off and running, back towards the lake house, back towards blood and death. I feel my heart slamming against my ribs, hear my tortured breathing. I'm out of time, out of ideas. He won't fall for the same trick twice.

Behind me I sense the 4x4, its sloping body, its metal grille. I imagine the look of savage satisfaction on Simon Rafferty's face.

Sorry, not sorry.

His words in the wine cellar, the night he kissed me.

Impact.

The Cayenne's wing strikes my hip, shattering it. Even before the pain hits I'm cartwheeling over the bonnet. An instant later my shoulder strikes the windscreen and punctures the glass. The rest of my body would follow it into the passenger cabin if not for the roof strut, which fractures three vertebrae and collapses my left lung before flinging me across the track. The landing might be when I break my right arm and elbow, or it might have already happened when I struck the car – my doctors will never figure that out. As I corkscrew across the ground, gravel shreds my skin like a macerator.

I come to a rest on my side, limbs twisted, one side of my face pressed to the track. A sound is coming out of me I don't recognize: a low-pitched drone that barely sounds human.

My vision skips, shudders. I see water, a glittering expanse. Dense pine forest rises behind it. On the near bank, a sun-blistered wooden sign tilts at a crazy angle. Its lettering is carved rather than painted: *Lago della Misericordia*. I don't speak much Italian, but I know how to translate it: *Mercy Lake*.

Little evidence the place deserves that moniker, from what I can see. And what I can see, beside the sign, is Simon's Porsche Cayenne, facing me from where it came to rest – at least that part of it within my field of view: a smashed headlight, buckled metal, a webbed windscreen.

Wow. I really did make a mess.

Its wheels spin, find traction. The 4x4 accelerates up the track towards the road.

This is the last time anyone will ever see that car. Italian police will never locate it. And while they'll put out an appeal once Simon reports it missing, they won't describe the damage, which would have made it so much more memorable to anyone who might have encountered it. Admittedly, the only person who could have told them was in a coma, but they found fragments from the broken head-light. Shockingly, they never even figured out I'd been hit.

My vision skips harder. The droning changes in pitch. It's so bright out here. So *hot*. I feel the sun frying my face, burning my wrecked arms and legs. I can't move, can't even turn my head for a moment's respite. My heart labours in my chest, pumping blood around a body that's going into shock. My mouth dries out, then my throat. Each breath of superheated air desiccates me from the inside out.

The sun arcs across the sky. Shadows swing away from the trees. For a while, time slows. A fox limps out of the scrub. I guess it could smell my flesh cooking. Maybe it heard my skin sizzling. It sticks around for a while. If not for my groaning, I think it would slink closer. At some point it disappears, and the sun continues to slide.

For a while I leave myself completely, drifting on tides of pain. When I return, the shadows have lengthened further. A red Jeep Cherokee is wending down the hill towards me, kicking up eddies of dust. It stops a short distance away. The front doors open. Simon and Nadia climb out.

Nadia starts to move in my direction, but Simon shouts at her to wait. He walks behind the car, opens the boot. When he reappears, he's clutching a torque wrench. Slowly, the couple approach.

'Phoebe,' I croak, determined to confront Simon with what he's done.

He glances at Nadia. Then he asks: 'What did you do, Keira? Why did you come? Where's Phoebe? Where's my *son*?'

When I lift my gaze to the lake house, the two of them break into a run. A minute later, I hear Nadia's scream.

Wise of Simon to return with a witness – to pretend that he's seeing all this for the first time. When he comes back outside, I don't see Nadia. Hopefully, she's looking after Ollie.

As Simon walks towards me, I realize he's still holding the torque wrench. 'You weren't meant to *be* here, Keira. Why you brought your *parents* I have no idea.'

He turns, checking the lake-house windows. Then he steps closer. I can't move my head, look up at him. All I can see are his shoes – and the bulbous head of the wrench. 'A fresh start,' he hisses. 'That's all I wanted. Without your sister taking half of everything. Was it *really* too much to ask?'

He sounds emotional. Angry and upset.

The torque wrench disappears from view. I imagine it rising in an arc like a golf club before a drive, hovering above Simon's shoulder, charged with potential energy.

I don't hear the air parting as it descends, aiming for those precious few millimetres of skull that protect my brain from trauma.

Goodbye, Keira Greenaway, I think. No more awkwardness. No more social anxiety.

The last thing I see is that old wooden sign, canted over near the water: *Lago della Misericordia*.

Mercy Lake.

And then I'm gone.

SEVENTY-FOUR

How long I lie there, staked out on Old Cobb's eastern slope, I can't fathom. I manage to brain myself once, retreating to the horrors of years past, but I don't attempt it again. If my only refuge is trauma, it's hardly a refuge at all.

On the horizon I see something monstrous: a meld of colours too rich to comprehend: blood and wine, lava and viscera. I know what it precedes because I can sense its approach – that sheer, inscrutable mass. I can feel the earth trembling beneath me, as if the entire hill is about to crack open, can feel my heels drumming against the ground, a pressure growing in my chest, a scream building . . .

. . . and then suddenly *there it is*, a sliver of red fire, a rising death, and although my scream comes then, it doesn't stop the sunrise, just encourages it.

I contort myself into every conceivable shape, the ropes carving ever deeper into my flesh, but nothing does any good. Soon, that sliver of sun has grown into a half-open eye.

I'm dying, here. At least, Mercy Lake is.

I cry for help until my voice goes. Then I weep until I've

no more tears. At some point I bite my tongue, so savagely that my mouth fills with blood.

In the east, the horizon surrenders its last grip. The sun floats free, a red orb gaining height. My bladder releases. Urine soaks my dungaree shorts, courses down my leg.

There are Day People and Night People, and I am absolutely the latter. While you can change once, you can't go back to what you were – that's what I've always said. It's lonelier at night, but at least it's safer. Being a victim is no fun.

And yet here I am again, a victim. If I can't go back to what I was, where can I go now? If Mercy Lake is dead, and Keira Greenaway before her, what's left?

The answer, of course, is nothing. And by the time that insight strikes me, I've stopped fighting, stopped caring. I rest my almost-very-nearly-crushed skull against the grass and listen to the birdsong.

The sun has risen even higher by the time Louis returns. He stands beside my head, staring down at me in silence. When he crouches, I wheeze out my breath, start to shake. Mercy Lake dies harder than Keira Greenaway, but this is the point she goes. What's left is a shell, an empty husk.

'Hey, Night Eyes,' he says, touching my forehead, unaware of what's just happened. 'Oh, you poor thing. Did you wet yourself? Come on, let's get you cleaned up.'

He puts his face next to mine. In the sunlight he looks artificial. An android with golden skin. Terrifying for Mercy – or for Keira, preceding her. For me, an empty husk, all I can do is stare.

'Did it work?' he asks. 'You're not struggling. You've done serious damage to your wrists, and we're going to have to fix that, but they'll heal.' He smiles. 'Look, Mercy. There's the sun. It doesn't burn, does it? Certainly not *this* early in the morning. It didn't kill you, either. You're here, alive. With me.'

How little he knows. But there is, I have to admit, a savage and terrible beauty to that swollen red mass.

I watch, stupefied, as Louis unties me. Ankles first, then wrists. My head lolls against his shoulder as he carries me to the campervan. When he rolls open the side door I see Little Guy, asleep on a rug.

Louis places me on the bench seat and buckles a seatbelt across my chest. I can't move, can't do anything but sit there with the buzz of my rope-burned wrists and ankles and the stench of my urine-soaked clothes. As we ride back down Old Cobb, I slip between different memories. I'm back inside the lake house with Phoebe; sprinting past Lago della Misericordia; bouncing over the Cayenne's bonnet; staring at Simon's shoes as the torque wrench rises out of sight.

Eventually, we end up at my flat. Real, not imagined. Louis carries me towards the bathroom, but I shake my head. 'Bed,' I croak. 'Sleep.'

I know that I stink, that I should strip off my wet clothes. But I just want to be alone, to burrow into darkness.

'Let me see those wrists,' Louis says, sitting on a corner of the mattress. Again, I shake my head.

He looks like he's about to insist. Instead, he gazes around the room. 'I'll leave you, then. Let you get some rest. And while you build back your strength I'll pay Simon Rafferty a visit. We both know why you came to Cranner's

Ford. And we both know you're not capable of doing it. You like to fix people, Mercy. That's your strength. The Angel of Cranner's Ford. But what you can't do, I can. It's what the universe wants of me, I think. I can end this chapter of our lives. Then, together, we can start a new one.'

'No.'

'Yes, Mercy. Because we can't stay—'

'Don't kill him,' I say. 'Don't lay a finger on him.'

Louis frowns. 'Simon Rafferty took *everything* from you. He took your sister, your parents. He ran you down outside that lake house, left you there to die. He took your balance, Mercy. He even took your *daylight*.'

I stare at him, focusing on my breathing. I recall what he told me, that night outside William the Navigator's window.

The universe engineers situations, presents us with choices. I'm convinced that's what was happening at the Texaco, Friday night. I'm convinced that's what pulled us back together. We can choose to be its agents – restore balance, preserve it. Or we can choose an alternative path.

Suddenly, it's all so clear. I close my eyes – and when I do, I catch a scrap of memory. Fleeting, tantalizing, but so incredibly beautiful.

I'm at the dinner table in my old house, Mum and Dad sitting opposite. Around me, I see birthday cards and torn paper. Dad gets up to dim the lights. And then Phoebe comes in, my magical sister, swerving all over the room with a cake, laughing and pretending to drop it. Together, my family starts to sing. Their faces glow with light and love.

The image dissolves, and when I blink my eyes free of tears I see the teal cremation urns on my mantelpiece and hear my teeth squealing in my mouth.

'You're wrong about what I'm capable of,' I say. 'I don't want you intervening on my behalf. That's not your right. Whatever we do about Simon Rafferty, we do together.'

Louis looks at me doubtfully. But really, how can he argue?

It's hard, this. Hard to keep talking. But I need to reinforce the point. 'Promise me. I've lived in this town a year, keeping my head down, keeping watch. You're not going to come along at the last minute and take him away from me. If you do . . .'

I swallow, force out the words. 'If you do, there's no us.'

Louis flinches. He studies me closely, head tilted. Then he nods. 'OK,' he says. 'I promise. I've got a couple of loose ends to tie up in town. Afterwards, we can tie up yours – move on from this, together.'

He leans in, kisses me. I shudder, pull the duvet over my head. My body feels like it's dying. As if I've been exposed to a massive dose of radiation that's eating me from within.

I've got a couple of loose ends to tie up in town.

I wonder what that can mean.

SEVENTY-FIVE

By Tuesday morning, Nadia's so sick with worry – and so exhausted from lack of sleep – she can barely function. Last night, Linda sat on the sofa and talked for hours about Hugo, about her failed marriage, about what might come next. By the time she left, it was starting to get light.

Two police officers arrive while Nadia's making Ollie breakfast. Simon leads them into his office and closes the door. When he emerges, twenty minutes later, he looks even sicker than she feels.

'I'm going with them to the station,' he tells her. 'To make a statement and see if there's any other way I can help.'

'Is Daddy in trouble?' the boy asks, once they've gone.

'Of course not,' Nadia replies, but the reality is that they all are. She can think of no reason to link Hugo's death to Keira, but she's convinced a link exists – worse, that it's a precursor to what might happen here if she doesn't accept Konstantin's help.

This morning, she's meant to be dropping Ollie at a forestry centre for a day of outdoor activities, but she daren't let him out of her sight. Instead, after a few phone calls, she drives him to a soft play in Old Town.

Traffic is heavy in Cranner's Ford. Everywhere Nadia looks, she sees Keira Greenaway: walking along the street; coming out of a café; jumping from a car or passing on a bike.

The soft play is a miniature hell on Earth; a place of screams and smells and shouted conversation. Konstantin arrives five minutes later, eating from a bag of wrinkled orange fruits. Sweat runs down his temples despite the aircon. Mothers at nearby tables throw him uneasy looks. Meeting him here feels perverse, but it's the safest and most public place Nadia could think of to bring Ollie.

'Have you made a decision?' he asks.

Nadia avoids his gaze. She feels no safer in his presence – more that she's traded one danger for another. 'I want you to frighten them,' she says. 'Badly, if you have to. Broken bones, I don't care. I just want them gone from Cranner's Ford. I want them to leave us alone.'

Konstantin is silent for a while. Then he says, 'I think you misunderstood.'

She frowns, glances over. 'What do you mean?'

'I offered to fix your problem. I never said you could dictate how.'

'What are you proposing, then?'

'That's not your concern.'

'Of course it's—'

'Do you want me to fix your problem?'

Nadia looks across the soft play, to where Ollie is swinging on a rope. Then she places her hands on her belly. According to her pregnancy app, her baby now measures two centimetres head to tail. Its face is beginning to form:

ears, nose, eyes now with pigment; a mouth with a tongue that's already developed taste buds.

What matters more in the world than these two innocents? Not her. Not Simon. Certainly not Keira Greenaway and her oddball friend.

Wondering if she's damning herself, Nadia whispers through clenched teeth: 'I want you to fix the problem.'

Konstantin sighs. An artery pulses beneath his sunburned scalp. His eyes flicker over her skin. When he touches her cheek, she tries not to flinch.

'Thank you,' he says, his expression beatific.

Back home, Nadia installs Ollie in front of the TV, activates the exterior alarms and arms herself with a kitchen knife. Only when she's investigated every room, checked every cupboard and looked under every bed does she pull out her phone and call Simon. His phone goes straight to voicemail. Perhaps he's still at the police station.

With nothing left to do except wait, she returns to her earlier thought – that Hugo and Keira might be connected in ways she hadn't suspected.

Making herself an espresso, she carries it through to Simon's office. Inside, she closes the door and goes to the four handsomely bound albums on his bookcase. They archive Sheergen's history in a series of press cuttings, photographs and press releases. Simon pays a media-monitoring service to keep them updated, both the ones he stores here and the duplicates at Sheergen's headquarters. According to Simon, Keira spent a short period working for him during her student years. Might her time there have overlapped with Hugo's?

Carrying the albums to the desk, Nadia opens the most recent one and starts leafing backwards. She finds nothing she hasn't seen before, or anything in the two that precede it. The oldest album features events during her employment at Sheergen's Italian office and even earlier. Inside it, she finds an image that turns her insides to water.

Nadia staggers to Simon's desk chair. For a minute, maybe longer, she can do nothing except sit and stare. Finally, she hauls out her mobile and dials Konstantin. They parted less than an hour ago. She has time to reverse her decision.

His phone rings and rings.

SEVENTY-SIX

Once Louis has gone, I scrunch up my eyes, curl into a ball, make it as dark as I possibly can. And then I cry.

I cry for my sister, for our parents, for my nephew. Most of all, I cry for me. Because I have no idea who I am. And because, right now, crushing self-pity is the least of my problems.

Afterwards, emerging from my cocoon, I stagger to the kitchen, fill a glass with water and drink. Mainly to rehydrate, but also to replenish my tears for the next blubathon. Stripping off my clothes, I hobble to the shower. I'm horribly unsteady on my feet. It feels like two years' worth of progress has vanished overnight. I sit on the shower floor, where it's safer, unwrap my bandages and carefully wash myself clean. From the bathroom I crawl to the bedroom and struggle into a T-shirt. Then I climb back into bed.

Around seven, I hear the building beginning to wake. Upstairs, Hazel starts clomping about. Getting dressed and eating breakfast, probably. Feeding her cats. People come down from the other flats. They go outside, start their cars. By nine, the place is quiet again.

Quiet is bad – it allows my mind to wander freely. Sometimes, to survive, the best option is to avoid all thought. To let events flow over you, to submit. But while I'd love to do that, I can't.

We both know why you came to Cranner's Ford. And we both know you're not capable of doing it.

Wrong.

Out there, right now, is a man who took everything from me. And from Keira Greenaway. And from Mercy Lake. Something needs to be done. And for five long years I've procrastinated.

I mix up some formula for Little Guy. Afterwards, I search through the fridge. I'm not hungry, but I know I need to eat. I toss down some pasta and pesto. Then I stumble to the bathroom and retch it all back up. For my second attempt – at food, not vomiting – I choose Heinz spaghetti hoops and toast. That goes down and stays down. I follow it with a couple of flapjacks.

Sitting at my workbench, trying to keep my mind off Louis, I check the news. Hugo's been named. The *Cranner's Ford Gazette* has the details. The photo they've used is a good one. In his face I see no suggestion of the malice I witnessed at Linda's. Then again, I see no suggestion of it in my own face, and I'm the one who killed him. Simon Rafferty is quoted in the article: *We're all devastated. Utterly heartbroken.* The police are appealing for information, particularly from motorists who might have dashcam footage of the local roads.

Around noon, I manage a few hours' sleep. When I wake I check my phone – no messages from Louis, no missed calls. In the kitchen, I remove every one of my knives from the drawer and line them up in a row. Then I open my laptop and go online. After watching a few You-Tube videos, I rummage through my workbench for the fist-sized spare padlock I keep for the bike shed. Then I root through my toolbox for a length of parachute cord. Tying one end around the padlock's hoop, I take it into the bedroom and give it an experimental twirl. When the padlock doesn't shoot off the cord I build up my speed, then bring it down hard on my storage chest. The lid disintegrates, the lock punching through the wood.

I stand there, imagining the damage my improvised weapon would do to a human skull. Then I start to shake. Mercy Lake is dead and I have no idea who I am. Returning to the kitchen, I put away the knives and dismantle my ridiculous improvised toy. I find my bear spray and tuck it inside my pocket.

Around five, I make another meal. An hour later, I strip off my dungarees and step into my red dress, tucking the bear spray inside my belt. In front of the bathroom mirror, I apply make-up. Afterwards, I paint my nails and wrap fresh bandages around my wrists. I look like one of the walking dead preparing for a date. Not someone who could reliably deliver vengeance. Returning to the kitchen, I open the cutlery drawer and look again at the knives. For the last year, I've travelled with one inside my cargo bag. So why do I suddenly feel such an aversion?

At 7 p.m., I call Louis. When he doesn't answer, I leave a voicemail. Then I grab the envelopes I retrieved from my post box on Sunday evening: one white, one red. They go into my rucksack along with anything else I might conceivably need: wallet, phone, mixtapes, refurbished Speak & Spell, binoculars, Tinker Bell outfit, Bubblicious gum.

At 8 p.m., I step outside my flat and creep up to the ground-floor hall. Through the transom window over the main entrance I see darkening sky. I stare at it for a moment before hurrying back downstairs.

I try again, ten minutes later. And again, five minutes after that. On my fourth attempt, I walk the entire length of the hall and put a bandaged hand on the building's outer door.

Am I really going to try this? Yes, I really am. Heart thumping, I peel open the door – and see red sunlight pouring through a gap between the townhouses. Cringing, I say a rude word and flee.

Back inside my flat, I recover my breath. Was my fear genuine? Or was it born merely of habit? It takes me a while to realize that I couldn't even have *contemplated* doing any of that yesterday. So something has changed, even if I can't say exactly what.

I test myself again, thirty minutes later. The sun has disappeared below the horizon, leaving a few bloodied clouds. I stand there for a good five seconds before slamming the door. I think I'll be able to do this.

Towards the end of civil twilight, I kiss Little Guy goodbye and carry my rucksack outside to my Jorvik. I zip it into my cargo bag and climb on to my seat.

Safety checks passed. Power engaged. Throttle up.

I ride beneath an indigo dome populated by waking stars. Never have I seen Cranner's Ford looking like this, touched by the day's last light. Never have I seen so many *people*. The pubs are open, the restaurants, too. There's traffic everywhere; headlights and horns and revving engines. Delivery drivers on mopeds zigzag around cars and pedestrians. A fire engine blasts past, siren blaring.

The air is rich with exhaust smoke and frying food. I ride past a chicken place, a kebab shop, a pizzeria – all open. My nose twitches like a starving rabbit's. I hear music and laughter; life, happening all around.

It's messy, frightening, overwhelming.

From Bartholomew Street I take Liphook Avenue, heading for Pincher's Mount. The drive-thru looks closed, its car park turned into an impromptu skatepark. I'm speeding past when I spot Lost Travis outside the restaurant, looking in. Detouring across the tarmac, I pull up alongside him. 'Hey, Travis. What's up?'

The big guy looks at me dolefully. 'Crash bang,' he says, reaching under his T-shirt to reveal his pendant. 'Becky right. Lightning bad omen. Came true.'

As he speaks, I notice the red-and-white-striped hazard tape strung across the main entrance. 'What happened?' I ask, peering through the windows. 'Why's it closed?'

'Bad thing,' Travis says. 'Found her this morning.'

'Found who?'

'Found Becky. All iced up.'

My stomach turns over. 'What do you mean?'

He gives me a haunted look 'Don't make sense. That freezer safe. Handle inside. Travis knows.'

'Becky was in the freezer?'

He nods.

'Is she OK?'

'Minus twenty, all night long. Hypo . . . Hypo—'

'Hypothermia?'

'Frostbite, too.' Travis wiggles his fingers. 'Gonna lose some, maybe all. And little piggies. What Gary tole me.'

I've got a couple of loose ends to tie up.

'Are you OK?' I ask.

'Travis safe now. Crash bang not for me.'

Touching his arm in goodbye, I ride across the car park to the main road. As I thread my way through the skaters, I spot a trio I haven't seen in a while. Dragon Back, Greasilocks and Wisp are practising their grinds on a section of kerb. They regard me sullenly when I pull up.

'Hell do *you* want?' Dragon Back mutters. 'We left you alone, didn't we? No need to set another psycho on us.'

I look him up and down. He's so *young*. Hard to believe I was ever frightened of him. 'Don't talk to me like that,' I tell him. 'It's rude and there's no need. One question and I'll leave. That night at the Texaco: what did he say to you?'

Dragon Back glances at the others. He watches an ambulance race along Liphook Avenue, blue lights flashing. Then he slouches over. 'He said if I didn't leave, he'd find out where I lived, that it'd take him less than a day's work to track me down, and then he'd break in one night when I was sleeping, tie me up . . . and after that he'd get my mum and he'd rape her in front of me. He'd cut her face, too, so that whenever I looked at her in future I'd see a reminder of him.'

He turns his head, spits. 'Guy was an utter psychopath.'

I wait until he meets my eyes again. Then I ask: 'Have you harassed any women since? Out late, like I was? Alone?'

'What the hell? No.'

'I guess his threat worked, then.'

Dragon Back flinches, takes a step back. 'Wow,' he says. 'Nice. You're as insane as he is. Can I go?'

I flick my head, dismissing him. Then I pull on to Liphook Avenue and continue east. I think of the night

Louis and I stood outside Lovesick Linda's and watched Hugo cart off her TV.

Sometimes, there's really only one solution to a problem. I love your creativity, Mercy – the ideas you dream up. But birdhouses and porch lights can only take you so far. Sometimes you have to tackle a situation head on.

Whiplash Becky locked in a freezer is head on. Three puppy farmers with shattered kneecaps is head on. So is White Knuckle Wanda's pulverized face. And Hugo Jepp plummeting from the Starcase.

That night on Pincher's Mount, minutes before Hugo fell, a new insight struck me: that in a world as cruel and random as this one, small acts of kindness are far less effective than fear.

Do I still believe that?

Halfway to Pincher's Mount, I reach the bridge that separates Old Town from new. There, I find the bench where I sometimes sit. Unzipping my rucksack, I retrieve the two envelopes, one white, one red, I brought from the flat. The paper is feathered where I've resealed them so many times.

I open the white one first, sliding out the card. On the front, a cartoon frog has its tongue stuck to a birthday cake. Inside is a handwritten message: *To our wacky, clever, kind, brilliant, funny and gorgeous daughter. Happy eighteenth birthday. We cannot wait to see what the future brings you. We just know it's going to be great. All our love, your equally wacky, clever, kind, brilliant, funny but not so gorgeous Mum and Dad xxx*

I stare at the handwriting for a while. My mind goes quiet. Carefully, I place the card on my lap. Then I reach into the red envelope. This card features a black-and-white image along with some nonsense gag I've never really understood. Inside, though, the message is far less cryptic: *To Keira. Wow, you actually made it! A fully grown adult. Cannot WAIT to celebrate with you later! From the best big sister in the world, Phoebe. Xxxxx*

As I read the words, my phone buzzes.

SEVENTY-SEVEN

Tuesday evening.

Eleven hours since Tapia met Nadia at the soft play. Seventeen hours since he discovered something profound near the summit of Old Cobb: his ghost-eyed girl, straddling heaven and Earth; the promise, at the moment of her death, of an experience utterly unique.

After checking out of his hotel late morning, he'd found a parking spot in one of the lanes and slept for seven hours straight, his dreams more vivid than they'd ever been. Afterwards, he drove into town and ate another bland meal: salmon and new potatoes, washed down with sparkling water.

Now that night has fallen, he checks over his inventory: jerry can of fuel; six litres of denatured alcohol; shackles and police-issue cuffs; syringes, needles and lidocaine. His shotgun is affixed by neodymium magnets to the underside of the van.

He places his phone in the dash cradle, where he can view the tracking app while driving. Keira Greenaway's buddy poses the greatest threat, so he'll pacify him first. Afterwards, he'll round up Keira and Nadia.

The campervan left the Seven Crosses campsite five minutes ago, heading towards town. Tapia intercepts it at the Texaco on Copper Beech Lane. He passes the garage without slowing and spots his target filling up at one of the pumps. Looping back, he tracks the vehicle through Old Town. It climbs the lane around Pincher's Mount and turns into a place marked Rycroft Hollow. Tapia pulls over a few hundred metres past the entrance. He grabs his rucksack and shotgun, climbs out and starts walking.

He sees the campervan parked at the far end of the gravel car park. The cabin lights are on, the curtains drawn. Threads of steam escape through a half-open side window. Tapia smells something cooking.

Using the darkness as cover, he can get to within a few metres without announcing his presence. Silent as a cruising stingray, Tapia does exactly that.

SEVENTY-EIGHT

It's a text message, not a call. Sent from Louis's phone.

COME TO ARCADIA HEIGHTS. MAIN GATE IS OPEN.

My scalp contracts. I stand up far too fast. The birthday cards fall from my lap and a gust of wind carries them through the railings. I watch them spiral into the river, where they gently float away.

I climb on to my Jorvik and grip the handlebars, ignoring the pain in my bandaged hands. Then I check for a break in traffic and pull on to the road.

From here, there's no going back, no return to the way things were. I'm not even sure I'd take that option if I could. For five long years I've been stuck in purgatory. Finally, maybe, there's a way out.

The cars ahead of me slow. To avoid them, I pull on to the pavement. When I hit the next turn I see the reason for all the traffic. Up ahead, the street is blocked with emergency vehicles. Three firefighters are aiming their hoses at a vehicle burning out of control. I guess I'm not the only one having a messed-up night. I can't get any closer, so I divert on to a side road.

Overhead, the sky has darkened further. Pincher's Mount, silhouetted, looms above me. At the next junction I turn right on to Abbot's Walk.

My Jorvik takes the strain as I wind my way up the hill. This is where the rich folk live, the powerful. The higher the walk climbs, the more impressive the homes.

Of them all, Arcadia Heights stands tallest. As I ride past the boundary wall, I close my mind to what lies behind it. When I reach the hydraulic gate, flanked by security cameras, I find it hanging open. For the first time in all my visits, I ride through.

The driveway swings left and right, beneath a leaf canopy dense enough to block out the night sky. My tyres make barely any sound on the smooth tarmac. When I emerge from the trees I see the house, my first view of it from this direction, and what a sight: stark cubes of concrete and glass, lit from within as if on fire. The front door is open. Through it I see a white entrance hall and a staircase of white marble.

I climb off my Jorvik, unzip my cargo bag and grab my rucksack, along with everything else I might need. Then I stand there a moment, looking up at the house.

Phoebe never saw this. She died years before Simon moved to Cranner's Ford. Perhaps, if she'd lived, she'd have counselled against such poor taste.

A few metres from the entrance, my brain pulls one of its tricks. I don't overbalance, but when I try to move the world smears, colours running to liquid before they settle. I place my feet deliberately, charting a path through the chaos.

It's bright inside the hall. White floor, white walls, white ceiling. I see only two patches of colour: on a side table, a vast display of flowers; at the base of the staircase, a few spots of blood.

Music is playing, somewhere deeper inside the house. I take a few steps, pause, take a few steps more. Around me the walls pulse and quiver. I pass an open doorway, leading into a room I recognize: the orangery where I've watched Daisy Double-Take practise her yoga.

In the cinema room, on one of the white leather sofas, I find Nadia. She's lying on her side, facing me. Her peach-coloured sarong has fallen open, revealing a single tanned leg. One foot wears a flip-flop. The other is bare.

Close up, she's even more striking than I expected, so flawless she hardly seems human. I pause in the doorway, waiting for my view to fully stabilize. I see no evidence of injury. Nothing to spoil that perfect physique.

When Nadia blinks, my heart thumps hard in response. Not dead, then, but I can't figure out why she's lying there like that – why she doesn't climb off the sofa and run. Still, I have no time to investigate. Turning from the doorway, I move further into the house.

I come to the kitchen, an oasis of marble and glass. Here is where the music is playing: 'Hold On, I'm Comin'', by Sam and Dave. Through the floor-to-ceiling windows I see a corner of the pool. At one of the bar stools I see Louis.

SEVENTY-NINE

Konstantin Tapia stares through the windscreen at the lights of Cranner's Ford. For two weeks, now, this town has been his home. Not a bad place, considering. Its Mexican restaurant was certainly the highlight.

His van is pointed down the slope. Far below him, he sees the road that crosses the river out of Old Town.

Tapia rolls his neck. The town's lights rotate for a while before they settle. He feels a rising numbness in his chest.

'*There* you are,' says a voice. 'I was worried I might have lost you again.'

When he notices Keira Greenaway's buddy examining him through the open side window, the recollections flood back: Rycroft Hollow; the campervan parked on the gravel; the smell of cooking food. He'd crept closer, shotgun at the ready.

Then: the flash of something metal in the dark: two fishhook probes attached by wires that turned him rigid and dropped him like a tipped-over door. Seconds after the current died, a chokehold put him out cold. He woke in the back of his van, trussed so tightly he couldn't move. Keira Greenaway's buddy sat opposite.

'I've been reading all about lidocaine,' the man said, when he saw that Tapia was awake. 'I'm guessing a spinal block isn't something a rookie should attempt solo, but you brought all the needles and I'm feeling confident. I've watched four YouTube videos, already. Think I can find your subarachnoid space? Think I can do it without killing you?'

The answer, it turned out, was yes – although not on the first attempt. How much of the isobaric lidocaine solution the man used, Tapia doesn't know, but thirty minutes later, sitting in the front seat and positioned upright, he can't feel anything below his waist and his legs don't respond when he tries to move them. His light-headedness might result from a natural drop in blood pressure due to the spinal block, or it might indicate something more serious. Right now, that's only one of his problems – because his hands are zip-tied to the steering wheel and his nose smarts with the fumes of spilled fuel.

'You can't intimidate me,' he says.

'Good to know,' the man replies. He reaches into the cabin and flicks on the van's headlights. Then he walks around to the passenger door and climbs in. 'You want to hear a story?' he asks. 'A few years ago, in South Africa's Kruger National Park, rangers found a human skull. Its owner was a rhino poacher who'd entered the park illegally. An elephant killed him. Then a pride of lions ate his body.'

The man smiles. 'I like that story. Don't you? I also think it illustrates perfectly what's happening here.'

Tapia's sudden nausea might be lidocaine-induced. Or it might be fear. Never has he experienced anything like it.

Beside him, Keira Greenaway's buddy takes out a matchbox. 'You can't use the brakes,' he says. 'Because your legs don't work. But you can steer. See that bridge, way down there below us? If you make it into the river, you might put out the flames.'

He pauses, glancing meaningfully at Tapia's zip-tied hands. 'Of course, that water's pretty deep, which gives you another puzzle to solve. You could always use those trees beyond the road as a hard stop instead. I don't know if any of this is helping.'

He strikes a match, inverts it.

Tapia watches the flame creep up the wood. 'Wait.'

'Nah,' the man says. He releases the handbrake, tosses the lit match into the back and hops out of the passenger seat. There's a whump of combustion behind Tapia, a blossoming of yellow light. Then the van begins to roll.

EIGHTY

On the worktop in front of Louis stands a bottle of white rum, uncapped. Beside it, on a chopping board, I see mint, sugar, squeezed limes, crushed ice, soda water.

'This place,' he says. 'Talk about well stocked. I made you a mojito. I know you don't drink, but I thought it might steady your nerves.' He holds out a glass. 'Here. They're not strong.'

I wave it away. 'Maybe later. Where's Ollie?'

'Your nephew's asleep in his bed.'

'I want to see him.'

'Sure. You want me to come up there with you? You don't look too steady on your feet.'

'I'll manage.' Indicating the chopping board and its contents, I add, 'You touched a lot of stuff.'

'I'll clean up. We have all night. Given enough time, we can make this place tell any story we want.'

The room slides apart. I breathe slow and hard, stitch it back together. Then I return to the hall. Clutching the stair rail, I climb to the mezzanine. I recognize this part of the house – I've seen it many times en route to Ollie's room.

Outside his door, I unzip my rucksack. If he wakes, I don't want to scare him. He knows me as Tinker Bell, so that's who he'll see. Off comes my red dress. On goes my lilac skirt and corset, my pink hair and fairy wings. Cautiously, I open the door.

It's dark inside. Slowly, my eyes adjust. I pick my way across a toy-strewn floor to Ollie's bed.

And there he is, asleep. My nephew. My sister's son.

His brow is gently furrowed. His eyes rove behind their lids. I wonder if the dream is a good one. Three years since I've been this close; so much of his life I've missed. Even longer since I've seen his mother.

That day in Italy, I spent hours lying broken beside the lake before Simon caved in my skull. I suffered a brain bleed on the way to hospital. After an emergency op, doctors induced me into a coma. When I woke, weeks later, I'd lost the ability to walk; even to talk. From there, it was a long road back.

By then, the police investigation had reached conclusions no one wanted to revisit, certainly not on the evidence of someone so obviously damaged. My memory wasn't reliable, they said, the slaughter at the lake house the result of a random burglary gone wrong.

Simon had booked that place as a retreat for just the three of them. Only once they arrived did he engineer a crisis at a Sheergen satellite office, setting up the beginnings of his alibi.

Phoebe, finding herself alone for a few days in a beautiful location, decided to fly me and my parents out there without telling him, thinking we'd be a huge surprise when he got back. We were, of course, but not the way she imagined. Straight after our flight, while Mum and Dad took a nap, I took the boat out on the lake. Phoebe's screams drew me back.

Police think she died first – and that her cries roused my parents. Dad died in the kitchen. Mum was killed in one of the bedrooms. If I'd gone straight upstairs the moment I rowed back to shore, maybe she would have survived. Instead, I called the police. Thanks to my garbled message and the lake house's remote location, help was late to arrive. Before it did, Simon returned with Nadia.

No evidence ever linked Simon to what happened; no motive was ever established for his involvement. His marriage to my sister, everyone said, was a happy one.

No matter that he married Nadia while Phoebe's coffin was still fresh in the ground. Finding solace in her arms wasn't a crime. What *was* a crime was to harass the couple like I did; to repeat my accusations long after anyone was listening; to follow them around; to break into their house; to abduct Ollie.

Still, I learned my lesson, however painful. Despite what Louis might think, I didn't come to Cranner's Ford to kill Simon. I came for one reason only: to see Ollie; to be close to him; to watch him grow. Because this boy is all the family I have left.

I lean over him now, inhaling his clean, biscuity scent. It's an elixir, filling me up. I still remember my excitement the day Phoebe told me she was pregnant. I remember every week of every trimester; every stage of Ollie's development.

I was seventeen when she gave birth. That was the year I did a month's work placement at Simon's office; the year they bought the big house – and the year he took me down to the wine cellar.

If I'd told Phoebe straight away, maybe my family would

still be still alive. Maybe she'd have started divorce proceedings and that would have kept them all safe. Instead, I chose to keep quiet and determine whether Simon's infidelity had been a one-off. I've always believed in second chances, even for a man who tried to seduce his sister-in-law mere weeks before his wife was due to give birth.

Of course, once I started watching him I learned that the wine-cellar incident was fairly typical behaviour. When Phoebe invited me to Italy, I'd already resolved to tell her. I took that boat out on the lake to summon my courage.

Now, gently, I reach out and touch my nephew – just my fingertips on his bare arm. This isn't only the closest I've come to Ollie these last three years. It's the closest I've come to my sister. In his face I see her features and sense her good heart.

Because of Simon, this boy never knew his mother. Because of Simon, he has no clear memories of his grandparents. Even his aunt is little more than a face at the window, a make-believe fantasy that was already on borrowed time.

Opening my rucksack, I take out the Speak & Spell. Since my brain injury, I've developed a number of weird obsessions. Fixing stuff that others have thrown away is one of them. There's little sense in repairing old Walkmans or VHS players – but it's sad for things to become unloved just because they no longer work as well as they once did. Particularly as I am one of those things.

Ollie doesn't need another refurbished vintage toy. He didn't need the vintage Tamagotchi, nor the Major Morgan or Little Professor. I tuck the Speak & Spell under his arm regardless. Then I kiss him on the forehead, cross the room and close his curtains tight.

Back down the stairs I go – to Louis and a mojito and whatever else awaits. But I don't head straight to the kitchen. Instead, I divert back to the cinema room, where I crouch in the darkness beside Nadia Rafferty. She's shifted position in my absence. Now, I see the zip-ties binding her ankles and wrists.

'Are you scared?' I whisper.

She nods.

'Do you want to live?'

Another nod.

'Do you want to answer a question for me?'

'Yes.'

'I'll know if you're lying.'

'I won't lie.'

'Honesty's always the best policy.'

'I'm pregnant,' she whispers.

'Then tell me everything I need to know.'

For the next minute, Nadia talks.

When she stops, I say, 'If you're wise, once this is over, you'll start again somewhere new.' Rising, I go to Simon's office, a little further along the hall. I turn on the lights, approach his desk. Then I retrace my steps to the kitchen. At the breakfast bar, Louis hands me a mojito. The sugar and fizz help me focus.

'When I sent that text, it wasn't fully dark,' he says. 'It wasn't even fully dark when you arrived.'

'No.'

'You rode here. In twilight.'

'I did.'

'So it worked.'

'Where's Simon?'

'Out by the pool. Are you ready for this?'

I take another gulp of my mojito. I think of my sister, my parents – the justice they never received. 'I'm ready,' I tell him, and indicate my drink. 'This is good.'

'You want another? We've got all night.'

'Later.'

I walk to the patio doors, thrown open to the night. There's the pool, glowing an ethereal green. At the deep end, inches from the water's edge, I see him. He's sitting on an aluminium pool chair, his ankles tied to its legs, his wrists tied to the arms. Duct tape covers his mouth. Blood is trickling down his face from a cut over his left eye. When he sees me, his back arches.

My stomach boils with acid. Gritting my teeth, I step outside. It's hard to contain my revulsion, especially as I draw closer, but I want to look into his eyes. For the first time since I've known him, the power balance between us has reversed.

I get to within a few metres before I stop. In his expression I see the arrogance and contempt I'd expected, but I also see fear.

'Do you ever think of her?' I ask.

Simon stares, lifts his chin.

I turn and walk back around the pool. Louis is waiting just inside the patio doors. 'You have a plan,' I say. 'Let's hear it.'

'We tip his chair over the edge, he drowns. We untie him, leave him floating face down in the pool.'

'What about Ollie?'

'They have a maid who turns up around six. We can keep watch until then, make sure he's safe. He'll probably sleep right through.'

'Nadia?'

'Nadia goes the same way. I know that sounds brutal, but once it's done, it's done. No loose ends.'

I return my gaze to Simon Rafferty. I think of Phoebe, lying dead in a crosshatch of her own blood. By comparison, drowning would be an easy fate. *Too* easy.

No matter. Because I have other plans for him.

EIGHTY-ONE

We walk back outside.

The temperature has dropped – far cooler than when I left my flat. Overhead, clouds have rolled across the sky. Around me the air feels heavy, expectant. I smell ozone, sharp and sweet; the promise of rain.

Simon watches my approach. I feel like explaining to him exactly what these last five years have been like – but I've never been good at conversation. Even less so since my brain injury. And really, why would I reveal my agony to him?

'If you want me to do it . . .' Louis begins, arriving at my side.

I shake my head, sliding from my waistband the chef's knife I took from my cargo bag. When Simon sees it, his breathing quickens.

I close my eyes, just briefly, and find myself back in the wine cellar. I feel his lips against mine, his tongue inside my mouth. Looking back, that was the precise moment at which everything in my life began to fall apart.

With my free hand I touch the depression near the base

of my skull, my permanent souvenir of Lago della Misericordia. I turn, glance up at Ollie's room, check that my nephew's curtains are still closed.

'The security cameras,' I say.

'Deactivated,' Louis replies. 'The ones around the pool. And those by the front gate.'

'Why gag him?'

'So you wouldn't have to listen to his poison.'

I nod. Then, knife clenched tightly in my bandaged palm, I plunge it into Louis's side.

He doesn't immediately react. When I pull out the blade, his blood splatters on to the flagstones.

Louis makes a sound of mild surprise, turns to face me. His green eyes find mine and I see a sudden dawning. In response I drive the knife into his stomach. This time he grunts, takes a forward step and grabs my wrist.

'No,' he mutters. 'Don't pull it out. What are you doing?'

I try to wrench myself free, but his grip is unrelenting. 'Going it alone,' I tell him. 'From here on in, it's just me.'

'Mercy—'

'Mercy Lake is dead. You left her up on Old Cobb.'

He groans as if he's eaten far too much food. 'You're not thinking straight. What's got into you?'

Again, I try to yank back my hand. Louis grimaces, squeezes my wrist – so hard I'm surprised it doesn't break. 'Stop, Mercy. Please. You've lost your mind.'

'Honesty's always the best policy,' I say. 'I never told you Simon's car hit me outside the lake house. And you couldn't have learned it from my scrapbook, nor anywhere else, because it was never reported. Simon wasn't behind the wheel that day, was he? He might have tried to silence me afterwards, but he didn't run me down.

Because you did. Just after you killed my sister, my mum and my dad.'

The pain in my wrist is extraordinary. When I abandon my grip on the knife, Louis drags me closer. His free hand clutches my throat, choking off my breath.

We're standing a lover's distance apart. Thanks to the pool lights, I can see the individual striations in his irises. Not just emerald but brown and copper and gold. His pupils are like whirlpools in a lagoon. Quite beautiful.

'I fell in love with you,' he whispers. 'We could have gone anywhere, done anything.'

I can't breathe, can't speak. I try to dislodge his fingers from my throat, but he's too strong. Changing tack, I fumble inside my waistband, raise my hand, close my eyes tightly and hit him with a full blast of bear spray.

The effect is instant. Louis gasps, releasing my wrist and throat. I rear backwards, out of range, before looking.

Bright orange liquid drips from Louis's face. He claws at his eyes, blind.

It's now or never. I take two forward steps, grasp the knife handle. I twist my grip as I tear it loose, opening him up. Then, one palm against his chest, I shove him backwards.

Louis falls into the pool, arms outstretched. A geyser of spray soaks my costume. He kicks out. Dark blood gushes from his wounds and stains the water. As it spreads out beneath him it looks, vaguely, like a pair of crimson wings.

His face breaks the surface. Before he can take a breath, the water closes over him again. I sink to my knees, watching as Louis kicks and twitches and, finally, goes still.

I close my eyes.

Just briefly, I return to the dinner table in my parents'

old house: Mum and Dad sitting opposite; Phoebe bringing in the cake. Then I let the image fade.

Louis's slip, at my flat earlier this morning, made me reassess everything – every conversation; every interaction.

I recalled once again his speech outside William the Navigator's window, the evening we put up the birdhouse: *The universe engineers situations, presents us with choices. I'm convinced that's what was happening at the Texaco, Friday night. I'm convinced that's what pulled us back together.* And yet Friday night at the Texaco was supposedly the first time our paths had crossed.

Then there was his reaction to my parents' urns, the night he stayed at my flat. An understandable one, perhaps, particularly after his claim that he wasn't good around death. But he had no problem stripping Hugo's corpse of evidence. What I saw in my living room, I now realize, was a man confronted with the consequences of an event he'd rather forget.

What about the dates of his overseas travel, plus the six months he claimed to have toured with Eleanor – a year in India, two in Southeast Asia, eighteen months in South America? Added together, they formed a perfect timeline back to that horror day in Italy.

Finally, there was my visit to Simon's office, a few minutes ago. On his desk, just as Nadia had promised, I found the folder archiving Sheergen's early history. Inside, near the front, I saw the photograph she discovered this morning: six people crammed inside a tiny and chaotic office, two of whom I recognized: Simon, leaning over a laptop with his shirt sleeves rolled, his hand clasping Louis's shoulder.

Nadia maintains that she hadn't suspected Simon's

involvement in Phoebe's death, even after confronting him with the photograph; that only when Louis arrived at the house did the truth become clear. Maybe I'm a fool, but I believe her. It's difficult, accepting that the person you care about is a monster. I can certainly empathize with that.

I have no such empathy for Simon Rafferty. Now, I turn my gaze on him.

EIGHTY-TWO

Slowly, carefully, I climb to my feet. Killing someone is hard – it takes a lot of energy and then it saps you of more.

The blood from Louis's body continues to feather the water. Cautiously, I crawl to the edge and swirl my knife beneath the surface. I remain there a while, marshalling my emotions, trying to cope with the trauma of what I've just done. Then I walk along the pool towards the deep end.

Simon Rafferty watches me close the distance. He glances at my knife, presses his spine into the chair. I advance steadily, taking my time, knowing how much I'm scaring him, extracting every possible ounce of fear.

When I step behind his chair he twists his head, grows frantic. Only when I touch the tip of my blade to his crown does he fall still.

'You know how much bone you've got here?' I ask. 'I've become quite the expert on skulls and what's inside them.' Applying no pressure, I let the blade slide down his scalp to the base of his neck. Simon shudders. I leave it there a moment, then remove it.

I'm shaking with adrenalin. I need to slow down a little, concentrate on what I'm doing.

From my rucksack I retrieve my phone. I open the camera app, switch to video and hit record. Then I step around to the front of Simon's chair, keeping the device hidden. Carefully, I pull the tape from his mouth. I imagine it was there to prevent Simon from implicating Louis – another indication of guilt, should any more have been needed.

'I have questions,' I say. 'I'd like honest answers. I think that's fair. Honesty's always the best policy. Do you agree?'

He swallows. 'Yes.'

I pause, point at Louis. 'He worked for you. Years ago. Employee number three.'

Simon stares at the body floating in the pool. 'Yes.'

'Did he . . . did he kill my family?'

No response to that. I study Simon for a while. Then, leaning forward, I touch the point of my blade to his cheek, tracing it upwards towards his eye.

He flinches, blinks. 'Yes, he did.'

'Did you pay him to do it?'

Simon takes a long, measured breath. 'Keira, I will give you whatever—'

I kick his chair. It skitters a few inches closer to the pool. He leans back as far as he can. 'Did you pay him?'

'It doesn't really—'

I kick the chair again. It stops a hair from the edge. Simon swears, clenches his teeth. 'Yes, I paid him – but only for Phoebe. I never commissioned a *slaughter*.'

'Meaning?'

'I'd set up a crisis at the Salerno office – a reason for me to leave the lake house for a few days. Phoebe was meant to be there alone. That's how it must have looked, when he first arrived. Your parents were asleep in a guest room and you were out on the lake. Only when he attacked her did you all come running – at which point I guess he panicked, killing your mum and dad and running you down on his way out of there. If only your sister hadn't gone behind my back, flown you all out in secret . . .'

'So it's Phoebe's fault.'

Simon closes his eyes.

'Don't do that,' I tell him. 'You don't get to tune out. We're having this conversation. Tell me, help me understand, because I really don't. How do you even *begin* to convince someone, an employee at your start-up, to kill your wife?'

When Simon opens his eyes, he throws a sour look towards the pool. 'Because he was a fuck-up, that's how. And because by then he was desperate. When he joined Sheergen, I paid him partly in stock options – standard practice for a lot of start-ups. My intention was always to take the company public, if it grew large enough. All he had to do was keep his head down and wait, but of course he couldn't. He took out bank loans, started spending. And I mean, *really* started spending. You name it, he was into it. Cars, casinos, women – he acted like he was James Bond. After he'd maxed out his loans and credit cards, he started finding money from other sources, got into drugs. That's when his *real* problems started.

'By then, because of his behaviour, I had no choice but to let him go. And as his stock options weren't fully vested, he lost out. When he approached me out of the blue, six months later, he looked like he'd been living in the woods. He begged for help, said he'd do anything. Whatever it took to buy himself a fresh start.'

'And my sister was the price you negotiated.'

Simon grimaces.

'What was he doing in Cranner's Ford? Why turn up now, after all this time?'

He shrugs. 'I only found out he was here last night. At first, I thought he wanted to extort more money, but that didn't seem to be his motivation at all. What the hell he was doing with *you*, I've no idea. Before you arrived, he was spouting a lot of weird stuff. Karma, the universe, the need to atone for old sins, achieve equilibrium.

'It seems he'd spent most of the last five years overseas, reinventing himself. Maybe that's where he picked up his batshit-crazy dogma. I suspect he had a breakdown somewhere along the way. Either that or some kind of psychotic episode. Maybe it was ongoing.'

I stare at him, reluctant to ask any more questions. Each time he speaks, I feel like another part of me is shrivelling up and dying. 'Why?' I ask finally. 'I know you alluded to it, that day at the lake house, but I still want to hear you say it clearly. If you didn't love her any more, why not just ask for a divorce?'

'I worked hard,' he says.

As if it's a valid answer. As if killing one's spouse to avoid a divorce settlement is a reasonable act. A logical one.

I look again at Louis. My feelings about what just happened – what I've involved myself with these last few weeks, what we did, how we lived – are far too complicated to unpick. I'm pretty sure I'll be unpicking them for years to come. Possibly with the aid of a horrifically expensive therapist. Either that or a counsellor working inside a prison – because from here I have no idea which direction my life will take.

I don't doubt a lot of what Louis told me – especially after what I just heard. Clearly, he came to Cranner's Ford seeking, in his own twisted way, atonement for past deeds. If our paths hadn't crossed at the Texaco, events might have played out very differently; and Simon, I suspect, would have been the one floating in the pool.

But our paths did cross, and Louis must have recognized the person he'd once left for dead. Doubtless, he'd have believed it had happened for a reason. He even said as much, that first evening on the garage forecourt: *Do you ever get the feeling that what at first seems random is actually something more mysterious?*

Who knows? Perhaps he was right. Perhaps the universe really did throw us back together. Although not for the reason Louis imagined.

One thing I *do* know is that his feelings for me were genuine. It's sick, obviously. Monstrous. But that doesn't change the reality.

To Simon, I say, 'There's still one thing I don't understand. If you went to all that effort to make sure you were in Salerno when it happened, why come back that same afternoon?'

'Because of Ollie,' he says. 'And because your sister never complied with a damned thing I ever asked. I'd arranged a childcare place for Ollie, so he'd be out of the way when it happened. I told Phoebe to relax, have a day to herself by the lake. The nursery would have raised the alarm when she didn't pick him up, but she didn't drop him off in the first place. I only found that out when I phoned the place. For all I knew, she was dead and Ollie was all on his own.'

I'm silent for a while, letting it sink in. Then I say, 'Tell me, in detail, how you paid him. How you transferred the money. All the individual steps. Don't leave anything out. I want the truth.'

Simon Rafferty sighs. As he recounts the specifics, I walk in circles around his chair, and every time I dip out of sight I check that the phone Louis bought me is still capturing his words.

I've no idea if this will change anything – whether it'll stand up in court or save me from jail. I do know, thanks to what happened on Old Cobb, that I'll be able to survive a little prison time – although for how long, and how well, I can't say.

Once Simon's finished, I save the video and reappear in front of him.

'I'm sorry,' he says, when our eyes meet. 'This has haunted me as much as you.'

His words stop me cold. I came here not to kill him but to save him. Ollie has already lost one parent. He doesn't deserve to lose another – death is simply too final. Still, if there was one thing Simon could say to change my mind, that was it.

I don't surrender to temptation. Instead, I bring up my keypad and dial 999. When an operator answers, I ask her to send police and an ambulance to Arcadia Heights. When she asks my name, I tell her Mercy Lake.

Mercy Lake might be dead. But she deserves a moment's reprieve – a chance to see this done.

EIGHTY-THREE

Upstairs, I wake Ollie. I do it gently, anxious not to frighten him. In the glow of his nightlight, he blinks his big brown eyes at me – Phoebe's eyes. His voice, when he speaks, is scratchy with sleep. 'You,' he says. 'Is this dreaming?'

'No. This is real. I need you to come with me, OK? Let's get you dressed.'

He nods, compliant. I find some clothes and help him pull them on.

'Where're we going?'

'A little night adventure.'

'Somewhere magical?'

'Maybe. You have a favourite blanket? A teddy?'

Ollie points at a straggle of turquoise cloth and a floppy-eared bunny.

'What's bunny's name?'

'Bunny,' he says solemnly.

One hand clutching the banister, I carry Ollie, Bunny and blanket downstairs. We go outside to my Jorvik and I sit them inside my cargo bag. 'You hold on tightly, OK? I won't go fast, but you must hold on tight.'

I switch on my lights and ride along the drive to Abbot's Walk. From there I head to the Monk's Brook and the bramble patch where I sometimes hide my Jorvik.

Together, we splash through the shallow water and traipse up the hill to my hollow. Amazing, how kids are so trusting. Then again, I'm his Tinker Bell. This last year we've grown pretty close.

I lay out Ollie's blanket and he curls up on it with Bunny. Once he's asleep, I slip out of my costume and back into my red dress. Hard enough to face what's coming. To attempt it dressed as a fairy would make life more difficult for everyone.

Already, a single police car is parked outside Arcadia Heights. In the distance, I see more coming – a daisy chain of lights, a multicoloured caterpillar worming its way through Georgian streets.

Once they've fished Louis from the pool, I'll go back down. I don't want Ollie to see what happened in his home.

I'll answer questions. I'll play the recording. I'll see if these police officers treat me differently to those in Salerno after I woke from my coma; after I relearned to talk; after I realized that Ollie Rafferty was the only one left from the family I loved so much.

I think of Louis in snatches. He took everything. And then he stole even more. But – and this is the hardest thing to accept – in some ways he remade me. Not Keira Greenaway, exactly. Not Mercy Lake. Someone new.

One thing he *didn't* destroy was my belief in the power of good works. Small acts of kindness, I've realized, might be less effective than fear. But, over time, they add up. They can make a difference. *I* can make a difference.

Overhead, stars are splayed across a bell jar of perfect black.

Just think of everything that had to align, Friday night, to bring us to this moment: your puncture, my empty fuel tank, those skaters . . .

As I look up at the sky, I consider the same question I asked myself a week ago. *Am* I being watched? From somewhere up there?

And if I am, who's watching?

And what exactly do they see?

ABOUT THE AUTHOR

Sam Lloyd grew up in Hampshire, where he learned his love of storytelling. These days he lives in Surrey with his wife, three young sons and a dog that likes to howl. His first thrillers, *The Memory Wood* and *The Rising Tide*, were published to huge critical acclaim in 2020 and 2021.

HAVE YOU READ SAM LLOYD'S CHILLING DEBUT THRILLER?

Elijah has lived in the Memory Wood
for as long as he can remember.

Elissa has only just arrived. And she'll
do everything she can to escape.

THE MUST-READ RICHARD & JUDY BOOK CLUB PICK.

'Beautifully told, with two superbly drawn young
protagonists, Lloyd is a rare new thriller talent.'
Daily Mail

'Superbly creepy, with an unexpected twist'
Guardian

'Brilliant writing, a terrifying story . . . If you enjoy dark,
twisty thrillers that stay with you, read this book.'
Samantha Downing, author of *My Lovely Wife*

OUT NOW

DON'T MISS SAM LLOYD'S
PULSE-POUNDING THRILLER

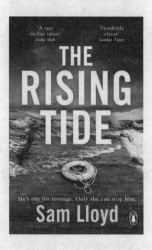

**A family pushed to its limits, set against the
backdrop of the most unforgiving of landscapes.**

'Lloyd is terrific on atmosphere, channelling
the hostile, volatile power of the sea both
literally and metaphorically . . . He excels at
taking readers to very dark places.'
Metro

'A thrilling family drama with dramatic
scenery and twisting reveals.'
Magic Radio Book Club

'Absorbing and deftly written . . . Each page promises the
literary equivalent of a fresh jab to the solar plexus.'
The Herald

OUT NOW

dead good

Looking for more gripping must-reads?

Head over to Dead Good –
the home of killer crime books,
TV and film.

Whether you're on the hunt for an intriguing
mystery, an action-packed thriller
or a creepy psychological drama,
we're here to keep you in the loop.

Get recommendations and reviews from
crime fans, grab discounted books at bargain
prices and enter exclusive giveaways
for the chance to read brand-new releases
before they hit the shelves.

**Sign up for the free newsletter:
www.deadgoodbooks.co.uk/newsletter**